AND SO THE
THUNDER
COMES

AND SO THE THUNDER COMES

NICHOLAS KENNEDY
& EMMA DARK

ARPress
45 Dan Road Suite 15
Canton MA 02021

Hotline: 1(800) 220-7660
Fax: 1(855) 752-6001

Ordering Information:
Quantity sales. Special discounts are available on quantity purchases by corporations, associations, and others. For details, contact the publisher at the address above.

Printed in the United States of America.

ISBN-13:   Paperback   979-8-89676-200-3
                  eBook   979-8-89676-201-0

Library of Congress Control Number: 2024925146

CONTENTS

The chirping of insects carried on the cool night air. It was bracing but not too cold. A small group of men gathered around a glowing fire to keep warm, whilst an old man spoke in a low rasping voice.

"Yes I knew him. He was everything the stories tell of him and more." The old man said. He adjusted his seating position to make himself more comfortable, as a cheeky grin broke across his face. He looked up at the others listening and his grin broadened. "Shall I tell you a tale?" He asked chuckling. No objections were voiced, so the old man laughed with delight, clapped his hands and cleared his throat. The group of travellers gathered closer to him and all attention centred on the old story teller as he began.

"I was a slave, chained to an oar on a galley when they dragged him in and threw him into the seat next to me. He was not so tall, but big, big as an ox with arms like a bear—" The audience scoffed, but the old man continued. "No it's true I tell you. He had a powerful body. His arms were each as big as both of mine. He was beaten, covered in blood, his eyes could barely open, all swollen and bloodied, just little slits left to see through. He was not like any other slave I had ever seen. No. This one, even in his beaten state, did not have the air of a slave about him, nor did he seem submissive as the rest of us learned so quickly to become." One of the men listening sighed and rolled his eyes. The old man's eyes flicked over to him, then just as quickly back to those who were interested.

"Just tell your tale old man." Another listener commented. The old man thought for a moment before he continued.

"They chained him to the same oar as me and slammed his hands down hard upon it, telling him not to remove them or they would be nailed in place."

"How did a galley slave rise to become a chieftain?" One young man sitting on the edge of the group asked.

"I was just about to tell you." The old man replied, somewhat disgruntled. He adjusted himself once more, leant back and smiled as his memories came flooding back. "Ah yes," he began again, "It goes something like this…"

THE GALLEY

The ship creaked and groaned as the swell of the Northern seas caressed its timbers. It was dark and damp below decks, where the slaves chained at their oars, rested for a time. A sickening odour of rotten seaweed, wet timber, pitch and sweat filled the air. The slavers secured the new slave at his oar and then moved towards the stern of the vessel as they cracked their whips. Once they were out of earshot, the young man chained next to the new slave whispered.

"Are you okay? Can you row? When we have to row again, you must pull with the rest of us or they will beat you some more. Can you hear me? Do you understand me?" The new slave raised his head a little. The young man stared at the bloodied hulk sat next to him. "Do you hear me?" He repeated. The blood-soaked mess turned his head slowly to face the youth. His blackened eyes struggled to open, even a fraction, just enough for the young man to see a pair of bright sapphires behind the curtain of matted, blood-caked blonde hair. "Good, you can hear me. Do you understand me?" The new slave slowly nodded his head. "Good. My name is Malik. What's yours?"

"Lubeck" The beaten man replied in a deep rumbling voice. Malik looked him over for a moment. "Your wounds will heal, I think, if you live long enough. From the look of you, you are from these parts. You're a Norseman, yes?" Lubeck turned his head a little to better view his inquisitor.

"Yes I am." He replied. "My ship was attacked just an hour ago. We were fishing, unarmed but for a couple of filleting knives, easy prey." Lubeck dropped his head as if ashamed.

"And the rest of your crew?" Malik asked.

"I don't know. Perhaps on the other ships, if they're alive." Lubeck nodded his head vaguely to indicate the other ships hidden by their enclosure. A voice rang out in the gloom of the galley. Men groaned as whips cracked. "We're off again." Malik whispered. "Row, row with me or they will beat you some more." Lubeck tightened his grip on the oar as he pulled in time with Malik. His muscles ached and blood oozed from some of the deeper cuts. He winced as pain shot through his beaten body and he ground his teeth against it.

"I will not die chained to this oar." Lubeck spat through clenched teeth. "I will break free and find my son before I stand with my forefathers in Valhalla."

"Quiet! Don't speak, Row!" A slaver shouted as he struck Lubeck across the back with his baton. The pain bit into him causing Lubeck to arch his back and pull hard against his restraints. He hissed as he ground his teeth even harder. The drum beat out a slow, steady rhythm for the slaves to keep time. Malik gave Lubeck a knowing nod and indicated with his eyes for him to comply. For now at least.

Lubeck wasn't sure how long had passed since he had been dragged half-dead on board this floating prison. Nor was he sure if it was night or day. A few rays of light slipped through the space where the oars passed through the ship's hull, so he assumed it was day time. As all of the slaves rested and the ship drifted with the tide, Lubeck looked around. The torches lighting the galley cast shadows, dancing like unearthly spirits in the half-light. Nobody was close or paying attention to what he was doing. So Lubeck once again, as he had done for the past few days, wrapped a coil of his chains around the metal eyelet through which it passed, securing him to the ship's deck. He twisted the chain, tightening it against the eyelet. He twisted even more, applying greater pressure. Suddenly, there was a sharp splintering sound that rang out like a bell in the silence. Lubeck ceased his actions immediately and put his foot over the eyelet, which had now become separated from the deck at one corner of the securing plate. The slavers jumped to their feet, shouting and striking slaves as they marched up the galley looking for what had made the noise. During this commotion, Lubeck pulled hard on his chains. The eyelet gave a little more. By now Malik was aware of what Lubeck had done.

"You have ten paces before he reaches us, nine, eight," Lubeck strained with all of his might. "Seven, six," Malik continued. Lubeck planted his feet firmly against the ships deck either side of the eyelet and took a firm grip with both hands gathering as much of the chain as possible. He heaved for all that he was worth. "Five, four," In a slight panic, Malik grabbed hold of Lubeck's chains to assist him. Heaving together, the eyelet broke free and the pair sprawled backwards onto the ships deck. The slaver looked up at the pair on the floor and immediately sprang at them drawing a sword as he came. As he swung the sword downward at Lubeck's head, Malik launched at their assailant, catching him in the ribs and knocking him into the laps of another pair of oarsmen. Delighted at their good fortune, they promptly wrapped a coil of chains around his neck and pulled hard. The slaver made a chocking sound and kicked furiously in an attempt to free himself. Two more of the crew started to descend upon the group of rebellious slaves. The drummer called to the rest of the crew above for help, as he grabbed a torch and followed his two shipmates.

By now Lubeck was on his feet and helping Malik back to his. The struggling slaver stopped and fell limp releasing his grip on the sword he had been carrying. As the other two crewmen closed down on them, Lubeck and Malik worked together to entangle the first of the two with the chain that, although free from the ships deck, still bound them together. Lubeck struck him hard in the face with his clenched fist rendering him unconscious, as Malik dropped to the floor tripping the second slaver, causing him to fall into the laps of another pair of oarsmen. They, as their galley mates had done, eagerly coiled their chains around his neck and pulled hard, enjoying a similar result as the others. Malik found a bunch of keys hanging from one of the slavers belts. Fumbling through the keys, while trying to open his shackles, he screamed a warning to Lubeck. Lubeck ducked as the drummer swung the torch at him missing wildly thanks to Lubeck's agility. On seeing that Malik had indeed found the right key and had released himself, the drummer realised Lubeck was now free to move independently. This realisation caused him to drop the torch, turn and run for safety. But he hadn't gone far before the other slaves tripped him and began to beat him with their fists.

Malik unlocked Lubeck's shackles and they fell to the deck. Then he turned and began trying keys in locks of the other slaves, releasing a couple of pairs just as reinforcements arrived from the upper decks. One of the slaves that had strangled the first crewman picked up the dropped sword and passed it to Lubeck. His fingers closed around the hilt and a slightly sadistic smile crept across his lips as he turned to face the slavers crew now flooding into the galley. With a blood curdling war cry, Lubeck ran full speed at his assailants. Now armed, he made very short work of the first two he encountered. Their swords, fallen to the deck were quickly picked up by other slaves joining the fight. With numbers swelling as more slaves were released by Malik and Lubeck killing anyone in arms reach, the ships crewmen retreated back to the upper decks. Unfortunately, during the commotion, nobody had noticed the torch the drummer had dropped. Its flames were now catching the few dry timbers and pitch within the galley area. The ship was ablaze in no time at all. Flames licked around the wooden structure and smoke filled the air. All of the released slaves were choking and coughing while retreating from the flames. Victory that had seemed so close was now being ripped from their grasp. Malik stumbled upon some small barrels of tar used to patch up any leaks in the hull. He handed one to Lubeck.

"Can you throw that as far as the heart of the fire?" He asked. Lubeck frowned in confusion and then as realisation came to him, he heaved it up over his head with both hands and hurled it at the fire. Malik passed him a second one. Lubeck treated it the same way. As Malik went to pass the third and final barrel, there was a resounding explosion which rocked the ship and ripped a gaping hole in its bow. Some of the slaves were unfortunately killed by the force of the blast and splintering wooden shards that flew in all directions. However, the majority picked themselves up and tried to climb away from the water that was now pouring in through the breached hull.

"Wait!" Malik shouted. "Wait for the water to fill the galley, take a deep breath and swim out through the hole in the hull." They didn't have chance to put his theory to the test, as the second barrel now exploded, ripping the entire bow section clean away from the rest of the ship. The ship went down in seconds after that point and men were washed out into the ocean like leaves on a breeze. All went dark and silence fell.

There are many seafaring tales of strange sea creatures, huge titans, like Krakens, Giant squid and monstrous whales. There are other tales of Mermaids, Sea Nymphs and Dolphins that may bring a sailor safely back to land when all but drowned. Who knows what happened or if magical forces were at work, but mysteriously none of the rebellious slaves were found by the crews of the accompanying ships. They had seen the fires, heard the commotion and witnessed the explosions followed by the sinking of their comrades, but on searching for survivors, they only found their own people and a few of the slaves that had been killed by the explosions. There was no sign of Lubeck, Malik or any of the other galley slaves. Perhaps they all drowned and sank to the bottom of the sea, they thought. Or maybe eaten by sharks or sea monsters. Whatever had happened, the other ships crews didn't care. They had recovered their fellow clansmen from the cold dark waters and the troublesome slaves were gone, swallowed by the sea or its inhabitants. Drums beat, oars moved and the two remaining ships slipped away and continued on their journey.

A Little Magic in the Air

Acooling sea breeze swept through the tower that perched on the edge of a cliff, overlooking a beach. A hawk screeched as it made its approach to land on the window ledge. Nearby, a lady brushed her flaming red hair as she hummed gently to herself. At the bird's arrival, she turned to greet him.

"Hello there, I wasn't expecting you back so soon." The hawk screeched again, lifted itself into the air and circled the tower. A little bewildered by this action, the woman went to the window, "Hey!" She called. "What's wrong with you?" She watched as the bird flew down to the beach and landed. The woman's gaze settled on some unfamiliar objects nearby. She frowned and stared trying to make out clearly what they were. They were too far away to see with any detail. She had walked these beaches for some ten years hence. Never before had she noticed anything there or even nearby. She gathered up the hem of her long blue dress and hurried down the stairs. On reaching the beach, she kicked off her slippers and ran barefoot across the sand. The objects lay just out of reach of the waves that lapped gently against the shore. The first one she reached, was a tall young man with olive skin and black hair. His back was covered in lash marks and his hands were callused. She rolled him over onto his back and checked for signs of life. He was breathing, all be it just. She rolled him back over onto his front and looked for the second. He was gone. Just six feet away from her a second person had been lying almost dead, like the first. Now, without her noticing anything, he had vanished. A wave of fear and panic washed over her momentarily. She turned to check all around searching the dunes for any sign of someone passing through them. Nothing, not even footprints in the sand. It was as if this second man had simply vanished into thin air.

"Like a ghost." She said under her breath. One last scan of the beach and the dunes beyond, then she looked at the young man still unconscious at her feet. A frown gripped her face as she thought. How was she going to get him all of the way up there? Her eyes settled on the tower in which she lived. The woman, hitched up her dress, pulled back her sleeves, bent down and gripped the young man under his arms then heaved. His limp body was heavy for her and she only managed to move him a little way from the water. She set him down in the soft dry sand and using the hem of her dress, wiped away the grains that covered his face. The young man coughed and stirred a little, but then fell still once more.

The red haired lady stood up tall to see all around looking for assistance. She looked again at the tower then back at the young man at her feet. She checked the beach and even the sky. When she was satisfied that she was in fact completely alone, she knelt down and whispered softly into the man's ear. He stirred a little and began to breathe more deeply. The woman stood again and began to quietly chant a low incantation. The gentle breeze became stronger. The sky darkened and the sea began to swell. Her incantations increased in volume as the woman raised her arms. Lightning flashed and a clap of thunder shook the ground, then all fell still. The sky cleared, the wind dropped and all was calm once more. Moments later a large black horse whinnied as it made its way down the rocky path from the cliff tops to the beach. The animal trotted up to the woman and stopped directly in front of her. She placed her hands on its head and stroked it gently. Without a spoken word, the beast knelt onto its fore legs and lowered its body closer to the sand. Dragging the young man onto the animal's back, the woman led the horse back up the rudimentary path to the top of the cliffs and then into the entrance to the tower.

Some way along the beach to the East, past an outcrop of rocks, a man's head broke the water's surface just yards from the shoreline. He gasped loudly and coughed choking as he swam. Struggling against the tide, he dragged himself onto the sand close to the rocks and once safely out of the water, he sat back and panted heavily trying hard to catch his breath. His huge chest heaved as he filled his lungs with air coughing up large amounts of water. When he had caught his breath and steadied himself, sticking close to the rocks, he edged his way around to take a look at the tower to the West. His eyes widened as he witnessed the scene before him.

"What in Odin's name?" He exclaimed. At that moment, a sharp biting pain, shot through his right thigh. He looked down to see that he was bleeding. The salt water was cleansing but stinging his wound. "Better do something about that." He muttered. Removing his belt and tied it tightly around his leg to help stem the blood flow. Looking around the beach from his hidden vantage point he saw in the distance, objects on the beach. He concentrated hard and screwed up his eyes in an effort to focus over such a distance. Could it be? Yes it was people. Some were lying on the sand motionless, some were moving about picking up and carrying those that were still. He pulled himself to his feet, slipped himself back into the water, then with a little look over his shoulder towards the tower, began to swim carefully and quietly away, towards the others further East around the headland. As he approached, the men on the beach started shouting and pointing in his direction. Two men waded into the water to help him out and onto the sand.

"Let's get that seen to." One of them said nodding at the wound on his thigh. Together they made their way up the beach and sat the tall, injured man down near the base of the dunes next to some other casualties.

"How's the leg?" A deep rumbling voice asked.

"I've had worse." The injured man replied, looking at the muscular frame sitting back on the rock he had been leant against. They both smiled in unspoken agreement, then again the man with the deep voice asked,

"What name do you go by?"

"They call me Thorsten." The tall man replied as he turned just a little, to look at his fellow survivor. "And you?" He asked in return.

"Lubeck." The muscular man replied. "You're a Norseman Thorsten, like me?" He continued in an attempt to make conversation. The tall man smiled as he replied.

"Yes, from the fiords in the North, as are you by your accent." Lubeck smiled and once again rested back against the rock he had been placed against. He looked his fellow countryman up and down. He was a giant of a man, with long blonde hair and beard. He had long limbs with a well developed muscular structure. His body was covered in scars, though Lubeck could not determine if they were from the whip or battle.

"I don't remember you from the galley." Lubeck commented attempting to keep the conversation going, after all, they had nothing else to do.

"No," Thorsten started to reply. "I was five or six rows behind you towards the bow of the ship. You wouldn't have noticed me up there in the shadows; the torch light rarely reached that far down unless a slaver brought one with him for some reason. I saw you though. I saw the state of you when they dragged you in and slammed you down next to that skinny young boy—"

"Malik?" Lubeck interrupted.

"Was that his name? I never had chance to speak with him. I didn't know him before the galley; don't know where he came from or anything about him—"

"Well, it doesn't matter now." Lubeck interrupted again. "He's gone I think. No sign of him here on the beach with the rest of us. I guess the sea took him, or sharks maybe?"

"No," Thorsten interjected. "He's here, I saw him just a few moments ago, just around the headland. A woman came and was examining him. I slipped back into the water while she was busy and not paying any attention to me. I swam round to those rocks." Thorsten pointed to the West, at the rocky outcrop some three hundred yards away. "From there, hidden from view I watched what she was doing."

"We have to go and get him back." Lubeck said struggling to get to his feet.

"No. Not yet." Thorsten replied reaching out to steady Lubeck and restrain his attempt to leave.

"She…" He paused and a troubled look came over his face.

"What is it?" Lubeck enquired.

"She's a witch!" Thorsten finally spat out.

"A witch? What would make you think such a thing? Witches are just old wives tales and stories we tell our children to stop them from straying at night, they're not real." Lubeck chuckled as he continued. "When I looked at you, I thought you were a mighty warrior, witches, really?" Thorsten looked Lubeck straight in the eyes.

"She's a witch I tell you. I saw it as sure as I'm sat here. She raised her arms and chanted some strange words, then the sky changed and the sea became angry. Then a horse came to her and carried Malik to a tower up on the cliffs round there to the West." Thorsten nodded to indicate the direction of the tower. "He's with her now as we speak." Lubeck moved to stand once more, but again Thorsten restrained him. "No wait," he began. "He is in no harm I'm sure of it. The witch could have killed Malik right there if she had desired it, but she rescued him of sorts and took him to her tower."

"We have to help him, I, we all owe him a debt. Malik helped me to free myself from the chains in that galley. He released all of you while I distracted the slavers." Lubeck protested.

"Distracted? Is that what you call it? We will retrieve Malik once we are better healed." Thorsten replied. "Be patient, once our strength returns, we will gather or make weapons and swell our numbers and then we march on the tower and release your friend." Lubeck pondered the proposal for a moment.

"You're right of course. I am no match for a witch like this." Lubeck raised his sights to the others on the beach. "Do you think these men will join us?" He asked with a vague air about his question. Thorsten looked around at the able bodied men still carrying and helping the injured slaves across the beach. Some eighty or so in total, more than half injured.

"I can't speak for them," Thorsten began, "but because you released me from my bonds, I promise my sword will be yours when the time comes." With that he held out his hand in friendship. Lubeck grinned and returned the gesture. They shook on it, smiled and both leant back as two other men approached, one commenting about treating their wounds and getting them both back on their feet.

In the tower, Malik stirred.

"Hold on there." A woman's voice said softly. "You'll pull those stiches and open that wound again if you're not careful." Malik paused, sighed and lay back again.

"Where am I?" He asked.

"You're safe." The woman replied, "But as for where, it's an Island called Thanos. Have you heard of it?" Malik looked confused.

"What?" He asked, his eyes searching the room for anything that might give him a clue as to the region of the globe he was in. There were items from all over the world as he knew it. Not helpful he thought to himself. "I don't know the name, but from the heat, I think we are a in the tropics somewhere. You don't look as though you are from the Tropics, so how come you are here?" He asked.

"Oh, it's a long story." The woman replied as she walked over to the bed where he lay. "I think we have a lot in common, you and I" she smiled as she sat on the edge of the bed and leant forward to check his stitches. "Good, they've held." She remarked, as she sat up straight again. "Where did you and your comrade come from?" She asked. Malik frowned with puzzlement.

"Comrade? What comrade?"

"There was another man with you when I found you. He was huge like a giant. I checked to see if you were alive, but when I looked up, he was gone, vanished like a ghost." Malik's confusion deepened.

"A giant, really, like the tales we tell our children." He laughed, but stopped abruptly as the wound on his torso pulled at his stitches. "I don't recall any giants." He said, holding his wound with one hand and pushing himself into a sitting position with the other. The woman looked hurt as she stood up and went to leave. "Wait!" Malik called to her quickly. "Wait, come sit, I meant no insult, but a giant really?" The woman turned and sat once more.

"He was enormous." She began. "I think he would be taller than my doorway." Nodding toward the opening across the room. "He was big too. Like a bear and covered in scars."

"I don't remember anyone like that." Malik said with a frown.

"It seemed to me, that he had pulled you out of the sea before collapsing himself, looking at the marks in the sand. I think you may owe him your life?"

"And you?" Malik asked. "How do you fit into this?"

"I found you on the beach, as I have already told you." She replied. "Finn alerted me to your presence"

"Finn?" Malik questioned "Is there someone else here?"

"No. Finn is a Hawk I have befriended. He comes to me daily and keeps me company for a while." Malik smiled and looked around the room once again.

"What are you looking for?" The woman asked.

"Do you live here alone?" Malik replied. The woman's face became filled with sadness as she turned and walked across to a window.

"Yes, I'm alone here; I've been alone here for some ten years or so." "Why?" Malik questioned. The woman smiled and turned to face him.

"That's another matter." She replied. "Don't worry yourself over that now, let's get you healthy again first"

"First?" Malik questioned again. "What do you mean first? First, then what?"

"Then we try to reunite you with your people, there is at least one other out there somewhere, I take it there were more?" The question hung in the air for a while unanswered, "It's alright." The woman continued. "I'm not going to harm you or your friends, I'm trying to help. It seems to me that you come from a very distrusting race. You don't trust me, when I've done you no harm, in fact, quite the opposite. Then the giant, he slipped away without a trace before I could offer him any assistance. I've brought you here from the beach where you were laying half dead. I brought you here to dry and warm you; I've cleaned your wound and stitched it closed so that it can heal. Then gave you a potion to restore your strength. Why then do you distrust me?"

Malik looked away as if ashamed. "I do appreciate all that you have done for me, a stranger to you, but I have survived a long time thanks to my distrust of strangers"

"I'm not a stranger." The woman replied.

"I don't even know your name." Malik snorted, in a low voice.

"It's Freyja." She said. "Now, what's yours?" Malik looked sheepishly at her, then almost against his will, he blurted out.

"Malik!"

"There." Freyja said delighted with a huge grin lighting up her face. "We're no longer strangers."

Along the beach to the East of the tower, men were working together to ensure all were treated and all were accounted for, as best they could. There were men of many races. Most looked Celtic in origin, some looked

African, others Norse, some oriental and others Moorish. Thorsten stood and surveyed their surroundings. He chuckled to himself, turned and offered a hand to Lubeck. Lubeck snorted, smiled and took up the offer. With both men now standing Thorsten said,

"Shall we make a start?" Lubeck nodded in agreement and the pair headed unsteadily along the beach.

"Hey, where are you going?" a man called after them.

"To look for wreckage, driftwood, food, anything useful." Thorsten called back. "We'll be back before night fall; you need to get everyone into the dunes and out of sight. We don't know where we are or who might be out there." Without a word, the other man gestured an agreement and returned to the tasks at hand. Lubeck gave Thorsten a slap on the back as the pair headed off again. While they walked, Thorsten realised that using his leg made it feel better. He passed his thoughts to Lubeck who agreed that he too felt better for being on the move. They had only walked for about half an hour, when Lubeck spotted something in the surf. "There!" He shouted pointing to some objects in the water. "What's that?" The two men hurried as best they could to the water's edge. Some wood coupled together with dowels and nails, covered in pitch.

"A piece of the ship." Lubeck declared.

"Yes and more over there" Thorsten replied moving through the water to retrieve other pieces. As they dragged the heavy wood to the shore and up the sand away from the water, Lubeck noticed some barrels bobbing about in the shallow waves. Three in total, tipping and rolling as the waves pushed them up against the sand.

"Quick," He snapped, before we lose them to the sea again. The two men reached the barrels in time and brought them to place with the rest of their bounty. Picking up a rock Thorsten said,

"Let me open one and see what's in it." Lubeck nodded and held the first barrel still while Thorsten struck the top with the rock. It took three solid blows before it finally yielded giving up its contents. Thorsten grinned as he raised a hand full of…

"Salted pork! Oden be praised." He exclaimed taking a great bite and chewing, grinning all the while. Lubeck joined him and the pair filled their bellies as they sat in the afternoon sun.

"What's in that one?" Lubeck gestured at another barrel.

"Let's see." Thorsten replied. Gripping it tight, he lifted it up and shook it vigorously. The barrel was large and heavy, but Thorsten made the task look easy. "Sounds like liquid, maybe ale." He grinned placing it back on the sand. He spotted a stopper pressed into an opening at one end. The two men worked together to remove it and taste the liquid inside.

"Water" Lubeck sighed. Thorsten looked disappointed. "It's water." Lubeck repeated. "The Gods truly smile on us this day." The pair drank their fill and then replaced the stopper. After a moments rest, Lubeck slapped Thorsten on the arm. "Come, let's take this back to the others, let them eat and drink as we have." They stashed the wood and the third barrel. Picked up one barrel each and heaved them onto their shoulders. It took an effort, but they managed to get them back to the others, who received the nourishment with great thanks.

"What was in the third barrel?" a man asked them.

"Don't know, we didn't open it." Lubeck replied.

"Perhaps that one contains ale." Laughed Thorsten. "Then the Gods will truly have smiled on us this day." Everyone within earshot laughed at Thorsten's thirst for ale. Lubeck looked to the sea, then around at their surroundings. He glanced at the injured and then addressed everyone in general.

"Tomorrow, we look for more. This time though, we move together, all of us, gathering as we go. We can't stay here; those slavers may sail back this way searching for survivors. That would be very problematic for us. So we move. Those who can walk carry those who can't, but together we all move at dawn." Nobody argued or even objected. Even the badly hurt nodded, laid back and attempted to sleep. No fires were lit that night; their glow would give away the men's position. Instead, the survivors huddled together to stave off the cold night air. None of them slept well that night. Everyone was cold, exhausted or in pain, but come sunrise, without complaint, they each gathered their strength and moved. They headed East, along the beach to where Lubeck and Thorsten had stashed the other barrel and wood. Some of the men found more pieces of wreckage as they moved slowly along the shoreline. More wood, ropes, one even found a sail which took three of them to pull ashore and gather up into a transportable bundle. Some of the wood, along with lengths of rope were constructed into makeshift stretchers to ease carrying the more severely injured. After a few hours Lubeck turned to Thorsten saying,

"I need to go back and take a look at that tower where Malik is being held."

"I don't know about that just yet Lubeck." Thorsten began to reply. "I told you, he's being held by a witch. She could use her magic against us and we're not in good enough shape yet to fight and we have no weapons." Lubeck frowned and thought for a short time.

"I just want to take a look, sound out the lay of the land and look for weak spots just as we would any normal foe."

"OK." Thorsten agreed reluctantly. "But we take a few able bodied men with us and we need to make some weapons of sorts." Lubeck nodded in agreement then indicated to an easy passage through the dunes they were approaching. Thorsten selected a group of healthy men and the party broke off after arranging to meet up again with the main group by nightfall.

Malik watched with great interest as Freyja stared into a small font of water set to one end of her chambers. She studied it intently, as Malik studied her. She was tall, pale skinned and he could see from the shape of her body under her long blue dress that she was quite athletic. His eyes moved over every curve, admiring the beauty that stood before him.

"See something you like?" She asked without breaking from her task.

"Sorry..." Malik apologised sheepishly. "It's just...err..." Freyja laughed quietly as she continued. "It's OK." She said. "Don't worry; I'm not offended, on the contrary. No man has ever looked at me that way. No man would ever come close enough to look at me at all, never mind with a lustfulness coursing through his veins." Malik hung his head with embarrassment. Then as he found a little more courage, he asked,

"What are you doing?"

"I'm watching your friends." She replied. Malik looked a little confused. Freyja smiled as she continued. "There is a large group of men approaching from the East. One is the giant I mentioned earlier. The others I have never seen before. One is maybe my height, but big in stature, broad across his shoulders with arms the size of my legs."

"Lubeck! He's alive then?" Malik called out.

"Shush!" Freyja hissed at him. "This one has evil in mind. He comes to destroy my home and kill all that dwell here. He's looking for something, no wait, someone. A young man he owes a debt to. He intends to free him from his captors." With that Freyja shook her head sharply and turned to look at Malik. "This Lubeck comes here to kill me and destroy my home because I helped you?"

"No! No! I think there has been a misunderstanding. Lubeck must believe that I am a captive here." He paused a moment, then fixing his gaze on Freyja he tentatively asked her. "Am I a captive here?"

"What? No, not at all. Why is it people always think the worst of me? Well, I will not be persecuted and attacked for trying to help those in need. This Lubeck will be sent running for his life when he tries to attack me here."

"No, wait, wait." Malik insisted. "I know Lubeck; He wouldn't attack you if he knew that I was in no danger. When he gets here, welcome him in; show him that you are not a threat to me or him. He will not be hostile then." Freyja frowned at him and then as she thought, her face softened.

"OK, we'll try it your way, but the first sign of aggression; I will unleash a nightmare upon them all." Malik slumped back on the bed in silence. He ran his fingers over his wound. It was already healed. With surprise he pressed a little harder, nothing, it was as if he had never been injured. As his thoughts ran wild through his head, a sudden realisation hit him.

"A witch." The words spilled out before he could stop them.

"What did you say?" Freyja snapped. She turned and advanced towards him. "What did you call me?" She demanded.

"Sorry! Sorry!" Malik repeated humbly   "I meant no harm."

"You called me witch," Freyja objected. "They have persecuted me for years using that name as an excuse for their actions and now you, you who I have only shown kindness to and helped selflessly. You, you call me WITCH too!" Her anger was growing as she spoke and Malik feared for what she might do to him.

"I'm sorry! I'm sorry!" He pleaded. "The words just slipped out without my intention. But tell me please, how could you see my friends? How did you heal my injuries so fast? I'm puzzled that's all."

"And that makes me a witch does it?" Freyja snapped. Malik made an apologetic gesture and bowed his head.

"No, not at all." He began. "I just don't understand, please explain and enlighten me." Freyja calmed a little, walked over to a window and stared out at the beach and sea beyond. She sighed, dropped her head then began to tell Malik of her plight.

"They took my sister some ten years ago. They called her a witch, but they didn't burn her as expected. No, slavers took her. They said they knew of a Warlord across the sea that would pay a handsome price for a witch of such youth, that he may be able to control and manipulate her before she reached an age where her own mind would prevail. I showed no signs of any abilities, but to be safe they imprisoned me here in this tower watching my every move. When I developed the power to heal the sick and injured, they called me WITCH and tried to burn this place down attempting to kill me. That's when I discovered that I could control the weather. I prayed for salvation, for someone to rescue me. The sea became stormy and the sky roared with thunder. Then the wind blew, the skies grew darker and rain fell in torrents dowsing the flames. I haven't seen my sister in all of this time and I miss her so very much. Sometimes when I gaze into my font, I can sense her, I can feel her presence and I pray for an army to come and help me, to find and rescue her. But as of yet, my prayers have been unheard." Malik looked a little puzzled and slightly embarrassed as he fidgeted uneasily.

"Can you do magic?" He asked uneasily. Freyja turned to face him with a disapproving frown on her face. But as she stared at him, a smile broke through.

"No." She replied. "Not magic, but as I said, I have the ability to heal the sick and injured. With the aid of my font, I can see into the hearts of men and understand their intentions. I can, of sorts, see that which has happened and sometimes that which may still come. I can talk to people in their dreams and perhaps influence their thoughts and decisions." She paused as she remembered the way the villagers had reacted when she had helped some of them in times of sickness and when one of the village boys had fallen, breaking an arm and both of his legs. Freyja had healed him and probably saved his young life and for this, they had tried to burn her in her bed. Her eyes filled with tears, but they didn't fall as the memories ran through her mind. Malik saw, but remained silent until the sound of a hawk landing on a window ledge caused them both to look round.

Freyja stared in silence at the bird for a moment, then, turned to Malik and announced. "He's here, the one I spoke of, the one who wants to kill me."

"No." Malik objected. "I've told you, Lubeck doesn't know what is happening here. He probably thinks that I am a prisoner. I need to talk with him, let him know of your plight—"

"Plight?" Freyja snapped. "What do you mean?" Malik swallowed hard before answering.

"I think that you would like our help to get your sister back, right? I mean, I know you haven't said it, but you would like us to help you find her and bring her back, yes?" Freyja's eyes drifted away in thought for a moment.

"Can you do that?" She asked. Malik smiled warmly as he answered.

"I'm sure that Lubeck will help. Especially if it means he gets a chance to kill slavers. He hates slavers, after being in chains on that galley for so long. Bring him in, talk with him; tell him what you have told me. Then you will see what is truly in his heart." Freyja nodded in agreement and walked over to her font. She raised her left hand and waved it slowly over the still water within. A mist developed inside the font shrouding the water's surface. As she waved her hand a little more, the mist cleared to reveal a vision. Two men, walking through tall grasses on sandy dunes. One was tall like a giant, the other shorter but heavy built with strong limbs and a deep chest. Freyja closed her eyes and concentrated. Malik watched with intrigue.

Out on the dunes Lubeck paused, mid conversation.

"Hey, what's up?" Thorsten asked tightening his grip on the crude club he was carrying and looking around for would be foes. Lubeck remained silent. A voice was echoing inside his head, a soft and gentle voice that beckoned him to be at peace and welcomed him. He shook his head hard as if trying to clear his thoughts, but the voice continued.

"Welcome Lubeck." The gentle voice said. "Come in peace, you have no enemies here. Come to the tower and see that your friend is unharmed and free to leave whenever he pleases. Please come and refresh yourself and your men. Eat, drink and rest in safety. None shall harm you here Lubeck, not under my roof." Lubeck frowned and stared at Thorsten.

"Did you hear that?" He asked.

"No." Thorsten replied. "What is it? Are we being watched?"

"We are indeed." Lubeck answered, "The witch knows we are here and welcomes us to dine with her. She says that we are all safe and welcome, that Malik is safe and free to leave when he pleases."

"The witch is in your head?" Thorsten gasped. "We must leave before she calls up demons to destroy us all."

"No." Lubeck replied. "No, this witch seems to want us alive, or surely she would have done so already?" Again the voice spoke to Lubeck inside his head. Again it wished him no harm and welcomed him. "Do we take this witch at her word?" Lubeck began. "Or do we run like frightened children?" The two men stood in silence for a moment. Then Lubeck began to walk, without caution towards the tower.

"What are you doing?" Thorsten called after him.

"I'm accepting her offer, I want to meet this witch that can know my thoughts and talk to me inside my head. After all, she knows we are here, so there is no point trying to cover our approach now is there?" Cautiously and reluctantly, Thorsten followed his would be leader.

"Alright then." He said as he caught up to Lubeck. "But just so you know, I think this is a bad idea."

"Noted." Replied Lubeck with a mischievous grin. Then signalling to the other men to follow, they continued openly towards the tower. The roof of the tower came into view long before the group reached the cliffs on which it stood. All seemed quiet and calm as they approached.

"No guards, no demons, no foes for us to fear Thorsten." Lubeck noted out loud. "It's no fortress, and there is no garrison stationed here, so, why does Malik remain?"

"Perhaps he is chained and cannot escape." Thorsten replied. Lubeck laughed softly while turning his attention back to the tower.

"We're here!" He called to whoever may be listening.

"Nobody is home." Thorsten said almost hoping to be right. Just then the large outer door creaked open and Malik stepped out to greet them.

"Come, come." He gestured towards the open door. "We are waiting for you, what took you so long?"

"Malik!" Lubeck called out with joy at seeing his friend again, smiling from ear to ear. The two men grasped in a hug slapping each other hard on the back. Thorsten relaxed at last and greeted Malik in a similar manner as did the other men that had accompanied them. All were relieved and happy to be reunited with their former galley mate.

"Come, come." Malik beckoned them all into the tower. "Come, there is someone I want you to meet." As they all mounted the stairs that led up to Freyja's chambers, Lubeck noted how warm the tower was, how clean and light. Unlike any other fortification he had frequented. They were usually dark and damp with cobwebs and dirt everywhere. On entering Freyja's chambers the light became even more intense. It was as if they were stood outside, mid-afternoon on a summer's day. A cool breeze wafted across his cheeks bringing with it the scent of summer flowers and other soft perfumes. Lubeck's eyes darted quickly around the room noting every detail before settling on the red haired beauty that stood towards the far end of the chamber, by a window. He looked her up and down drinking in her femininity and beauty. Could this really be a witch? He thought to himself. Or is this some mind trick, concealing her true form, designed to encourage them to lower their guard, so that she could spring her trap? Freyja laughed out loud. Then speaking to Lubeck telepathically, she said,

"That could well be Lubeck. Perhaps you are right?"

"You're in my head again witch." Lubeck replied in a calm gentle voice. "Is this how you ensnare your victims? You trick their eyes and catch them off guard? Then kill them, or eat them or perhaps enslave them selling their souls to whatever evil God will bargain for them with you?"

"No, No!" protested Malik. "She's kind and gentle; she healed my injuries and regained my health. She has brought you here to request our help."

"She brought us here?" Laughed Lubeck. "I thought we came here at my command."

"That's what I wanted you to believe." Freyja interjected. "Malik is correct. I brought you here because I would like your help—"

"With what?" Thorsten snapped cutting her short. Freyja's gaze drifted from Lubeck to Thorsten. A smile broke across her lips as she continued.

"You, more than any should appreciate what I am about to request."
"What does that mean?" Thorsten demanded becoming more agitated.

"Your son." Freyja began. "Was taken by slavers some ten years ago, right? That's why you were out alone, searching for him. Trying to track them down, which you did, but you were heavily outnumbered. You were overpowered and became enslaved yourself." Thorsten's gaze dropped to the floor as he remembered the way his son had cried out for help the day he was taken. He remembered the hunt for the slavers and the battle that ensued when he caught up with them. More than a dozen dead slavers to his credit, but it was not enough. He had been overpowered and enslaved and had never seen his son since. "I feel your pain." Freyja said softly. "You are not alone, others have suffered the same." Her eyes suddenly shot to an older man towards the rear of the group. "Hagar." She began. "Your daughter was also taken some three years earlier, by these same slavers and you, like Thorsten, hunted them to try and reclaim her, only to suffer the same fate." The older man also dropped his eyes to the floor and nodded. "And you Lubeck." Freyja continued "You don't know what has become of your son. You were fishing when they struck you, easy prey being unarmed and only four in number, one being a young boy too." Lubeck's jaw tightened and his fists clenched as his thoughts drifted back to that spring morning fishing on the fjords.

"Where is he? What became of Hafthor?" Lubeck said, his voice beginning to fill with hate. "If you can see and know these things, you can tell me what became of my son."

"No." Freyja replied. "I cannot. I can only see through you, I can only see what is in your heart. But I can help you. I can help you find them, find them all and claim them back."

"How?" Demanded Lubeck. "Tell us how you can do this. Why would you do this? What is it you need from us?"

"I can help. I can guide you in your search and help you find the men who enslaved your families—" "How?" Thorsten interrupted.

"I can see things, things that have not happened yet and things that are happening now, but only through your eyes and minds. I can see what you see, hear what you hear, feel what you feel and so on. I can also see your possible futures, your pasts and through your emotional connections to loved ones, I can catch glimpses of their surroundings, hear, see and feel as they feel. Distance is a minor barrier, but this Island is a bigger one. I can't leave this place, not until the spell that holds me here is broken. This I can only do when my sister is safe. The same slavers that took you and your families, also took my sister. I want you to hunt them down and return my sister safely to me."

"And how do we do that? With no weapons and no ships, how do we find and defeat these slavers?" Hagar asked gruffly.

"Weapons and supplies I have right here and can give them to you for your journey. As for a ship, I know of a place where a ship builder lives. A man who has also lost family to slavers. I have spoken to him; and persuaded him to help you."

"And how did you know to do that before we arrived?" Thorsten asked.

"I saw you all in my dreams and influenced your decisions through yours."

"And this is how you will guide us? Through our dreams? Talking to us as we sleep?" Lubeck asked.

Freyja lowered her eyes and nodded.

"I want my sister back, as much as you want your children." She said almost sobbing.

"I for one will go." Malik said rising to his feet from where he had been sitting during these discussions.

"I will also." Declared Hagar. Lubeck turned to face Thorsten and asked him. "Will you trust this witch if I put my faith in her? I want my son back—" "As do I." Thorsten interrupted.

"Then we go?" Lubeck waited for an answer, his eyes searching his friend's troubled face. "Thorsten?" He continued. "It seems to me that if we want to get our loved ones back, we are going to need a little help. This woman is offering us that help. Witch or no witch, if she can get me weapons and a ship, then by all the Gods, I will embrace her as an ally." Lubeck's eyes changed their focus from Thorsten to Freyja as he continued. "If she betrays us for whatever reason, then no tower, no demons, or any dark powers known to man or God will protect her from my wrath. Even if I have to kill Odin himself to reach her. That is my promise to you, to all of you." The room fell still with an uneasy silence. The chill of Lubeck's cold and Icy words hung in the air menacing and spine chilling as if the Gods themselves were afraid of his threat. Then slowly and reluctantly Thorsten nodded his head in agreement. Lubeck walked slowly and intimidatingly across the room towards Freyja. He stood so close to her, that as he spoke his breath moved the fine wispy hair that was not tied back and hung loosely by her cheeks. "I will help you recover your sister in return for your help to recover our loved ones. If you do anything that is not in our best interests undertaking this quest, I will come for you and all your powers will be useless against me. Even if I have to come back from the dead, I will find you and I will feast on your still beating heart after I tear it from your chest with my bare hands." Freyja's eyes lifted slightly to make contact with Lubeck's. She looked deep into them, deep into his soul and shivered. Never had she seen a man with such an intimidating presence. Fear began to turn her blood to ice. It was almost as if this man were already returned from the dead and she felt deep inside, that he would indeed tear out her heart and eat it, still beating if he believed that she had betrayed them in some way.

"You… you have my word." She stuttered. "I will not betray you, any of you." Lubeck moved away slowly and returned to Thorsten's side. The silence that had fallen around the room hung in the air with an unsettling atmosphere. No one dared to speak or make eye contact with anyone else, until finally Malik's light hearted voice rang out.

"Well, Now that we're all friends…." Laughter rolled around the room and the mood lightened as everyone began to talk at once trying desperately to change the subject.

"Can I help you, all of you with your wounds?" Freyja's voice lifted above the rest.

Thorsten stepped towards her.

"If you could, I would appreciate that. My leg has been uncomfortable since the ship sank. It would be good if you could fix me the way you did Malik."

"I'll do what I can. I will try my best to heal you all." With that Freyja removed the crude dressing from Thorsten's leg and inspected the damage. "This should not be too hard." She said in a cheerful voice as she smiled. Then gathering a small box from a nearby table, she began to thread a hooked needle with a fine twine and headed back towards Thorsten. "Remove your garments so that I can clean and stitch that." Thorsten did as she asked and Freyja got to work. Lubeck watched for a moment then beckoned Malik, who came over to sit beside his old galley mate. Lubeck proceeded to explain about the rest of the survivors who would be waiting for them at the rendezvous later that evening.

"Are you well enough to make the rendezvous and bring them all here by tomorrow noon?" He asked.

"It will be tough to make that journey in such a short time. What's the urgency?" Malik asked in reply.

"I don't fully trust her, the greater our numbers, the harder it will be to be entrapped here." Lubeck commented. Malik thought for a moment, his mind torn slightly. Freyja had been very kind and helpful to him and he felt a little sympathy for her plight. But one thing he had learned about Lubeck during their time together, was that he had an uncanny insight and an instinct for survival second to none.

"I will go and be back before noon tomorrow." Malik said sombrely. Lubeck slapped him on the shoulder and smiled, then turned towards Freyja, calling,

"Freyja, I need to see these weapons you spoke of, are they here?"

"Yes." She replied. "Give me a moment to finish this and I will take you to them." Once finished stitching up Thorsten's leg, Freyja began decanting various coloured powders from stone jars and mixing them with leaves and herbs crushing them and grinding them with a rudimentary pestle and mortar. Once ground finely enough, she added a little water to form a paste.

"Here." She said handing it to one of the wounded men. "Cover your cuts with some of this and pass it around for you all to do the same. Your wounds will heal much faster with this." The man looked at Lubeck, who nodded his permission to do so. Soon all of the group's open wounds were smothered in a blueish, green paste that smelled surprisingly of wild flowers. At inhaling the scent, Lubeck's thoughts drifted away to memories of his home. Home, so long ago now, or so it felt. He broke into a warm smile, as thoughts of his wife and son flooded into his head. He closed his eyes and sighed. Freyja's voice broke the moment.

"Your turn." She said gesturing for Lubeck to remove the remnants of his shirt. He sighed, curling up the edge of his lip as he complied with the request. Freyja examined his injuries. "The ones on the outside are superficial." She said. Then placing her hands on his chest, she closed her eyes and concentrated. "You have some internal injuries. I can heal them, but you will have to trust me." Lubeck looked at Thorsten and Hagar for reassurance. Hagar nodded silently and Lubeck agreed. Freyja walked over to the table, removed the lid from a small stone jar and poured some purple powder into her hand. She then returned to where Lubeck was sitting on the floor, knelt down beside him and gently blew the powder into his face. Lubeck coughed a little but immediately felt himself drifting off to sleep. Thorsten jumped to his feet grabbing his club as he moved. Freyja waved her hand and he flew backwards across the room as if thrown by some invisible beast. He landed on the bed, unharmed. The other men in the room gasped and uneasily gripped whatever weapons they had been carrying.

"Be still." Freyja commanded raising her hand a little higher. Thorsten sat up shaking his head as if to clear it and attempted to stand again. "Don't!" Freyja snapped glaring at him with steely eyes.

"You." She began, pointing at a man sitting nearby. "Pick him up and place him on the bed." Then turning to Hagar she added. "Help him." With that the two men lifted Lubeck and carried him to the bed, urging Thorsten to move as they did. Freyja followed them and as soon as Lubeck was laid safe, she began to chant a soft low incantation. The men watched on uneasily, but accepted that Freyja was in fact trying to help. When she paused, Freyja looked up and smiled at Thorsten.

"It's done." She stated. "Now we just have to wait and see if the Gods have heard my prayer."

Everyone in the room continued to eat, drink and rest while the paste Freyja had mixed worked its magic. A low murmuring filled the room as the men talked, interspaced with short bouts of laughter. Darkness slowly fell and the chatter died down and finally gave way to snoring. Shadows danced along the walls as the torch flames flickered their final moments. Freyja surveyed the room and her sleeping guests. One last check on Lubeck, then she too settled herself, closed her eyes and drifted off to sleep.

ARMS OF THE GODS

A light breeze gently moved Freyja's hair, as she drifted in and out of sleep, sitting in a chair next to the bed where Lubeck lay. It tickled her face and awakened her fully as she swept it behind her ear with her slender fingers. It was not yet fully light, just enough to make out her house guests still sleeping. She looked at Lubeck. He was still asleep with no signs of any movement since he had been laid there the evening before. She moved to a window and looked down to the beach below. In the gloomy morning light, she could just make out the white edges of the small breakers that lapped up and down the shoreline. As she watched, she could see a faint shadow moving along the beach towards her tower. She strained her eyes to focus in the dim light.

"Don't worry." A voice came from very close behind her. "It's Thorsten, he went to fetch breakfast." Freyja turned startled at the proximity of Hagar, who was less than an arm's length away. "I'm starving." He continued. "Let's hope he was successful huh?"

Thorsten climbed the stairway that led to and from the beach. He entered the room and unceremoniously dropped a dozen fish strung together, onto the table. The look on his face and the knowing shrug said it all.

"But," He began, "I did manage to get these." With a grin, he pulled a crude sack from his belt and laid it gently on the table. He released the tie at the top and revealed a large number of eggs. "Better than fish." He said with a grin. By now the rest of the group were beginning to stir.

Voices began to fill the air and sporadic laughter rang out from time to time. Freyja checked Lubeck again for signs of improvement, nothing yet.

"Don't worry, he'll be fine." Hagar said to her. "He's a tough one that one. Even the Gods would find it difficult to kill him." Freyja smiled and joined the rest of the men to feast on Thorsten's catch. "Malik should be back soon." Thorsten pointed out. "By noon I believe Lubeck told him."

"Yes." Hagar replied. "So long as he doesn't run into anything unexpected."

"He had best not be late." A deep voice rumbled from the far side of the room. The men looked round to see Lubeck sat up and slowly swinging his legs out of the bed to stand. "Is there any left for me?" He asked with a grin. Freyja squealed with excitement and quickly carried over a plate of eggs.

"How do you feel?" She asked him. Lubeck's face revealed little as to how he felt, but he replied.

"I feel strong again, the pain has left me and I have a clear head." He reached out and took the eggs gratefully. The sullen atmosphere was lifted and chatter filled the room once more. Men checked their own injuries, which had all miraculously healed without trace. The early morning light was by now spilling in through the windows as the sun rose in the clear sky. Soon the eating and removing of dressings ebbed and quiet befell the large tower room again. Thorsten, ever eager for a fight, lifted his club and gestured across the room to Lubeck who nodded silently, then Lubeck turned his attention to Freyja.

"Now that we are all friends and you have healed every one. Shall we take a look at these weapons you mentioned?"

"Of course." She replied. "Follow me." They proceeded from the room and down the stairs. When the stairs came to an end, with one door to the beach and walls to all other sides Lubeck looked at Freyja with Distrust.

"Where now?" He asked. Freyja smiled and raised her hands, closed her eyes and whispered a short verse. The ground shook, not fiercely, just enough for the men to become a little uneasy. Then the wall to their right began to move. Dust and sand fell as the stones shifted to reveal a passage way with more stairs leading underground. Freyja clapped her hands once and a low golden light glowed far away in the depths of the earth beneath them. Cautiously Hagar stepped forward and peered down the newly revealed stairway.

"Don't be afraid." Freyja began, "The weapons you desire are at the bottom of those stairs. Come." She continued. "Follow me." With that she pushed past Hagar and started to descend the steps to the chamber below. Cautiously a dozen or so men followed her. Lubeck thrust his arm across Thorsten's chest as he attempted to enter the staircase, stopping him in his tracks.

"Wait here." Lubeck said. "If it's a trap, I don't want us all caught like rats." Thorsten nodded and indicated to a further group of men to take up a rear guard and to remain alert. Lubeck then slowly and cautiously descended the steps towards the hidden chamber below. The intensity of the light increased the deeper he descended. Ahead of him the voices of his men were cheerful and somewhat optimistic. Excitement oozed from the chamber as he approached. Then as his eyes blinked against the light, he stopped and stared in amazement. There before him was an armoury filled with every weapon imaginable, shields, vestments, breastplates and helmets. All shone with highly polished finishes. Men were picking up swords, axes, bows and spears, inspecting them with admiration. Hagar approached Lubeck carrying a sword. He had an expression of admiration and bewilderment on his face. He lifted the sword and offering it to Lubeck he said,

"Here, feel the weight of this sword, I don't understand it." Lubeck reached out and took the sword from him. It was not at all what he was expecting. It was a large sword and ornately decorated with a Lions head on both sides of the cross guard. It also had a Dragons claw grasping a large Sapphire as the pommel. The hilt was a hand and a half with a broad fluted, double edged blade, longer than his arm. A very heavy sword, but yet it wasn't. There was almost no weight to it at all; a child could wield it.

"How can this be?" Hagar asked. "How can they be so light?"

"Probably have no strength, they'll break as soon as they are used." Retorted another man carrying a large shield. Without warning, Lubeck raised the sword and swung it overhead striking at the man. An ear splitting sound rang out like a bell as the would-be target raised the shield just in time to deflect Lubeck's blow. He fell under the force of it. A small cloud of dust rose as he hit the ground. Everyone in the chamber stopped what they were doing and stared at Lubeck, gripping tightly whatever weapon they held, as they prepared to defend themselves.

Lubeck reached down and helped the man back to his feet assuring him that everything was okay. He took the shield from him and examined it. Not so much as a scratch. Lubeck turned his attention to the sword he had used, again, no damage to the edge of the blade. No marks at all on either item. All in the chamber looked on in wonderment, still a little uneasy with the events of a moment ago. Lubeck then placed the shield on the ground and requested the axe another man was holding. The man handed it to Lubeck warily. Lubeck hoisted it up and over his head with both hands. His huge arms and shoulders flexed and bulged with the power of his swing. Every muscle in his body worked together to create an enormously powerful strike. He brought the axe down on the shield with such ferocity that most of the men recoiled for safety. Once more, the sound of metal against metal rang out like a huge bell, filling the air with a noise that could not only be heard, but felt deep inside one's body. When the dust had settled, Lubeck once again examined the shield for damage. There was no sign that it had ever been struck. An audible gasp of amazement filled the chamber as everyone stared in disbelief. Lubeck checked the edge of the axe he had used. Again, not so much as a scratch appeared on either edge of the double head. Lubeck grinned widely and looked across at Freyja.

"Are they all like this?" He asked. Freyja smiled as she replied,

"Yes, all of them, everything in here is made in the same way. Where they came from, I don't know. I begged the Gods to send me an army and the weapons they would need to hunt down and defeat my enemies. I discovered this chamber some days later, filled with all you can see. I concealed the entrance and thanked the Gods for them. Then waited for my army to arrive, and now, here you are. Praise the Gods and protect you all on our quest."

"Just a moment." Lubeck began. "We're not an army, not yet anyway and we have our own agendas to address first."

"No." Freyja objected, "You are an army. With these weapons and armour no man shall stand in your way and your agendas are the same as my own. I have kept my word, now you must keep yours. Take what you need from here and follow me to Antonio, who will build you a ship. Such a ship will never have been seen before. Your numbers will grow as more will join your cause. You will become an army and you will have a fleet of ships at your command. Then, you will hunt down these slavers to their homelands and destroy them all, recover your loved ones and return my sister to me." A cheer of support echoed around the chamber. All of the men were looking to Lubeck for approval. With a frown on his face, Lubeck picked up the sword once more. It felt good in his hand, almost as if it were part of him. Thinking hard about his lost wife and his son missing since the slavers had attacked; he felt the anger and hatred rise within him. He raised his eyes, which settled on a strange looking item in the centre of the armoury. It was a shaft about three feet in length with a spear head and backward facing hook resembling a boat hook at one end and a vicious looking mace at the other. He stepped forward and gripped it in the middle. It, as with all of the other weapons, felt surprisingly light and well balanced. Then looking at Freyja, Lubeck announced.

"Take me to Antonio."

All of the men were now fully equipped with weapons and armour of their choice. Indications of their origins depicted by their choices including Thorsten and the ten men who had helped him watch the entrance earlier. There were men from all corners of the globe, some obviously from the same regions. It appeared that in their small band of men, almost all of the world's races were represented. Lubeck cast an eye around the band. He noticed there were ten men of oriental and Middle-Eastern origins that had chosen bows and filled quivers. A tall African and five others had all chosen spears. Most of the Scandinavian and Celtic types had chosen swords or axes but all of them regardless of origin carried additional weaponry tucked into belts or boots or strapped to their backs. Lubeck himself carried the odd looking hooked weapon, along with the lion headed sword on his hip and two daggers, one in his boot, the other tucked into his belt at the small of his back. A Saracen was sat to one side, two slim curved swords strapped to his back and two daggers arranged similarly to Lubeck and finished off with a short bow with a quiver of arrows slung around his waist. This man, now, clothed and armed took on a new light that Lubeck had never noticed before. He looked like one of the Moorish demons he had encountered some years ago while exploring new lands as his people often did. A shudder ran down his spine as he remembered how these men had been unbelievably fast and could wield one of those slim curved swords equally well with each hand simultaneously making them very hard to defeat. Just then, a large double headed axe thumped to the floor in front of him. At the other end of its long shaft was Thorsten grinning widely, covered now in leather and chain mail. Knee length fur boots covered his lower legs and his head was crowned with a conical animal skin hat finished with a metal spike in the centre and flaps that fell down to cover his ears. Laces dangled from these flaps, that could be tied below his chin if need be.

"And what are you meant to be?" Asked Lubeck with a grin.

"Terrifying yes? My enemies will run in fear just from the sight of me, No?" Lubeck stood up and removed the Mongol headgear that Thorsten was wearing, replacing it with a metal helmet which had chain mail covering the wearer's neck and shoulders. A face plate covered all but his eyes and mouth. When combined with Thorsten's immense height, it made him look very intimidating indeed.

"That's better." Lubeck stated. "Now you really do look like a demon, summoned from someone's worst nightmares." Both men laughed and Lubeck picked out some armour of his own. He picked up a round shield with a Dragon embossed at its centre and walked off to climb the stairs back to the daylight of the beach. Both men stood by the tower entrance and observed the other men now gathering on the beach. All of them fully healed, fed, watered, fully rested and equipped for battle thanks to the Gods, or at least that's what Freyja would have them believe.

"Fearsome are they not?" Hagar asked rhetorically. "Strangely fit and strong to a man." Lubeck's mouth broke into a lopsided smile as he looked at Freyja.

"Yes, strange that." He admitted. "But now we are starting to look like an army, though we are few in number—"

"For now." Thorsten interrupted. "But we will recruit more, of that I'm sure." Hagar looked up to the sky.

"Malik should be here with the rest of the men soon." He said. Lubeck and Thorsten looked skyward.

"Let's hope so." Thorsten added. Then turning to Lubeck, he continued. "Do you think Freyja will see them coming?"

"She saw us didn't she?" Lubeck replied. But just to make sure she would, Lubeck approached her and asked her if it would be possible for her to try and see where they were and if they were in any danger. Freyja agreed and returned to the tower and her font to take a look. Meanwhile, Hagar gathered the men together and started to organise them. He explained that in order for them to be successful, they would need to work together and to fight as a single entity. He arranged them into groups, archers in one, and spear-men in another and so on. Lubeck watched on from a short distance seated on a rock.

"How long do we wait here?" Thorsten asked him.

"Until Malik gets here with the rest." Lubeck replied. Then looking up at his large companion he asked him. "Why do you all treat me as if I were your leader? Why do you all look to me as if I were your chieftain?" Thorsten pondered for a moment, then after much thought he replied.

"Who else would we follow? You freed us from our chains and helped us escape from that Galley. When we had all but accepted our fates, you showed us the way to freedom. You took the initiative and broke our bonds. You, as any leader should, looked to the wellbeing of his men and saw to their needs before your own. You are a natural born leader and a mighty warrior too."

"Nearly got you all killed more like." Lubeck replied with regret in his voice. Thorsten raised an eyebrow and sighed as he replied.

"Some died, most survived. You found food and drink, gathered broken men and gave them a reason to go on. You give us hope that we will see our loved ones again. When men were at their weakest, you stood strong and refused to accept your fate. I for one would follow you to the gates of Valhalla, as would most, if not all of these men."

"I am not your born chieftain." Lubeck countered.

"No." Thorsten interjected. "You are better than that, you are our chosen chieftain. The men look to you to lead them. They trust your judgment and the strength of your heart. You're also a mighty warrior, not so mighty as me." He laughed. "But a mighty warrior all the same and the men respect that as much as your judgment and wisdom. Accept it, embrace it, you were born to lead. So lead us and make good on your promises." With a heavy sigh, Lubeck stood up and tossed the pebble he was toying with over his shoulder and strode towards the group. Calling for their attention, he addressed them.

"It is time to decide on a leader. Time to decide where you go, what you do and who does what."

"I thought that you were our leader?" A voice called out from the group and mummers of agreement rippled through the men.

"I have pledged my service and my sword to Freyja's quest." Lubeck began. "Though I cannot speak for you all. You must decide what you want to do and where you want to go, not me. I can only speak for myself."

"Freyja's quest is the same as mine." Another voice stated. "I want my family back from these slavers, if you go, I will follow." More sounds of agreement rippled around the group. Another man stepped forward to make himself heard.

"I have no family." He began. "I would still be shackled to that Galley if you had not freed us. I too will follow, if you lead us Lubeck." Several other men sounded in agreement to that also.

"Anyone else have anything to say on the matter?" Thorsten called out in general.

"There is one who might not agree to your lead Lubeck." A man called from the rear of the group. "He is the Celt that took charge when we were all washed up on the shore half dead. Kei, I think is the name he goes by. He was not as badly hurt as the rest of us and assumed command organising those of us who were able, to help those who were not. He may not be so keen to relinquish his position to you. This could be a problem."

"Then we shall face this problem when he arrives with Malik later today." Thorsten answered. "Maybe sooner." Hagar indicated towards the tower. Freyja was signalling to them from a window. "They're here." She called. "About three miles away, maybe less. About forty of them all told."

On hearing this news, the group of men started to gather with anticipation and an air of excitement at the prospect of being reunited with the rest of their shipmates. Lubeck however, had a different feeling about the reunion. If this Kei did in fact consider himself leader, then this could indeed be problematic and could tear the group apart, or worse, it could lead to fighting amongst them and they could incur fatalities resulting in a vast reduction in their numbers, instead of increasing them. He pondered this for some time, long enough for Freyja to descend the tower and make her way to where he was sitting.

"You look troubled my Lord." She began. "What is so disturbing?" She continued.

"Being called My Lord for one." He laughed. "I'm no Lord. I'm just a simple man who has been declared leader of this group of survivors. There could be trouble when Malik arrives with the rest of the men. A man called—"

"Kei." Freyja interrupted. "Do not concern yourself with him. He will accept the way things are, but do not trust him either. He has his own agenda and will betray you all for his own gain. When the time comes, Thorsten will deal with Kei, I have seen this already." Lubeck looked round towards Thorsten. The giant was organising the men and preparing them for the possible trouble that may lie ahead.

"Have you seen all of our futures?" Lubeck asked.

"No." Freyja replied. "Only the ones that affect my sister's return."

"Do I come under that heading?" Lubeck enquired warily.

"Yes, but I have only seen your near future, not what lies years ahead."

"Do I have years ahead?" Lubeck pressed. Freyja frowned at him and then replied.

"I can look deep into your future, if you really want me to see. Do you really want to know exactly when and how you are going to die?"

"So, I am going to die then?" Lubeck replied with a sigh.

"We're all going to die, but when and how? Is something best left unseen, don't you think?" Thorsten now approached them, stating that they were ready. Lubeck looked up at the tower.

"Place a lookout up there, I want to know what their approach is like." Thorsten frowned in confusion.

"Do they approach openly without fear? Or do they try to conceal their approach or mislead us as to their numbers?" Thorsten nodded, a little embarrassed that he had to be reminded about something so simple. Walking back to the group he barked an order to one of the men at the front, who instantly ran off in the direction of the tower to take up his position. Thorsten continued to bark orders and men left in various directions to take up positions and conceal themselves. After a short while, the lookout pointed East and assured Lubeck that the group following Kei was approaching openly and without caution, Malik heading up the group, followed closely by Kei.

"May I?" Lubeck said to Freyja gesturing towards the tower.

"Of course." She replied. Then, with a sharp whistle to Thorsten, they moved up the stairway back into the tower. Thorsten joined them followed closely by Hagar and five other men. The rest of them stayed in their positions waiting to see what might develop. Malik and the remaining survivors approached the tower and stood before it in the midday sun. Hot, tired, hungry and weak. Dressed in rags, as their clothing was torn and holed from service on the Galley and the wreck caused by Lubeck's rebellion.

"Freyja! Lubeck!" Malik called. "We're here, let us in!" The big doors opened and Lubeck strode out to greet his shipmate.

"You are all well?" He enquired.

"Hungry, thirsty and tired from the journey. Many of these men still suffer from their injuries, they need Freyja's help." Malik replied.

"Come then, let's see what she is willing to do." Stepping aside and gesturing for them to enter, Lubeck watched them with suspicion. How many, he wondered would side with Kei if it came to a power struggle. He watched them pass by him, weak and injured. They were no match for him and his followers now fully healed and fed. But, soon this group would be too, with Freyja's help. If they accepted the way things are and joined his growing force, they would have enough men to fully man a long ship, a big long ship. One that would be capable of mounting a raid and possibly rescuing their families. As the survivors filed past, Lubeck felt something that he had not felt since the day he and his son were taken by the slavers, Hope. Hope began to rise inside of him. With these men, the armour, the weapons, the ship Freyja had promised them and her help. It just might be possible to find and rescue their families. His heart raced and pounded in his chest. He could feel his blood surging through his veins. His muscles tightened and he took a deep calming breath. Yes, yes, it was indeed possible, but first they need to learn to fight and not just fight, they need to learn to fight as one. Eighty of them altogether now. If eighty strong, healthy Norsemen, fighting as a single unit, disciplined and following orders. There were none that could stand in their way, unless sheer numbers were to overpower them. But these were not all Norsemen. Only a few were. But could these few teach the rest in time? Then, stopping his thoughts from running away with him, Lubeck remembered the Saracen. Lubeck had fought the Saracens before, a few years back now, but the memories of that time were still fresh in his mind. Never before had he fought such men. Highly skilled with swords, lances and bows, but more than this, they had magic. Well, it seemed like magic at the time. Fighting the Saracens, Lubeck remembered, they had used fireballs that exploded and punched holes in their shield walls. They had devices that hurled these fireballs from far away. His raiding party suffered heavy losses from this onslaught before they were in range to fight at close quarter. Then, the skills these Saracens had displayed and their ability to kill, was heart stopping. "Yes, the Saracen." Lubeck said under his breath. "I need to talk with this man."

By the time Lubeck returned from his thoughts, all of the survivors were inside and Hagar was beckoning for Lubeck to come back inside also. He did and the big doors of the tower were closed tight behind him. Thorsten had by now summoned the rest of the men to join them from their positions and Freyja's main chamber was filled to capacity with eighty men all clambering to greet each other. The room was filled with talk and laughter. Spirits were high as the fit tended the injured. Food and drink flowed to fill the bellies of those who had not eaten for a day or two. Freyja sat on a window ledge watching as the frivolities continued. Lubeck joined her with a smile.

"Can you heal them please? As you did with us?" He asked her.

"I will." She replied. "Just as soon as they are all settled. Then tomorrow, I will take you all to Antonio." Lubeck smiled.

"Good" He said then moved over to Thorsten and whispered something in his ear. Thorsten moved across the room and spoke to the Saracen who was sat with two similar looking countrymen. He looked up and located Lubeck, then nodded. Standing, he slowly and inconspicuously made his way over. Lubeck turned and left the room making his way down to the beach. The Saracen followed silently as the rest of the men began to settle for the night. Once both men were alone on the beach, Lubeck asked him about Saracen fireballs and fighting skills. The two spoke for some time before Thorsten summoned them both back to the tower. They returned to find Kei waiting for them.

"We need to talk Lubeck." He said.

"As you wish." Lubeck replied.

"Not here, not where we can awaken the men, out there." Kei indicated to the entrance hall they had passed through as they came into the tower. Lubeck gestured for Kei to lead the way. In the hallway Kei voiced his concerns and his claim to leadership.

"I was elected leader by my men." Lubeck explained.

"Well that was then, I am here now, so you can step aside and I will lead us." Kei retorted.

"No, I don't think that is going to happen." Lubeck began. "I was elected by Thirty five men, unanimously."

"I was not here then, but now I am." Kei interrupted. "You will step down as leader and let me take my place as Chieftain."

"What if I don't want to?" Lubeck countered.

"Then I will remove you." Kei snapped reaching for the fishing knife tucked into his waist band. As he did, the Saracen stepped out of the shadows where he had concealed himself. One of the slim curved swords unsheathed and held up to Kei's throat with such speed that neither Kei nor Lubeck had time to react.

"Put that away." A soft almost whispering voice with a heavy Middle Eastern accent said. Kei's fingers gripped tighter around the handle of the knife.

Don't, The voice warned tilting Kei's head back by pressing the sword edge against his skin. A thin trickle of blood seeped out and ran down his throat to his collar bone. "I will not speak again." The voice continued. Kei let go of the knife and the Saracen lowered his sword.

"I think that says everything." Lubeck began. "I will put your claim of leadership to the men in the morning. Until then, may I suggest that you keep your hands well away from anything that could be mistaken for a weapon. You wouldn't want to lose it would you?" Lubeck turned to return to the main chamber as Kei called after him.

"Your Saracen bodyguard can't watch you every second of every night Lubeck!"

"He doesn't need to." Lubeck replied. "The Gods themselves watch over me." With that, he continued to walk to the main chamber, the Saracen at his back. As Kei stood there in the dim light of the hall, two more Saracens stepped from the shadows and followed their countryman. Kei spun around looking for more and panted uneasily as he did.

"Like ghosts!" He exclaimed. Reaching to his throat, he wiped away the blood with the back of his hand. As he turned to return to the main chamber, a huge fist struck him square in the face, felling him and rendering him unconscious.

DRAGON SHIP

As morning broke, Kei awakened to find himself lying on Freyja's bed. The small cut to his throat was healed, his jaw did not ache and he was rested.

"I trust you are well?" Freyja asked him. Kei didn't answer but looked around the room. It was empty.

"Where is everyone?" He asked.

"They are all on the beach waiting for you to join them. Come, I'll show you the way." Freyja replied. They both walked down the stairway to the beach where the rest of the men were assembled. All fit and well now and dressed in full shining breast plates and chain mail, with weapons to match. Thorsten was standing on a rock addressing them with reference to the contention for leadership. He broke off as Freyja and Kei approached.

"How do you feel?" Lubeck asked.

"Strangely, well." Kei replied. Lubeck laughed as he continued.

"Yes, Freyja has some healing abilities. She treated you last night as you slept—"

"Slept?" Kei objected, "I was attacked and rendered unconscious, but I don't understand, why for so long?"

"I did that to you." Freyja began, "I kept you asleep while the potion did its work." Kei scowled at her. Freyja shrugged her shoulders and walked across the sand to sit on a rock and listen. Thorsten continued addressing the men, as he had been before the interruption. He told the men of Kei's claim to leadership and that Lubeck had agreed to let the men decide once more. Again there was a resounding roar for Lubeck. There were some seventy one men siding with Lubeck and only a hand full supporting Kei.

"I show in favour of myself." Lubeck stated. "And I think you do for yourself?" Lubeck continued turning his attention to Kei. Kei nodded without a word.

"That makes it seventy two in favour of Lubeck and eight in favour of Kei." Thorsten announced. Those in favour of Kei moved over to stand by his side. Kei looked at the small army stood by Lubeck, including the three Saracens and the huge giant, Thorsten.

"It is decided then!" Announced Freyja standing up. "Lubeck will be your chosen chieftain." The men cheered and slammed swords against shields in support of the decision. Thorsten stepped forward to address Kei directly.

"You can accept the decision of the men and stay with us, or you can take your followers and leave. I would suggest the former if I were you. We don't know these lands and we don't know what waits for us out there. You would do better if you stayed with us. Greater numbers, means better chances of staying alive, but it's up to you." Kei pondered this for a moment, then lowered his head and asked for acceptance. Lubeck granted it and Kei with his followers re-joined the group. Lubeck leaned close to Thorsten and spoke quietly to him. Thorsten frowned and nodded, then walked over to Hagar and repeated what Lubeck had told him. Lubeck looked over his shoulder to find three Saracens standing close by.

"Thank you for last night." Lubeck began, "I feel that I can trust you and your countrymen, I hope that I am right?"

"You can." One of the Saracens announced.

"What name do you go by?" Lubeck asked him as he looked at the three mysterious figures.

"Tarique, and this is Jaffa and Jamal." He replied gesturing to the other Saracens. Lubeck once again looked the three men over curiously, his eyes taking in every detail.

"I need to talk to you about my request last night." He said. "Will you help me?"

"Yes." Tarique answered "Our people have used these methods for centuries, we can teach you, if this is your wish?"

"Good. It is." Lubeck grinned. "We will have time while we are waiting for Antonio to build us a ship." Lubeck jumped up onto a rock and addressed the group as a whole.

"Gather food, water, any other provisions you consider necessary, carry as much as you can. We are going to need it. Hurry, we leave for Antonio as soon as we are ready." Freyja looked at the tower and lowered her head. A great sadness befell her expression as she spoke to Lubeck.

"I'm a prisoner here, I can't leave this place. Antonio is on the far reaches of where I am permitted to travel. He moved closer to me so that I could talk with him regularly. He knows my predicament and he sympathises with it. He has offered to help, if I could get my army together. To break the spell that binds me here, I must have my sister returned unharmed, or I can never leave."

"Then we must not fail." Replied Lubeck. "Get me this ship. I will sail when it's ready and I will return with your sister by my side. This I promise you." Freyja nodded gently and turned towards the tower.

"I'll prepare for the journey. It's two days travel from here. I'll take you there and secure your ship." With that she was gone, hurrying towards the tower. Head still hanging low. Lubeck watched as she walked away. What strange magic held her here? Or was it simply fear for her sister's life? Perhaps that was it? Perhaps that is why her sister has to be returned to her unharmed? She fears that the slavers will kill her if Freyja left these shores. It's not that her sister is a powerful witch at all. It's Freyja they fear. It's Freyja that has the power and the slavers are using her sister to control her, keeping her here so that they know where she is when they want her? Perhaps they don't need to sail far away at all? Maybe if they cause some irritation to the slavers in some way, they might return here to force Freyja to help them put an end to it? Maybe we don't have to find them? Maybe they will come to us? Lubeck grinned to himself. His mind in a whirl, a plan was hatching to lure the slavers to him.

Provisions gathered and distributed amongst the men, all fully armed and dressed for battle. They stood ready to leave by the tower's great door. Freyja headed the group as Thorsten opened the door and everyone began to advance, following Freyja in tidy, neat columns of two.

"They look almost professional don't they?" Hagar commented.

"They will be professional by the time we sail." Lubeck replied, slapping his friend on the back and heading off following the rest. Thorsten pulled the big doors closed again as the last of the men passed through it, then joined the rear of the column and walked on to whatever adventure lay ahead. As they left the tower behind, Lubeck ordered scouts to forge ahead and also a rear guard to cover their movements. All of the men knew to stay alert and not to let themselves be caught off guard. They talked as they walked, but their eyes were always checking their flanks as the column moved on.

"Rotate the men every Five miles." Lubeck told Thorsten. "I don't want them getting tired and missing signs of a possible ambush." Thorsten acknowledged the order and started detailing the relief groups to go scouting or rear guard. The first day passed uneventfully and the party made an encampment for the night. Fires were lit and sentries posted. Watch rotas worked out so that every man got a fair amount of food and sleep.

"We have made good time today." Hagar pointed out.

"Yes, We should reach Antonio by midday tomorrow, much sooner than I thought." Freyja replied.

"Good." Lubeck began. "The sooner the ship is started the better."

"The ship is already started." Freyja replied. "Antonio has been working on it since last summer. I told him that before it was complete, I would provide a crew to man it." Lubeck looked at her suspiciously. "I saw your escape." Freyja continued "I saw your coming to me and I saw your army grow. It is all as I have foreseen." Thorsten smiled and dropped his huge frame onto a rudimentary bed on the ground close to the fire.

"Then I hope you have foreseen our success in your font little witch." He said with playful mocking in his voice. Freyja frowned at the big man and Thorsten laughed, lying back and doing his best to make himself comfortable. The night passed uneventfully and on rising, the band disassembled the temporary encampment and continued on their journey.

The morning was bright as the sun rose. No clouds in the sky, no harsh wind, just a gentle breeze that helped to cool the band as they walked cheerfully but cautiously towards their goal. By the time the sun was high in the sky, Freyja pointed towards a narrow path that led down the side of a cliff towards a beach below. As they made their way down, they passed through forests of tall broad trees that meandered almost to the water's edge. An estuary now blocked their path and Freyja directed the men to walk inland along the banks. The forest became thicker and it became difficult for them to pass through. Lubeck studied the water in the estuary as he walked. It was deep and wide. Wide enough and deep enough for a ship to pass through. He smiled as he continued to walk.

"What are you smiling at?" Thorsten asked him.

"He's clever this Antonio. Nobody would expect to find a ship builder down here. On the shoreline maybe? Perhaps at the mouth of the estuary? But, this far up stream? Not exactly a prime ship building location. I like that. The ship will be built in secret."

"Why does it matter if people know of the ship's existence?" Thorsten asked, screwing up his face with contemplation.

"If word got out about a fighting ship being built, would they not come to find out why? This kind of curiosity would get the attention of the slavers who might decide to come to investigate for themselves." Lubeck replied. Thorsten thought for a moment before asking,

"But would this not be a good thing? It would bring our enemies to us."

"No Thorsten, it would not be a good thing. They would catch us before we were ready to face them and they would burn our ship before it ever sailed. No, we need to stay hidden for now, until we are ready to sail. Then we let them know that we are here, by raiding some of their settlements and taking their supplies, maybe even free some more slaves and increase our numbers. We could build this army that Freyja talks about. You know, for the first time since being captured, I think we might have a chance to do this." Lubeck grinned widely and slapped the giant on the back as they continued to make their way to meet with Antonio.

"We're here!" proclaimed Freyja as they passed into a small clearing. The men all gasped as their eyes beheld the main frame structure of a large ship, already two thirds of the way through its construction.

"She's huge." Lubeck said, his eyes darting all over the framework of the mighty hull that sat majestically on a slope to the bank not too far from them now. He could already see that the ship would have two decks when finished. It was also some one hundred and fifty feet in length.

Long and narrow, with an impressive Dragon mounted way out front as an intimidating figure head.

"She looks fast" Lubeck pointed out.

"She'd better be. I've worked long and hard on my designs to make sure she will be the fastest ship this world has ever seen." A jolly voice rang out from inside the ship's hull. With that, a balding head with short white hair framing the shining dome popped up and hazel eyes looked over the group with interest. "I've been wondering when you would finally pay us a visit Lubeck." The man said, his eyes settling firmly on Lubeck's face. Then his gaze swapped to Freyja as she made her way forward. "Freyja my darling, how lovely to see you. Come, come. I could do with a break, come and join me." With that, the middle aged man scrambled out of the partially build ship and beckoned them to follow him, as he scurried away along the bank towards a small hut.

"He knows me?" Lubeck enquired to Freyja as they followed Antonio towards the hut.

"Yes, I have told you before, I have seen it all and shown Antonio to convince him to build this ship for you." She replied. Lubeck reached out and ran his hand along the ship as they walked past.

"So smooth." He said with curiosity in his voice.

"Yes, it helps the way she will glide over the water and the air will not drag her back, less drag, more speed." Antonio shouted back at them as they approached the hut. "She will lift as she moves forward, not so much ploughing her way through the water, but almost skimming over it. Her hull is designed to flex and give a little when the sea becomes wild. This will make her more durable in bad weather, reducing the possibility of her back breaking with the swells." Antonio spoke with such enthusiasm in his voice, it was almost infectious. "I had hoped to have her ready for your arrival, but it's slow work, cutting trees and sawing wood then securing it all into place on one's own." He continued.

"Well, you're not alone anymore." Lubeck began, "And we have eighty strong pairs of hands to lighten your burden."

"Good! Good!" Antonio shouted with delight "The sooner she's finished, the sooner we can sail." "We?" Thorsten questioned.

"Yes, why?" The reply came back from Antonio. "You don't think that I'm going to build the fastest, finest fighting ship this world has ever seen, then just hand her over to a bunch of thugs who will get her smashed or burned in no time at all, do you? Who's going to put her back together again then?"

"Then you come too." Lubeck stated, "Now, let's eat and drink, it's been a long journey." They all sat around the hut and the band of warrior's unpacked food and drink, then settled back to enjoy the peace and tranquillity of the place. After they had finished eating and rested, Hagar organised the men into groups to assist Antonio with the heavier work which allowed him to focus his efforts on designing and planning. They cut the trees required, sawed wood and hammered fixings into place, all under Antonio's supervision. Lubeck, Thorsten and Hagar were not excused labours either. They too worked alongside their men, sweating and straining with the rest of them. Treating sore hands and the occasional bloodied finger from misplaced hammer blows as they worked. Soon the ship was taking shape and as it did, it became less manpower intensive. Therefore Lubeck reorganised the men's working groups, so that while some were working on the ship, others were training in the arts of war. Thorsten took each group and instructed them on how to make a shield wall, the mainstay of any Norse battle tactics. Interlocking their shields to form an impenetrable wall. Each man protecting the man to his left from knee to neck in the top row and the bottom row protecting from knee to floor. Then by Lubeck's command, this was modified, with help from a couple of crewmen from Greek origin, into a Phalanx. Now the men were not only protected from the front, but from 360 degrees all round and above. The men soon learned to swap between the two methods of defence at the sounding of a Viking horn and within seconds could turn it around from one to the other. This was a good result Lubeck thought to himself.

So, now he questioned every crewman about the techniques used by their people to attack and defend on the battlefield. The months passed quickly and with each new technique they learned, the crew became more and more formidable, a very efficient fighting force.

"Now they are starting to look like an army." Lubeck announced as he smiled.

"A fierce raiding party yes, but we need more numbers to be an army." Thorsten replied.

"Your numbers will grow with each raid you carry out." Freyja stated.

"Raids will cost lives, but hopefully not so many that we can't increase our numbers with replacements. But losing men, good men like these, is not a favourable outcome. We need to ensure that we're trained to such efficiency, that our foes cannot defeat us. Our losses must stay low and our spoils high." Lubeck looked to the other two with a hope. "Perhaps with this mixture of tactics and skills, we will make such a force that our enemies yield without a fight?"

"Where's the fun in that?" Thorsten responded.

"To be feared." Freyja answered. "To be so feared, that the mere mention of our name will terrify our enemies and send them running like scared children."

"And what name shall that be?" Lubeck enquired. Freyja smiled thoughtfully and said. "Our ship shall be known as, Thunder Child, our soldiers known as—"

"Gurlemek." Tarique interrupted. All eyes focused on the Saracen as silence fell upon the group. They waited in anticipation for him to elaborate. Tarique simply shrugged his shoulders and said, "It means Thunder in my language." Everyone still stared at him in silence. "I'm a Turk." He continued, "Gurlemek means Thunder in Turkish." The group laughed lightly amongst themselves, trying out phrases to fit their suggested name.

"Run! Run for your lives the Gurlemek are coming!" Thorsten shouted mockingly.

"No." Tarique corrected him. "It would be, run for your lives the Gurlemek IS coming." Hagar added his thoughts to the conversation.

"Perhaps our enemies will run and hide if we made a noise like the sound of thunder as we approached?"

"Yeah." Malik laughed, "Maybe Thorsten could point his huge arse in the direction of our enemies and fart at them? That would sound like thunder." The whole group were laughing at the thoughts and suggestions except Lubeck, who silently rose to his feet, then stated,

"No, our enemies will look from their fortress walls as the Thunder Child approaches and their hearts will grow heavy as they think to themselves and so the Gurlemek comes."

"And so the Thunder comes." Freyja translated, almost in a whisper.

"And so the Thunder comes." They all repeated in a low, hushed murmur.

"Gurlemek!" Thorsten exclaimed loudly. "Gurlemek! This will be a name the enemy will grow to fear and dread."

"It sounds like a leviathan from ancient Greece." Announced Hagar. "Like the Kraken or Harpies."

"By the time we're finished." Lubeck began, "The Gurlemek will be even more feared than any Leviathan."

The training continued and the men became more adept at their new and exotic battlefield techniques. Faster and faster. Easier and more natural the manoeuvres became. Strange at first, but they became increasingly familiar with practice. Men that were particularly skilful with bows coached those who were not, until they too, became proficient and could hit moving targets with relative ease. Men practiced with recently made wooden training swords. Lubeck also, was not excused class. Thorsten wielded his mighty axe and demonstrated how difficult it could be to get close enough to strike a killing blow against an opponent who was armed with such a weapon. Until the moment Tarique stepped forward carrying two wooden training swords, one in each hand. Thorsten laughed.

"You'll need a lance or a spear at least, to have a chance to strike even the slightest blow, never mind kill an opponent armed with this." He said holding up his huge axe. Tarique smiled and shook his head while staring at the ground.

"I don't think so." He replied. Everyone stopped their training and gathered around to watch. The men helping Antonio build the Thunder Child included. Leaning close to Freyja, Lubeck said in a hushed voice.

"This should be good." Malik, never one to pass up an opportunity, quickly started taking bets as to who would be triumphant. Men started staking trivial commodities such as sweet fruits and trading workloads as wagers. Antonio was worried for the two men's safety and expressed his concerns to Lubeck, who merely chuckled and told the ship builder to relax.

"Tarique is too skilful for Thorsten to catch him and he is only armed with wooden swords, so he won't hurt Thorsten with them."

"But what if Thorsten hits Tarique with his axe? That axe is not wooden." Antonio protested.

"Thorsten is too slow to catch Tarique with any blow that could hurt him, don't worry, watch and enjoy the entertainment." Lubeck replied in a relaxed manner.

"I hope you're right." Freyja commented in a worried voice. Lubeck smiled and moved to a slightly better vantage point just as Thorsten took a swing at Tarique with his axe. Tarique simply stepped backwards out of the axes long reach and the head sailed past harmlessly almost overbalancing Thorsten. Tarique walked calmly around Thorsten staying just out of reach and rotating both swords simultaneously in a menacing display of ambidextrous ability. Thorsten roared as he hoisted his axe high overhead and took a step towards his opponent. This was the moment Tarique had been waiting for. He leapt forwards towards the giant and performed a forward roll under the arc of the huge axe. As he rotated fully over to an upright position kneeling on one knee in front of the huge warrior, he struck him hard with one sword across the abdomen, then continuing his forward rolling technique, rolled past Thorsten's right hip and again struck the big man. This time, across his back. Thorsten roared with pain and rage. He spun round swinging his axe at waist level. Tarique jumped vertically and tucked up his legs bringing his knees in tight to his shoulders, allowing the head of the axe to pass harmlessly underneath him. As he landed, Tarique dropped to the floor and drove the sole of his right foot against the back of the unbalanced giant's knee. Thorsten buckled and fell to his knees as Tarique jumped to his feet and cracked the side of Thorsten's head with one of his swords. The crowd winced and groaned as if feeling the pain themselves. Thorsten's head rang from the blow. He shook it as if trying clear his thoughts. Tarique smiled at the big man as he offered a hand to help him to his feet. Thorsten grunted loudly as he accepted the hand and climbed back to a standing position. His eyes flicked across the crowd, all were eagerly waiting for the next event. Thorsten thought for a moment then suddenly lurched forward at Tarique who skipped to his left to avoid the hulk's attack. Thorsten however, had anticipated this and mid stride checked himself and spun around to his right bringing his elbow up and striking the surprised Saracen squarely on the forehead stopping him instantly. The force of the blow stunned the Turk who instinctively dropped to the floor and rolled away from any immediate danger. The huge Viking quickly stepped towards his disorientated foe and kicked at him as he moved. His foot caught Tarique on his hip, spinning him further away. Tarique used this opportunity and momentum to his advantage and allowed himself to roll with the force of the blow, which brought him back up to his feet just in time to deflect another attempt from Thorsten to kick him. As he rotated away from the attempted kick, he spun fully round and caught Thorsten across the back of his head with another blow from one of his swords. Thorsten reeled from the blow and staggered forward managing to retain his balance. Tarique followed up with another swing with his other sword, but Thorsten caught the sword in one hand and jabbed his axe head into Tarique's stomach with the other. The crowd gasped as air rushed out of Tarique's mouth with such force that it could be heard above the cheers of support from their crew mates. Thorsten now pulled on the sword he had just caught, ripping it from Tarique's grip and swiping it across the side of his head. Tarique lurched backwards from the impact of the blow. But, as he fell to his knees, he too jabbed out with his second sword and caught Thorsten squarely on the stomach winding him too. The giant fell to his knees also gasping for breath. But, as he did, he reached out and grabbed Tarique by the throat with one of his enormous hands and began to choke the Saracen.

"Stop this!" Freyja pleaded, worried for Tarique's life. At that precise moment, Tarique struck Thorsten hard on the side of his head with the hilt of his wooden sword. The blow bit deep into Thorsten's skull and pain shot through his whole body. His grip on Tarique however did not loosen. Tarique, beginning to cough and splutter now gripped the giant's wrist. With a huge effort and dropping himself onto his back, he drove his feet into Thorsten's stomach lifting him into the air and over the top, slamming him down hard onto his back and forcing him to release his grip on Tarique's throat. The two men lay there in the dirt panting, as Lubeck stepped forward laughing loudly at the pair. As their breathing steadied Lubeck reached down with both hands and assisted both men back to their feet. Looking at Thorsten he declared.

"An even match I think, though Tarique did behead you at least once or was it twice?" Lubeck laughed as the big Norseman rubbed his head where it had been struck by Tarique's wooden sword. Laughter filled the air as everyone returned to whatever task they had been performing before the entertainment break. Antonio approached as the men walked towards the ship.

"I'm just about to put the figure head in place." He announced excitedly.

"But the ship has a figurehead." Lubeck replied a little confused, pointing towards the huge dragon at the bows of the ship.

"Yes, yes I know, but I'm not on about that snarling dragon. He watches over the waters ahead and keeps us safe from what awaits us there. No, I'm talking about this." By now the group had reached the ship and had climbed aboard as they were talking. Antonio reached out and patted another figure wrapped in a white cloth that was mounted at the stern of the ship overlooking the decks and crew. "What do you think?" Antonio asked as he pulled away the cover to reveal an ornately carved bust, bearing an uncanny resemblance to Freyja. The men stared at it stunned by its intricate detail and craftsmanship. "She can't come with us in body, but at least she can watch over us in soul, don't you think?" At that moment Freyja stepped up onto the ship to join them. Her eyes caught sight of the carving and she took a second glance at it in a mixture of surprise and admiration for the workmanship that had created such a piece. She now stared at it, unmoving and silent. Antonio's face filled with concern. "What's wrong Freyja, don't you like it?"

"No, it's not that." She replied. "I'm… I'm stunned. I don't know what to say."

"Good, you like it then?" Antonio asked, laughing as he planted a big kiss on the cheek of the figure he had created. "I for one will sleep better at night knowing that you are watching over us every minute of each day and night."

"Me too." Lubeck muttered almost to himself. Freyja caught his eye as she turned towards him. Lubeck dropped his gaze and uncharacteristically looked a little embarrassed as he realised that she had heard him. "It's a fine piece of work." He continued loudly, as if to trying to erase his former comment and slapping Antonio on the back in congratulation they stepped away and off the ship.

Freyja remained for a moment and stared herself in the face. A strange feeling filled her soul as she did. A deep but gentle voice came from behind her.

"How does it feel to come face to face with oneself?" She turned round to find Hagar there smiling warmly at her. "I'd bet there isn't a man amongst us that will not sleep soundly being watched over by you." He said as he slipped past her to leave the ship. Freyja's gaze returned to the carving and she smiled.

"I'll do more than simply watch over you all." She said as she fumbled around in the small sack she was carrying. Her hand located the small leather bound book she had been searching for and lifted it out discretely. She flipped through some of the pages and stopped at a particular verse. Her eyes quickly scanned over the page, then removing a small ampule of green liquid from a pocket in her dress, she began to utter the words she had just read from the page. As she completed the verse, she removed the stopper from the ampule and poured the liquid over the head of the carving. Freyja took a deep breath and held it in anticipation. For a moment nothing happened and Freyja thought that she had misinterpreted the words. Disappointment crept into her heart as she waited. Then just as she was about to give up and accept failure, the figure moved. Not a lot, just a little, just enough to catch her eye. Freyja gazed at it waiting for it to move some more, for another sign that her plan had worked, but no, nothing. Had she succeeded? Or was it that, what she thought she had seen, had simply been a trick of the light? She waited a little longer, only to be disappointed as nothing more seemed to happen. With a frown and a sigh, she hitched up the hem of her long dress and stepped down from the ship and headed towards the hut where the rest had gone for some refreshment. She had only made it about half way there when the carved figure moved again. This time though there was no doubt, it moved, it was no trick of the light. But there was nobody around to witness the wooden figurehead open its eyes and take a slow deliberate look around at its surroundings before closing them again and returning to its inanimate state.

THE FIRST ROLL OF THUNDER

The following day found the ship almost ready to sail. All of the men worked together to ready the slipway and prepare to launch her. But before that happened, Lubeck gathered Tarique, Antonio and Freyja together to discuss one last modification.

"When I fought the Saracens in the East, they destroyed a quarter of our fleet before we could release a single arrow. Their ships hurled thunderbolts at us and burned our ships before we could get in range. How could they throw fire balls at us with such force and range?" Lubeck enquired of the Turk. Tarique smiled as he answered.

"I don't know how they achieved this, though I too have seen it from afar. But Jamal knows of these things. He used to help make such devices. Shall I go and bring him here?" Lubeck nodded and turned to Antonio informing him.

"Whatever Jamal tells you about these devices, I need you to listen. I want them mounted on the Thunder Child before we sail. With such devices, our dragon guardian up front will not only look fierce, but will also breathe fire." Jamal arrived and began to discuss the devices with Antonio, then between them, they devised a plan to manufacture and install them. Lubeck instructed that he wanted two of them at the bows of the ship and one at the stern. Antonio scratched his head as he tried to figure out a way to achieve everything Lubeck wanted, but finally drawings were made and work began.

Some weeks later and with lots more training to their credit, the ship and crew were ready. The launch went ahead without incident and the Thunder Child was afloat on the river and looking ready for war. Brightly painted, round shields were secured along both sides of the gunwales. The sail was black in colour, but gathered and secured away, so as not to catch the wind just yet. A fierce Dragon looked out over the waters ahead, with a fearsome looking ram breaking the water surface below it, while a friendly face looked down over the crew from astern. She was big, bigger than any ship the crew had ever seen. Almost two thirds longer and half as wide again than anything they had laid eyes upon before. Two decks deep, but very different from the Galley they had all been slaves on some ten months prior. These decks were not made for slaves. The upper deck was open with benched seats for the crew to man their oars; there were no chains in these benches though. Two small shelters, one forward and one aft provided for those who may be injured or needing relief from the sun. The lower deck was divided into two halves. One provided stabling for twenty horses, the other sleeping quarters for the crew. Unlike the slavers Galley, each crewman on this ship had his own bed to sleep in when weary.

The Thunder Child sat on the water glistening and new, looking like some mythical monster in the midday sun. She rocked gently, which gave her the appearance of a giant creature at rest breathing deeply as it slept. Antonio and the others looked on with admiration.

"A fine piece of work my friend." Announced Thorsten with a wide grin. "She'll strike fear and dread into our enemies when they see her bearing down on them, breathing fire as she comes for their souls." Utterances of agreement rippled through the onlookers, but there was a slight tension in the air. This was broken by Malik as he spoke without thinking as always.

"Is she fast?" He asked without a care. Silence fell upon the crew and everyone including Lubeck stared at Antonio with anticipation.

"Fast?" He began, "I hope so, that's what I had in mind when I designed her, but these extra modifications and her size, well, well I'm not sure if speed has been compromised for strength."

"Only one way to find out." Lubeck interjected. "All hands on deck!" He shouted. "Cast off and man the oars! Make ready for sea and man the sail!"

The crew sprang into action. Men clamoured for the benches and began to push oars against the river banks as others released the mighty ship's moorings. Men pulled on ropes and climbed aloft to release the sail as the Thunder Child slipped away from the bank and began to move majestically downstream towards the mouth of the river and the open sea beyond. Men heaved on oars and the ship picked up speed. Everyone worked together as free men and achieved their goal efficiently. The Thunder Child's sail rippled and lashed as it tried to catch the wind. Crewmen fought with ropes tightening and loosening them trying to control the huge expanse of canvas that formed the great black sail. Antonio clutched Freyja close to him as they stood at the stern watching with wonder at the hive of activity that surrounded them. Both were filled with excitement and wonderment, mixed with just a little apprehension. A giant fire breathing dragon, wings spread wide and claws out stretched, all in Gold centred against the vast black square, roared like thunder as the huge sail bellowed catching the wind and filling fully. A vicious jolt shot through the ship as she suddenly picked up speed.

"Stow the oars!" Yelled Lubeck.

"Make fast the sail!" Added Thorsten. Men hurried about their tasks, not needing any more guidance. Hagar heaved on the tiller to bring the bow of the mighty ship around to meet the open sea ahead.

"Hold on tight!" Called Antonio from the stern. "As we leave the river mouth, the wind will catch us as it comes down from the cliffs behind!" No sooner did the words leave his lips, the golden dragon roared again. The vast sail lashed as the wind strengthened and stretched the canvas fully tight, as if the dragon had taken a deep breath. Salt spray dampened the air and soaked the crew from head to foot as the bow of the Thunder Child lifted from the water. "Now!" yelled Antonio. "Now you'll see her fly!" As the wind strengthened, the ship lifted in the water so that its hull merely skimmed the surface rather than ploughed through the waves. As it did, there was yet another noticeable increase in speed. Some of the crew clung desperately to ropes and railings with a hint of fear in their hearts. Others laughed and whooped with joy at the way the Thunder Child sped across the crest of each and every wave as if the Gods themselves were aiding her along.

"Now this is a ship!" Lubeck rejoiced, with a wide grin. Thorsten, Malik, Antonio and everyone aboard this ship of ships whooped and cried out with excitement and pride for their achievement. But their celebrations were cut suddenly short, as Freyja cried out in pain, wavered then fell to the deck. Antonio knelt to aid her. There was no visible reason for her fainting. She was breathing, but erratically, and her forehead was extremely hot to the touch.

"What is it?" Asked Lubeck, still holding onto a nearby rope to steady himself against the motion of the ship's great speed.

"I don't know." Antonio began, but then realisation befell him as he looked outward towards the quickly disappearing shoreline. "The distance, we're too far out. The curse, we have to get her back closer to the shore, we're too far out damn it!" The severity of the situation hit him like a thunderbolt. Lubeck looked up at the distance they had travelled in such a short space of time. Freyja had told him that she couldn't go with them because she was cursed to remain in these parts until her sister was returned to her unharmed. The shoreline now appeared to be a low shadow on the horizon. Lubeck looked toward Hagar on the tiller.

"Bring her about!" He yelled. "Bring her about hard! Take us back to shore!"

"Aye captain!" Hagar replied heaving on the tiller for all his worth. Thorsten jumped to assist him and together they pulled the Thunder Child around to head back home.

"We'll have to tack against the wind." Antonio informed them.

"That will take too long." Lubeck replied. "Gather the sail, break out the oars!" He called. Men gathered up the sail and secured it safely away, while the rest jumped onto the benches and lowered the oars into the water. Thorsten and Lubeck both jumped to man an oar also.

"Steady, Together, Heave!" Antonio called out. "Heave together, stay in time, heave, listen to the drum!" With that Antonio grabbed the hammers and began to beat out a steady rhythm on the big drums mounted at the stern of the top deck just below the carving of Freyja. The Thunder Child sitting heavy in the water began to move against the wind and back towards the shore. "Pick it up!" Antonio called, "Pick it up, faster!" The tempo of the drum increased and the huge oars moved to keep time with it. The bows of the ship cut through the water increasing forward momentum with every stroke. The crew grimaced and strained as they heaved for all they were worth. Soon the shoreline became more visible and they could make out individual trees along the forest edges. The Mouth of the river could now be seen cutting into the land mass and dividing the woodland where they had hidden the ship during its construction. Freyja moaned and grimaced in her unconscious state as the Thunder Child slowed and entered the estuary heading cautiously back to her moorings by the river bank. Thorsten carefully lifted Freyja and carried her back to the little cabin on the edge of the woods. Antonio, Lubeck, Malik and Tarique followed anxiously. Hagar took charge of securing the ship and preparing it again for sea. The crew busied themselves securing all moorings and swabbing down the sea spray from the decks. This time though, the men began to fill the armoury with weapons and tools. They stocked the hold with food and water supplies and made ready the stables to receive horses.

"We prepare the stables for horses we don't have." Complained one crewman.

"I guess Lubeck has something in mind to rectify that." His shipmate answered with a soft chuckle.

"You have a lot of faith in him don't you?" The first crewman asked in response.

"As do most of us." His companion responded again "He set us free from the Galley, he found Freyja and she healed our injuries, fed and watered us, gave us shelter and lead us to Antonio. Now we have a ship worthy of the Gods themselves and Lubeck has trained us all to be professional soldiers. Lubeck has done right by us and transformed us from slaves into free men with a means of gaining our revenge and recovering our families. Do you not have faith in a man who has achieved so much in so little time?" The first crewman grunted and shrugged his shoulders indiscriminately.

"When you lay it all out like that…." He trailed off not really reaching any conclusion in his own mind but continued with his given chores without any more questions. His mind troubled him though. Loyalties split between Kei, the man who had pulled him from the water and dragged him up the beach, saving his life and Lubeck, the democratically voted leader who had, as correctly stated by his shipmate, freed them all from slavery in the first place and given them hope, purpose, and the ability to take back their loved ones. His split loyalties troubled him deeply, but he continued his duties as directed and prayed quietly to himself for guidance from the Gods, to show him where his path should lay.

In the little cabin, Freyja's condition had not changed. She lay in the small bed usually used by Antonio when he lived there alone. Still unconscious and showing no signs of coming round.

"What do we do now?" Asked Thorsten, pacing like a trapped animal. Sighs hissed around the cabin as all inside had no idea what they could do.

"This is a dark magic right?" Lubeck's question broke the uneasy silence.

"Yes, I believe so." Antonio replied in puzzlement. Lubeck frowned and rubbed his chin in thought.

"We need a witch or a Warlock to break this curse then?"

"It's not that easy." Replied Antonio. "Only the one who set the curse can remove it and she's on the other side of the world I think."

"Who? Who was it that set the curse?" Lubeck demanded. Antonio dropped his head reluctant to disclose Freyja's secret, but also resigning himself to the fact that he had no choice.

"It was her sister, Agatha. When the slavers took her, they were afraid that Freyja might become a witch like Agatha. So they forced Agatha to cast a spell to imprison Freyja on this Island, where they could watch her and come back for her if she developed the same sort of powers as her sister. As yet they haven't returned for her."

"Has she tried to leave before?" Lubeck enquired thoughtfully.

"Yes, just once, about six years ago. She bought passage on a trading ship and left with them. As they reached about the same distance from shore as we did, the same thing happened."

"How do you know this?" Thorsten asked. Antonio chuckled to himself a lightly.

"I was the captain of that trading ship. I thought nothing of it at first; merely that she wasn't much of a sailor. But, the sky became darker and a storm blew in from nowhere. The sea grew angry and we had to gather our sails to avoid losing them. Then, thunder roared and lightning destroyed my ship sending her to the bottom in an instant. I lost most of my crew that day. I grabbed Freyja and managed to slowly swim back to shore bringing her with me and then later, to the tower. I watched over her before Morgana turned up and tended her until the curse broke its hold on her some days later."

"If both of you knew what would happen, why did you allow her to remain aboard during our test voyage?" Lubeck asked gruffly. Antonio looked up with surprise in his eyes.

"We didn't expect the Thunder Child to be quite so fast. I mean, I know I built her for speed, but she excelled anything I ever expected of her. We covered more water than either of us thought she would in such a short voyage. Caught us both by surprise."

"Why didn't the curse destroy us like it did your vessel?" Malik asked.

"I don't know to be honest. That's what I feared at first. I thought the curse would destroy the Thunder Child, once I realised how far out we were. I can only assume that she is so fast, that we returned to shore before the storm came. I did not return to shore that day, I continued to sail away from the Island, and perhaps that's where the difference lays?"

"So, we wait then and see if she recovers like last time?" Malik enquired with a hopeful exuberance.

"Not quite." Antonio replied. "There's a woman in the village to the East, It has no name, she, is the one I referred to, called Morgana. Morgana helped last time. She stayed, tending Freyja for a few days. Then one morning she simply left and a couple of hours later, Freyja awoke. I don't know what Morgana did if anything, but it might be worth tracking her down and enlisting her help again this time."

"On it!" Announced Malik jumping to his feet. Lubeck turned his head and nodded at Tarique, who without a word, followed Malik out of the cabin calling his two countrymen. The trio escorted Malik off into the forest heading East.

"I'll keep an eye on her." Antonio began, addressing Lubeck. "You go and get the ship ready to sail. We should cast off as soon as Freyja is well enough to watch over our voyage." Lubeck nodded silently, then reluctantly left the cabin and turned his attention to preparing the ship. Day turned to night; night turned to day and still no word from Malik. Lubeck stood at the bow of the ship staring out over the water while leaning heavily against the back of the ornate Dragon figurehead.

"It's only been a day." Thorsten's voice came from behind him. "It will take them a few days at least to make the return journey. She will be ok my friend I'm sure of it."

"It's not her I'm worried about; it's my men out there, on foot and so few in numbers." Lubeck snorted. Thorsten laughed as he slapped Lubeck on the back.

"You can tell yourself whatever you like but you don't disguise your worries. I know how you feel about her, so do most of us. You can lie to yourself, but you can't lie to us. Malik will be fine too. He has three Saracen demons escorting him. Tarique on his own is enough to ensure a safe return, but Jaffa and Jamal are with them also. There is no need to worry about anything. Come, relax, our friends will return soon bringing this Morgana with them."

"Suppose she doesn't want to help?" Lubeck asked.

"Ha! I didn't say anything about them returning with a willing helper. Those four will return with her, willing or otherwise. Then, if she's not willing to help, I think circumstances will be inclined to help sway her mind." Thorsten grinned widely and dragged Lubeck away from the ship. The two friends headed towards the cabin where Hagar was now tending Freyja.

"No change." He reported as the two entered. Lubeck knelt by Freyja's side and placed a cloth, moist with cool water across her brow. He bent forward and placed an ear close to her face to listen to her breathing.

"It's as if she were simply sleeping." He noted. Hagar nodded as he replied.

"She's been that way all morning. She has a fever, but peaceful, as if in a deep sleep, yes."

"I'll sit with her for a while." Lubeck instructed. "You two go and put the men through their paces again, keep them busy, don't let them get idle. Tell them that everything is being taken care of and that they need to stay sharp, for soon we sail to pick a fight with some slavers in the Western approaches."

"Yes, Earl Lubeck." Hagar replied as he moved towards the door. Thorsten bowed his head slightly, slapped his fist against his chest uttering.

"Earl Lubeck." As he too headed towards the door. Outside, the crew were milling around idly as the two men approached. They quickly snapped to attention as Thorsten yelled out orders for them to report to their instructors for training. To a man, they jumped to it without question. Hagar smiled.

"Now they are behaving like professional soldiers. Now we may have a good chance for our revenge."

"I can't wait." Thorsten growled heading off to grab a bow. "Time for me to try and get a little better with this thing." He called back to Hagar as he held the bow aloft grinning as he went.

"The Gods themselves couldn't teach you how to use that, you big ox. You should stick to that axe of yours!" Hagar laughed as he replied. Thorsten laughed and then was gone. Hagar looked up to the sentries placed on the vantage points around the encampment, two men at each of three locations. Raising a hand to signal to them in turn. Each lookout returned a hand signal back indicating all was well. He took a deep breath and sighed. "Come on Malik, hurry." He thought out loud.

Far off to the East, Malik and the three Saracens could see the village in the distance from the top of the ridge they had surmounted. Lying close to the ground to hide their position, they observed what they could.

"We need to get closer." Malik stated to the others. "Tell me again, why are we creeping up unseen, like thieves or assassins? Why can't we just walk right into the village like simple travellers?"

"Suppose they are hostile?" Tarique suggested.

"Suppose they're not?" Malik retorted. Jamal nudged them both and pointed towards a one horse cart being driven slowly but surely towards the village gates. It was inconspicuous and unhurried as it approached the dilapidated perimeter fence and the rudimentary gate with only two men guarding it. Entry into the village for the cart was uneventful and quite nonchalant. The gate was opened after a cursory look by the guards. The cart, empty as it was, manned by two men and a woman, passed through and continued on its journey almost uninterrupted.

"There." said Malik, "That looked simple enough."

"Perhaps the guards knew them?" Tarique offered back.

"Perhaps these people are not aggressive?" Malik retorted.

"May I suggest something?" Jamal asked. "Let Malik, accompanied by one of us approach the gates. If they pass through unchallenged, all is good. If not the remaining two will have to rescue them." Tarique frowned, as he thought for a moment.

"No." He replied. "Malik can go down there alone. We are not dressed so as not to attract attention or suspicion. Saracens are not a common sight in this part of the world. We would raise too many questions if we were to approach the gates."

"Alone? I don't like the sound of that." Malik said nervously.

"Why?" Tarique replied. "You are the one who says that they are probably not aggressive are you not?"

"Yes, but—"

"But nothing." Tarique cut him off. "Go down there and test your theory my friend. We will have your back if something goes wrong."

"If something goes wrong, I will be a dead man and will have no need of your help." Malik replied ungraciously. Jaffa tapped his bow.

"They'll be dead before they can draw breath my friend, do not be afraid, we will have your back."

"You will have to be much closer." Malik stated.

"We will be, trust us." Jamal answered. Malik groaned as he looked at the three Saracens.

"Ok, but you must pay attention, I have no desire to die today, or any day, come to that."

"That's okay." Tarique began, "They probably won't kill you straight away. They'll probably capture you. That will give us lots of time to find Morgana and spirit her away while they are busy torturing you."

"Capture! Torture!" Malik gasped, panting with fear at the thought. The three Saracens laughed. Malik had never seen them laugh before. "You're kidding me right? It's a joke yes?" He asked rhetorically. Simultaneously, the Saracens stopped their laughing. Serious expressions befell their faces once again.

"Torture is no joke my friend." Tarique said in a sombre voice. "It hurts, a lot." Malik swallowed hard and fidgeted nervously.

"Err, maybe—" Giggling stopped him completing his response. Again the three Saracens were laughing.

"Go my friend." Tarique told him. "Go, we will not let them take you."

"Alive anyway." Jamal added as laughter broke out again.

"Funny, you're funny guys." Malik protested. But with that, he began to descend the ridge and make his way to the village gates. He looked back over his shoulder for reassurance from the Saracens, but they were gone. No sign that they had ever been there. The sun was beginning to set as Malik approached the gates. The two guards watched him as he advanced.

"Hold it there! State your business stranger!" One of them called out to him.

"I'm lost my friends. I've been wondering around out there for days. I just stumbled upon this place by the will of the Gods." Malik replied.

"Wait there, don't come any closer." A guard said in an authoritative voice. "Where have you come from?" The questioning continued.

"From across the sea. I was marooned here by a flea infested son of a baboon that claimed to be captain of the ship I stowed away on. He really wasn't very sympathetic to my predicament at all."

"What ship was that?" The guard continued. "There hasn't been a ship put in on this Island for months." Malik swallowed hard, his mouth drying as he realised this wasn't going to be as easy as he had first thought.

"I don't recall the name of the vessel. I just jumped aboard and concealed myself before it sailed. I didn't really pay much attention to what it was called or where it was going. I was in a bit of a hurry to get out of there."

"Get out of where? And why?" The guards continued to question. Malik wracked his brain for a quick answer.

"Pentecost." He announced. "I got into a little bit of trouble with a maidens father and four brothers." He grinned mischievously. "You can see why I needed a rapid escape, no?" The guards laughed, but then one said.

"Pentecost? I've never heard of it, what shore is that on? And as I have already said, no ship has put in here for months." Malik thought quickly.

"It's far to the East, past the usual trading routes, past the lands of spices and silk, and as I was about to explain. The ship didn't put into port. The captain merely came close to shore and tossed me overboard. I had to swim almost a mile to make it to this Island. I thought the sharks would get me for sure. But, thanks to the Gods, I made it somehow. I haven't eaten for a couple of days now and I'm awful thirsty too. Please have mercy and let me in."

"Do you have any way to pay for food and drink?" A guard asked. Again Malik tried to think quickly.

"No, but I am a skilled carpenter. I would be willing to work for food, water and shelter." The guards looked Malik over. Pondering for a moment before continuing their interrogation.

"Those clothes are not those of a carpenter." One pointed out.

"No." Malik began. "They are stolen from one of the many chests stowed in the hold of the ship I stowed away on."

"Why did you need to steal clothes." Another guard asked.

"Err, did you not hear me when I said I ran into a little trouble with a maiden's father and four brothers? I didn't really have time to dress before making my escape." Malik replied with sarcasm in his tone. The Guards laughed loudly and began to open the gates.

"Thank the Gods." Malik exclaimed as he stepped forwards to enter the village.

"Not so fast!" A guard called stepping into Malik's path. "You must report to the great hall and explain your situation to the village elders before we can let you run loose. You will have to repeat your story to them and let them decide if they will allow you to stay. Come, I will escort you there." With that, the guard took Malik by the arm and walked him towards the great hall at the centre of the village. Malik looked around anxiously. Where were the Saracens?

It didn't take long to reach the great hall and the guard explained to an elder the situation concerning Malik. The elder frowned at him, tutted and indicated for Malik to follow him. They reached a dining hall in a short time and Malik again had to recite his tale of woe. The elders were not impressed by his antics but they did grant him sanctuary for a short time on the condition that he proves to them, that he could be trusted and was in fact a skilled carpenter as he claimed to be. Malik was taken to a tavern and provided food and drink then taken upstairs to a room.

"You can stay here until you repair two of my tables and four chairs that have been broken for some time now." The landlord said. "Then maybe, we can see about finding you real employment so that you can earn enough to pay for what you eat and the room you use." The land lord left him in the room, and Malik slumped onto the small bed in the corner. He had not stopped bouncing from his ungainly flop, when the small window on the other side of the room slowly slipped open and one by one the Saracens dropped quietly from the roof and into the room to join him.

"Where have you been?" Malik demanded. Tarique smiled a crooked smile as he replied.

"Don't worry my friend, we were with you all of the way. While you bored the guards to death with your sob story we gained entry unseen.

We have also located a woman that one villager called out to. They called her Morgana as they beckoned her over. We now know where she lives. So don't get comfortable, we have work to do." Malik smiled at the prospect of their task being completed so soon as he replied to Tarique's instructions.

"Take me to her then, I'll see if I can charm her into coming with us."

"If not, we will convince her to accompany us." Jamal smiled. Malik left via the small door he had entered by and the Saracens vanished the way they had come in, silently as always, like spirits. Malik left the tavern and began to walk through the gloomy streets. A small pebble struck him on the back of his head. He flinched and looked around. In the shadows by a wood shed Jamal beckoned him over.

"This way, that hut over there, the one with a dim light in the window, by the well, see it?" Jamal pointed as he questioned. Malik nodded and made for the hut Jamal had directed him to. He approached the main door and knocked on it gently. A soft voice came from inside.

"Come in Malik." Malik froze, and the Saracens disappeared into the shadows once more. "Don't be afraid, I've been expecting you." The voice continued. Malik swallowed hard, then, hesitantly pushed the door open. An early middle aged woman stood by a small fire in the hearth. She was well presented in a long purple dress and her long brown hair tied back in a tight French plait. She was lean, as Malik had noticed earlier, so were most of the people in the village. She stopped tending the pot of stew which slowly simmered in a pot over the fire and straightened up to address Malik as he entered her home. "Don't be afraid, I have been waiting for you for a day or so since I received a vision from Freyja. She's hurt and needs my help again doesn't she?" Malik nodded in silence. Apprehension gripping his face and he uneasily fidgeted as he advanced towards her.

"You are Morgana?" He asked, drawing close beside her, as she still stood by the fire.

"Yes. Freyja and I are sisters, not of blood you understand, but of soul." Morgana looked for signs of understanding in Malik's face, but all she saw was confusion. She smiled, then offering him some stew she continued. "We are of the same vein. She has the power to heal, so do I. She can see the future, of sorts. So can I. She can summon violent storms to do her bidding…" Morgana paused for a second before continuing. "I can summon something much worse if need be." Malik's eyes widened as thoughts danced around his head. Morgana sniggered and smiled at him. "Don't worry yourself." She said. "My monsters will only harm those who would harm me, just as Freyja's storms only harm those who would harm her." Malik took the bowl he had been offered and set himself at Morgana's table. "Make yourself at home." She said mockingly.

"Apologies." Malik began, "I mean no disrespect."

"Don't worry your pretty little head over it." Morgana reassured him. "But tell me, why are your friends skulking in the shadows outside? Are they not hungry too?" Malik's eyes lifted to stare at her, but as he was about to speak, Morgana cut him short. "Don't even try to deny it, I see everything, you know that already, you've seen Freyja do it haven't you?" Malik nodded and lowered his gaze. As he did a Saracen appeared in the doorway. "Ah, there you are." Morgana sighed with a smile. "And your two friends?" A hand on her shoulder made her jump. As she turned to face its owner, Jamal said.

"You didn't see that, did you witch?" Shock captured Morgana's face as she backed away from the silent assassin who had caught her so completely unawares, but as she did, she bumped straight into Jaffa who had also spirited himself into her home, completely unseen both by her eyes or her abilities.

"Demons!" She spat. "How can you appear from nowhere like that? How could I not see you?" Her calm self-assurance now shaken as a feeling of vulnerability swept over her. Malik smiled as his confidence rose again.

"You might be able to summon monsters, but my demons would take your soul before you finished conjuring them." He said shaking his head playfully. "Now sit and listen." He ordered, taking a mouthful of the stew. "This is good." He commented. "Come eat and let us discuss what is going to happen now." Tarqiue closed the door, then helped himself to a bowl of stew and indicated to the others to do the same.

"Hey! Ladies first." Malik objected with a scornful look towards the Saracen.

"Apologies my lady." Tarique muttered, offering his bowl to Morgana. She took the bowl, settled at the table and began to eat. Joining her, the Saracens seated themselves, each with a bowl of the freshly made stew.

"Now, we mean you no harm, but you are coming with us this night." Malik said firmly. "Freyja needs your help and we have been sent to bring you to her. Willing or unwilling, you are coming with us just as soon as we finish this incredibly tasty stew."

"So it would appear." Morgana retorted. "But if Freyja needs my help, I will offer it willingly. As I said, we're sisters and that's what sisters do, look after each other."

"Good, then we can all be friends?" Malik asked rhetorically, his face creasing around the eyes as he smiled.

"We leave as soon as we finish." Tarique said in a stern tone.

"Really? I'm tired, it's dark and I'm in no mood to walk all the way to the tower at this time of night." Morgana stated defiantly.

"Yes really." Malik answered. "Freyja is unconscious and has been for about two days now I'd say, but we're not going to the tower. Freyja isn't there. We're headed way up the coast from there."

"How far?" Morgana asked.

"Two days travel from the tower. Maybe more from here." Malik replied as he continued to eat. Morgana frowned. If Freyja had been unconscious for that length of time she didn't have long left, if left untreated.

"We'll never make it in time on foot. We'll need horses. We'll have to travel light and move fast, even on horseback." The Saracens looked at each other and grinned. Then almost as if they had never been there, they were gone. "I wish they wouldn't do that." Morgana hissed. "It's unnatural and unnerving, they're like ghostly demons."

"I know, but it makes you feel safe when they're on your side." Malik said as he grinned at her. Morgana began to fill a small bag with vials of coloured liquids, powders and various herbs. Then grabbing her cloak and wrapping it around her shoulders, she looked towards Malik and asked him.

"Well, what are we waiting for? Let's get on our way. Hurry, time is against us." Malik raised a hand and indicated for her to wait. He moved to the door and peering through the small gap as he partially opened it and peered into the darkness outside. He could see no signs of movement from any corner of the village.

"What is it?" Morgana questioned.

"There is nobody outside, no villagers wandering the streets. No guards patrolling either. Where is everybody?" Malik asked.

"It's not so unusual." She replied. "People turn in about now around here. The guards only patrol once in a while, as there are no perceived threats usually. In fact, I think the last time we were under any kind of threat was when Freyja summoned a thunder storm which doused the flames that engulfed her tower, the night they tried to burn it down with her still in it." Malik raised his hand to silence her again. A group of horses approached. Malik pushed the door almost closed and crouched. The horses stopped right in front of the small hut. They snorted softly and scraped their feet impatiently. Malik closed his eyes as if praying. One of the riders dismounted and stepped onto the wooden flooring in front of the door without a sound. Malik drew a slender, double edged dagger from his right boot and indicated for Morgana to back away. Just then, there was a gentle tap at the door. Malik and Morgana froze. A second tap came, a little louder than the first. The rider remained motionless by the door and the horses continued to fidget in the dark. Malik raised his dagger in preparation to kill the unwanted visitor, as he grasped the door handle making ready to snatch it open.

"Please don't do that." Jamal's voice came from behind him inside the hut. Malik and Morgana span round in a mixture of surprise and relief. "Get up; we're waiting for you outside with horses. When you didn't answer the door, we thought something had happened to you both." As he spoke Tarique pushed the door open and gave a look of irritability towards Malik, slapping him sharply on the back of his head.

"Aww!" Malik yelped, rubbing the spot where Tarique's hand had struck. The group left the hut, mounted the horses and disappeared into the night. They passed through the village gates, which were no longer manned and rode off into the darkness towards the river where the others would be eagerly waiting for their return.

"What happened to the guards?" Morgana asked as they passed through the gates.

"They're okay. We put them to sleep for a short time with some powders of our own. We used these in times of war to do exactly what we have just done. They will wake in a few moments believing they simply fell asleep while on watch. I doubt they will be willing to make a fuss about it at all, do you?" Tarique replied. Malik looked at the small clay jar that was tucked into Tarique's belt. Jaffa and Jamal had similar jars in their belts too.

"You made this powder yourselves?" Malik enquired. Tarique's broad smile said more than words.

"I've seen this powder before." Morgana stated. "I used to make it to help people sleep while they had limbs removed due to injuries or infection. When they breathe it in, it's as if they are dead, yet they still breathe. Where did you learn how to make this?" She asked, her gaze falling upon Tarique.

"My people use it for many things, but we were taught by our combat masters in our old country. They learned about it from their quests in the Far East. I dare say that our Mongol and Oriental friends know of it too." Jaffa and Jamal nodded and murmured in agreement with the suggestion. The group rode all night and deep into the next day before reaching the river side encampment. Some of the crewmen jumped down from the Thunder Child and took care of the horses, laughing at the thought of now having five horses and tack to add to their growing inventory. Malik and Morgana rushed over to the hut where Freyja lay unconscious still, with Antonio fussing and doing his best to keep her comfortable.

"Make way, let her see Freyja." Malik commanded as they approached. Antonio sighed with relief as he stepped away and made room for Morgana to do what she did best. The door swung open and Lubeck stepped into the room. No words were spoken, but eyes and nodded heads said everything. A large hand patted him on the shoulder from behind and Thorsten's deep voice uttered in his ear.

"Come Lubeck, leave them to it. You can do nothing here. She is in good hands now. We must continue to make preparations for the voyage. We must be ready to sail, as soon as Freyja recovers." Lubeck reluctantly dragged himself away from the hut and followed Thorsten down to the ship where he began to help the rest of the men filling her hold with stores of food, water, weapons, tar, planks of wood and every conceivable item they may require to launch a fully committed raid. All would be set by the end of the day. They just needed Freyja to recover in time.

Hagar smiled as he looked over the horses. Running his hand gently across the withers of one of the tired animals, he turned to Jamal declaring.

"Fine beasts, where exactly did you find them?"

"In a stable on the outskirts of the village where Morgana lives." Jamal replied with a smile.

Raising his eyebrows and scoffing in a light-hearted manner, Hagar responded.

"What? They were just astray, lost, wondering aimlessly in a secure stable without a care in the world? Nobody there to watch over them? I guess you rescued them from such a dangerous situation then?" Jamal recognised the sarcasm in his voice and frowned as he replied with a flamboyant bow.

"I shall go immediately, back to the village and find the stable owner so that I can pay him most generously for the use of his fine beasts." There was a moment's pause, then both men roared with laughter at the very idea. Then, as the laughter subsided, Hagar retorted.

"You know Saracen, we are going to require more fine beasts like these. Did you notice if there were any other horses in danger and in need of rescuing?" Jamal raised one eyebrow with a mischievous expression. Hagar grinned as he continued. "Then I'll leave it in your hands to execute such a rescue my friend, but it must be done by first light, two days from now. We sail then, with or without your rescued horses. With or without YOU my friend and I fear, with or without Freyja." Slapping Jamal on the back as he left, Hagar headed towards the ship and the rest of the crew, who were still working steadily preparing for sea. At his approach Lubeck looked up.

"How close are we?" He asked. Hagar sighed as he replied.

"I think that we will acquire a few more horses by the day after tomorrow, first light I believe. Do you think that we can wait for them to arrive?"

Lubeck nodded then looked to the sky. The sun shone brightly bathing his bare torso, causing the beads of sweat from the hard toil to glisten against his tanned skin. A soft breeze licked at his hair lifting the ends of it gently. He looked down again at Hagar remarking.

"It's hot here in this place. Not like home. There's no snow, ice or frozen hard earth. Just look around you at the variety of vegetation that grows here. Look at the riches in the sea and hunting in the forest. A man could make a future here for himself don't you think?" Hagar looked worried momentarily, then letting out a long heavy sigh, he replied.

"You feel it too? I thought I was the only one. I want to see my loved ones again and I want revenge for the deaths of those I have lost. But when I'm done with that, it would be nice to settle here, grow old and fat surrounded by trusted friends and family. Is that wrong of me to feel this way? Am I going soft? Or is this place casting some kind of a spell over me? Making me weak?" Lubeck scoffed quietly, shook his head gently as he said in reply.

"If this place is casting a spell, it's not on you alone my friend. I feel it too and I share your desire to grow old and fat here. I too, have a blood thirst to be quenched before I can allow myself such dreams. I promise you this though. Once we have our revenge and our loved ones are returned to us, I will bring the Thunder Child back to her birth place and settle with whoever will settle with me. Those who do not wish to, will be free to follow their own path. The Thunder Child will remain here, but they will be given other ships to continue along whatever path they have chosen. They will always have safe haven here, but I for one will not be raiding for the sake of raiding once my thirst for revenge has been satisfied." The two men sat and pondered for a moment enjoying the warmth of the sun and slipping into dreamscapes of what might be. Then Malik's voice brought them both back with a bump as he called to them, informing them of Freyja's awakening. On entering the hut Lubeck and Hagar were met by the sight of Freyja sitting upright in the bed smiling.

"So, when do you sail?" She asked as if nothing had happened. Clearing his throat Lubeck replied.

"As soon as you are well enough to guide us."

"Tomorrow it is then." She stated.

"No, at first light the day after." Hagar corrected. "The Saracens, they need the time to return with the horses."

"First light, the day after tomorrow, with or without our Saracens and the horses." Lubeck decreed. There were grunts of acknowledgement as Lubeck left the hut to return to the ship once more. Freyja turned to Morgana asking her to tell all about the events of the past few days. The two women settled into conversation as Morgana did as requested, like two siblings that hadn't seen each other for some time. The following day came and went without event, except for Freyja venturing out into the sun for a walk to strengthen her legs, Morgana glued to her side. It lifted the hearts of the crew to see her up and about and appearing so well. They settled to their tasks and had the Thunder Child ready to sail ahead of schedule. All they had to do now was wait; wait for the return of the three Saracens, with the horses they had gone to collect. As the sun rose the next morning Lubeck looked to the East with a heavy heart.

"They'll be here." Thorsten tried to reassure him.

"No, we cannot wait, they had their orders. Make the ship ready to sail. We leave in one hour." Thorsten dropped his head and walked away in the direction of the ship. His movements were heavy and laboured as he went. Freyja approached with Morgana in tow.

"Tarique and the others are not in danger." She began. "You must sail as planned. They will be here in time. They do not have far to travel, but the tide is not going to wait for any man. You must sail as planned or lose another day and a half." Lubeck grimaced, took a deep breath then replied.

"I will sail before the tide cuts me off, but I will give my Saracens as long as I can before leaving them behind." With that he brushed past the two women and made his way to the Thunder Child. The morning advanced with no sign of the three Saracens or the horses they had gone to acquire. Lubeck paced the main deck of the ship like an expectant father, his internal turmoil showed in the troubled expression on his face.

"Earl Lubeck!" Thorsten caught his attention. "We cannot wait any longer. The tide has already turned and we will not have enough water to reach the open sea if we don't sail now." Lubeck stopped his pacing and gazed to the East once more.

"Cast off." He growled with a sigh of reluctant acceptance. Thorsten shouted orders and men pulled at ropes, grabbed oars and began to release the ship from her moorings. As they attempted to raise the gangway, Morgana stepped onto it and headed towards the ships main deck.

"What do you think you are doing?" Thorsten snarled.

"I'm to accompany you on this raid." Morgana announced in reply.

"No! No you're not!" Lubeck yelled as he approached the pair.

"You need me on this voyage, Freyja said that I'm to come with you and—"

"Hold!" Cried Thorsten cutting Morgana off. "Hold those moorings steady her, hold her tight!" His voice drowning out Morgana's objections.

"I don't have time for this. Get off my ship!" Lubeck yelled at her.

"Earl Lubeck!" One of the crewmen called.

"What now!" Lubeck snarled back.

"Up there, on the ridge." The crewman replied. They looked up to see horses, a dozen or so, moving along the ridge and down through the trees towards the encampment. Tarique bringing up the rear. Lubeck looked around at the tide, it was already ebbing fast. He dropped a sounding line overboard checking the depth of water under the ship.

"We have but moments before we run out of water. The men must hold her until Tarique gets aboard." He declared. The crew manned the moorings, holding the Thunder Child and preventing her from moving down stream with the ebbing tide. Their bodies ached as their muscles strained.

"Hold her! Hold her!" Thorsten shouted grabbing a hand full of rope to help restrain the huge ship. The Horses thundered closer and Jamal called out for people to get out of the way. Hooves clattered onto the wooden deck and horses whinnied with confusion and frustration as they found themselves suddenly with nowhere to go. Chaos ensued and in the commotion, crewmen were distracted and the moorings slipped. The huge hull moved away from the river bank and the gangway splashed into the water as the gap between ship and land grew. Tarique now found himself with two loose horses plus the one he rode with a long jump ahead of them. He corralled the horses around and began their approach urging them on harshly. The three horses bolted towards the ship.

"No! No! There's not enough room!" Screamed Malik as he saw what Tarique was attempting. But it was too late. Suddenly, three tons of horse flesh flew through the air with nowhere to land safely. They hit the deck of the ship like thunder bolts, crashing into the first group of horses which were already panic stricken, bucking and prancing around on the main deck. Men dived for cover trying to avoid being trampled in the chaos. Horses reared onto their hind legs flailing their forelegs wildly, some striking crewmen and knocking them to the ground with deep cuts to their heads and shoulders. Tarique's horse slammed into two that were in its path. The sudden impact sent Tarique sailing through the air and over the side into the shallow water below.

"Man overboard!" Thorsten called out, attempting to be heard over the turmoil. Antonio, who had instinctively grabbed Morgana and pulled her out of danger, now grabbed a coil of rope from a storage bin. He tied it around a rail and looked over the side for signs of Tarique. The rest of the crew, at Lubeck's order released the moorings and allowed the ship to run free with the tide. Antonio spotted Tarique bobbing unconscious in the quickly shallowing water. He climbed on the guard rail ready to jump in, but a hand on his leg stopped him.

"Give it to me, quickly." A tall dark haired crewman said as he stripped off his shirt. "Tie it around my waist, hurry." Antonio did as requested and the crewman was gone, over the side and swimming for all he was worth against the current towards the limp body of Tarique. Other crewmen steadied and calmed the horses and one by one began to lead them down the ramp to the lower decks and the stable stalls awaiting them. Some of the crew were focused on ensuring the ship made its way safely towards the mouth of the river, while others helped those who were injured by the frightened horses. Thorsten and Lubeck answered Antonio's call and came to the side of the ship where he was watching apprehensively as the dark haired crewman continued to battle the current. He slowly made his way to where Tarique had become snagged on some small rocks which were now breaking the water's surface as the tide continued to ebb.

"He'll never make it." Thorsten said.

"Yes he will." Malik retorted as he joined them. "I know that man. His name is Mauro, he is from the Mediterranean. He and his people practically live in the sea. He swims like a fish. If anyone can reach Tarique, he can." The group looked on with expectant anticipation. Lubeck noticed the rope would run out before Mauro could reach Tarique. He called for another rope to be tied to the first extending its length. The task was quickly done and the rope, now double its original length appeared to be long enough to allow the rescue to be performed.

"As soon as he has Tarique, haul them both in, fast." Lubeck ordered. Mauro, now just a few strokes from his target, was beginning to tire. His progress slowed and his breathing became sporadic as he coughed and spluttered, choking on the fast flowing water. With a massive effort, he held his breath and kicked hard. Now he could feel the rocks under his feet. He dug in and using his hands and feet together dragged himself across the wet and slippery rock, shaking from the effort required to overcome the force of the water pushing against him. Mauro was tired and bleeding as he reached out as far as his long arms would allow. His fingers caught in Tarique's tunic and he pulled with determination. Tarique's tunic tore and the two men came away from the rocks and into the main stream of the current.

"Heave!" Lubeck called. "Haul them in quickly!" The whole group, Malik, Thorsten, Lubeck, Antonio and even Morgana, grabbed the ropes and pulled hand over hand, reeling in their friends. Mauro and Tarique bounced off sand banks and rocks in the shallow water as they were hauled towards the ship. The combination of the ship's speed, moving with the current and their friends reeling them in, made it very hard for Mauro to keep both his and Tarique's heads above the surface. This ordeal didn't last long before Thorsten's huge hands had Tarique by the tunic hoisting him over the guard rails and onto the ships deck. Mauro followed shortly after, manhandled aboard by Lubeck and Antonio, dropping him onto the deck next to Tarique. Morgana checked Tarique for signs of breathing and then rolled him over onto his side where he coughed and vomited what appeared to be gallons of water. His eyes flickered open.

"By all the Gods, he's alive." Thorsten announced with a relieved tone to his voice.

"It's by the will of Allah." Tarique corrected him as he panted, attempting to sit up.

"No, it's by the will of Mauro." Declared Lubeck, reaching a hand down to assist the exhausted swimmer to sit up. "If it were not for this fish, you would have surely been lost and become food for the crabs by now. What on earth did you think you were doing? The ship had cast off, we were in the ebbing tide, you could have killed us all."

"It was Allah's will that you have these horses, you need them for the voyage ahead. It was also Allah's will that I come on this voyage, to keep you safe Earl Lubeck." Tarique replied with a cheeky smile. Lubeck grunted and helped the Saracen to his feet. Then he turned to Mauro.

"We owe you a debt Mauro. Tarique lives and is with us still, because of you."

"Are we not brothers?" Mauro replied. "Do we not watch over each other? You owe me nothing Earl Lubeck." He continued, bowing his head in respect before heading below decks to rest in his bunk. Lubeck returned a respectful nod in reply. Then turning to Thorsten, he instructed the big man.

"See to it that this man rests as long as he needs before he returns to his duties. Make sure his wounds are treated too." Then Lubeck turned his attention to Morgana. "Well, thanks to the unexpected activities, it looks as though we are stuck with you now. You had best make yourself useful and help those who are injured. Just tell me, why did Freyja want you to come with us on this raid?"

"To be her eyes and ears my Lord." Morgana replied. "What I see, she will see. What I hear, she will hear. Together we can guide you to your prey, watch over you and try to keep you all safe." Lubeck simply grunted and gestured for her to go. Then he turned his attention to the safe passage of the ship to the open sea. Morgana set about helping the injured and slowly the ship returned to quiet tranquillity as they slipped out of the river mouth and into the wide open, crystal blue ocean beyond. Antonio approached Lubeck and with a little relieved humour in his voice, he noted.

"Her birth was not an easy delivery, but she's arrived into this world. Now let us see our enemies tremble and see the skies glow red with fire as we bring the Thunder down upon them." Lubeck smiled discreetly as he looked towards the horizon.

"Make ready for war, I want this ship alert and ready at all times. We are in hostile waters. The slavers use this route constantly, that's why we were all washed ashore on your Island. They pass by here regularly, so there must be a port and settlement close by. Let's not get caught unawares. I want a sharp eye on the horizon in all directions at all times, day and night. First sight of a sail, and we're ready for action. Now, set the sail, make ready for war and let's go hunting."

Night of the Sea Dragon

The sky was clear blue, as a steady breeze moved the Thunder Child swiftly across the water. The crew occupied themselves with menial tasks so as not to get too bored. Lubeck approached Hagar who was manning the tiller.

"What course my Lord?" Hagar asked as Lubeck drew near.

"To tell the truth, I'm not really sure." Lubeck replied with a troubled look. Hagar raised an eyebrow and sighed.

"Perhaps you should ask Morgana?" He offered as a suggestion.

"Perhaps I will." Lubeck replied. He looked around the main deck for his unwelcome passenger. "Where is she?"

"I believe she's below decks with your Saracen." Hagar replied, chuckling with friendly concern.

"He's not my Saracen." Lubeck objected. "He just seems to have taken on the role of personal bodyguard. Not that I'm complaining. Do you know of a better one than he?" Hagar shook his head.

"No I do not. The three of them are like ghosts. By the time you know they are there, it's already too late by far."

"This is very true my friend." Jamal said stepping out from behind the rear figurehead and up to Lubeck's shoulder. Both Lubeck and Hagar jumped with surprise at his disclosure.

"See?" Hagar protested. "Even in broad daylight they simply appear as if by magic." Jamal smiled widely.

"We never sleep either." He laughed.

"Jamal, Could you go and find Morgana for me please? Ask her to come and talk with me?" Lubeck requested.

"Certainly, it will be my great pleasure." Jamal replied as he bowed politely and went about his task. When Morgana arrived, Lubeck took her to the rear figurehead where they spoke for some time. She agreed to help, using the powers of sight which she possessed. She went to her sleeping area and opened the rough bag she had brought with her for the voyage. From it she removed a smooth, opaque orb and a small stand. She dripped a few drops of two different potions over its surface, then began to quietly recite a verse from a small book. The misty effect within the orb began to clear as she peered into it. Her eyes widened as she watched. Moments later the mists began to reappear. Morgana covered the orb again and returned it to its resting place. She reached for two small stone jars and gathered them up before returning to the main deck. She approached the rear figurehead and quietly spoke to it in a whisper. Nobody paid her much attention, so nobody noticed the figurehead open its eyes and move its lips as it replied to her. After consulting with the statue, Morgana took up a place at Lubeck's side.

"Your quarry is to the North East of here, in that direction about half a day's sailing." She stated firmly pointing her slender finger. Lubeck looked to where she indicated. He couldn't see anything on the horizon as yet.

"Are you sure?" He asked her firmly. Morgana lowered her head slightly as she answered his question.

"Yes, I have seen their vessel. It is much smaller than this one, with only twenty men on board though it could carry more. They are armed, but they will pose no threat to you. You will take their ship and they will disclose the location of their port to you. Come now, half a day in that direction." Lubeck looked to Hagar still manning the tiller.

"You heard the lady." He said. Hagar pulled on the tiller bringing the ships bow to bear in the direction indicated. The shift in direction caught the crew's attention.

"Make ready for battle men. We have a ship to take." Lubeck bellowed. The men cheered and began to don armour, helmets and side arms. Eighty armed warriors ready for battle, their prey, a much smaller ship with only twenty aboard. This should not be much more than a training session. As the crew busied themselves, Morgana moved to the front of the ship unnoticed and stood by the dragon figurehead on the bow. She took the stone jars from her dress pocket and poured some of the powder from each jar into her hands. Blowing the powder over the figurehead she recited a prayer. Everyone was busy and did not notice her as she then returned to her sleeping area below deck. A few hours later at full sail, the lookout called down from on high while pointing North East.

"Sail! Sail on the horizon!" The crew looked to where he was pointing. Thorsten highlighted, that if we could see them, then they could see us.

"More speed, we need more speed." Lubeck directed to Antonio.

"She's heavy with horses, supplies and crew. She will out run them in time, but to get more speed, we would need more sail. Unless the men row at the same time?" He suggested. Lubeck looked round at Thorsten and without a word he jumped into action, getting the crew onto the benches and manning the oars. As they rowed, the ship picked up speed. Her hull lifting in the water as it had before. The distance between the little ship and the Thunder Child decreased with every passing moment. Lubeck's eyes were fixed on his prey.

On the small ship, the slavers had just become aware of the colossal ship closing in on them. The captain looked at the ship in the distance and without much of a care pointed out to his second.

"They are far too big to catch us. We are much faster than that big lump. Set the sail and put them to our stern. Once we are in port, we can gather more ships and track them down together. I'm sure their cargo and crew will bring a handsome price." His crew set their sail and their little ship picked up speed. "Head for port!" Their captain called. But as his eyes scanned along the horizon, he noticed that his pursuer's ship looked much larger now. He frowned and strained his eyes attempting to calculate how far behind, this unknown vessel was.

"Perhaps they are heading for port also captain?" His second in command suggested hopefully.

"No, I don't think so." His captain began. "Most ships would run parallel to us if they had the same destination. This one is heading straight at us on a collision course and it would appear to be closing on us. How is this possible? Get the crew ready for battle. It would appear that our unknown pursuers mean to find themselves in chains by the end of this day."

"Aye sir!" Replied his second and off he went to get the crew ready. The slaver captain squinted at the approaching ship.

"Who are you?" He whispered to himself. Within the hour, the Thunder Child was bearing down on the slave ship.

"Stow the oars and make ready to board her!" Lubeck yelled to his crew. The Thunder Child's momentum and swift design meant that now the distance was lost; there was no escape for the slave ship. Flaming arrows poured from the sky and hit the Thunder Child's decks. Water was thrown onto the small fires dowsing them quickly. Antonio took charge of preparing the two catapults at the bows. Midway through loading them Lubeck called.

"No, not those, I want this ship intact." Another volley of flaming arrows peppered the Thunder Child. Again the flames were dowsed.

"Reply to that, will you?" Lubeck called to Thorsten. With that, Thorsten gathered a dozen archers and returned fire. These arrows though were not aflame. They struck into the slave ship killing two of the crew. The captain had a sudden realisation.

"They're after my ship!" He snarled to his second. "They want our ship! They would have replied with fire if they merely wanted to kill us. They want this ship intact." As he was contemplating these thoughts, a second volley came from the Thunder Child. This time only a single crewman was hit.

"Captain, they are almost upon us!" A crewman yelled, his voice tainted with fear. His captain looked round and gasped.

"How? How could you move so fast? Prepare to repel boarders!" He shouted grabbing a sword and moving into position. The Thunder Child slammed into the side of the slave ship pushing it through the water as the great ship's momentum and weight proved superior. Arrows were once again loosed by the slavers, but most of them thudded harmlessly into the shield wall that had been erected moments earlier by Lubeck's men. Others though, found a target. One crewman that had been preparing grappling hooks fell to the deck clutching at two arrows which had found their mark. Before the slavers archers could ready more arrows, the shield wall broke open and more than forty well equipped and well trained warriors jumped across the void and onto the deck of the smaller ship, bristling with ferocious aggression. Swords chimed like bells as they clashed against each other and men screamed as axes thumped into their flesh. Blood flowed like water and limbs fell to the deck severed from their hosts.

The fight didn't last long, as the slavers were inferior in ability and numbers. Lubeck approached the slavers captain, who rushed at him in rage fuelled by what had just befallen his ship. Lubeck parried the slashing attempt to cut him down with his sword and while his attacker was off balance, Lubeck struck him hard in the side of his head with his left fist. The slaver had never felt such force and dropped his sword involuntarily as the power behind the blow stunned and horrified him. He tried to clear the swirling in his head as he grabbed a boat hook from a nearby stowage. Its long shaft should keep the Norseman far enough away to avoid another punch like the last one. The slaver lunged at Lubeck hoping to spear him with the sharp point on the end of the hooks head. Lubeck caught the boat hook by the shaft just below the head and pulled the slaver into him. The slaver pulled out a dagger from his belt and thrust it towards Lubeck's chest. Lubeck turned his body just enough for the attempt to miss and the dagger cut through nothing but air. The action pulled the slaver off balance, causing him to lurch forwards. As he tried to regain his footing and stand upright again, Lubeck slammed his fist straight into the middle of his opponents face, breaking his nose and spraying blood and cartilage across the ships deck. The man screamed with pain and reeled backwards. His remaining crew were by now overpowered and disarmed. They were powerless to help, and could only stand and watch as their captain took a beating at the hands of this powerful Viking. Lubeck looked at his opponent inquisitively.

"You had enough yet?" He asked. The slaver screamed as he launched himself at Lubeck once more, slashing maniacally at him with the dagger he had somehow managed to retain. Lubeck ducked and weaved avoiding the cutting attempts and was successful, until one finally caught him on the shoulder cutting into his flesh and making him wince. That was the signal for Lubeck to end this. As the slaver spun around to launch another onslaught, Lubeck caught him by the wrist gripping it tight and slamming it into the guard rail on the side of the ship. The man screamed again as his wrist snapped and he dropped the knife. Without pause, Lubeck took a grip of the slavers belt and hoisted him up and over his head. Lubeck's huge arms flexed and his shoulders locked as he held his opponent aloft. With a half step and a mighty heave, he threw the man overboard and into the sea. Jaffa drew his bow and in a flash had loosed an arrow into the water after him. A cloud of red oozed across the surface and the captain was motionless. Lubeck waved an arm in the general direction of the prisoners,

"Chain them up and question them. I want to know where they were headed." He snarled. "Antonio, check both ships for damage. Make good what you can, secure them together until we're done." Antonio nodded and proceeded with his given tasks. Ropes were passed between the ships to secure them together and the prisoners were chained below decks on board the Thunder Child. The dead were tossed unceremoniously overboard and the decks washed down with sea water to clear away most of the blood. Antonio beckoned Mauro, who came to see what he wanted.

"Do you think that you could dive down and see if there is any damage under the hulls of both ships?" He asked.

"Yes it shouldn't be a problem." Mauro replied. "But I will have to wait a while I think." He nodded in the direction of the sea. Antonio looked to where Mauro had indicated. Sharks, a half dozen or more. Cleaning up the bodies that were littering the sea around the two vessels.

"Hum, how long do you think?" Antonio asked grimacing because he thought he already knew the answer.

"One, maybe two hours I would guess. We could move away from the bodies, put a little distance between us and them. Then I could drop over the side and take a look."

"We could give that a try, better than waiting so long. In that time we could all be shark bait if we have a leak. I'll check below decks for signs of water seepage, you go and let Lubeck know what needs to be done." Antonio directed as he scurried off below decks. The two men went their separate ways. Mauro informed Lubeck of the situation and of his plan to distance themselves from the corpses in the water and thereby the sharks they had attracted. Lubeck agreed and readied the ship to move on. Meanwhile Antonio was checking the ships interior for signs of seepage. He checked everywhere that would be of vital importance first, then moved onto less vital areas. There was nothing that would become a problem anytime soon. Satisfied that the ship appeared to be watertight still, Antonio returned to the main deck where he could see the Thunder

Child was now being rowed with the small slaver's ship in tow, heading away from the floating dead and the sharks.

The crew had been rowing at a steady pace for about a half hour, before Mauro announced that he felt safe enough to drop over the side to inspect the hulls of both ships. Lubeck ordered a few archers to stand watch just in case any inquisitive sharks passed a little too close for comfort. Mauro smiled appreciatively as he readied himself for the plunge. He dropped majestically into the deep blue waters and disappeared beneath the Thunder Child's huge hull. Some of the crew continued to tidy up the ship, removing burned arrows from the deck and mast, tossing them overboard and rubbing down the splintered wooden timbers from around the points of impact. Scorched ropes were inspected for signs of weakness and replaced if in any doubt. Antonio, Lubeck, Malik and Thorsten were looking over the side at the water's surface for any signs of their shipmate. Malik and Thorsten moved over to the opposite side of the ship and searched the water below. Looking back towards Lubeck, Thorsten shook his head with a worried expression.

"It's been a while now." Antonio said with a hint of concern in his voice. Lubeck began to strip off his armour and chain mail, preparing to dive in and look for Mauro himself. But just as he removed his shirt, the water splashed and a breathless Mauro called up to the ship.

"All looks good so far! I'll take another dive and check the front!" With a deep breath, he was gone again. Lubeck sighed with relief.

"Well, at least you didn't get wet" Antonio laughed.

"I told you, he's like a fish." Malik reminded them. "He practically lives in the water."

Three more dives and Mauro had surveyed both ships. There was some minor damage to the slaver's ship, probably from the collision with the Thunder Child's ram. Antonio took three men with him and got to work on the repairs straight away as Thorsten's enormous hands reached down to help Mauro back on board. Lubeck approached Hagar asking him how many men would be required to sail the small ship they had in tow.

"Twenty at most I think." He replied.

"Twenty to manage the ship and another fifteen as a raiding party, thirty five in all." Lubeck muttered as he calculated how best to split his crew in the most effective way. "The Thunder Child has ten oars on each side, two men per oar, twenty per side forty in all needed to row. Seventy five men required to man both vessels. We number eighty in all, just enough to do it but there will be little rest for any of us."

"eighty one." Antonio corrected.

"Err, eighty two." Morgana countered.

"No, eighty one." Thorsten interrupted. "We lost Niles during the attack. Hit by archers." Lubeck nodded solemnly in recognition of their loss.

"We need to bolster our numbers. Taking that ship was the first step. The prisoners have revealed their intended destination. Now we sail to the port of Ibis where we shall commandeer another ship or even more, plunder their riches and free their slaves who will join us and swell our numbers."

"Ibis, never heard of it. How far is that? And what if the slaves refuse to join us?" Thorsten asked.

"I don't know how far, but Morgana has told me that we will reach it soon. Morgana also told me that Freyja has seen through the minds of the prisoners, where the slaves are located. She placed her hands upon their heads and all of their thoughts were disclosed to her and also to Freyja." Lubeck replied. Thorsten frowned then voiced another opinion.

"If we can find this port, we should be cautious, scout it out first, land our forces unseen and undermine their defences before we make our attack."

"We will indeed." Retorted Lubeck. "But we will divide our forces and use their own ship to gain safe passage through their harbour fortifications. Once inside, the crew will land and undermine their defences. We will sit just out of sight on the Thunder Child and wait for a signal that their defences are compromised. Then we bring her round and use these devices Tarique introduced to us, to smash their castle walls and bring the port to its knees. The landing party will continue to cause as much chaos as possible from inside their own walls. They will find themselves fighting on two fronts, caught in a cross fire. Their harbour will fall before they have chance to defend it." Thorsten raised his eyebrows.

"It could work." He began. "But the landing party would have to be made up from our best men in order to be successful."

"Agreed." Lubeck said in reply. "That's why you will be leading it. Tarique, Jamal and Jaffa are the most able to get in and out of somewhere undetected, so they will be with you, as will Kei. Take thirty more of your own choosing and man the slaver's ship. We sail together until we reach Ibis. We will wait for dusk so that they can see the ship, but not be able to make out individual faces on board. You pass through and moor up. Get ashore as soon as possible and disappear into the shadows. I will leave it to you to decide when it is the right time to make your move, but if we haven't seen a signal by early dawn, we will bring the Thunder Child about and attack from the sea anyway. In this case we will suffer heavy damage from the outer defences, so make sure you do your thing and take them down first." Thorsten grinned widely.

"Finally, time to strike back and let them know that now they are the hunted." He stated as he headed off and began to select the men who would form his raiding party. The raiding party crossed to the smaller slaver and cast themselves free from the Thunder child. The two ships sailed together following a heading that Lubeck had insisted the port of Ibis lay. Some of the men were not entirely convinced that anything lay way out here in the middle of the ocean, but they followed with blind devotion, the man who had brought them so far from the chains of that dark, damp prison that was the Galley.

They sailed for the rest of that day and most of the night before a lookout noticed lights on the horizon. His warning jolted the crew into action as they scrambled to catch a glimpse of their target. Swords rattled and shields clattered as men made ready for the fight. Their armour and chain mail made metallic sounds resembling notes from a tune as the men moved in performance of their preparations. Lubeck also tightened the leather straps on his chain mail and draped his sword across his back. As he reached for the peculiar weapon he had found in Freyja's tower armoury, Morgana's hand touched him on the shoulder.

"Wait." She said. "There are too many ships and men resting in the bay right now. They will sail in the morning and only a quarter of their number will remain. Tomorrow evening would be a better time to execute your plan." Lubeck dwelled on her advice for a moment.

"How do you know this?" He asked.

"The same way I knew how to find this place." She replied. Lubeck turned to face the wooden figurehead at the rear of the ship and sighed, dropping his head in submission.

"If I take this advice, you had better be right." He growled, under his breath. He called to his crew and told them to stand down for now. They would remain at a distance to avoid giving away their presence and thereby losing the element of surprise. This as you can imagine didn't sit well with them. Thorsten especially, was disgruntled by the delay, but as he had done since their escape from the Galley, he followed Lubeck trusting in his judgment. The two ships drifted gently with the tide for the remainder of the night. The men split into shifts keeping their position just far enough away from the land to remain hidden from sight. No lights were visible on either ship lest they would be seen by the port's lookouts. The ships creaked and groaned quietly in the dark and men spoke in whispers so as not to let their voices carry on the night air.

The next morning came at long last, and the lookout from the Thunder Child's tall mast whistled down to the crew below, pointing towards the port. Just as Morgana had predicted seven ships sailed out of port heading North in a small armada.

"Must be around Two hundred maybe Two hundred and fifty men in total aboard those ships." Hagar pointed out. "Thank the Gods we didn't raid last night, it would have been short lived." Lubeck turned to look at Morgana curling up one corner of his mouth in an uneven smile. He noted the fleet's course and drew up a rudimentary map and calculated a possible heading. From his knowledge and experience and after consulting with Antonio and Hagar, he had a good idea where they may be sailing to. He wanted to pursue them and stop them from taking more slaves to sell for profit. However, his small band was no match for hardened dealers in human flesh in such vast numbers. They all knew that they needed to increase their force before they could launch such an attack. So, all thoughts were back to the raid on the port of Ibis.

The day passed very, very slowly and the crew grew restless. But, with words of encouragement from Lubeck and Thorsten, they remained focused on the forthcoming task. As the sun began its slow decent, the small ship slipped away from the huge Thunder Child and made its way towards the distant Port. The crew were anxious but eager to strike a blow at their enemy. They had only sailed for an hour or so when Thorsten called to his raiding party to make ready.

"They will have spotted our sail by now men, so let's not give them any reason to suspect us. We are one of their own returning as planned. They have no reason to challenge us as we approach, but just in case, I want to be ready for a fight."

The sun was low in the sky and long shadows covered the ship's deck, making it difficult for the ports lookouts to see clearly who was aboard as they passed the outer defences. The guards in the towers on either side of the ports entrance waved them through without incident, recognising the sail and the ship as one of their own, just as Lubeck had predicted. They silently passed deeper into the harbour. Thorsten noted that both towers had been armed with devices resembling those Lubeck had insisted on installing at the bow and stern of the Thunder Child. In addition to these, each tower was manned by at least a dozen archers and small flames flickered from braziers. Thorsten had seen this sort of thing before in his previous life, before he had been taken as a slave. Large cauldrons of oil were also mounted on the battlements. These he knew would be heated and poured through purpose made fluid ways that would release the boiling oil through the mouths of the gargoyles carved at various positions around the top of the battlements, dissuading would be attackers from climbing the tower walls. This oil would also spill out onto the surface of the sea. Flaming arrows would then be loosed to ignite the oil and form a barrier across the mouth of the harbour, preventing any ship from entering. These defences would have to be destroyed to ensure the safety of the main force that was to follow.

Two more ships lay alongside at their moorings inside the safety of the harbour. They were both bigger than the one they were aboard. Neither was ready to sail and were unmanned. As the small ship drew closer to the docks, Thorsten's crew could hear music and laughter carrying on the evening breeze. Lights were visible from the various taverns littering the bay. A stronghold was also visible now, a little way up the hill from the main docks a garrison of men were enjoying a little relaxation from their guard duties in the towers. Thorsten estimated their numbers to be in excess of forty. A large wall was also visible, winding its way around the entire port and positioned at regular intervals, were up to four small towers, each manned by a group of soldiers. Thorsten's heart raced as the ship pulled up alongside. Two men came along the jetty to assist with mooring it securely. To avoid suspicion, the raiding party threw ropes without hesitation or conversation. The two men tied them off routinely then offered up a gangway to be taken and secured by the ship's crew. Thorsten appeared at the top of this as the two port workers looked up unsuspectingly. Their expressions changed to one of horror as their eyes beheld the mountain of a man bearing down upon them. Before they could sound an alarm, they were grasped from behind and their throats cut quickly and precisely by two Saracens who appeared from the darkness, silent and deadly. The two bodies were taken aboard the small ship and concealed where they wouldn't be discovered. Jamal and Jaffa cleaned off their daggers and together with Tarique, disappeared into the night.

"Where are they going?" Kei asked Thorsten as they disembarked.

"They are going to make sure that the Thunder Child remains safe from those towers we passed on the way in." He replied. Three men remained aboard the small ship while the remainder slipped away into the dark following Thorsten's lead. They travelled light without shields or armour to avoid unwanted attention if seen. But each man was heavily armed, carrying daggers swords and axes. Quietly, they made their way from the jetty and into the streets of the port towards the strong hold they had seen earlier. As they approached, Thorsten could see that most of the off duty guards were inside the building which had large wooden doors at one end. These doors had big iron handles to assist in opening and closing the heavy structures. He grinned as an idea came to him. He moved silently to the doors and up turning a bench located nearby; he wedged it underneath one of the door's handles, bracing the door shut. Kei followed his lead and did the same to the other with another bench that had been used as seating for the men when outside. Another crewman stepped up with a length of rope and tied the handles together. Now the only way for the guards to exit the building, was via the solitary window which faced the harbour. Thorsten detailed two archers to stand guard over it and ensure any attempt to leave by this route would be discouraged instantly.

"There." Kei pointed to another building on the outskirts of the main town. It was made mostly of stone with thick walls and bars on the windows. There were no lights showing from inside, but there were faint sounds of weeping from within.

Thorsten nodded wordlessly in agreement. This had to be where the slaves were locked away for the night. Two guards sat outside some twenty feet away from the door. They were not being particularly mindful of their task, but were instead, drinking ale and eating heartily. Four of Thorsten's men made their way around behind them. Then before the guards had time to realize what was happening, they pounced, killing them quickly and quietly. The guard's bodies were dragged away into the shadows and their clothing removed. Two of the raiding party appeared dressed as the guards and replaced them sitting by the small fire. One of the men pulled at the ill-fitting clothing, gesturing that he was not convincing. Thorsten scowled at him and the man took up his position without any more objections.

Now the remainder of the party moved further into the town, staying under cover of the shadows and avoiding contact with any of the inhabitants. They made their way around the perimeter wall visiting each small tower along its length in turn. At the base of each tower, there was a small wooden door. The raiders placed thatch, which they had removed from some of the roof tops as they had made their way around and set the bases of small fires at each door as they went. They soaked each pile of thatch and the door itself with oil or tar from some of the torches which lit the alleyways along their route. So far, they had remained unnoticed. They had not run into any resistance and they still moved freely without being challenged.

Elsewhere, the Saracens had made their way unseen, to the first of the large watch towers forming the ports outer defences. Two guards were looking out towards the sea, while others were sitting around small fires, eating and drinking. The large catapult was the saboteurs' target. This had to be rendered useless in order to protect Lubeck's forces as they came to help complete their raid. Tarique slipped invisibly to the device. Then with his dagger, cut two thirds of the way through two of the ropes which were vital for the device's correct operation. As he did so, Jaffa removed the wooden wedges that restricted the movement of the wheels and prevented the device from rolling away from its position. Jamal meanwhile, took some of the oil from one of the cauldrons and laid a trail across the floor, to a rack containing a score of bows and a host of arrows. He covered the weapons in oil and trailed what was left away to a safe distance. He set a candle he had removed from the window ledge of a small house as he had passed. He cut its length to give them a little time before the flame would burn it down to the floor. Placing the candle into the trail of oil, he lit it carefully from another he borrowed from a nearby table then slipped away, still unnoticed. The three Saracens now made their way down to the water's edge. They quietly lowered themselves into the cold dark water and swam carefully, so as to not draw any unwanted attention, across the bay to the other side. They climbed out and up the rough stonework of the second tower. On reaching the top, they proceeded in a similar fashion to that previously, but this time Jamal didn't have a candle to set as he had before. So instead, he laid the trail of oil to the edge of one of the braziers. He then took a small piece of wood from the nearby pile and passed one end of it through the grate, leaving the other end sticking out above the oil. The three Saracens retreated back into the shadows and disappeared once more.

All was now set and as the raiding party met up again near the docks, Thorsten asked about a signal to inform Lubeck they were ready for the main attack. However, the little piece of wood Jamal had set as a makeshift fuse, burned through prematurely. It broke away and fell to the ground. The hot embers landed directly in the oil as planned. The oil ignited and a fiery worm streaked across the tower floor. It reached the weapons rack, which ignited into an orange blaze in moments. Guards shouted, raising the alarm and the raiding party were forced to change their plans. The flames from the burning weapons illuminated the night sky. Lubeck and the rest of the crew saw the glow against the dark backdrop and took it to be the signal they had been waiting for. The order was given and the crew manned the oars to row the ship into position to launch their attack. The devices at the bow were loaded with tar soaked projectiles and primed, ready to launch.

Now the candle Jamal had set made its way to the oil. The flame ran along the path laid by Jamal and again found the weapon racks as planned. This time though, the guards were already lifting out their bows and making ready to defend the port. The oil transferred to the soldier's hands and they attempted to clean them by wiping them against their tunics. Unfortunately, it smeared all over their clothes spreading and covering them with the potential catalyst. The burning oil trail reached the guards and leapt from man to man engulfing them in fiery terror as they screamed in pain and fear. One, in his panic, tried desperately to smother the flames. He stumbled, falling against one of the oil filled cauldrons, spilling its contents across the tower floor. In seconds the whole tower was ablaze. Men screamed and flailed helplessly as they burned.

Lubeck frowned as he realised this second fire was not part of the signal. Calling for more speed, he donned his helmet and drew his sword ready to join the raid. As the Thunder Child came into position, more flames were visible within the town. These were the small fires set by Thorsten's group, at the base of the doors to the small towers, earlier. The guards within were now captive and unable to defend the port.

Thorsten's raiders had to change their plans and were now forced to reveal themselves in order to make the best of a bad situation. The guards in the stronghold attempted to leave by the door, only to find it barred. A couple of them attempted to exit via the window, only to be cut down by Thorsten's archers. By now the whole port was in chaos. Soldiers were running in all directions trying to find their attackers. A dozen or so soldiers who had been enjoying some rest time in one of the taverns now gathered themselves, picking up their weapons and heading into the streets. They headed for the stronghold hoping to discover what was happening. As they approached, they saw Thorsten's archers keeping the guards locked inside. Four of the soldiers drew their bows and loosed a volley towards them, hitting one in the leg and sending him reeling backwards in pain.

The second ducked for cover which gave some of the guards enough time to jump free of the window and out into the street. They headed straight for the position they had last seen the archers hiding, drawing their swords as they moved. But before they got far, they too were brought down by a volley of arrows from the rest of Thorsten's raiders, who by now had returned to the harbour in an attempt to return to their ship. The soldiers from the tavern now turned their attention to Thorsten's men. Thorsten roared loudly as he charged like a raging bull towards them. Lifting his huge axe and swinging it viciously at his startled foes. It's mighty head cut through two of them felling them like wheat before the scythe. The rest of the guards did not have time to contemplate what they had just seen, as the rest of the raiders were upon them. Swords rattled and men screamed as a vicious fight ensued.

The ports two towers of the outer defences were now ablaze. The catapult device of one was not affected by the fire. Some of the guards loaded it as the Thunder Child drew closer. They tensioned the device and released the projectile. The ropes which Tarique had cut, now snapped under the strain. The whole device flew backwards and the missing restraining wedges allowed it to recoil crashing into the wall behind. The projectile was thrust erratically into the air and fell short of its intended target, splashing harmlessly into the water ahead of the Thunder Child. The huge ship answered with two projectiles of its own. The tar soaked rocks had been ignited before they were released. Two balls of fire hurtled towards the tower smashing into it and bursting into an inferno as they struck. With both towers now burning uncontrollably, there was nothing to prevent the Ship moving into the harbour.

Arrows showered the deck of the Thunder Child, but did little more than make noise as they hit. The ship rolled in and as she came alongside the jetty, twenty warriors jumped ashore to assist their comrades who were already fighting in the streets. With the arrival of Lubeck and the rest of the Thunder Child's crew, the fighting didn't last long. The remaining soldiers were overwhelmed by the sheer ferocity and skill of their attackers. The port burned and the few surviving soldiers were rounded up and chained. The keep that had once housed sobbing slaves, now housed the remnants of the ports garrison. The slaves were freed from their bonds and Lubeck approached with an offer to join him. Some merely wanted to return home but others like Lubeck and his men wanted revenge. Lubeck smiled as he watched the freed slaves join his small army. He now had four ships in total and more than one hundred and fifty men at his command. All of the ships were manned and cast off to make for the open sea. The Thunder Child waited until the other three had passed the harbour mouth and into the darkness beyond, before slowly backing out herself.

The crew manned the oars and rowed gently, backing the huge ship away from the devastation in the bay. The smoke from the fires now filled the air and as the ship moved through it, a survivor lifted his head to see a huge dragon's head staring back at him through the smoke. Lubeck barked an order and two more fire balls were launched at the town as a final declaration of victory. The smoke made the survivor's eyes water, blurring his vision. He screamed in fear as he saw what appeared to be, a huge fire breathing dragon destroy the port as it returned to the sea from where it had come. The night sky was bright with an orange glow from the burning port.

Once they had cleared the harbour mouth, Lubeck turned the ship around and made after his newly acquired vessels. The sun was beginning to rise now and it wasn't long before the three smaller ships were visible against the lightening horizon. The Thunder Child caught up with them and all four ships headed North, the same heading as the seven slavers ships had followed.

Revenge Is Best Served Cold

Four ships of various sizes, tiny specks floating on the vast sparkling oceans, sailed with purpose heading North. North as they had done for the past few days. Their holds still held enough food and fresh water to last for a few more. Aboard the Thunder Child, the horses and the few prisoners from the first captured slave ship, rested uneasily below decks.

"I heard some of the crew talking last night. The fighting a few nights ago was these Gurlemek as they refer to themselves, destroying the port of Ibis." One of the prisoners told the others.

They all looked around at each other with worried expressions. One of them replied to the comment.

"If they can destroy Ibis, then they really are a force to take seriously. I saw what their leader did to our captain; he picked him up and threw him overboard like he was a child, but not before humiliating him and beating him first. Our captain was a fine swordsman was he not? This barbarian defeated him with as little effort as if he were a tavern wench. He is strong too. He has the strength of a bear. That giant they call Thorsten..." he trailed off in thought. Then after short contemplation, he continued. "I think these Norsemen are on a blood hunt. I don't know for sure, but I think they are going after our people. It doesn't feel as if we have changed course in days and by the drop in temperature, I would say we have been heading North."

"Perhaps they are returning home?" Another man suggested.

"Perhaps, but I know that our ships were going to head North on another collection for the markets in Altear. I think these Barbarians are set to attack our ships and kill our people…" He paused for a moment again in short reflection. "If they can destroy Ibis, they can destroy our ships too."

"Why do you think they spared us?" One of the others asked.

"Who says they have?" Came the reply. A couple of the prisoners pulled dejectedly at their chains then slumped back down, hopelessness gripping them. Up on the main deck, the crew were busy with the usual tasks involved with sailing such a large ship. Lubeck was standing at the stern by the figurehead of Freyja, accompanied by Morgana. He spoke to her in a hushed tone, for fear of the crew overhearing their conversation.

"Have you seen when we shall make landfall?" He asked her.

"Freyja spoke to me in my dreams last night my Earl. She told me that we will make landfall by mid-afternoon today."

"Mid-afternoon, that's impossible." Lubeck remarked, scanning the horizon for signs of land. "There is nothing out there but ocean. If we are to make landfall today, we should be able to see it by now."

"It's there my lord, trust me." Morgana reassured him. "We must change course and head North West for the rest of the morning. We will make land fall by mid-afternoon. But beware, we must land unseen and remain hidden until we have fortified our landing site and can keep our ships protected."

"Don't tell me how to mount a raid. I know how best to conduct a campaign. I have fought many times, before I was enslaved. War was my birth right." Lubeck reminded her. Morgana bowed her head slightly and backed away, looking at the Dragon figurehead at the ship's bow before moving on to take a seat in the morning sun. Lubeck watched her curiously for a moment, then, moved his gaze to the Dragon. What was it about that figurehead? Lubeck thought to himself. It's not the first time she has given it a strange stare. "New heading. North by North West!" Lubeck called loudly.

Hagar heaved on the tiller and crewmen pulled and loosened rope to keep the wind in their sail. The lookout high on the mast called out to the other ships signalling their new course. Thorsten, aboard one of the others noted this and passed on the information to the other ships by way of hand signals following a long blast on a Viking horn to attract the other crew's attention. All four ships were now on the new heading and making good time as the sun rose higher in the morning sky, warming the crew against the cold Northern air. They sailed on for the rest of the morning before the lookout reported that he could see land. The crew cheered and looked to Lubeck for orders. "Take us in close to the coast. We will hug the shoreline as much as possible until we find a suitable landing site. We must keep our presence a secret from our quarry until we are ready to engage them." Lubeck instructed. The Thunder Child led the way and the smaller ships followed.

By mid-afternoon just as Morgana had foreseen, they found a suitable landing site. They pulled their ships in and unloaded the horses from the Thunder Child's lower decks. The animals were unsteady on their feet at first, but seemed very pleased to be back on dry land with sweet, sweet grass to graze on instead of the dry hay and oats they had eaten for weeks. The crews unloaded their supplies and began to fortify their position. The ships were camouflaged as best as the crews could and within the week, shelters were built. Tarique and the other Saracens were charged with scouting and mapping the surrounding area.

"Scouting parties will be sent out every day in all directions until we locate our foe. Then we will draw up plans to engage them and make them pay for what they have taken from us." Lubeck's voice was laced with vengeance as he addressed what had now become his council members.

"A thoughtful and tactical leader will bring victory to us." Hagar began tentatively. "A good and clear headed leader could do this for us, but not a vengeful one my Earl. Vengeance clouds the mind and blinds you to what needs to be done. Bad decisions can be made in hateful haste and many men can fall because of such decisions." Lubeck's eyes narrowed as he cast his gaze upon the older Northman.

"My head is clear old man. I have hate in my heart for these dogs, but I do not forget the burden of leadership which I carry each day. My mind is calm and my thoughts are clear. My blood does not boil as you may think. It is ice that runs through my veins and when we catch these murderers, rapists and child takers, my vengeance will be calm, cold and calculated. Vengeance, my friend, is a dish best served cold and mine shall be frozen." Hagar and the rest of the group took a deep breath as the air felt sinister. Lubeck left the recently finished hut and walked alone to the water's edge.

He allowed his mind to wander and reflect on the time before he was enslaved and his son Hafthor had been taken from him. He thought of his wife too and how he missed her. Then, remembering the day he had been captured, one man in particular stuck in his head. He had been dressed in red, with a black bull emblem embroidered on his tunic. Tall and heavy with dark hair and eyes, carrying a scar on his right check. Lubeck's fists clenched as he remembered this man pulling Hafthor away from his grasp while his soldiers held him fast. Then, without mercy he beat Lubeck to within an inch of his life while the soldiers still held him fast. Lubeck's heart pounded in his chest as his thoughts raced. This man was the one he was going to kill personally. This, brutal coward, was the one man above all others he wanted the pleasure of killing. His jaw tightened and his teeth ground hard as the hatred he felt began to boil over. The blood in his veins burned and he could feel it racing through his body. But, as the rage began to swell within him, he began to feel sleep taking over him. His eyes grew heavy and he found it hard to keep them open. His heart began to slow as his eyelids fell shut. Lubeck fell back against the grassy shoreline, the sun warming his skin against the cool Northern air. Peace befell him and he drifted off to sleep.

"Sleep, sleep." A whispered voice said to him in his head. "Calm yourself, dream pleasant dreams. Be still, be still and sleep." Freyja's voice faded and soon a peaceful slumber took him. Lubeck slept for some time as he dreamed sweet dreams.

Lubeck awoke to the sounds of a commotion within the camp. Men were shouting and gearing. Scrambling to his feet, he made his way back to the main encampment with haste. There he saw Tarique and the other Saracens driving two prisoners, hands bound and disarmed before them. The men were showing their anger to the prisoners, who wore the tunics bearing the bull emblem of the slavers. Thorsten approached them as Tarique explained they had stumbled across these men during their latest scouting run.

"I thought they might be able to tell us exactly where their main camp is." Tarique explained.

"Nice work. I'm sure Lubeck will be pleased by this." Thorsten replied.

"Indeed he is." Lubeck stated approaching the group. "Bring them in here." Lubeck opened the door to one of the larger huts and the prisoners were hurled inside unceremoniously. Thorsten and the Saracens followed, as did Morgana and Malik. The door closed and Lubeck glared at the two frightened men laying on the clay floor.

"Now." He began. "You are going to tell me everything I want to know, or you are going to suffer a very long and extremely painful death. Do you understand?" The two prisoners froze with fear as they looked at Lubeck's huge arms flexing as he picked up a heavy stool moving it a little closer to them, before setting it down and sitting on it. "Now." He began again. "I would like very much to know where your encampment is located." The two men remained silent in stern defiance, keeping their eyes fixed firmly on the ground. "Have it your way." Lubeck sighed. He turned to Malik and instructed him to go and get Untumi and the others from his tribe. Malik looked a little confused but did as requested. It didn't take long, but it was a lifetime for the prisoners, before Malik returned with five men of African origin. Each had tribal scaring on their faces and chests. Lubeck glanced over his shoulder as they entered the room. "Augh." He sighed. "These men are cannibals." Untumi and his countrymen looked confused and insulted. Lubeck passed them a mischievous wink while his head was turned. "We feed them our dead enemies. I'm afraid they haven't eaten for a few days now and they're very hungry. However, dead men can't talk, so I'm going to let them eat you a little bit at a time, not all at once." The prisoners looked at the Africans and shuffled uneasily. Lubeck beckoned Untumi over and invited him to choose which pieces they would like him to cut off, for them to eat first. Untumi moved closer and began to look inquisitively over the two frightened men. He reached out and began to poke and prod them as if checking for tender parts.

"No! No! Please no!" One of the prisoners sobbed.

"What?" Lubeck asked.

"Don't, don't let them eat us." The prisoners begged.

"Then tell me what I want to know." Lubeck demanded as he frowned at them. The two men became silent once more. Untumi continued to prod and poke while the two men squirmed and wriggled trying to keep him at bay. Then Untumi smiled and grasped one of the men by an arm.

"This feels good." He said, smiling and revealing his long teeth glowing white against the dark skin of his face.

"That one?" Lubeck confirmed. "Alright then. Thorsten, get your axe. Jamal, prepare a brazier; I don't want him to lose too much blood when we remove that arm. I want to keep him alive to answer my questions. Cauterise the wound to stop the bleeding as soon as the arm is removed. Then give the arm to Untumi so that he and his men can have some dinner tonight." Thorsten left the hut followed by Jamal. The two prisoners sobbed quietly in the corner as Lubeck took Malik and Morgana outside leaving the other two Saracens to keep watch.

"You're not really going to cut off his arm are you?" Morgana queried once they were clear of the hut.

"Only if I have to, in order to make my point. I hope they will yield before it comes to that, but if they call my bluff, one of them at least, will be very, very sorry."

"Untumi and the others, are they really cannibals? Would you really feed them that man's arm?" A disturbed Malik asked. Lubeck looked at him trying not to laugh.

"Of course they're not, no more than you or I, but they don't know that do they? I'm just trying to frighten them into believing that they are going to be eaten piece by piece unless they tell me what I want to know. We'll soon know if my ruse works." Malik laughed uneasily, not sure if Lubeck was kidding. He looked around the camp and noticed a hog roast being prepared for that evening's meal. He swallowed hard at the thought of Untumi and his friends eating the prisoners.

Jamal returned with the brazier and began to set it up inside the hut in clear view of the two prisoners, who watched with terrified eyes. Thorsten entered the room carrying his huge axe and the prisoner marked by Untumi, swallowed hard and began to breathe rapidly with fear. Lubeck returned to the hut and prevented Morgana from entering. He instructed her to wait elsewhere before he re-entered the hut. He looked at the glowing brazier and checked the irons that by this time were glowing white hot. Tarique carried a block of wood, about four inches thick and placed it on the ground in front of the first prisoner.

"Now, one last time. Tell me what I want to know and I'll spare you your arm. If not, Untumi and his men eat well tonight." Lubeck stated with growing irritation.

"Go to hell!" The prisoner replied.

"Wrong answer!" Lubeck snapped indicating to the Saracens to ready the man for retribution. The three men stepped forward and tore off the prisoner's tunic. They pulled him over to the block of wood and pinned him to the ground with one arm outstretched over it. The prisoner cried out and panted with fear, struggling against the Saracens as they held him. But still he refused to talk. Lubeck frowned and told Thorsten to ready his axe. Thorsten loomed over the frightened man, who now froze with terror.

"Last chance." Thorsten's deep voice rumbled. The prisoner shook his head. Thorsten looked to Lubeck, who reluctantly nodded his head. Thorsten raised the axe, one swift, powerful blow and the man was separated from his arm. Screams could be heard by all around the camp. Jamal moved swiftly and pressed one of the white hot irons against the prisoner's bleeding shoulder. The blood instantly boiled and hissed. A foul stench of burning flesh filled the hut forcing Malik to cough and choke. The second prisoner soiled himself emptying his bladder with fear at the scene he had just witnessed. Thorsten reached down and picked up the severed arm holding it out to Lubeck. "What shall I do with this?" He asked.

"Give it to Untumi as planned." Lubeck replied angrily. Thorsten stepped outside taking the arm with him. As he stepped through the door, Morgana blocked his path staring at the severed limb in his hand.

"I think you might be needed inside now." Thorsten said gently pushing her aside and continuing on his way. The scene inside the hut was horrific as Morgana entered. One prisoner was shaking in the corner, covered in his own urine and sobbing uncontrollably as he stared at the unconscious, mutilated body of his comrade laying just feet away. Morgana moved quickly to the unconscious man and began to tend his wound.

"What, what's she doing?" The terrified prisoner enquired nervously.

"She's keeping him alive so that we can ask him more questions when he awakens." Lubeck stated menacingly. "But until he does, your turn." The man panicked and began crying uncontrollably pushing himself as far into the corner of the room as possible. "I'm going to take a walk." Lubeck stated. "When I get back, I will ask you the same question. Think long and hard about your answer." With that, Lubeck left the hut and walked towards the shoreline. Malik followed him at a scamper.

"What are you going to do now?" He asked catching up with his friend.

"I don't know really. I didn't expect them to call my bluff. But now it's done, I hope they will not be tempted to do it again." Lubeck replied gruffly. Malik looked round at the sea, the sky, the encampment then back to Lubeck.

"And what if they do?" Malik tentatively enquired. Lubeck frowned hard as he thought before answering his young friend.

"I am going to have to frighten them so much; they will do anything I say out of fear. I have to make them believe that Untumi and his friends are going to eat them piece by piece until they talk." He too looked around. He saw his men drinking and talking. Laughing and making merry as the sun began to set. The flames of the fire glowed bright and fat spat from the roasting pig over it. The smell of cooking was heavy on the air and it made Lubeck feel hungry. He smiled and chuckled to himself. "I have an idea." He said with an evil twinkle in his eye. The pair rose to their feet and Malik followed as Lubeck made his way to the hog roast. He asked for a piece of meat still attached to the bone, to be put onto one of their roughly carved wooden plates. Then getting Untumi and a couple of his friends to accompany him, they returned to the hut where the prisoners were being held. When Lubeck entered the hut, the two prisoners cowered into the corner, one terrified and sobbing the other still in shock after losing his arm. Untumi grinned as he took a bite from the roast pork Lubeck had passed to him as they entered the hut. He chewed as he spoke in a language that none of them understood and gestured towards the men huddled in the corner. Lubeck merely shrugged and turned to face the prisoners.

"What, what did he say?" The frightened men asked. Lubeck replied with a nonchalant shrug and unconcerned expression.

"He says that your friends' arm tastes good and wonders if you will taste the same. He's trying to decide which bit of you they want to taste after they have finished eating his arm. He thinks maybe your leg or perhaps your manhood. I've heard that they are very partial to a man's manhood, it's a delicacy." The prisoners wailed and sobbed loudly rocking like infants. Lubeck sighed heavily as he said. "Of course if you simply told me what I want to know, well…." He stopped as the men began to cry loudly. Lubeck frowned as he continued. "I'm getting a little tired of waiting. I have other things to occupy my time with. So if you're not going to talk I'll just leave Untumi with you so he can eat his fill." He turned away and handed Untumi a large knife uttering, "I'll let Thorsten know he is to remove whatever parts of these two you want to eat next. They're all yours."

"No, no I'll tell you, I'll tell you what you want!" The man in the corner wailed. Lubeck stopped and without turning back said.

"I'm listening." The prisoner spent the next hour passing details of the slavers operation. Their location, numbers and what kind of defences they had implemented. He continued to disclose how many slaves they had collected and how much longer they intended to remain, before heading for the markets in Altear. As the man finished answering all of the questions put to him, Lubeck sat back on the stool and sighed with a smug satisfaction. He reached out and picked up what was left of the roast pork from Untumi's plate and took a big bite. The prisoner was horrified as he watched. Lubeck rose and told Tarique to feed and water the prisoners and also to make sure they were comfortable for the night. He left the hut and moved over to the fire. A man tending the hog roast handed him a fresh plate of hot meat. Lubeck took it gratefully and proceeded to eat.

"It tastes much better hot, than cold." He noted. Malik had also joined him and agreed that the food did taste good.

"So what will you do with them now?" He asked referring to the prisoners.

"I'm not sure. Perhaps I should set them free? Or maybe use them as slaves to work around the encampment?" Lubeck replied.

"Perhaps you should give them the choice?" Morgana interrupted as she approached. Malik and Lubeck looked at her, confused at her suggestion.

"Give them the choice?" Malik questioned.

"Yes, I think they will choose to stay and help out around here. You see, they can't go back. If they do and try to inform their leaders as to what they have done by informing us of their numbers and plans, they will most likely be executed for disloyalty. If they merely wonder around out there, surviving locals will recognise them for what they are and most likely kill them on sight, or worse. So I think they will choose to stay here and work by their own free will."

They pondered the idea for a little while. Then Lubeck announced that he thought Morgana was right and that he would offer the prisoners their freedom come morning. Thorsten and Jaffa joined the little group and began to eat as Malik told them of the discussion they just had. Thorsten gave a complacent shrug, stating that he thought it would be safer and easier to simply kill them and have done with it. But if the decision had already been made, then he would go with it as always. The group ate their fill and drank perhaps a little too much of the ale they had plundered from Ibis, then slipped into deep restful sleep.

With the morning, came a new sense of direction. They had the location, numbers and defences of their quarry. Now it was time to draw up plans to destroy them and have their revenge. Council was called and all of Lubeck's closest and trusted friends gathered to discuss the forthcoming events. Their numbers were not that different. The slavers perhaps had the advantage of a few dozen or so extra swords. Lubeck and the others were quite sure they had superior skill. Taking the port of Ibis without loss and only a few casualties had boosted their confidence. They also had the element of surprise. As yet the slavers were unaware of their presence. The Saracens were tasked to lead a scouting party to map the land around the slavers encampment. The party was not to be large, as large numbers of armed men make lots of noise and that would attract attention. So no more than six would go. Three Saracens and three others of Tarique's choice. Once they had a clear picture of the land surrounding the slavers stronghold, carefully planned battle tactics could be drawn.

Tarique began to choose his scouts. He chose two Mongols. He had heard they were extremely capable horsemen. This would be the time to put that to the test. The last member was a quiet, bald headed Oriental man of middle age, slight of build but wiry. Tarique had witnessed this man fight empty handed during the destruction of Ibis. He killed at least four men single handed while unarmed. Something Tarique had heard about, but never witnessed first-hand.

They prepared their horses, packed saddle bags with supplies, slung on their armour and weaponry, then with the briefest of goodbyes, rode off into the wilderness. The scouting party would be gone for a week or so. In the meantime the remainder of the main group would be preparing for a campaign and if necessary, a siege of the slavers encampment. The latter would not be a preferred option, so Lubeck decided they would have to draw them out into open battle. They had to kick the hornet's nest as it were.

The original crew trained the newcomers in the fighting skills they had learned from their time during the building of the Thunder Child. Sharing their knowledge and increasing the efficiency of their growing army. The newcomers didn't want to die in the inevitable battle, so they were eager to learn. Thorsten, Lubeck and Malik drummed it into them, they had to fight as one, no weak links in the chain. Every man must know what to do and when to do it without having to be told. They also had to trust their commanders. They had to trust that they knew what they were doing and to follow orders quickly without question, if they wanted to survive. Discipline, military discipline was being ingrained into each and every man. Lubeck was turning ordinary men, once slaves into a professional army.

Morgana approached Lubeck, who was now sat on a rock by the beach and asked him about the fate of the women and children they had also rescued from Ibis. They had come straight here in rapid pursuit of the slave ships that left the morning of the attack. They did not have time to drop them off anywhere, so had brought them along.

"They are all still in danger while they are here." She stated in a concerned manner.

"I know this, but they are safer here under our protection than out there undefended. I will return them to their homes or offer them new if they wish to settle with us when this is over." Lubeck replied in an attempt to reassure her.

"Settle? Where?" Morgana enquired.

"I don't know yet, but I have some ideas. I need you to watch over them while we are away. I will not leave you undefended. I will leave some men behind with you. If we don't return before the last full moon, you must take one of the smaller ships, destroy the rest and sail for home. Do you understand me?" Morgana dropped her head but acknowledged Lubeck's command. Then lifting her head again, she asked.

"When this is all over, do you have a woman in mind with whom you might settle?"

"Are you offering?" Lubeck retorted with a smile. Morgana lifted one eyebrow and smiled. Then with playfulness in her voice, she replied.

"Perhaps, perhaps not. If I thought the position was open to be filled, then perhaps I might." Lubeck grinned at her and without reply stood up and returned to help with the training. Morgana watched him leave and sighed. Had she just embarrassed herself? Or was there a real possibility that she could become Lubeck's wife? She knew that Lubeck had a wife but what she did not know is what had become of her. Was she still living in his home in the North? Or was she Killed during the slavers raids? Perhaps she no longer lived due to natural causes? Or maybe died in child birth? Her head began to spin as she filled it with endless possibilities as to the fate of Lubeck's wife. He never spoke of her, just his son, who he longed to find and bring home with him. Lubeck loved his son, that was obvious. But he never spoke of his wife. Why?

The sun shone bright and a light breeze flowed through the tower, as Freyja looked into her font. She watched with longing eyes, as the men in the raiding party trained and practiced. How she wished she too could be there, indeed, how she longed to be anywhere but where she had been for these long years past. In the waters of the font, the vision now focused on Tarique and his scouts. Freyja was trying her best to watch over all of the men, women and children who were under Lubeck's protection. All appeared to be going well. The presence of the scouting party was still unknown to the slavers as they continued to enslave more individuals from the surrounding area. Each day they would head out armed, carrying chains. Each evening they would return with fewer and fewer slaves. Their searches would have to go deeper inland and take longer if they were to fill their ships with enough slaves to make the money they hoped to in Altear. Tarique and the scouts watched intently and noted all movements. They mapped the surrounding areas and marked what they considered to be good vantage points and prospective battle grounds to engage their enemy.

Freyja watched and tried to reach them with her mind and guide them through possible dangers. Tarique's mind was strong and difficult to reach so far away. Jamal however, was a little easier, not because he was weak minded, but because he was a little more open to suggestion. She reached out to him and a little voice in the back of his head warned him, the path they were taking was a dangerous one.

"Why do you protest so Jamal?" Tarique questioned him.

"I don't know, it's just a feeling, call it instinct or maybe a warning from our ancestors, but something is not right about talking this path. We're walking into a trap, I feel it."

"A trap? But no one knows of our presence here. How could there be a trap in wait for us if no one knows we are here?" Tarique countered. Jamal screwed up his face with frustration as he replied.

"I don't know, but you have known me a long time my brother, do you not trust our instincts?" Tarique thought for a moment.

"Alright, dismount, conceal the horses and ourselves. Let's see what has got you so spooked Jamal." The scouts did as instructed, but no sooner had they dismounted, they heard soldiers approaching from ahead of them. Suddenly, all of their ears were tuned into the sounds which surrounded them. Twigs snapped to their right, rocks crunched to their left and the sound of boots marching towards them from ahead.

"We're surrounded." Jaffa pointed out.

"Really? I hadn't noticed." Tarique replied with deep sarcasm. The group tethered their horses and drew their weapons. The Saracens and the Oriental disappeared while the two Mongols remained visible though not obviously so. The men to their flanks moved closer, still under the illusion they had not been discovered. The soldiers on the road ahead of them continued in full sight and apparently without concern. As the main group drew closer, the hidden soldiers sprang their trap. Three came down from the right, swords drawn and shields up racing towards the two Mongols. Three more appeared from the left with spears running head long at the two scouts trapping them in a simple pincer movement. The Mongol scouts turned back to back to engage their attackers. The first spear head glanced off the defending shield of the first Mongol as the attacker attempted to skewer him on his approach. The Mongols reply was to drop to one knee and bring his sword around cutting deep into his attacker's abdomen. The man screamed and fell to the ground clutching at his fatal wound. Swords clashed behind him as his friend engaged the three men from their right. Swinging around each other and swapping places, the Mongols slayed two more assailants with quick unanswered strikes. Two more attackers were slain from behind as Jamal and the Oriental scout appeared and assisted their comrades. The one remaining slaver realising he was out numbered and outclassed ran towards the approaching main group marching up the road ahead. The Oriental quickly draw a small knife from his belt and threw it hitting the runaway in the back of the neck. The man stopped instantly, dropped his sword and shield, fell first to his knees, then forwards landing on his face in the dust on the road.

The commotion now caused the six advancing soldiers to break into a run. They approached the scene and instantly charged at the four scouts. Their number was quickly reduced by two, as arrows struck them from behind. Tarique and Jaffa had circled around behind the main group and were now assisting their fellow scouts. These soldiers fought briefly before joining their colleagues in the afterlife. They wore uniforms and marched like soldiers, but they certainly lacked the skills the scouts displayed. A dozen less slavers to worry about. The scouts dragged the bodies away and concealed them in the undergrowth.

"It won't be long until they are missed." Tarique stated with concern. "Once these bodies are discovered, it won't be long before they come searching for those responsible." The group mounted their horses and made for home.

In the slaver's camp one man reported to a tall, heavy, dark haired man wearing a red tunic bearing a black bull emblem.

"Two of our scouts have been missing for a while now sir. They were due back a couple of days ago but have failed to return. It could be nothing. They could merely be making a more thorough sweep of the area they were sent to sir." The red clothed man thought for a moment before he replied.

"A day maybe, but not two. Two days late raises concern and sends tingles through my blood. Something is not right. Which direction were they sent?"

"East sir. We had already looked in that direction with nothing to report, but one of our men thought that he had seen a sail a few weeks ago. He didn't report it straight away as he thought it a trick of the light, for when he cleared his eyes and looked again, the sail had gone. Just a glimpse nothing solid sir, but when he informed his commander, we sent out a couple of scouts to take a look."

"When was this?" The tall man asked.

"It was about three weeks ago sir. As I said, they were due back two days ago, but have yet to return." The soldier replied.

"Then I think we need to go and take a look to the East. Let us see what is there that has prevented our men from returning. I want fifty men, armed and ready. Before this day is done, we will be on the road heading East in numbers to locate our missing men and unravel this mystery."

"Very good sir." The man retorted snapping his heels together and bowing his head before heading off to ready the search party.

Back at Lubeck's encampment, Morgana stood on the main deck of the Thunder Child in front of the figure head of Freyja. She appeared to be in conversation with the wooden effigy as Thorsten climbed aboard. The conversation ceased and Morgana gathered herself as he approached. Thorsten's eyes played tricks on him he thought as he stared at the wooden image.

"Why do you stare so?" Morgana asked him. Thorsten as if awakened from a dream shook his head and blinked, but always keeping his eyes fixed on the figurehead, he replied.

"I thought..." He laughed nervously as he began. "No, couldn't be."

"What? What is it that troubles you?" Morgana pressed again.

"I thought I saw her close her eyes." He answered with puzzlement in his voice.

"Have you been drinking too much ale again Thorsten?" Morgana laughed softly.

"Not at all." He objected with a dark expression taking over his face. "What were you doing just now? It looked as though you were talking to her as if she were here."

"I was talking to her. It comforts me to talk to her, like some talk to the Gods through idols and alters. Is there wrong in that?" Morgana gathered her things and brushed past the big man leaving the ship and heading towards what had now become a small village within the encampment.

"What did you want Thorsten?" She called back over her shoulder. Thorsten, his eyes still fixed on the wooden statue muttered.

"I wondered if you would like to ….." He drifted off, not finishing what he began.

"Would like to what?" Morgana called back. Surprised that she had heard him, Thorsten's gaze broke and turned towards Morgana, who by now was already some fifty feet away.

"Would like to eat with me tonight?" He finished almost under his breath.

"I'd like that." Morgana's voice fading with the distance carried on the breeze.

"Huh?" Thorsten was shocked that she had heard him yet again and even more so that she had accepted his offer. A huge grin spread across his face as he turned back to look at the figurehead once more. Was it just him? Or did the carved face appear to be softly smiling. Thorsten shook his head trying to clear it. He shrugged and with a light heart and a smile on his lips, he stepped away and off the ship returning to the main encampment. He playfully slapped one of the watchmen on the shoulder as he passed, remarking.

"Keep up the good work!" The watchman seemed a little bewildered by Thorsten's actions but simply replied.

"Thank you, I will." The figurehead once more opened its eyes and looked towards the dragon at the bows of the mighty ship.

"Stay alert, danger comes this way soon. Beware, stay mindful." A whispered voice, drifted like rustling leaves on the breeze. The eyes slowly closed once more while the dragon's chest heaved as if taking a deep breath. Then both figureheads returned to stillness.

A single ship left the slavers encampment and headed East along the coast three days after the heavy dark haired man left with fifty soldiers heading overland in the same direction. The Oriental scout accompanying Tarique, noticed the sail from their elevated position and pointed to it. The scouting party stopped their journey to take note. It was hard to tell how many men were aboard, but the ship was not overly large.

"Looks like we are going to have company soon." Jamal pointed out. The men tried to calculate how long it would take for the ship to round the headland and follow the coast before stumbling on their landing site. Most of the day, but no more. The ship would find them by night fall. They had to ride and ride hard to make it home before the ship would get there. They had to make it and warn the rest of the forthcoming danger.

"If they have discovered the bodies, they will have sent out a land party too. They must not be far behind. We have to ride fast, don't worry about concealing our presence any longer, let's just get home in time." Tarique said as they kicked their horses into action and rode like the wind in the direction of the landing site. A lookout near the camp, called out as the scouts approached. Lubeck could see that something was wrong by the way they were riding without concerns for covering their tracks. He called the men to arms. A horn sounded and men rushed to gather their arms, as women grabbed children clambering to hide them as best they could. A half dozen of the women then joined the men arming themselves and joining the ranks. A group of men headed by Hagar, had mounted horses forming a light cavalry. They rode out to meet the returning scouts and covered their return to camp. A few of the horsemen broke off and ventured out in search of signs of pursuers, returning very quickly to report that a large group were not too far behind, a day at most.

Tarique reported to Lubeck about the ship coming along the coast and the returning horsemen told of the land party so close behind the scouts.

"Looks as though you kicked the hornet's nest." Lubeck remarked. Orders were given and men made ready. The camps defences were primed and within an hour they were ready for their unwelcome guests. The ship appeared first. It sailed by apparently harmlessly, as if they hadn't noticed the landing site. But then it turned abruptly and made for land just a short distance East of the camp.

"They'll come down the coast and try to burn our ships to prevent our escape." Thorsten pointed out.

"That's what I would do." Agreed Lubeck. "Take a dozen men and intercept them. Hold them as best you can." He ordered. Thorsten did as he was told and within moments his band were weaving their way through the long rough grasses of the shoreline dunes heading East. Reinforcing the number of guards around the ships, Lubeck then returned to the main group in the middle of the camp. He divided the remaining forces into three units. One large and two smaller ones. The large unit was to stand their ground in plain sight of the approaching enemy as if defying them to proceed any further. It would appear that they were prepared to meet their attackers head on like the Vikings in the North. Meanwhile, the two smaller groups would flank their approaching quarry and at a given signal, descend upon them from both sides, forcing them to defend on three fronts. A difficult task for any commander and one Lubeck hoped would be unachievable for this slaver and his inferior troops.

Thorsten's group came across the crew from the ship uncomfortably close to the encampment. They were carrying pots of thick oil and tar mixed to make a sticky flammable substance resembling pitch. The torches they were carrying began to glow against the failing light of the setting sun. Thorsten knew they had come with the goal of burning their ships as he had first thought. With a sharp hand signal his group advanced upon the slavers at pace. Thorsten's gigantic frame leading the way. He lofted his huge axe and with a single blow cleaved the first of his enemies almost in half. Men screamed as swords clashed and fighting ensued. Unfortunately, two men broke away from the main group and managed to traverse the small battle unseen. They made their way around to the place where Lubeck's ships were moored. Once there they continued with their mission to burn the ships. The first, was a small lightweight ship. They poured the contents of one pot over the deck and put a torch to it. Flames flicked and danced as they grew and spread across the vessel. Once the men were sure the fire had taken, they moved to the next.

On hearing the commotion and seeing the flames, the guards Lubeck had stationed there mounted an attempt to extinguish the fires and save the ship. Preoccupied with this, they didn't notice the two intruders move on. The smoke from the burning ship and the failing light made it easier for them to move unseen. The second ship was a little larger than the first. As they moved around it to locate the best position to set their fire, the first man froze in his tracks staring up at the massive dragon mounted on the front of the mighty Thunder Child. The second man also stopped and stared in amazement at the magnificent ship. It would be a shame to destroy such an awesome vessel, but that was their charge, so they set about the task. They set the fire on the second ship, but as they did, sharp gusts of wind would extinguish the flames before they had chance to take fully. A third and then a fourth attempt before the flames stayed alight. The sound of creaking wood and whooshing of air that resembled heavy breathing filled the arsonist's ears. The water around their waists, swirled and splashed as if some large fish were swimming and thrashing nearby. The two men looked at each other bewildered as to what was causing this effect. Then as they made to move onto the Thunder Child, they froze in shock and fear. Through the smoke and shadows of the dusky light, an enormous dragon's head lurched towards them followed closely by a huge hand like claw. With a roar, like a hellish demon, the dragon sunk its long teeth into the first of the arsonists killing him instantly. The second was taken by the claw that reached out of the smoke and gripped him tight lifting him high into the air. The dragon's head came towards him now, mouth wide open and roaring once more. The man screamed at the sight, but not for long. The huge jaws closed around him biting him clean in half and silencing his screams. The mighty claws crashed back down into the estuary splashing water high into the air. It fell back like torrents of rain onto the burning ship extinguishing the flames with a loud hiss and clouds of steam. All of the ships moored nearby bobbed and rocked with the motion of the water. The guards could not save the first ship and it burned brightly illuminating the darkening sky.

The leader of the slavers saw the orange glow against the dark backdrop and realised that his strategy was working. He decided that victory must be close at hand, so pushed his men onward. The demonic roars emanating from the temporary dock caught Thorsten's attention. Finishing off the last few slavers, he recalled his men to return to the ships and investigate. The glow of the flames from the burning ship fuelled their efforts and encouraged their haste. When they reached the ships, the first was all but sunk. Its mast was broken and had fallen to the side and its hull was charred black and smouldering with just the smallest of fires still burning. As they approached, guards challenged them not recognising their own people in the dark and smoke.

"What happened here?" Thorsten asked looking down at the bodies on the jetty next to the Thunder Child.

"We don't know Thorsten. Some sort of wild beast I think." One guard replied. Thorsten looked at the guard in disbelief.

"Look at the size of those teeth marks. This beast would have been a giant, about fifty feet tall.

Where is it now?" He asked clutching his axe.

"I don't know. We didn't see it come in or leave." The guard reported.

"Then it's been here all along. Perhaps we have settled within its nest?" Thorsten added, looking around for signs of the beast that might lead to its whereabouts. There was nothing however. It was as if this beast simply appeared then disappeared perhaps by magic. By magic, Thorsten thought to himself. He looked around again uneasily.

"I hate magic." He grunted to himself as he looked up at the dragon figurehead on the Thunder Child's bow. "Was it you?" He called up to it, thinking to himself that he might be losing his mind. While he was looking up at the huge dragon, a droplet of blood hit him in the middle of his forehead. Thorsten wiped it away with his fingers and looked at the red liquid glistening under the now full moon. Cold shivers ran down his spine and he quickly ushered his men away to lend support to the main group, who were just about to engage the enemy. He looked back, just the once as he followed them and caught a glimpse of what appeared to be, the dragon resting back into its original position before freezing, motionless again. He blinked, not trusting his eyes. Had he just seen what he thought he'd seen? Or was it a trick of the moon light and the ship rocking on the water?

About half a mile away from the main encampment Lubeck and his men stood their ground, blocking the way of the approaching slavers. As they came into view their dark haired leader called for them to form ranks. His men jostled and formed three lines. The front line with their shields facing Lubeck's men and advancing at a steady pace with the other two ranks following a pace and a half behind. As they drew closer, Lubeck called to his men.

"Shield wall!" The former slaves reacted immediately, two rows of men, the front kneeling, the second standing, interlocked their shields forming a solid wall of brightly painted Viking shields resembling the scales of some mythical creature. The slavers stopped and set their own shields, but unlike Lubeck's men, these shields were not dug into the ground. They merely held their shields protecting themselves from the knees to the neck in a flimsy row across their front rank only. At a command from their leader, they dropped to their knees and archers stood up from behind drawing their bows.

"Phalanx!" Yelled Lubeck and swiftly his men from the rear rushed forward and interlocked their shields overhead and around the flanks of their comrades. The wave of arrows rained down glancing off shields harmlessly. A second volley came down with the same result. The slaver's dark haired leader frowned as he watched two more waves of arrows have very little effect. He raised his hand and the archers stopped.

"Recover!" At Lubeck's command, his men disassembled the phalanx and returned to the simpler shield wall. His opponent glared at them, under the full moon's silvery light. Not a single casualty. A whistling sound grew louder as he watched.

"Arrows!" He called. His men held up their shields in an attempt to defend themselves. Arrows bit into shields with a thud and men screamed with pain as some found their mark. A half dozen men fell to the floor clutching at legs arms and some fell lifeless as arrows stuck fatally. The dark haired leader cursed and in his rage ordered a full charge.

"Brace!" Lubeck called to his men. The sound of charging feet and the war cries of the slavers grew louder as they drew near. "Brace!" Lubeck instructed his men. With an almighty crash, the wave of soldiers broke against the shield wall like waves on rocks. Men hurled themselves at the obstacle, only to find they were thrown back into the path of their advancing comrades behind.

"Thrust!" Lubeck gave the order to his troops. The shield wall parted slightly and through the spaces, a third row of men thrust spears, lunging some three feet past the shields and skewering numerous slavers wounding them to varying degrees.

"Recover!" The next order came and the shield wall clamped tight again. "Advance!" The shield wall moved in unison, one step, two steps three steps. Now Lubeck's men were stepping on the wounded slavers who had fallen in front of the wall. These men were slain as Gurlemek passed over them. Enraged to an even higher level by this, the leader of the slavers ordered a full charge with the few mounted men he had brought with him. Men still fought at the wall. Swords rang against shields and occasional screams echoed loud above the noise as men were stabbed by Viking swords slipping through the shields and striking the undisciplined horde in front of them.

"Cavalry!" Lubeck called loudly. A horn sounded and the thundering of hooves rumbled up from behind his own lines. Hagar leading the Gurlemek cavalry, charged forward to meet the opposition. The fighting at the shield wall broke as Hagar's cavalry approached at speed. The wall parted to allow them through and the slavers on the other side turned and ran as the horsemen began to cut them down. The slaver's own horsemen passed through their retreating troops and engaged Hagar's men. Horses slammed into one another sending their riders plummeting to the ground. Others fought on horseback with swords ringing and shattering under heavy axe blows. Another horn sounded and Lubeck's flanking warriors moved into position to prevent the retreating foot soldiers from escaping. Unseated riders from both sides picked themselves up and continued fighting on foot. The men forming the shield wall now broke ranks and joined the onslaught.

Having suffered heavy losses and being out skilled, the slavers were soon overwhelmed and defeated. Lubeck now in the thick of the fight was finishing off two slavers who had made the fatal mistake of thinking they could kill him if they worked together. The Lion headed sword in one hand and his unique hooked weapon in the other, Lubeck parried blows and ducked attempts to behead him with graceful capability. It was as though he were merely toying with the men, frustrating their attempts to kill him with nonchalant ease. Then as Thorsten arrived with the rest of the men, Lubeck drove his sword deep into the middle of one attacker's chest. The second, pulled a spear from a dead soldier and launched it at Lubeck while he was preoccupied killing the first. Thorsten's shield intercepted the weapon midway and the man turned to run. Lubeck sheathed his sword, swapped hands with his hook like weapon and then hurled it at the fleeing slaver like a spear. The head of the brutal weapon thumped hard into the man's back between his shoulder blades, severing his spine. He fell to the ground emitting a short scream before falling silent. Victorious, Lubeck's men rounded up the remaining slavers and herded them like sheep to kneel before him.

"You're covered in blood, are you injured?" Thorsten enquired looking at Lubeck. Wiping his face with the back of his hand, Lubeck replied.

"It's not mine. How did we fare?"

"We lost five men as I see it. Can't say for sure yet. They lost..." He looked around at the dead littering the field. "Perhaps forty or more here plus another twenty in the dunes, around sixty all told at a guess." Thorsten replied smiling contentedly.

"Sixty of theirs for five of our own, I like those odds, but if they only brought what, seventy? That means there are many more still at their encampment." He looked down at the few prisoners and pointed to one particularly scared individual. "You, return to your people and inform them of what happened here. Tell them I'm coming for them, all of them and if they try to run, my ships will destroy them out there on the oceans and I will cut them to pieces. Alive or dead I will feed them to the sharks." With that he waved a hand in dismissal and the man was released and sent on his way. Lubeck then turned to Malik and asked him the names of the Gurlemeck soldiers who had died and if they had any family. Malik told Lubeck everything he could about the men who had died, then informed him that arrangements would be made for their funerals and one man had a wife that was freed at the same time as he had been, during the attack on Ibis. It soon became clear that all of the men who had died were from the Port raid. None of Lubeck's original crew had been killed in either battle.

"They were not ready for battle. They needed more training." Malik stated.

"Which is why we must keep it up, never let it lapse. Practice makes perfect, perfect makes unbeatable, unbeatable means survival." Lubeck snarled in response.

Malik nodded and moved away to initiate proceedings for the men's funerals and to ensure the widowed woman would be taken care of. Lubeck now turned his attention to the prisoners they had taken that night. Especially the heavily built, dark haired leader of this attack, who wore the red tunic and whom Lubeck had recognised immediately.

"Lock this lot up with the others from Ibis, but bring him to me." Lubeck growled pointing at the man wearing the red tunic. Obeying his order immediately, Lubeck's men separated the leader from the rest of his men and dragged him to the landing site and the fire still burning in the middle. There, they stopped and threw the man to the ground at Lubeck's feet.

"Do you recognise me?" Lubeck asked him sternly. The prisoner looked up at the steely blue eyes glaring down at him.

"Should I?" He retorted defiantly.

"It was about five years ago. Your people descended on my fishing boat, you killed one of us and took the rest as slaves." Lubeck snorted in disgust.

"That's what we do, we take slaves—" The man was cut short by Lubeck slamming his fist into the side of the man's face knocking him flat against the dirt.

"I didn't give you permission to speak you son of a whore. Speak out of turn again and I will do more than slap your face." Lubeck snarled with vicious hatred. The prisoner used the back of his bound hands to wipe away the blood that trickled from the corner of his mouth, but remained silent.

"YOU ordered your men to beat me because I tried to save my son. YOU dragged a little boy away from his father and sent him to be sold in Altear. YOUR men almost killed me before chaining me to an oar in the belly of one of your Galleys. Now YOU are going to tell me where they took my son. So, where is my son?" Lubeck roared.

"I don't recall the incident you refer to. I don't remember what happened last month, never mind what happened in some insignificant little fiord in the North five years ago." The prisoner laughed as he tried to remember.

"So you do remember after all. I didn't tell you where it happened, just when. So tell me, where is my son?" Lubeck glared at the man, clenching his teeth and biting his lip, trying to curb his anger.

"You injured six of my men that day before we could finally take you and your boy. He's probably dead by now, in the salt mines of Bakar or maybe he was sold to some boy lovers in some far off land. I don't know and I don't care. I took him to Altear where I got a fair price for him." The prisoner replied attempting to get to his feet. Lubeck subdued the desire to kill the man there and then. He needed to continue questioning him. He asked about the location of Altear and what had happened to the rest of the slaves they had taken. All answers led back to Altear. This was where he had to head for next, as soon as they had dealt with the remainder of the slavers from this raiding party. After almost an hour of questioning, Lubeck was satisfied that he had enough information to continue their search.

"Cut him loose." Lubeck commanded. His men were confused and uncertain as to what they should do. "I said cut him loose." Lubeck repeated. The Prisoner laughed as he held out his hands so that his bonds could be cut.

"I will return with more men and kill you Barbarian, you know this."

"No, you won't." Lubeck replied as he turned his back on the man and began to walk away. As soon as his hands were free, the prisoner grabbed the knife from the man who had released him and raced towards Lubeck, attempting to kill him from behind. Lubeck had anticipated this action and was far from surprised. He spun around with lightning speed and slammed his fist straight into his attacker's face. The man was stunned as blood burst from his mouth and nose simultaneously. He fell to his knees dropping the knife. Lubeck stepped behind him and wrapped his powerful arms around the neck of his attacker in a lethal strangle hold. The man choked and pounded at Lubeck's arms. With a sharp crack, Lubeck snapped the man's neck like a dry twig. Emotionless and cold, Lubeck regarded the dead man on the ground at his feet. He kicked sand at the corpse in disgust as he looked to his men ordering;

"Eat, rest and rotate the guards at two hour intervals. We march midmorning and destroy the rats nest along the coast. The women and children can prepare the ships for sea while we are away. We will destroy the slavers and free the slaves they have taken. Then we sail for Altear." The men bowed slightly in respectful obedience and set about their tasks. Then looking again at the body on the ground, Lubeck ordered. "Throw this pig to the crows. Let them feast on his eyes so that he will never see, in whatever afterlife awaits him. Let the jackals eat his flesh and tear out his innards, so that the maggots and beetles can also feast on this stinking son of a whore."

"Yes Earl Lubeck!" A man replied as he grabbed a colleague to help him move the body. Morgana stared at him in disbelief. She was used to men killing in the heat of battle. She had even thought it an admirable quality at times. But Lubeck had killed this man with cold, emotionless calculation. Something she had never expected of him. This was a side to Lubeck she had not known was there.

"It was cold revenge for taking his son." Thorsten told her as the door to the hut closed behind Lubeck. "He needed to get it out, before it consumed him from within. I've seen hatred and the desire for revenge destroy men. It is best that it was done this way. Revenge is a dish best served cold. If he had killed this man in the heat of battle, the thirst would never have been quenched. At least now it's done and Lubeck will be able to think with a clear head and secure the return of our loved ones." Morgana was not entirely settled by this, but she accepted Thorsten's explanation and followed him back to the hut where Antonio and Malik had started eating, before trying to get a few hours' sleep. Thorsten paused by the door and glared at the Thunder Child as it bathed in the silvery sheen of the full moon. Morgana noticed this and enquired.

"Why do you stare so at the ship? What troubles you?"

"I'm not sure, but I think there is magic at work this night. I may be losing my mind, but I don't fully trust that dragon." Thorsten replied gruffly still staring at the ship.

"Whatever do you mean?" Morgana laughed softly. Thorsten frowned, turning away from the ship and opening the door to the hut he uttered under his breath.

"That Dragon is alive, I know it, I feel it in my gut, but I also know it can't be unless magic is involved. I don't like magic. I don't trust it or those who use it."

"You trust me don't you? And Freyja?" Morgana objected.

"Of course he trusts you both, don't you?" Malik asked rhetorically as they entered the hut. "Why would you ask such a thing Morgana?" He continued. Thorsten stopped and stood tall in the middle of the hut. He had a troubled look on his face. Then, clearing his throat and at the risk of sounding crazy he announced.

"The dragon figurehead on the Thunder Child, it killed two men tonight. I don't know how, yes it's made of wood, it's just a carving, but I know what I heard and saw tonight."

"You saw it kill these men?" Antonio gasped.

"No, not exactly. I heard a fierce roar and men screamed. When I got there, they were already dead. One had been bitten by something big—"

"It could have been any wild creature." Malik interrupted.

"No, I looked around for the beast ready to defend myself and my men. I looked up, because I thought I saw the dragon move—" Thorsten continued.

"Probably just the motion of the water." Antonio butted in. Thorsten shrugged.

"Perhaps, but something wet hit me on the forehead, when I wiped it away, I saw that it was blood. I looked closely at the dragon; it had blood dripping from its teeth." Silence fell upon the room as the occupants pondered what they had just listened to.

"We should go and take a look, all of us together. If Thorsten did indeed see what he thinks he saw, then magic is indeed at work here and we need to tell Lubeck." Antonio suggested. Nobody seemed to be particularly keen on the idea, but they all decided to go and investigate. They left together and made their way down to where the ships were moored. The smouldering wreck of the ship the slavers had managed to burn in the attack earlier, made the air heavy with the scent of charred wood and smoke. The subtle motion of the waters movement rocked the ships gently and the Thunder Child's dragon moved with it, which did indeed make it appear as though it were alive.

"A simple trick of the light and the adrenaline of battle I think." Antonio remarked staring at the immense carving on the bow. Thorsten moved a little closer and hesitantly climbed aboard the huge ship. He made his way forward until he could reach the beast with his hands. Touching it made him wary as he imagined it coming to life and slaying them all. Before he realised what he was doing, he had climbed onto the carving's back and was almost at its head when the tension was smashed by a deep rumbling voice behind him.

"What, by all the Gods are you doing?" Morgana screamed, Antonio and Malik gasped and reeled away from the ship, while Thorsten trying to draw his sword, overbalanced and went tumbling into the water below with an almighty splash. Lubeck stood by the figurehead sighing with disillusionment. He stared down at the giant, floundering in the shallow water choking and thrashing about like a disgruntled child. Lubeck shook his head and the frightened gasps turned to laughter, as the three on the jetty looked upon the mighty Thorsten spouting water from his lips and pulling sea weed from his hair.

"By Odin's beard Lubeck, I could have killed you creeping up on me like that." Thorsten declared trying to gain a modicum of dignity.

"Not from down there you couldn't." Lubeck retorted, chuckling at the scene in front of him. Thorsten took a deep breath and dived below the surface, returning with his sword having retrieved it from the soft sand of the sea bed. He had dropped it prior to his fall, in a futile attempt to grasp a hand on anything to prevent his humiliation. He tossed it to the jetty then swam the short distance to follow it. Malik helped him out of the water and Morgana, using the hem of her dress wiped and dried his face. The four friends stood together on the jetty looking up at Lubeck standing by the dragon. The giggles subsided and a more serious air befell the group.

"I repeat my question." Lubeck broke the silence staring down at his comrades. Their complexions paled, their jaws dropped in terror as Thorsten scrambled to pick up his sword.

"Lubeck, look out! Run!" Malik cried in horror. Alerted, Lubeck followed the gaze of his friend's eyes over his shoulder. The sight that befell him was one of terrifying wonder. The immense wooden dragon had somehow turned its head and now stared down at the group of startled and frightened individuals. Instinctively Lubeck sprang away from the figurehead drawing his sword as he moved. The dragon did not react further. It remained motionless and inanimate as it had been since its completion. The group did likewise, nerves on edge, senses tingling with a primeval instinct to survive. Slowly Thorsten edged his way towards Morgana, quietly ushering her to move away to a small storage place on the side of the jetty. Malik followed suit as did Antonio. Lubeck moved a little closer and squinted, looking intently at the wooden creature for further signs of life.

"What are you doing?" Thorsten whispered, his hushed voice carrying on the early morning breeze.

Lubeck raised a hand to silence Thorsten as he moved a little closer. He stopped, a voice sounding softly in his head.

"Be still Lubeck, Fear not, this guardian means you no harm. He watches over you and your growing fleet, keeping all safe and will warn you of impending danger. He's with you at my hand and will protect the Thunder Child and her crew whenever he is needed." Freyja's voice faded with the breeze and Lubeck shook his head trying to clear it once more. The sound of straining timbers mixed with a sigh from the huge carving raised Lubeck from his trance. The dragon had returned to its original position and was now as inanimate as it had ever been. Lubeck rested his hand on the beast's back patting it as one would an obedient guard dog.

"It would appear that our little witch has a long reach indeed." Lubeck announced, without fear of disturbing the resting creature. Hesitantly Thorsten and the others came out from their refuge and crept closer to the ship. Their eyes fixed on the immense statue searching for the first signs of life. "It would appear that our friend in the tower is a witch after all. For bringing this beast to life is a little more than having the ability to heal the sick, wouldn't you agree?" Lubeck's voice was laced with annoyance and relief as he posed his rhetorical question.

"Freyja did this? Why? How? " Malik enquired in bewilderment.

"Apparently to protect and watch over us. Perhaps we should ask her accomplice as to how?" Lubeck answered turning his attention to Morgana as he jumped down from the ships deck landing on the jetty beside his friends. Morgana hung her head resigning to the fact that her covert actions had been discovered. She began to tell the others about the pact she had with Freyja and the instructions the young witch had given her. As she spoke, a loud roar emitted from the dragon, catching the attention of all in the group.

"Cover!" Thorsten called knocking Morgana to the ground as he moved to shield her. An arrow sailed wide of its intended target, as the shock at hearing the beast's warning, distracted the assassin momentarily affecting his aim. He turned to run as Lubeck, Thorsten and Malik all gave chase simultaneously. They spread out attempting to restrict the assassin's options for escape. Another fleeting shot narrowly missed Lubeck as he dived for cover. Malik drew the archer's attention by hurling a rock in his direction. Pausing to notch another arrow, the assassin carefully gauged distance and wind then, drew a bead on Malik who had stood tall in order to throw. Another roar caused the archer to momentarily switch his focus as fear began to disrupt his concentration. The arrow missed its mark but caught Malik in the thigh, bringing him to the ground, as he cried out in pain. The delay in the assassin's escape had given time for Thorsten to close down his quarry. The archer turned to run, only to meet with Thorsten's sword sweeping downward towards him. With not even enough time to scream, the assassin was cleaved from neck to navel in the single swift and powerful blow. Before the body of the slain man had hit the ground Lubeck appeared beside his trusted countryman. He spat at the corps in disgust. Moans of pain caught their ears, as Malik attempted to stand. As he wobbled trying not to bear any weight on his injured leg, a firm hand steadied him. Tarique ducked his head under Malik's arm and helped to share the load aiding him back to the jetty where Morgana and Antonio were still hidden behind some barrels of fresh water. Jamal and Jaffa, along with the Oriental scout had accompanied Tarique on hearing the commotion and were already scouring the dunes for more hidden archers. After the search was completed and Lubeck was satisfied that no more assassins were hiding in the dunes, they all returned to the main camp. Malik's leg was treated, guards doubled and the chance for a little rest seized before dawn.

When the new day came, Hagar took a salvage party to retrieve the slavers ship which had put into shore just around the headland. All of its crew were now dead and the ship lay vacant just a quarter of a mile away. They recovered it without incident and tied it up alongside their own, moored against the temporary jetty. By the time the task was completed, the remainder of the main party were ready to march and attack what remained of the slavers. Given just enough time to catch their breath and quench their thirst, Hagar and his men joined the ranks alongside their colleagues. Having given his instructions to those who would remain at the camp, Malik now included among them, Lubeck took the head of the column mounted on a fine looking Black Friesian mare alongside Thorsten riding a huge Piebald Shire horse.

"That thing is meant to pull carts, not to ride into battle." Lubeck commented as he settled into place.

"It's the only horse big enough to carry me." Thorsten laughed in reply. With almost one hundred men at their backs, all armed and clad in armour, the pair raised their arms in signal for the march to begin. They moved out in unison, a hundred men moving as one body. They marched across the grassy hillsides and open plains for most of the morning. As the coast line came into view, Lubeck checked to see two of his ships moving close to the shoreline with the same heading as themselves. Pleased with what he saw, Lubeck settled back into his saddle and set his mind to the task ahead. His forces now outnumbered those of the remaining slavers, but they were held up in a fortified encampment. He was ill equipped for a siege, especially if it were to become a lengthy one. He needed to finish this swiftly to prevent heavy losses on his part. They marched all that day, rested overnight and continued the following morning. From a high vantage point Thorsten could see their ships sat just off the shore awaiting the prearranged signal to close. As he scanned the lay of the land, he saw the slavers encampment in the distance. No alarms had been raised as yet, no scouts or lookouts even. It was as if the slavers were not expecting an attack at all. As he watched, his eyes settled on a small dust cloud that appeared to be heading their way. He narrowed his eyes in an attempt to focus more clearly. Tarique and his scouts were riding back at speed.

"To arms!" Thorsten called. Lubeck rallied his troops and instinctively as they had trained for months to do so, his men formed defensive formations to face the incoming foe. But, as Tarique and his scouts rode up, there was no sign of pursuers.

"Lubeck! Lubeck!" Tarique called out as he approached "They're gone, they're all gone!"

"AAAGGHHHH!" Lubeck's roar was one of unmistakable anguish. Tarique began a full report of the reconnaissance he and his scouts had made. The slavers, the slaves they had captured and the ships, all had gone.

"It would appear your sending the survivor spurred them into immediate departure." Thorsten stated.

"No, my warning of doing so was clear. On foot and injured, it was impossible for the messenger to have made it here in time to give enough warning for them to flee so quickly." Lubeck pondered. "He could have only made it here late last night or even early this morning. Even if they made haste, their ships should still be in the bay and only a few miles out. So where are they? How did they get such early warning? How could that injured soldier have made it back here with such speed?"

"On a horse perhaps?" Mauro suggested. Lubeck rubbed his forehead hard with his hands as if trying to pull the solution physically from his head.

"Where would he get a horse from? We gathered all of the loose horses after the battle and stabled them with our own. Even with a horse, he couldn't have made it here so far ahead of us, which was the whole idea behind sending him back. To let them know we were right behind him and that they didn't have time to run before we would be upon them." Lubeck was becoming more agitated as his frustration grew. The sound of a Viking horn sounding interrupted the discussion. Everyone looked to see where the sound had come from. On the other side of the small valley they were overlooking, an outrider was signalling to them and pointing out to sea. Lubeck dug his heels into his mounts haunches and the beast sprang into a canter. He rode across the valley and up the other side followed by Thorsten and twenty other horsemen. There, approaching the horizon were the slavers ships. A few heading Eastward and three heading South.

"Why would they split their forces?" Jamal asked.

"Altear is in that direction; South is where we have come from. Their main force is heading for Altear to warn them of our imminent attack. I don't know why they would send ships South again retracing our journey here." Thorsten enlightened the rest.

"Damn the Gods!" Lubeck growled. "How did this happen? They have too much of a head start on us. Even if we ride without sleep, we will not reach our ships in time to give chase. Signal the two off shore to come in, it will be faster by sea to return and launch the rest of the fleet."

"Earl Lubeck! Earl Lubeck!" A voice called from the other side of the small valley. Lubeck looked towards the man frantically yelling. The Thunder Child was rounding the headland just a half mile off shore.

"By all the Gods. What is she doing here?" Thorsten gasped.

"Who cares? Let's ride." Lubeck roared, kicking his horse into a gallop and heading to the slavers encampment and the port therein. The other two ships were now heading towards the port also, and by the time Lubeck arrived, the first of them was already approaching the wooden jetty the slavers had built some years earlier. Lubeck waved them further down informing them that the Thunder Child was coming in too. Both ships made their way past and deeper into the port leaving the much wider and deeper part open for the mighty ship to berth. As she came around the mouth of the estuary, Lubeck noticed that the Thunder Child was towing two other smaller ships with her.

The rest of the mounted men were now walking their horses to the docks. About five minutes behind them the Gurlemek foot soldiers were heading towards the encampment also. Antonio leaned over the guard rails of the Thunder Child as she docked.

"Lubeck, are we too late?" He called as he gathered up ropes and helped to tie the ship alongside.

"For the battle yes, to rescue the situation, no. Tell me, why did you bring the Thunder Child here?" Lubeck replied.

"It's Morgana; she foresaw this and Kei's treachery. Quick get them aboard, I'll explain as we sail." Lubeck's men began to load the horses aboard the Thunder Child as the rest of his men arrived on foot. By the time everyone was there, the horses were stabled below decks and men were starting to prepare the two smaller ships for sea. The men scrambled aboard the five ships distributing themselves as best they could between them.

"Tell me of Morgana's vision and Kei's treachery then." Lubeck snarled, addressing Antonio.

"Of course, of course, it was Kei who helped the man you sent back. He took two horses and left the camp in the confusion that night. While we were down at the jetty, he rode out to find the survivor. He helped him to return and give the slavers time to escape."

"Kei! I'll kill that mongrel swine when I get my hands on him!" Thorsten declared.

"Did Morgana see where they were headed?" Lubeck asked being a little more constructive.

"Yes. They will take their main force to warn Altear of your impending attack. But they have also sent a small force to return to the tower and kill Freyja. They believe she is the heart of your success so far."

"How do they know of Freyja?" Jaffa asked.

"Kei of course!" Lubeck snapped back irritably.

"I swear by all the Gods I'll—"

"I know, I know…" Lubeck cut Thorsten short. "I can't stop both forces at the same time." He continued.

"Perhaps you can." Hagar suggested as he joined the meeting. "We can do as they have. Send our main force to Altear as planned and at the same time, we send a smaller force to intercept those sent to kill Freyja. Or we could just send one force in one direction. Whatever you decide to do, you need to do it fast or they will be too far ahead to catch." Lubeck thought for a moment, before replying.

"I'll take the Thunder Child to protect Freyja. She's the fastest thing on the water. We should arrive ahead of the slavers and should be in place ready to ambush them. Thorsten will follow with one of the other ships. Hagar, you take the rest of our fleet to Altear. Judge the situation yourself when you get there, only begin your attack if you think there is a good chance for success. Take these remaining ships and return to our encampment. Man all of the others. Take all of the women and children too. Put them onto two ships and keep them off shore away from trouble. If things go wrong, they are to sail back to their homes or anywhere they want, so long as they remain free. Thorsten, you take Jamal and his

Oriental friend with you. Hagar you take Jaffa and those Mongol scouts with you as well as Mauro, you may have need of his swimming abilities. Tarique comes with me. Malik, are you able to fight and accompany me or do you need to stay with the women and children?"

"I'm ok, or at least I will be by the time we reach Thanos. I'm with you." Malik replied scowling at Lubeck's insulting remark. Lubeck looked around as men were manning the ships making ready to give chase.

"We need more men, this was not supposed to happen yet." He commented.

"I might be able to help with that. I was going to mention it earlier but never really got the chance." Hagar sighed.

"What is it? What do you mean?" Lubeck asked. Hagar began to explain himself.

"I know of a chieftain two days sail from here, further North. I might be able to convince him to lend a hand, perhaps join our cause or maybe increase our ranks by sending some of his men to aid us. It's a long shot, but it's possible that he could be convinced."

"Do you know him well?" Lubeck enquired.

"Well enough I suppose. I've known him all of my life since before I was a small boy. I think he is part of my earliest memories."

"Then this is good is it not?" Lubeck smiled. Hagar frowned in thought before replying.

"We've never been on particularly good terms, even as small boys together. I can't say that he will help with any certainty. Do you want me to take the time to go and ask?" Lubeck thought on it, but before he could reply Thorsten cut in and questioned.

"If you are not on good terms even though you have known each other for so long, what makes you think he might help?"

"Because our mother will probably tell him to, I'm sure she will insist that Magnus should come to the aid of his younger brother. I doubt he will ignore her, especially if it ultimately could lead to the return of her granddaughter." Hagar answered as he stared at the ground in embarrassment. Everyone was stunned into silence and a few moments passed before Lubeck broke it.

"You are the brother of a chieftain, Earl Magnus no less. I've heard of him and yet you are happy for me to lead you, why?" Hagar lifted his eyes to look at Lubeck as he replied.

"Because I believe you are worthy, you have the makings of a great Earl, maybe one day even a King and I would gladly follow such a King as you."

Silence returned to the group momentarily, until a voice called out from a vantage point nearby. The slavers ships had reached the horizon. They needed to sail now if they were going to stay with them. Lubeck made his decision; he turned to Hagar giving him instruction.

"Go to your brother and ask him for aid in this venture. We split the men as I have already indicated. The lost time seeking aid from Earl Magnus will mean that Altear will be well prepared for your attack, so don't. Land well away from the main cities and towns. Fortify your landing site and wait for our return. Scout the land and make maps of the area around the main markets. I want a full reconnaissance done by the time we arrive."

"And if you don't?" Hagar asked tentatively.

"Give us three weeks after you land, if we're not with you by then, the fleet and crews are yours to command. Do as you will, though I hope you will free our families. I would sit much happier in Valhalla knowing my son was free again." Hagar nodded in silence before Lubeck called them to sail. The men divided themselves as Lubeck had ordered and moments later, the ships were on the open seas heading in their separate directions.

A Sisters Kiss

Anxious in case they had been pursued by Lubeck and the rest of the Gurlemek, the captain of the slaver's ships scoured the horizon for the slightest sign of a sail. A small dark patch against the fading line of the mainland was all he had as an indication, but was that a sail? Or was it just his eyes playing tricks as they strained to see anything over such a distance.

"They couldn't possibly catch us with this much of a head start." He stated to the Saxon standing by his side.

"If Lubeck is coming, which I'm sure he will be, his ship is the swiftest ship I have ever seen. One day's advantage is no advantage at all." Kei informed him.

"Then it is lucky that we have brought *her* with us, isn't it?" The two men looked across at a young woman, tall and slender with wild red hair that lifted and fell in the wind as she looked out to sea. "I have yet to see swords defeat sorcery and Agatha is such an accomplished sorceress. I think that your Lubeck will be in for a surprise when he comes." The slaver captain laughed to himself as he walked back to his cabin leaving Kei alone on deck. Kei looked to where the captain thought he had seen a sail. His eyes strained, but he also could not determine if the dark patch was indeed a sail. He turned his gaze ahead of them and saw nothing but open water. If they were being followed by the Thunder Child, she would be upon them within two days he thought. Agatha looked around to set her eyes on Kei.

"You are afraid of this man who pursues us. This Lubeck. Why do you fear him so?"

"Who says I'm afraid of him?" Kei replied.

"I see it in your head and feel it in your heart, you fear him greatly." Agatha informed the Saxon.

"When you meet him, you'll fear him too. He does not fear anything, not even magic. You will have difficulty in killing him, even with your sorcery." Kei commented shifting his feet uneasily. Agatha tossed her head back and laughed.

"He's a simple Barbarian who has frightened you all into following him because he is big and strong with a bad temper."

"He is protected by a witch and the Gods themselves." Kei corrected her. "His men follow him because they believe in him, not because they are afraid."

"A witch?" Agatha enquired. Curiosity creeping in.

"Yes, we head there now so that Mormont can kill her, removing Lubeck's protection." Kei continued with an uneasy tone. Agatha's eyes fell to the deck.

"Mormont didn't mention anything about a witch to me. Just this North man Lubeck and how he needed my help to defeat him. Where is this witch?" She asked.

"The witch is of no concern to you Agatha." Mormont's voice interrupted as he returned to the main deck. "I simply need you to counter her magic and leave the rest to me and my men." Agatha glared at him with tight lips. She turned and departed his company returning to solitude as she stood by the ships starboard guard rails. Her mind racing at the news she had just learned. A crewman released a pigeon into the air and it flew off, East bound at speed. Kei watched as it quickly disappeared with the increasing distance.

"Where is that going?" He asked Mormont, though he thought he already knew the answer.

"It's carrying a message to Lord Ballan, informing him of the events of the past few weeks. I'm sure he will be displeased with this Lubeck for killing so many of his men and destroying Ibis as well. Lord Ballan will want retribution I'm sure. I have asked him to send ten ships with arms to meet with us when we land. We shall see how this North man fairs against such odds, shall we?"

On the deck of the Thunder Child, Lubeck stared at the horizon. He could see the dark patches of ships sails far off in the distance.

"We're making good time." He commented to Malik, who was standing by his side.

"Yes but I'm afraid they will see us giving chase." Lubeck looked back over his shoulder at the ever decreasing land mass behind them.

"I think they will find it hard to make us out against the land for now. We will not become truly visible until we are another half a days' sail out. Then we will stand out against the horizon as do they." He looked at the darkening clouds ahead of them. "I pray those clouds bring a storm. They will be preoccupied with staying afloat instead of looking for us."

"A storm, you wish for a storm, we do not need a storm." Malik gulped.

"We will be fine in a storm. This ship will weather it well, but I fear their inferior ships may not. I think we will follow undetected for some time if that storm strikes. Besides, we have a guardian watching over us." Malik looked at the Dragon figurehead.

"I don't see how that will help."

"Not that creature, Freyja, she watches over all on this ship. She knows that we race to protect her, she will ensure our safety to do so." Lubeck laughed as he replied.

In her tower, Freyja watched the events of the recent days, she was not afraid of the approaching menace or the sorceress that accompanied him. All of this had been foreseen. She also knew that Lubeck would land ahead of Mormont and his men. She even knew of the pigeon that had been dispatched to Lord Ballan. None of this worried her as she watched. There was one thing that played on her mind though, she was sure the sorceress was known to her, just a faint notion, but it was there all the same.

On the slave ship, Agatha looked troubled. Her face betraying her thoughts. A feeling of being watched, a feeling of intrusion. Someone was inside of her mind, searching her thoughts and memories but she couldn't block them. Was this the witch she had been told about? Was she prying for information? Something to aid her in the conflict to come? She might not be able to block this magic, but she might be able to stop it at its source. She closed her eyes and concentrated, mumbling an ancient incantation barely audibly. Her mind focused on the mysterious sorcery that aided this invasion of her thoughts. Then with the incantation reaching a crescendo and a thrust of one hand, her eyes opened wide.

"I see you!" She snapped.

In the tower, Freyja reeled backwards as a hand thrust out of the font almost clutching her by the throat, emerald green eyes staring out at her and a voice in her head stating 'I see you!' made her hurry to break the connection and rid her of the sorceress who obviously possessed equal though different powers to her own. With the connection broken, the font returned to normal. Perhaps she would not try such a feat again. If this sorceress could cross the astral bridge so easily. It might not be a good idea to invite her to do so again. Instead, Freyja turned her attention to Lubeck and Thorsten following behind. She peered into the font again, this time to view the Thunder Child and her crew. She closed her eyes and chanted a verse from an ancient script. The scene in the waters of the font showed a mist developing. A thick fog descended and began to encompass the ships as they made good time and closed the gap between themselves and their prey. Mormont watched with interest as the mist developed behind them.

"It seems we are fortunate. If we were being pursued, they shall have difficulty in following through that." He laughed.

"It's the work of the witch. She hides their approach. Beware, for a Dragon hunts you down and advances through his smoky breath." Agatha warned in a trance like state. Her eyes all a glaze and staring into nothing. As they watched, the mist advanced towards them. Soon the slavers too were engulfed in thick blinding fog.

"Hells teeth!" Mormont cursed "Archers! Where are my archers?" Two archers reported to Mormont as he demanded. "Set your arrows with flame, fire ahead of the ship every few minutes. I know we should not encounter any obstacles, but let's play safe shall we?" The archers did as directed and the first arrow flew, its orange flame glowed against the mist before it extinguished with a hiss in the water ahead. This action was repeated every few minutes as directed.

Aboard the Thunder Child, the lookout called to those below and pointed to their starboard bow. Everyone looked to where he was pointing. The brief orange glow drew closer each time and Malik noted they were gaining on the slavers.

"We shall be upon them within the hour." He commented.

"We shall pass them unobserved in this mist. Once passed, I want full sail. I want to be clear of them before this fog lifts." Lubeck grunted in reply.

"Full sail? But how will we be sure not to run aground? We don't send up flame as they do for fear of giving away our position. So how do we steer once in front?" Malik questioned, fearfully.

"Shall we say, someone watches over us, she will guide us and keep us safe." Lubeck replied. He walked over to the figurehead at the rear of the ship and stood in front of it. "Guide us Freyja, keep us safe and give us speed to land before these slavers who would harm you." As he spoke the eyes of the figurehead opened to look at him.

"Alter your course to the West. Sail straight at full sail for two days. You will not run aground or come to any harm. Mormont is off course in the mist and will take a day to correct it. This should give you time to land and prepare for his arrival. You will land at Antonio's boat yard." With that the eyes closed again and the carving returned to lifelessness. Lubeck spoke to his helmsman.

"Steer to the West and maintain that heading." The man acknowledged the order and made the adjustment. The crew noticed the change in course and wondered why they had done so. Lubeck explained that the slavers were off course and would emerge from the fog in the wrong place. He went on to explain how they would land before them and have plenty of time to prepare for the slaver's arrival.

"We need to let Thorsten know of this somehow." Malik pointed out.

"No need at all, look." Lubeck pointed to the rear of the ship. The fog was lifting behind them and they could just make out the sail of Thorsten's ship a few miles astern. "He'll see our change of course and follow our lead." Lubeck declared and within a few moments the Thunder Child was clear of the fog and under clear skies again, at full sail. Constant checking of Thorsten's progress noted that he too had changed course and was approximately a half days' sail behind them.

"By the time we make land, he will be about one full day behind." Malik noted. Lubeck nodded with a thoughtful grunt.

"I hope he is no more than that. This Mormont as he is called has sent word to a warlord called Ballan that he is in need of assistance. We may be facing over three hundred men by the time they arrive. We number but fifty at most, including Thorsten's crew. My mind is troubled by this, I need strategy, a way to reduce their numbers or a way to make their numbers count for less."

"How do you know this?" Malik asked.

"Freyja." Lubeck smiled. "She talks to me inside my head like a dream, but I'm awake. She has seen what is happening and warning me, to give us an advantage." They sailed for the remainder of that day and all through the night. With the sunrise, the lookout called down informing them that land was on the horizon.

"Make for the river and Antonio's jetty!" Lubeck ordered the helmsman. They drifted cautiously down the estuary and docked where the Thunder Child had been born. "Off load the horses, conceal the ship, make ready for combat and ride light, carry weapons, armour and water only. We ride as soon as all are ready." Lubeck's orders were superfluous; his men were well trained and knew what they were there to do. They needed no direction in getting ready for war. Each man had his own reason to fight. This was why they had joined Lubeck, for the chance to kill the slavers who had destroyed their homes and imprisoned their families. None needed a rousing speech for encouragement. They all rallied to a common cause and were ready to die for the chance to strike back. This was it and they needed no prompting. Within the hour the ship was concealed as best they could and they were all in the saddle. Thirty mounted, highly trained warriors set on making a difference, to strike a blow that would most likely open the gates of Hell and bring forward the Devil himself, Ballan. If they could draw him out, they could cut off the head of the snake. Then his empire built on the sweat, blood tears and lives of those he had enslaved, would come crashing down with him. But first, they had to protect Freyja and survive the next few days. They rode relentlessly for the rest of the day and made it to the tower by nightfall. The horses were hot and covered in foamy sweat from the hard ride. They dismounted and Tarique took charge of a few men to take care of the horses and ensure they were rested ready for the following day. Meanwhile Lubeck and the others entered the tower looking for Freyja. They found her, safely resting in her chambers. She grinned widely as Lubeck entered.

"We need to fortify this place before Mormont lands." He said without any other greeting

"Well hello to you too!" Freyja snapped back.

"I don't have time for niceties, there is too much to do."

"No, there isn't, steady yourself and rest, be calm. Mormont will not land until tomorrow afternoon. He has just two ships, with forty men at most. This tower is easily defended and I am in no danger from him. It's the sorceress that might pose a problem. She is powerful and she has abilities different to mine. I fear that I may not be able to protect you all from her." Freyja looked worried as she spoke.

"I fear no sorceress and if Ballan has not sent assistance, I feel our chances of victory are much improved." Lubeck reassured her. Freyja looked at him, concern etched across her face.

"Ballan is coming. He will be here in four days, from now and he brings ten ships, each with thirty men."

"First we defeat this Mormont and then we prepare for Ballan. It's time to move!" Lubeck exited barking orders to his men. At Malik's suggestion they began to prepare bales of dried grasses gathered from the nearby fields. They coated these grasses with oils and rested them in strategic positions along the cliff tops. They dug trenches in the sand around the base of the tower, lined the base of the trench with dried grasses and again poured oils onto it. Archers were designated their positions along the cliff tops to give them high vantage points enabling them to pick their targets. A few light horsemen were briefed to wait in hiding, in case they were needed to sway the balance of power if things didn't go well for them.

"I may not have the brawn of a warrior, but my mind has kept me alive this long." Malik said as he watched his suggestions being put into place. Lubeck smiled at his young companion, seeing the wisdom and strategy behind Malik's ideas. The preparations continued most of the night, with men snatching only a few hours sleep before continuing the next morning. As Lubeck and his men rested and gathered their strength, sails were spotted closing fast. The ships had swung around the headland to cover their approach and it had almost worked.

Luckily, Lubeck was well versed and experienced in war and had anticipated this practice. His lookouts had spotted the sails and raised the alarm with time to spare. All was set; all they had to do now was wait to see what Mormont would do. His ships drew close and drove their bows onto the beach and crewmen jumped down securing them. The rest of Mormont's men scrambled ashore and began to prepare for battle. Thinking that they had landed ahead of Lubeck, there was no urgency in their movements. Mormont ordered his horses to be brought ashore and Lubeck winced, as this was not something he had anticipated. As he watched, his mind ran wild trying to reconsider his strategies.

At the same time Thorsten's men were also ashore and heading towards the tower from the inlet they had landed in just a mile along the coast. Lubeck was unaware of this, so could not count on his friend being there in time. Raising one arm, Lubeck signalled his archers. They ignited their arrows and let them fly towards the beached ships. Mormont's men immediately took cover behind their shields and scrutinised the cliff tops for signs of their attackers. The ships behind them began to smoke as the flames from the arrows caught. A second volley thumped into the ships setting yet more small fires alight. Some of Mormont's men ran to the ships trying to combat the flames and save them. As they did, Lubeck's archers lit the bales of dried grasses and unleashed them from the tops of the cliffs. The burning bales tumbled down to the beach below and rolled at great speed towards the slavers taking cover behind their shields. The bales, fully burning smashed into the barrier below and burst into clouds of flame. Men screamed in fear and pain, their clothing ablaze and sparks blinding their eyes. Some of the men rolled in the sand attempting to extinguish the flames. Lubeck gave the order and along with a dozen men ran out to engage the confused and disorientated enemy on the beach. Again a volley of arrows thumped into the ships, some hitting the men attempting to put out the fires. Mormont rallied his men and engaged with Lubeck as he and his men descended upon them.

Though having lost a number of soldiers, Mormont's force still outnumbered Lubeck's on the beach. Lubeck's archers were now disengaging, being cautious of killing their own men, as the small battle began below. As the former slaves fought the slavers, Mormont and a dozen of his men, Kei amongst them, mounted their horses. Swords and shields clashed, men cried out in pain and rage as the two sides collided on the soft surface of the beach. Smoke wafted across the battlefield from the burning ships, making it difficult to see clearly. Blood flowed over the sand mixing with the sea water that lapped against the shoreline turning it red. A light breeze cleared the smoke momentarily as Lubeck slayed one more opponent. Through the clearing swirl, he saw a dozen horsemen charging towards him at speed. The ground trembled and the thunder of hooves grew louder as Mormont led his horsemen through the battle lines knocking down Lubeck's men as they came. Lubeck grabbed a spear from the body of a slain slaver and hurled it with all of his might at the advancing cavalry. Missing his intended target of Mormont, the spear struck and buried its head deep into the chest of the rider next to him unseating the man as he crashed to the sand. Lubeck held his shield high as Mormont galloped past striking at him with his sword knocking him to the ground. Disorientated, Lubeck frantically searched for where the cavalry were headed. A blood curdling scream captured his attention. One of the slavers attempted to finish what Mormont had started, by driving his spear into Lubeck as he lay on the sand. Malik had seen this in time and intervened, driving his sword deep into the assailants back.

"The tower! They're headed for the tower!" Lubeck shouted, pointing in that direction. Malik sounded the horn that was slung across his torso. On hearing this, Lubeck's archers lit their arrows. Raising their aim high, they loosed them towards the tower. The arrows hit their mark just in time. The oil soaked grasses in the bottom of the trench encircling the base of the tower, burst into flame in moments. Mormont's cavalry stopped in their tracks, some horses reared up throwing their riders in fear of the sudden, scorching wall blocking their path. One rider fell from his horse and landed in the trench. He screamed loudly as the burning oils covered his clothing. Mormont looked on helpless as the man writhed in pain and panic, covered from head to toe in fierce orange flames. The man's suffering ceased as a second volley of arrows struck him down along with three more of Mormont's men and two horses. The horn sounded a second time. Now Lubeck's horsemen charged out from their secluded position and headed directly towards Mormont and what remained of his cavalry. With a wall of fire in front, the sea to his left and advancing cavalry to his right, Mormont ordered his horsemen to return back along the beach from where they had come. Back through the fading foot battle and their only route for escape.

As they charged back, Lubeck had regained his footing. Malik, Tarique and six other men stood facing them on foot while the rest of Lubeck's men finished what remained of Mormont's forces. The horses pounded towards them. Tarique dropped to one knee, drew his bow and loosed an arrow. It thumped home knocking a rider to the ground. The others dug their shields into the sand forming a low barrier forcing the horses to jump. As they did, Malik lunged upward with a spear into another rider, effectively impaling him. Lubeck swung his sword, sweeping it high and cleaving a rider's leg. One of Mormont's horsemen turned in his saddle and released an arrow as he continued to retreat. The arrow flew straight to its target hitting Lubeck just above his left hip, finding a small gap as his chain mail vestment rode up during the swing of his sword. Lubeck fell as Mormont and his remaining horsemen continued to ride away pursued by Lubeck's cavalry. Their path however was soon blocked by Thorsten accompanied by more than twenty men. They formed a much larger shield wall ahead of them. Mormont's horsemen tried to change direction, but had nowhere left to run. Lubeck's cavalry cut into them with vicious ferocity. Men from both sides fell from their horses and scrambled to their feet to continue fighting on foot, Kei and Mormont among them. Thorsten and his men advanced to assist their comrades.

As the fighting continued, Kei found himself staring straight into the eyes of Thorsten bearing down on him, axe in hand. Kei raised his shield and swung his sword at the approaching giant missing widely as Thorsten checked his stride and leaned backwards away from the menacing blade. As Kei over reached, he tried to regain his balance. Thorsten kicked him hard, knocking him to the ground. A spear head came close to Thorsten's face, distracting him as he deflected an attempt from another attacker to skewer him. Seizing this chance, Kei picked himself up and thrust at Thorsten with his sword. The attempt was thwarted by a shield being pushed between them by one of Thorsten's men. Thorsten charged at Kei, swinging his axe high in the air and screaming,

"Traitor!" In a thunderous voice. The huge axe head cleaved Kei almost in two, from collar to hip in a single blow. Realising defeat was inevitable, Mormont scrambled back onto a stray horse and dug his heals in hard. The horse reared up and then charged away from the slaughter.

Seeing a possible escape from the beach, Mormont rode for it. Before he had travelled far, a deep roaring voice called to him,

"Mormont, we have your witch!" Mormont paused just momentarily, to see Agatha being held by Malik and Tarique as Lubeck stood defiant in front. The arrow still sticking out from just above his hip, blood streaking down his left leg. No shield on his arm, just an odd looking shaft resembling a boat hook held in his right hand. Turning his mount sharply, Mormont thundered headlong at Lubeck, who stood steady as a rock monitoring his enemies approach. The horse drew closer, Mormont wielding his sword as he came and leaning over to the right hand side of his mount. Judging his assailant's approach perfectly, Lubeck's timing was impeccable. He pivoted around to the left hand side of the approaching horse. Swinging his weapon in a high backhand and catching Mormont on the left side of his chest. The force of the blow unseated him, breaking his clavicle with the heavy club like pommel. Mormont landed on the sand with a thump screaming in agony. Lubeck took a moment to survey the remnants of the battle. Mormont's forces were all but done with few losses on Lubeck's side. Moans from the injured carried on the air and the crackling sound of the burning ships seemed loud in Lubeck's ears as he stood just a few feet away. Mormont cursed as he tried to get to his feet. His broken collar bone hindering his efforts as pain surged through his body with every movement. He reached down and retrieved the sword he had dropped, as if to continue the fight. Lubeck wagged a finger at him to gesture that this was not a good idea.

"I'll kill you yet!" Mormont spat at Lubeck straining to lift the heavy weapon.

"Not this day." Lubeck retorted. A quiet voice reciting an ancient rhythmic verse drifted across the beach. It came from Agatha, who had started to mutter her incantation in a strange language. Tarique attempted to prevent her, but she turned her head sharply to glare at him. Tarique was thrust across the sand, as if picked up by some invisible giant and tossed aside like a rag doll. Malik, taken by surprise, released his grip on Agatha's arm. She instantly thrust her hands out front as if trying to push Lubeck over while her chanting reached a crescendo. Lubeck was knocked to the ground with immense force, the arrow in his side was pushed clean through and the head emerged from the left side of his lower back.

Mormont seized the opportunity and raised his sword in preparation to strike Lubeck a fatal blow. As Lubeck cleared the sand from his eyes, he reached to his side where the arrow had travelled two thirds of its length through and increased his pain. On seeing Mormont's approach, Lubeck filled with adrenaline and determination snapped the shaft of the arrow and pulled hard on the head protruding from his back, removing it through torn and bleeding flesh. He cried out as the pain washed over him, but some primeval instinct to survive drove him on. He rolled towards Mormont and drove the arrow straight through his leading foot and deep into the sand below. Mormont screamed in agony as flesh, tendons and bone gave way allowing the arrow to pass through. Struggling to his feet, Lubeck drew the large Lion headed sword from the scabbard on his belt and deflected the weak attempt from Mormont, which was little better than a child's attack. Agatha began to chant again. Malik found himself unable to move and could merely watch as Lubeck deflected a second attempt from Mormont. As Agatha's chanting grew louder, it suddenly stopped with a thud. She fell to the sand unconscious, revealing Freyja standing behind her clutching a piece of charred wood she had retrieved from one of the burning ships. Mormont lurched forward, clumsily attempting to thrust his sword into Lubeck once more. This time, Lubeck stepped to one side to avoid being skewered and drove his own sword deep into the side of Mormont's throat. Blood spurted out in all directions and Mormont coughed and choked as he began to drown on it. He fell to his knees, his arms falling limp as he dropped his sword. He looked at Lubeck as he coughed once more, spilling blood from lips as his mouth filled and overflowed. Then, with a final thud he fell, face down on the sand turning it scarlet as his body drained.

The noise of battle faded, as Thorsten's group following the remnants of the cavalry regrouped where Lubeck now exhausted, fell to the ground beside his slain opponent. With Agatha unconscious, Malik was free to move again and looked to Tarique for assistance. Tarique picked himself up and ran to Lubeck's aid. Together they carried him to Freyja's chambers at the top of the tower. While Thorsten slung the unconscious Agatha over his huge shoulder and followed. Once there, Agatha was laid on a pile of pillows in a corner, watched over by a very cautious Tarique. Lubeck was once more laid on Freyja's bed in order for her to treat his injuries.

"The wound is severe and will take some time to heal, even with my abilities." Freyja announced.

"But Ballan is on his way you said." Malik objected. Freyja looked solemnly at the war battered crew that filled her chambers.

"He is and we are too few to defeat him." She replied.

"No, we will be ready. Few will stand against many, as they have many times in the past. With shrewd planning and concealing our numbers, we can inflict such losses that Ballan will lose heart and leave." Thorsten announced attempting to motivate and encourage his weary men. Some of the men muttered as they too, looked around at their battered brothers in arms. They were tired, injured, hungry and about to face a foe with overwhelming numbers. They had landed with over fifty men, now their numbers were less than forty, another ten injured including their chieftain.

"But we do have the Thunder Child, and Freyja." Malik informed them with almost boyish exuberance.

"Yes! We shall sink his fleet before it lands. The Thunder Child could do this. She has the Saracens devices to hurl fire balls at them from a distance. She has the size and speed to ram and smash them. They will be sacrificed to the Njord, God of the sea and those who do make it ashore, will be slaughtered by our fire traps and archers before they can recover their senses." Thorsten roared raising his men from the dark place they were entering in their minds.

"Yes you are right. The Thunder Child could destroy most of Ballan's fleet before he lands. But you would have to catch him from behind, so as not to be seen approaching or he will scatter his ships making him harder to stop." Freyja pointed out.

"This could be done, if a certain mist were to develop and conceal her approach, clearing only once she was so close that no action could be taken to avoid her wrath." Malik suggested with a wry smile.

"I will see what I could do about that." Freyja said looking towards the table and her books there on.

"And perhaps Thor might lend a hand?" Thorsten dropped into the discussion.

"Thor?" Tarique asked hesitantly.

"Perhaps, if he will answer my call. I will try my best, but the storms will not care whose ships it destroys. It could be dangerous if I can't concentrate enough to fully guide the lightning bolts." Freyja replied understanding what Thorsten was implying.

"And what of me?" a soft voice came from the corner of the room. Everyone looked to see Agatha slowly sitting up and rubbing the back of her head.

"You sister, will behave yourself and do as you are told, unless you want to be burned at the stake by these pagan barbarians for being a witch." Freyja warned.

"I'll kill the first one to come near to me." Agatha spat.

"You'll do no such thing sister, or you will be forced to kill me too. Is that what you want?" Freyja stared at her sister waiting for a reply. Agatha shuffled uneasily then smiled at her sibling as she replied.

"You have grown into a fine woman little sister, are your powers so grown as well?"

"Grown more than you can imagine." Freyja replied in a menacing tone. Agatha raised her hands reciting a verse in a long forgotten language. Tarique ducked for cover, he had been on the receiving end of this one before. Freyja planted her hands on her hips and tapped her foot irritably. All was still, Agatha repeated the verse, a little louder this time. Still nothing. Freyja sighed, dropped her arms by her side and returned to tend to Lubeck calling back over her shoulder as she did.

"Your powers won't work here, not in this place. Only I have any abilities inside these walls. Don't you remember? Or has it been so long?" Agatha frowned as she tried to remember her childhood. Dreamlike glimpses of a life long ago flickered in her head, but she was unable to pick out the exact memory Freyja referred to. Silently she sat and pondered as everyone else continued to make plans for what lay ahead. After a short while, Malik carried some food and a drink over to Agatha and sat down beside her. He noticed that her gruff exterior had slipped somewhat and she now appeared a little subdued and vulnerable. Offering her the refreshment, Malik began a conversation with Agatha about her childhood and her relationship with Freyja. As they spoke, Agatha warmed a little and periodically smiled as fond memories broke through the shadows of her mind.

"She never gave up looking for you, you know. She brought us here somehow, she brought us all together in order for us to find you and reunite you both." Malik told her softly.

"Really? I thought Mormont brought me here to help destroy a bunch of slaves that had gone wild." Agatha said giving him a condescending look.

"Yeah, we thought that too. I mean, we all thought that we were in control of our own destinies as well, but no. It was revealed that your sister controlled events that brought us together. Freyja touched us as we slept and planted the seeds of ideas in our heads. Lubeck acted on these ideas as they grew. Now we are all free of our bonds and helping the woman that guided our destinies." Malik laughed softly. Agatha looked at the young man beside her. She saw the admiration in his face as he spoke about his friend.

"Lubeck, you like him don't you? You all like him?" She asked. Malik's expression lifted a little.

"We would all risk our lives for him. He freed us from slavery, provided us with food and water, he has led us along a dangerous but profitable path and we are all so close to finding our missing families. He treats us all like equals. He does not see himself as an Earl, but we all treat him so and call him Earl. Every one of us would give our life for his, because he would do the same for any one of us." Agatha turned her gaze towards Lubeck still sleeping on Freyja's bed.

"You are very lucky to have such a leader. I fear those whom I have served would not be so generous or caring for my wellbeing. I doubt Ballan will lose any sleep when he knows what has happened here today."

"Perhaps you should think about your allegiances—"

"Allegiances?" Agatha interrupted. "I was taken against my will as a child and forced to work for Ballan. I have never had a choice, or been free to pick my allegiance."

"You are now. Join your sister and Lubeck. Help us to defeat Ballan when he comes." Malik replied with hope in his voice.

"There is no defeating Ballan. You're all going to die. My sister cannot leave here, bar for a few miles and Lubeck is all but dead. The giant over there has no head for leadership and you young man, are no warrior, not like them anyway. The Saracen though, I know his people, he might have what is needed to get you all away to safety, if you leave now, before Ballan arrives." Agatha replied with contempt. Tarique's sharp ears overheard this remark as he addressed the group discussing strategies. All eyes turned to

Agatha and the conversation ceased. Freyja turned slowly to face her sister, making her feel a little awkward under the attention.

"Come sister, share your plan with us." She offered. There was a moment's pause, before reluctantly Agatha spoke.

"I was telling Malik that you are all going to die when Ballan gets here. His forces are too strong and too many for your small rag tag group of criminals. You are leaderless with Lubeck practically dead and the only one among you with any kind of head for war is possibly the Saracen there." Agatha raised a finger and pointed it towards Tarique, who immediately flinched with uncomfortable expectation of another shockwave to throw him across the room. "If you expect to survive this at all, you must flee. You must leave here and draw Ballan away from this tower." Still pointing at Tarique, Agatha continued, "He, must lead your forces away and devise a plan to cut Ballan's numbers, Guerrilla tactics will have to be used. Stay hidden, strike and run. You cannot defeat him in open battle, not with so few men. Ambush, traps archers from afar. All must be used to cut his numbers with few losses of your own. Freyja can help from the safety of this stronghold if he, can keep Ballan's attention away from here." Thorsten rose to his full enormous height.

"I will cut Ballan's forces with my axe; they shall fall before it like wheat in the harvest—"

"And you will die a fool's death." Agatha cut him short. "Big and mighty as you obviously are, Ballan's troops will flow over you like the waves of the sea crashing on the shoreline."

"Well sister, it seems that you have it all worked out." Freyja commented with a little irritation. Pointing again at Tarique, Agatha asked,

"What's his name?"

"Tarique." Tarique replied.

"Tarique, good. Well it depends how long Tarique here can keep hurting Ballan without getting himself and all of you killed." Agatha then moved menacingly towards Freyja's bed. Then looking down at Lubeck's motionless body she continued. "None of you know who he is, do you?" All in the room looked to one and other in confusion, as they didn't understand the question.

"He's Lubeck of course. He's our appointed Earl and close friend." Replied Thorsten defiantly.

Mummers of agreement sounded around the group.

"He's a natural leader isn't he? You feel it, when he speaks you listen, he leads, you all follow without question, because it is as if he were born to lead? Yes?" Agatha retorted questioningly.

"What are you getting at sister?" Freyja enquired, irritation gripping her voice.

"As I said, you don't know who he is do you? Yes his name is Lubeck. I was there the day he was captured. It was no accident that Ballan's ships were there that day. They were sent there to take him. This man lying here half dead is Lubeck alright, Lubeck Jorgensen." The name hung in the air like an ominous thunder cloud. Freyja, Tarique and Malik all looked confused, but Thorsten gasped as Agatha smiled.

"Jorgensen? Like Gunter Jorgensen?" He asked angrily. Agatha smiled and turned to face the big man.

"You know Gunter Jorgensen then?" She enquired.

"Not personally, but I know of him." Thorsten's tone had changed, it became more sinister and he dropped his head as he spoke.

"You do well to hang your head." Agatha continued. "But this could work to our advantage—"

"Our advantage?" Freyja interrupted. Agatha smiled uneasily, but then continued,

"I think Gunter will be very interested to know of his son's whereabouts and health."

"Gunter Jorgensen's son! By all the God's we're doomed. If Ballan doesn't kill us all, Gunter is likely to." Thorsten roared with rage and anguish. Now totally confused, Freyja and the others all chattered at once. A torrent of inaudible noise erupted within the group.

"Quiet!" Malik yelled and silence fell. "Who is Gunter Jorgensen?" He asked.

"Tell them, why don't you?" Agatha said looking towards Thorsten. Thorsten stepped forward towering over the woman as he stared down at her. A look of foreboding gripped his face. He shuffled a little uncomfortably, looked around the room noticing that a couple of other Norse men had recognised the name as well. Then, he addressed the rest of the group.

"Gunter Jorgensen is the right hand man to King Rogan Magnusson of the Northern tribes in my homelands. King Rogan commands more than twelve Earls and all of their people. Rogan has some twenty thousand warriors at his disposal. He is possibly the most powerful king I know of and Gunter commands his armies."

"That's fantastic; maybe he will help us once he knows his son is alive and well?" Malik suggested innocently. Thorsten looked at Malik, anger filling his soul.

"Gunter went on the rampage on hearing the news that his son and grandson were killed by rival tribes. He destroyed many settlements over the following three years, mine included." His chest heaved as he remembered the events, his eyes welled with tears. "I swore to avenge those who were lost. I swore that I would track Gunter down and kill him and his family, ending his blood line." Everyone stood in stunned silence staring at the Giant who was now breaking under the pressures of conflict inside of his soul. The big man's head dropped and his huge arms fell limp. "Lubeck Jorgensen. How the Gods mock me." Thorsten half laughed, almost to himself. With that he dropped to the floor and squatted against a wall covering his head with his hands, sighing and muttering to himself. "Jorgensen, I've befriended, fought along-side and followed a man I have sworn to kill. Oh how the Gods have their fun with me. I was working on a ship with my son Bjorn when Gunter sacked my village. We heard the screams, and hurried back, only to find everyone slain and the village burned. It was while I was hunting Gunter, that the slavers took Bjorn." Agatha stepped up and gently placed her hand on the big man's shoulder in a soothing gesture.

"Now you have Gunter's son at your mercy, you could have your revenge at any time. What is your dilemma then? Pick up your axe and have your revenge."

"He would be dead before he could strike a single blow!" Tarique objected stepping forward, fingers closing around the hilt of one of his slender, curved swords. Malik also stepped up as Freyja moved herself in between the bed and the conflicted giant.

"My what a loyal following he has, this Lubeck." Agatha noted looking at the group of friends. Thorsten slowly stood and rose to his full height, then glaring down at Agatha, he menacingly growled.

"I owe that man my life. We are brothers in arms, and he is my countryman, shipmate and friend. Your serpent's tongue will not make me harm him. Even if I was of a mind to kill him, I would not do it this way. I would wait until he was strong enough to face me with a sword in his hand."

"This is a man who is truly blessed by the Gods it would appear. If they watch over him as you all do. Perhaps events will not go as I had thought when Ballan arrives." Agatha retorted. With that, she moved to the edge of the room and seated herself on the floor against the wall from where she had stepped up earlier. The tension in the room eased a little following Thorsten's declaration and all breathed more freely. Thorsten is a big man and a mighty warrior. Not even Tarique wanted to face him in mortal combat, but all in the room would willingly risk their lives to save Lubeck's, as he would for them. Gunter Jorgensen's son or not, it made no odds to them, not even the giant who had sworn to kill him in a previous life. Freyja watched Thorsten as he battled silently with thoughts cascading through his mind. A troubled expression etched onto his face. She moved over to him, offering a cup of ale she had thoughtfully collected as she moved. Thorsten received it with thanks and fidgeted uncomfortably as his thoughts raced uncontrollably. Smiling reassuringly, Freyja placed her hand on the big man's, steadying their restlessness. Then speaking in a gentle, soft voice she asked him.

"Will you be able to calm your head and think straight when Ballan gets here?"

"There's nothing to focus a mind like battle." Thorsten scoffed "I will be fine once I see the sails of our enemy approaching." With a heavy sigh, the giant leaned back against the wall and drank some of the ale Freyja had given him.

"What troubles you so much Thorsten?" Freyja asked. Thorsten dropped his head shaking it mournfully.

"I'm not a stupid hills man without a brain. I think of Lubeck as a brother now. We have suffered together as slaves and fought side by side as free men. What troubles me is…" He paused in thought for a moment, then sighed and continued. "What troubles me is that I have seen with my own eyes, the faceless demon known as The Valkyrie."

"Valkyrie? You mean the Angel of Death?" Freyja frowned as she questioned. Thorsten slowly nodded as he replied.

"The Valkyrie's face was always covered by the face guard of the helmet he wore. I will never forget the first time I saw him in battle. He had the strength of a bear and the speed of a striking snake. His swordsmanship was like something I have never seen. He was as a God, supreme and invincible. As soon as he appeared on the field of battle, his enemies would flee, the ones with sense anyway. I dreamed of serving such a man and fighting by his side for honour and glory. If this man, our Lubeck really is The Mighty Valkyrie I have seen in battle, how were the slavers able to capture him so? Also, I have fought alongside this man, he is a mighty warrior, but he does not resemble the Valkyrie. If the Valkyrie and our Lubeck are in fact one and the same, why has he not yet shown his worth? He fights well, but not with the ferocity and efficiency of the Valkyrie. If they are the same man, he must be holding back, going through the motions of battle. If so, what is he waiting for?"

"I can tell you some of what you ask. At least as to how he was captured so easily. If you want me to that is?" Agatha's voice interrupted. Freyja and Thorsten looked round at the woman sat in the corner nearby.

"I want to hear it." Thorsten said looking back towards Freyja as he spoke. Freyja nodded and indicated for Agatha to continue.

"It's simple, it was a misty morning and they took him by surprise. He, and a few others, his son included were fishing as the slavers drifted silently onto them. By the time Lubeck realised what was happening, the slavers were to close for him to get away. He was unarmed, but he fought and fought hard. I think he killed more than six of the crew before one of them captured his son Hafthor. The threat to kill him was all it took to tame the Valkyrie. That was that, they chained and beat him. He endured everything in order to protect Hafthor' s life. It was only a few moments later, they chained him next to you." Freyja and Thorsten looked to where Agatha was pointing. Malik had been listening and now stared open mouthed as Agatha dragged him into the conversation.

"I knew there was something about him when they brought him in. He never seemed submissive like the rest of us. He always had an air about him, that he was no ordinary slave." He laughed softly to himself before continuing. "I have no idea who this Valkyrie is, I'm not a Norseman, but I have heard of Rogan. Before I was enslaved, I travelled many countries in search of fortune. King Rogan was a name I heard in the North. I had heard that his armies were formidable and the men that commanded them were Gods, fearless and unbeatable. I was warned not to try and make my fortune in Rogan's lands, his retribution would be terrible."

"Retribution? For making a living? I don't understand." Freyja questioned.

"He was a thief, a thief who got caught and sold into slavery. If he had been caught in King Rogan's lands, he would not have been so lucky." Thorsten enlightened her. Another Norseman approached from the other side of the room and offered a suggestion as how to identify Lubeck more positively.

"I fought the Valkyrie once. I was with King Akhola in the Southlands back home. Akhola, has tried many times to overthrow Rogan, but has always failed because Gunter and the Valkyrie have always been too strong. With those two by his side, Rogan's reign is safe. Anyway, during one battle, I found myself facing the Valkyrie alone. Fear gripped my soul and I thought I was a dead man—"

"If you truly faced the Valkyrie alone, then I am talking to a ghost." Thorsten interrupted.

"Shush! Let him continue." Freyja snapped. The man nodded his head in gratitude before continuing.

"He made short work of me. I was no match for him. I lay on the ground seriously wounded and dying. Three of my comrades attacked him from behind and he left me to deal with them. During this skirmish, His helmet was knocked off, I only saw him from behind, I didn't see his face. I picked up an axe from the ground where I lay and threw it for all I was worth. It struck the back of his head, biting deep into his skull. He turned so fast, it was just a blur. He kicked me in the head. The next thing I remember, I was being cared for in one of our settlements some days later. If this man truly is the Valkyrie. He should have a scar, on the back of his head, under his hair line. I would think it to be about as long as my hand, right in the middle." Freyja moved over to where Lubeck lay, still sleeping under the influence of the potions she had treated him with. She gently lifted his head and parted his hair. All in the room waited with baited breath. Laying his head back into the pillows, Freyja nodded confirming that the scar existed.

"Satisfied little sister?" Agatha asked.

"Then it's true? Lubeck truly is the one we called the Valkyrie?" Thorsten enquired. Freyja silently nodded again and Thorsten emitted a loud sigh of disgruntled acceptance. Malik broke the tension in the room as he enquired.

"I still don't understand. So Lubeck is this Valkyrie. If his father is Gunter Jorgensen who commands King Rogan's armies, how is this a bad thing? We could use all of the help we can get, right?"

"Yes, Malik is right. When Ballan comes, we will need help." Freyja replied to Malik's open question.

"Ballan? It's not Ballan you need to worry about, though he is most likely to kill you all when he gets here. No, it's Akhola who poses the biggest threat to your lives." Agatha laughed.

"Akhola? Why?" Enquired Thorsten, becoming ever more confused.

"Because it was Akhola who ordered Ballan to take Lubeck as a slave." Freyja replied with a sudden realisation. "With Lubeck, the Valkyrie removed, his father Gunter would seek revenge, as in fact he did. Now with both the Valkyrie and Gunter gone from King Rogan's side, the way is open for Akhola to invade and defeat Rogan. Half his armies are following Gunter across the North lands seeking revenge for his son and Grandson's deaths. In doing so, the people are turning against Gunter and looking to Akhola for protection. Rogan's forces are divided while Akhola's are growing. If Akhola wants to overthrow Rogan, now would be the perfect time to do so."

"Well done little sister. You finally figured it out." Retorted Agatha smiling as she spoke. "Yes it's Akhola behind everything. He has called the tune and we have all danced to it, Rogan included." The room fell quiet for a moment before Tarique broke the silence with a question.

"So, where do we all fit into Akhola's plan?"

"We don't. Akhola wasn't planning on Lubeck escaping. But now that he has, what we need to be thinking about is what might happen when Gunter discovers that his son is still alive and who is responsible for his disappearance." Thorsten replied. "It doesn't matter who knows what, at this stage. Our own agendas will have to take a pause for now. It appears that open war is upon our homelands and I think it is time that we pick a side." Everyone stared at the Norseman, knowing he was right. Finding and freeing their families and loved ones would have to wait. This new turn of events was bigger, much bigger than any of them had imagined. If war couldn't be avoided, then it needed to be won and they needed to choose a side or they may not have a home to return to with their families once they are freed.

With heavy hearts they all set about their individual tasks with their preparations for the arrival of Ballan's fleet. The men split into working groups as they had done previously anticipating Mormont's arrival. They began to prepare various traps and defences. Trenches were dug for the second time and lined as before with dried grasses, hay and straw soaked in oil. This time though, Thorsten had ordered them to be dug in such a way, that when burning, they would leave one particular channel for Ballan's men to flow through. Again the trench around the base of the tower was lined in a similar manner, but this time Tarique ordered sharpened stakes to be embedded into the base of the trench. Arrows were placed along the cliff tops as before and bales of dried grasses and straw soaked in oil were once again suspended ready for release to the beach below. These bales were placed in such a manner, that when released, they would tumble straight down the channel left by the burning trenches. Malik took charge of a group embedding sharpened stakes into the beach, under the water's surface at the extremities of the trenches. The idea being to prevent Ballan's men from skirting around the back of them thereby avoiding being channelled in the direction Thorsten wanted them to come. Everyone worked hard with direction and haste. Even Agatha assisted where she could, much to the surprise of Freyja, who was pleased to see her sister slowly coming round to the plight of the band of runaway slaves. Freyja in the meantime tended Lubeck. She could not understand why he wasn't healing faster. She knew, as did everyone, that he would be needed when the battle commences. She sat on the side of the bed where he lay, checked his wounds, which were healing quite well, but a fever had set in, to spite her best efforts. Lubeck's body glistened with sweat in the morning light as Freyja wiped him down with a cool moist cloth. She uttered quiet verses from books written by people years before, but to no avail.

"Would you like me to try sister?" Agatha's voice broke the quiet of Freyja's chambers. "I know some crafts that may speed things up a little."

"And why would you do that?" Freyja retorted.

"Oh, shall we say, I have no desire to go back to being Ballan's little play thing. I don't want to be like a trinket that he can use then toss aside when he's bored. I want my freedom as do you. You can't leave here until WE break the spell that holds you here. I can't use my powers within these walls, so, I will teach you a little something that might just benefit us both. If it works and by some miracle we survive this mess, I want my freedom to go wherever I want, unharmed and unrestricted. Will you agree sister?" Freyja thought for a moment before answering.

"I have never had anything to do with what has happened to you. But you, you imprisoned me here on this Island, Why?"

"Because I love you sister. I cast that spell to protect you. You are of no use to Ballan or Akhola if you can't leave this place. So they left you alone, in peace. My powers were bound by a power greater than mine every time I returned here. So even if Ballan brought me back to break the spell, I couldn't. That's why I say WE need to break the spell that holds you here." Agatha smiled.

"How can I help?" Freyja protested. Agatha joined her by the bed and looked Freyja straight in the eyes.

"Who cast that spell? It was not me, and you couldn't have done it at that time. So there has to be another with the abilities that we share. Someone with powers equal to or greater than mine. Who is it? Tell me. We have to get them to remove it so that I can free you and thereby myself." Agatha pleaded. Freyja sighed and frowned as she thought before replying.

"I have no idea my sister. I don't know anyone with that degree of abilities. In fact the only person I know with any abilities is…." She paused as realisation hit her. "Morgana." She whispered to herself.

"What was that? What was that name?" Agatha asked. Freyja looked up into her sister's eyes. "If I'm right. The person you seek is a long way from here in Altear. She can't help us now."

"Altear! What in the name of all that is wrong with this world is she doing in Altear?" Agatha screamed.

"It doesn't matter. I may not be right. I could be way off with my thinking and even if I am right, she's too far away to help now." Freyja dropped her head in anguish. "It looks as though we're stuck doesn't it?"

"No sister, YOU are stuck here as you always have been. I on the other hand, can leave whenever I want. Remember?" Agatha snapped.

"If Freyja cannot leave, then you will not either." A deep booming voice echoed around the room. The two women looked around to see Thorsten and Tarique had returned from their preparations outside.

"So I'm a prisoner here then?" Agatha asked in protest. Freyja sighed as she reached for her sister's hand.

"Not a prisoner no, but there is so much at stake here that we can't afford to leave anything to chance. We need to know that you are with us. If you're not, you will have to stay here until this is over. Then it doesn't matter if we win or lose, you will be free to leave."

"We could step outside of these walls, to the beach below. My powers would not be harnessed there and I could break the spell that holds you." Agatha offered.

"No, you now need to be outside of the whole area, some three miles from this tower. That's the way the binding spell works. You entered the tower, once you did that, the range of the binding extended to the outer reaches of my own confinement. We need the person that did this, so that you can free me." Agatha slumped to the floor and sat back against the wall in stony silence as she stared at the two men standing across the room. She knew that if she tried to leave they would simply catch her and bring her back. Without her abilities, there was no way she could travel three miles before they would catch her. So she was stuck, free to move around, but not to leave. Thorsten and Tarique spoke quietly with Freyja in low muffled tones. The two men nodded and then they left. Freyja turned and walked over to a window. She closed her eyes and stood in silence for a moment.

As she opened them again, a smile broke across her lips. She scanned the sky for a moment before returning to the bed to check on Lubeck once more. His condition had not changed and Freyja seemed anxious about that. She moved to a table and consulted more books making notes as she read. Agatha watched her as she worked. Then noting the glint in Freyja's eyes as she tended Lubeck, Agatha asked.

"You care for this Lubeck, don't you sister?" Freyja stopped what she was doing and looked her sister in the eyes before answering.

"I care about all of them. They are good men who have suffered much over the years. They are also my friends and I don't have so many of those as I can afford to turn any away. But yes, I care for Lubeck, perhaps a little more than the others. Why do you ask?" Agatha sighed and reclined against the wall a once again.

"You know that if you want any of them to survive this, you are going to have to get help? You need to get a message to Gunter Jorgensen and let him know that his son is alive and needs his help." As she spoke, a Hawk flew in and landed on the bed post with a low screech.

"Aaghh, Finn." Freyja said with a smile. "What is the name of this place?" She asked Agatha.

Agatha looked confused, but replied.

"Thanos, It's a small Island —"

"I know what it is. I just didn't know its name." Freyja replied cutting her sibling short. She rolled up the small piece of parchment she had been writing on. Placed it into a small capsule and tied it around one of Finn's legs. Then she reached out touching him on the head and closed her eyes once more. Finn gave a short screech and lifted into the air and was gone.

"I take it you have just sent word to Gunter as I suggested?" Agatha snorted. Freyja looked at her sister without comment. She went over to her books once more and began to study again, scribbling notes as she read. Agatha watched intently as Freyja began to collect small jars filled with coloured powders and various liquids. She mixed some of the contents together and began to heat the mixture over a small flame. The mixture started to bubble and thicken into a thin paste as she stirred.

"Do you need a hand little sister? I too know the art of healing." Agatha asked, the offer sounding genuine. Freyja paused a moment before replying.

"If you really want to help me, you could check that I have this right before I apply it to his wounds."

"If it's what I think it is, you mixed it correctly, but you need to let it boil before you can administer it. Otherwise, it will not be sterile and you will cause infection." Freyja thought momentarily before returning the mixture to the heat.

"If you're advice is wrong and—"

"If my advice is wrong, that giant will cut me in two with that huge axe of his I'll bet. I see that you care for this Lubeck. I care for you believe it or not. If helping him helps you…..." Agatha trailed off.

Freyja brought the mixture to the boil, then allowed it to cool a moment. Once it had, she spread it over Lubeck's wounds. She cooled his brow with a dampened cloth and kissed him gently on the cheek. Agatha smiled to herself.

"Why don't you go and get a little food sister? You must be hungry. I haven't seen you eat since I was brought here. The food being cooked outside smells divine, it's making my belly rumble, so you could bring me some back when you're done. I'll keep an eye on this one while you are eating. He'll be fine, I promise." Agatha attempted to reassure her sister. Freyja moved to the window and smelled the aromas wafting up from the beach below. Agatha was right, it did smell divine and her stomach rumbled with anticipation as she inhaled. She was surprised as to how hungry she had suddenly become. She looked over her shoulder once more at Lubeck, then reluctantly agreed with her sister.

"I'll be back shortly. I will collect two bowls and return here to eat with you." She said moving with haste.

"Fine." Agatha said with irritation. Freyja left the room and descended the stairs to the beach. As soon as she was out of sight and earshot, Agatha moved over to the still unconscious Lubeck as he lay in the bed. She laid her head on his chest and listened. Then she whispered in his ear. She crossed to the table and searched the small jars that Freyja had used earlier. A broad smile stretched her lips as she located what she was looking for. She opened the jar and took a small quantity of its contents into her mouth. Replacing the jar exactly as she had found it, she returned to Lubeck's side, bent close and kissed him slowly on the lips while gently passing the dark blue liquid from her own mouth to his. Lubeck coughed and stirred a little before settling again to his deep unconscious sleep. Agatha smiled to herself, glanced around, then gently kissed him again. Standing, she took the hem of her dress and wiped his lips clean so as not to alert anyone to what she had done. Footsteps on the stairs alerted her to Freyja's return. She quickly moved to the window and rested against the sill as Freyja entered carrying two bowls of food.

Out on the beach work was almost complete. Malik checked everything one last time as Thorsten drew up a roster for watch keepers to guard their preparations and to ensure that Ballan did not slip ashore unseen that night. His ships should be landing at first light, if Freyja was correct. All was set. All were fed, most now sleeping to regain their strength. Thorsten returned to the tower to speak with Freyja.

"If you can call your storms when Ballan comes, it would be very helpful." The big warrior sheepishly asked.

"I can call it. I can't promise it will help, but I hope it will." Freyja sighed, a little fear shaking her voice as she spoke. Thorsten touched her gently on the shoulder in a reassuring manner.

"It will be fine I'm sure. Malik is taking some men to the Thunder Child as we speak. I hope he doesn't get her sunk. Lubeck will not be impressed if that happens." They both laughed nervously at the prospect. Thorsten nodded towards Lubeck still struggling with the fever that had gripped him. "We will miss his sword tomorrow. His head for war too, but we shall do what we can and the Gods willing, we will be triumphant." He bent slightly to kiss Freyja on the forehead. "Try and rest. Tomorrow is going to be a long and terrifying day." Then he turned and left the room.

THE SOUND OF THUNDER

Seagulls cawed in the morning air as Freyja's eyes flickered open. She scrambled to the bed where Lubeck lay still unresponsive as she touched his skin. Surprise lightened her face at the realisation his fever had broken. His skin was cool and dry to the touch and his breathing was steady and deep. No longer ragged and shallow as it had been the previous days. She threw herself over him embracing him with delight. As she did, a sweet aroma caught her attention. Freyja sniffed around him like a hound after a trail. The sweet aroma was coming from his lips. Gently and carefully, she opened his mouth. The aroma became stronger. Looking into Lubeck's open mouth, Freyja could see a dark blue tint to his tongue. She bit her lip hard with agitation. Turning to call her sister, she was struck dumb as Agatha enquired,

"His fever has broken then?"

"You did this? You used Hydra blood to break his fever? How could you administer that? It has to be done at body temperature. You were not alone with him long enough to have brought it up to the correct temperature without me knowing….." she stopped as she saw Agatha opening her mouth wide revealing her dark blue tongue. With a mischievous giggle Agatha admitted.

"I merely kissed your handsome patient. Now he seems to be on the mend." Freyja restrained the urge to throttle her sibling screaming at her instead.

"You could have killed the pair of you. What were you thinking? If you were just a degree out, you would both be laying here dead this morning."

"Agghhh, but we're not now are we?" Agatha retorted. "And this handsome beast is well on the way to recovery I believe. Now stop your whining and do your thing. Get him back on his feet. I am going out there to see what I can do to help. Ballan will be here soon and I have no desire to go back with him. So you had best get this dispatcher of death on his feet with a sword in his hand, fast." Though it troubled Freyja to admit it, she knew that her sister was right. The risk she had taken the previous night had worked and now the main thing was to get Lubeck onto his feet and into the battle. By breaking his fever, Agatha had reduced Lubeck's required healing time by at least four days. Was this going to be enough? Nobody could tell. Lubeck was a strong man, but even strong men need time to heal. Agatha left the room and went out to the beach where Thorsten was raising the few men they had to confront whatever forces landed on the beach. Tarique was up on the cliffs with a hand full of accomplished archers. While Malik had the Thunder Child ready for sea awaiting a signal and hopefully a mist to hide his approach. Everything was set, all any of them could do now was wait. Lubeck stirred a little in the bed as Freyja tended his wounds. These had healed well but were not fully there yet. As he settled again, Freyja whispered to him.

"Get up Lubeck, you need to come back. Come back to aid your friends who fight this day for freedom and families. They need you, they need your sword. Come back to us and unleash the Valkyrie upon our oppressors." She waited, waited for a sign that he was returning to the living, but to no avail. She concentrated and stared at him trying to break through the mists of that lonely place between life and death. Where was he? As she looked deeper and deeper, her concentration was broken by the sound of horns being blown in warning of Ballan's approaching fleet. She rushed to the window to take a look at the situation. Ships covered the horizon maybe a couple of hours away. She turned her gaze along the coast. She couldn't see, but she knew the Thunder Child would be underway at the sound of the horns. Malik was relying on her, she had to leave Lubeck for now and raise a mist to conceal the mighty ship from Ballan's men. She had to give Malik a chance to get close enough to take them by surprise. "Lubeck! Get up!" She yelled as she moved to another window to recite her incantation. Raising her arms and closing her eyes, she began. Low and steady at first. Slowly picking up speed and volume as the incantation continued. The morning sky began to darken, filling with storm clouds and a mist began to form along the coast, slowly thickening and moving gradually out to sea. On Ballan's ship, his crew became agitated at the sudden development.

"This looks like witchcraft to me!" One man shouted. A roar of agreement erupted around the vessel.

"Quiet you dogs! It's a mere trick to frighten children. Get back to your stations. Make ready for war and keep your eyes open, WIDE!" Ballan yelled. The mist grew thicker as it began to form a barrier between Ballan's fleet and the shoreline ahead. Malik saw this and moved the Thunder Child to sail with it. Quietly and steadily the mighty ship moved to circumnavigate Ballan's ships, hidden from view by the thick band of fog. Malik allowed his mind to empty and he relaxed almost to a trance. In his mind he could see the positions of Ballan's fleet along with his own. It was as if he were stood in the highest part of the tower looking down on the scene below. Now he knew where to position the Thunder Child for the best effect. In the tower, Freyja blinked her eyes waking from her connection. She turned, moving back to the other window, kicking the bed as she passed.

"Get up dam you! Get up and help!" She yelled as she kicked the bed again. On reaching the second window, she once again closed her eyes and concentrated. Now the skies filled with thunder, the winds grew stronger and the sea began to swell. On the beach below Thorsten rallied his men to ready themselves.

"I've seen this before!" He cried. "Take up your positions, things are going to get a little freaky any time now, but hold your nerve, no matter what you see!" Above the roar of the wind and the crashing thunder, Tarique's lookouts sounded their horns again. This time in warning. Ballan had suspected something might happen and instead of moving away from the mist, he had turned the whole fleet to head into it. This was something unexpected and not planned for. If Ballan's fleet engaged the Thunder Child too early. Their surprise attack would be foiled. Freyja thought quickly. She needed to turn him around and get him to follow the course they had planned for him. She went to her font and removed the covering. Waving her hand over it as she had done many times before. Frowning into the waters within, she thought about what needed to be done. The skies darkened further and lightening licked through the air like the cracking of celestial whips.

Freyja projected her thoughts through her visions to Malik below. Now he was aware that Ballan's fleet were almost upon him and that he needed to alter course to avoid being discovered. The orders went out and the mighty ship disappeared into the fog. Freyja looked around as Lubeck stirred. Desperation began to set in as she realised that she couldn't do everything alone.

"Get up!" She screamed at him, "Get up and help!" Her frustrations and fear sending shock waves through the celestial plains she had opened through the font.

On a ship's deck, far off to the North, Morgana suddenly opened her eyes wide declaring.

"It has begun." Hagar turned to look upon her.

"The battle? The battle has begun?" He asked.

"Yes, but all does not go well. Something is wrong. Freyja is afraid." She closed her eyes once more and uttered a verse in a strange language. Visions rolled around her head and then with enlightenment she told Hagar what was happening back in Thanos.

"Lubeck mortally wounded and not in the battle will not fare well with the others. Freyja is scared and things are not going as planned. I think we should get this rescue done as quickly as possible and then head for home at speed." Hagar declared.

"Home? You now think of Thanos as home?" Morgana enquired.

"It will be once we get those slaves freed and on board with us. Though Hafthor is not among them I think that one of those young men might be Thorsten's son Bjorn and I'm almost sure there is a young woman among them that could well be my daughter. The others I'm sure are also related to some of our men. I think we may have found most of our families. Let's get this done and get home."

"I need a little privacy while you and the men are planning your assault." Morgana declared.

"Not a problem, you may use my quarters below as you please." Hagar replied heading to convene his council. Morgana went below decks to Hagar's quarters. She ensured that no one was within earshot, then placed some small objects in particular order on the floor in a random circle. Chanting quietly to herself, visions began to formulate in her mind. Thick fog was all she could see at first, but then as realisation of what she was viewing made her whisper a single word.

"Awaken."

Back in Thanos, the Thunder Child moved silently through the mist where she successfully out flanked Ballan's fleet. The thick fog conjured by Freyja totally engulfed the entire fleet. As the mighty ship bore down on the rear most of the invaders, the dragon figurehead opened its eyes and stared at its prey. In the tower, Lubeck stirred then suddenly opened his eyes. Freyja called to him.

"It's about time. Ballan is upon us. Thorsten has only a handful of men and needs your sword down there with him. Can you stand? Can you fight? Can you hear me?" Frustration rife in her voice.

Out on the water, the Thunder Child had caught the first of Ballan's ships. In the thick fog, nobody saw the dragon mounted on the Thunder Child's bow, snarl and grab the smaller ship in its huge jaws. Men screamed as timbers splintered and smashed. As Malik ran to the front of the ship he thought his eyes deceived him. For as their bows cut through the shattered remains of a ship with its crew dead or drowning, he saw the dragon settling back into position. He looked down at the bodies of the stricken ship's crew. Arrows flew from his own deck killing those in the water that were not already dead. Cries for help and the sound of smashing timbers came from way out in front of them, as now a lightning bolt pierced the darkening skies and destroyed a second ship. Alarms sounded and Ballan called for his fleet to change course. A third ship crashed to an abrupt halt, as a second bolt of lightning struck, breaking the vessel as if the Gods had slammed a mighty fist down upon a fragile toy. Then as Malik leant against the huge dragon carving, his support shifted and his balance was lost causing him to jump away quickly to avoid falling overboard. The dragon had moved, stretching its long neck down and gripping a fourth ship, lifting it out of the water and shaking it until its crew fell to the sea below. Screams filled Malik's ears and timbers splintered again. The Thunder Child was alive and her figurehead was destroying ships all by itself. With a magical storm destroying his ships ahead and the Thunder Child attacking ships from behind, Ballan made the decision to head towards shore and to get his forces onto land as soon as possible. Something unworldly was happening within this fog and he wanted to be free of it.

Lubeck still lay on the bed, awake but not moving. A voice in his head told him to rise. As he attempted to, a woman's hand caught his arm to assist him. Agatha had returned from the beach and had noticed Lubeck's attempt as she had entered the room.

"Here let me help." She said as Lubeck took her arm and heaved his body to a standing position.

"Get him his sword! It's by the table, his armour too." Freyja called to her, still trying to sway the balance of power on the seas below. Agatha helped Lubeck don his armour and sword. Lubeck looked around the room until he found his hooked weapon. Taking hold of it in one hand and slipping a couple of large daggers into his boot and belt with the other, he headed for the door, his stride strengthening with each step.

Out on the water, the storm was sinking another of Ballan's ships. It's crew struggling for life in the stormy seas. The main body of the fleet had almost reached the shoreline. The Thunder Child's devices, now unleashed raging thunder bolts of fire towards the trailing ships. Ropes lashed and timbers smashed and burned as the projectiles crashed into them, but it was too little to prevent Ballan's main forces from landing. Again and again, the Thunder Child unleashed fire balls at the vessels lining the shore. More of them burst into flame and burned with black smoke filling the air. Even with almost half of his fleet destroyed, Ballan's forces numbered more than five times that of Thorsten's men. Malik knew this. He had not been able to sink as many ships as he had hoped. He made the decision to turn the Thunder Child towards shore and bring his crew into the inevitable fight on the beach.

The storm grew stronger as Malik's men waded through the breakers some way down the coast. His ship safely moored and just a few men left behind to guard it. The crew moved at speed to assist their colleagues past the tower. As they approached, they could see their preparations had not been in vain. Ballan and his men were being funnelled by the burning trenches towards a waiting Thorsten. As they charged, burning bales of straw and grasses hurtled down the cliff faces and across the beach careering into slavers setting them ablaze on impact. Screams and wailing filled the air and it was difficult to see clearly through the thick smoke. Panic stricken and confused, slavers ran as a rabble towards Thorsten's organised shield wall. Tarique's archers loosed volley after volley cutting them down as they charged. Realising that chaos was going to defeat him, Ballan rallied his men and began to restore order and discipline to what was left of his forces. A respite in the fighting followed.

Tarique checked on the supply of arrows he and his archers had left. It did not look good. Perhaps another full volley if they were lucky. It was about this time that Lubeck reached the cliff top and Tarique greeted him gladly. Together they surveyed the scene below. Thorsten's shield wall had as yet, not been engaged. But glimpses through the smoke showed them that Ballan was preparing archers of his own now. Also a band of around twenty men had broken away from the main group and were attempting to find a way through the slowly dying trench fires in an attempt to flank him.

"We need to intercept them." Lubeck instructed pointing at the breakaway group. "If they get behind Thorsten, the shield wall will fall." Three archers were left to do what they could from their elevated position, while the rest gathered to Lubeck's side. At Tarique's signal a horn sounded. All on the beach looked up to see what was occurring. Thunder clapped and lightening flashed silhouetting Lubeck's mighty figure, sword held aloft, creating a fearsome sight for his enemies to behold.

"Nice touch sister." Agatha laughed looking out of the window from Freyja's chambers.

"I'm all but done. I'm afraid it's up to them now." Freyja announced with a sigh. Both women watched together, heart in mouth, to see what the outcome might be.

On the beach, Ballan's blood ran cold as fear began to grip his soul. He knew this man on the cliff, he had seen him before. His heart sank at the realisation that the Valkyrie was still alive and not only alive, but coming for him. He gave the signal and his archers loosed their bows. Arrows flew and thumped into the shield wall in front of them. While being covered by their archers, keeping Thorsten's men with their heads down. Ballan's forces rushed the wall, crashing into it in a vain attempt to find a weakness.

"Hold! Hold!" Thorsten commanded. As the slavers recoiled back from their assault, Tarique's few remaining archers loosed, cutting down a handful more of their enemy as they scrambled on the sand.

"Advance!" Called Thorsten. The shield wall moved in unison, stepping on fallen slavers and moving over them to a new position. In its wake, the fallen were slaughtered by Thorsten's men. Seeing this efficiency, Ballan called for his men to fall back and regroup.

Meanwhile, further along the beach, the breakaway group had found their way through the flames and were attempting to flank the shield wall. As they skirted along the cliff face, Lubeck's group blocked their path. Seeing that their opponent's numbers were very few, the slavers charged head long at them. With too few men to form an effective shield wall, Lubeck did away with any organised defence and charged likewise at his attackers. Men screamed as swords rattled and armour rang with blow after blow. Lubeck was a wild beast, cutting down three of his attackers in quick clinical succession. Sword in one hand, his hooked weapon in the other, he ducked, twisted, turned and jumped avoiding every attempt to strike him, countering each and every thrust with a killing blow from his own enchanted weapons. Within seconds, he had carved a path straight through his opponents like a plough through well-tended soil. Never before had Tarique seen such ferocity, power and agility combined with flawless technique. There was no doubt in his mind now. This truly was the Valkyrie the others had talked about and were so afraid of. Fueled by his friend's demonstration of supremacy, Tarique and the others engaged their attackers alongside their Earl making short work of any resistance. When the skirmish was over, none of the slaver's stood.

The group followed the path the slavers had taken during their attempt to flank the shield wall. The fires in the trenches were all but done and the field of battle was widening. Thorsten's wall was now ineffective. Some of his men at the edges were being killed as slavers were finding weakness due to lack of numbers. They began to fall back trying hard to stay in formation and protect one another. Lubeck looked to the sea; some of the survivors from Ballan's sunken ships were gathering themselves on the shoreline and readying to join the fight. Lubeck's mind was split as to who to engage first. Did he attack this new threat from the sea? Or did he aid Thorsten at the wall? Fortunately, this decision was made for him as Malik, followed by the rest of the Thunder Child's crew hurtled impulsively into battle with the drenched survivors.

"By all the Gods, Malik!" Lubeck exclaimed. Now there was only one thing to do, help Thorsten. He left the half drowned slavers for his friend to deal with and ran to assist the giant defending the beach by the tower.

As they approached the fight, Lubeck stopped his men from charging blindly through the smoke wafting across their path. Instead he ordered a horn to be sounded catching the full attention of his enemy. Ballan's men disengaged from their attack on Thorsten, who was still managing to hold some kind of wall together despite his losses. Forming a rear guard, Ballan's forces turned to engage this new threat from behind. His men dug into defensive positions and waited with apprehension. Thorsten and his men welcomed the pause for breath and used the lull to reform and drag their wounded clear of further harm.

Ballan waited, staring into the smoke. His men were tired and bloodied, breathing heavily and all were afraid. As they peered through the thinning smoke, shadowy figures could be seen moving slowly towards them. Ballan ordered his archers to fire upon them. As they did, almost as one, the shadows dropped to the ground and sheltered behind their shields. The arrows struck them and glanced away falling harmlessly to the sand. The shadows rose and continued to move towards their foes. As the smoke cleared a little more, Ballan could see clearly who was advancing towards him. A mixture of fear and rage gripped him and he charged recklessly towards the advancing enemy. His troops following suit in a desperate attempt to escape the nightmare they had plunged into. At seeing this, Thorsten ordered his men to attack and the wall broke formation, following Ballan's men and trapping them in a bloody pincer movement, forcing them to fight on two fronts. The skirmish didn't last long as Lubeck fought like a demon from the underworld, effortlessly cutting down any opponent within arm's reach. The screams died away and the clash of steel against steel subsided. Soon there was all but no resistance left. Ballan knelt on the sand bloodied and panting, though still defiant. The few men he had left were unarmed and moaning in pain from their wounds. Only Ballan still had fight left in him. Thorsten cast a long shadow over him as he approached axe in hand.

"Wait!" Lubeck called steadying his huge friend. "We need to question him."

"I'll tell you nothing" Ballan spat.

"Then you will die a slow and agonising death. I've been here before many times, the last was your man Mormont. He, like you was defiant to the end. But before he died, he told me what I wanted to know, as will you." Lubeck retorted. Ballan mad a feeble attempt to strike Lubeck with his sword. Fatigue and injury sapping all of the vigour and power from his efforts. Thorsten easily blocked the thrust with his axe, knocking the sword from his hand. Ballan fell onto all fours on the sand at Lubeck's feet. Lubeck looked out to the shoreline where some of Ballan's burnt ships lay half submerged in the shallow waters. He saw shark fins moving erratically as they fed on the bodies of fallen soldiers, turning the surf red with blood which in turn attracted more of their kind to join the feast.

"The tide is flooding. I have an idea." Lubeck commented. He instructed a hand full of men to embed a tall rudimentary stake into the sand, about half a ship's length out, waist deep in water. "If he won't tell us what we want to know, tie him to it. The tide will continue to flood for another few hours. If he doesn't drown, the sharks will eat him. One way or another, it is all in his own hands." Thorsten took charge and carried out Lubeck's orders. Ballan struggled in vain as he was dragged into the water and tied to the stake. The water had reached his ribs by the time Lubeck asked him the first question.

"Where is my son Hafthor?" He boomed, anger hardening his voice. Ballan refused to talk, remaining silent as the waters rose slowly. The body of one of his crewmen floated past some twenty feet away from him. It twitched and appeared to jump, before the tall black fin appeared from below the surface. Ballan realised that the sharks had not yet finished their feast and as he watched two or three more appeared momentarily taking bites and tearing flesh away from his dead crewman.

"There's no need for you to die this day Ballan. Answer my questions and my men will cut you loose and bring you back in." Lubeck offered. Ballan's breathing became heavier and more erratic as fear began to grip him. Lubeck's voice being drowned out by the sound of his own heart pounding in his ears. The questions kept coming and Ballan remained silent. Until the water reached his chest. By this time, the number of feeding sharks had risen to alarming numbers. One came close and bumped Ballan in his stomach with an investigatory nudge. Ballan couldn't help but yell in fear as the demonic beast circled the stake with curiosity. Another, then another each moving a little closer. Soon, everywhere Ballan looked there were large black monsters getting ever closer and more curious. It was a simple matter of time before the inevitable happened. Ballan omitted a blood curdling scream as one of the beasts took a bite from his side. It's teeth sank deep, tearing a lump of flesh away as it pulled and twisted. The pain was immense as Ballan could feel himself being pulled at by the great fish. He coughed and spluttered as water and blood filled his mouth.

"Help! Help me!" He screamed.

"Not until you tell me what I want to know!" Lubeck replied. A second shark sunk its teeth deep into Ballan's thigh. He screamed again as the pain shot through him and the fear tortured his mind with the knowledge that he was being eaten alive.

"Akhola will destroy you! He will destroy all that you hold dear when he overthrows Rogan. Your son will watch his father and grandfather torn limb from limb and fed to the wolves before he is tortured and slowly, painfully killed. AAAGGGHHH!" Ballan screamed again as yet another shark bit into him removing more of his flesh, spilling blood and tissue into the water. Smaller fish gathered, pecking at the scraps of torn flesh floating in the blood filled waters. Ballan now hung limply from his arms, which were tied overhead. Whimpering and moaning in pain.

"Shall I go and retrieve him?" Thorsten asked. Lubeck said nothing. He merely nodded a solitary nod. and walked away, up the beach towards the tower. Passing Freyja and Agatha, who now stood on the sand where Thorsten had formed the shield wall earlier. Agatha looked frustrated and angry.

"That's it? He lives? A scrap of information. Something we already knew and you let him live?" Lubeck stopped and looked her in the eye.

"He's dead already. I doubt he'll survive the night." Agatha looked past Lubeck watching Thorsten and two other men, as they lashed at the water fending off sharks as they cut down Ballan's blood drenched body. They supported him and dragged him ashore slung between two of them as others helped to defend their retreat from the hungry fish. As she watched, rage began to take over Agatha's thoughts. She grabbed a dagger from Lubeck's belt and ran down the beach towards the group leaving the water. Freyja called after her but to no avail. Agatha hurtled towards the soaked group and plunged the dagger deep into Ballan's chest. Ballan gasped as he tried to focus on his assailant. Agatha withdrew the blade and thumped it home again and again until Thorsten finally grasped her arm and removed the weapon from her grip. Lubeck raised an unconcerned eyebrow.

"Well?" He called. Thorsten shook his head as he reached down to a sobbing Agatha helping her back to her feet from where she had slumped when disarmed.

"I think your sister could do with a hand." Lubeck suggested softly to Freyja as he calmly walked past, heading for the cliffs. "Get her to help with the wounded and tell Tarique to arrange a pyre to dispose of the dead. Once that is done, we all get some rest. Tomorrow I hold a council to plan our next move. Talk to your sister, I'll need both of you when we sail."

"I can't–"

"Leave that to me." Lubeck interrupted. "I think your friend Morgana is a more powerful witch than she lets on. It was her that woke me from my sleep. If she can reach me from Altear, then she can break this spell that holds you here."

"Morgana?" Freyja asked puzzled. Lubeck stared at her.

"You didn't know she could do this?" Freyja dropped her head and looked at the sand.

"I had my doubts. I could feel something whenever she was near. I would wake at night sometimes as if knowing that someone was using the arts, but I could never see who."

"It would appear that she is more powerful than you or your sister, but doubtful if she is more powerful than you both together." Lubeck scoffed. Freyja looked a little offended.

"Do you feel that she is a danger?" She asked. Lubeck cocked a lop sided grin.

"We'll find out soon enough." He said as he resumed his path. Then stopping for a moment he spoke over his shoulder. "The Thunder and lightning was a nice touch, it helped raise fear in the hearts of our enemies and made us look like demons." Then with a wry laugh he continued on his way.

REUNITED

Off the shores of Altear, a small fleet of ships sailed into the night. Their crews happy with a job well done. Their holds filled with women and children, men young and old, all with their chains of slavery being methodically removed. On the upper deck of the lead ship, Hagar stood with a flagon of ale in his hand laughing and drinking while Morgana tried to tend the deep gash on his head that poured blood down the side of his face matting his long thick hair and beard.

"Hold still you big ox. How do you expect me to do anything when you're like this? Hold still." Morgana snapped with irritation.

"Don't worry I'm fine, I'm more than fine." He laughed swigging more ale.

"You won't be if you lose any more blood. Now be still for a moment while I sort this out." Morgana continued to treat the head wound as best she could while Hagar continued with his frivolities. Behind them, the dancing flames of a burning Altear illuminated the night sky. The rescue had gone well and all of Hagar's ships were filled with slaves young and old. The crews were in high spirits as many of them had been reunited with lost family members. Only a few were less so, having lost friends during the raid. A tall young man, taller than the rest, came up on the main deck for some fresh air. He rubbed the marks on his wrists left by his recently removed shackles. Morgana stopped treating Hagar and left him to his drinking.

"Bjorn is it?" She enquired in a quiet and calm manner.

"Yes." The young man answered.

"I know your father Thorsten. He is a friend and he is looking for you. He will be so pleased to see you again." She said beckoning him to come and sit by her.

"My father? My father is dead. He was killed when they took me slave." The youth responded,

"No, no he's not. At least he wasn't a few days ago." Morgana protested. The youth looked at her in puzzlement. "Come sit, let me tell you of your father, a giant of a man and how he searches for you." Morgana continued as the youth accepted her offer. He sat beside her and as Hagar broke into song, she began to tell the tale as she knew it.

Gunter Jorgensen sat by the Grand Lodge of the settlement he loved to visit when not at the strong hold of King Rogan. He bit into an apple as he watched the sun rise over the nearby hills. His grey hair wafted gently in the early morning breeze. He looked to the sky and sighed. Six long years had passed since he received the news of his son and grandson's deaths. His vengeance for this act had been running for five of those up to now. His actions though, had strengthened the resolve of those who would oppose King Rogan, something Rogan himself had taken a dim view of. He had ordered Gunter to cease his rampage under pain of banishment. Gunter, under duress had obeyed his King, but hung up his sword and resigned his position at Rogan's side. Now with no purpose, he whiled away his days in this secluded settlement, trying to help out with any tasks in need of fulfilling. He was well known to the villagers here, all knew who he was and who he had served, so he still commanded a high degree of respect from everyone there. As he sat enjoying the morning sun on his face, a young boy ran to him with a message. He was to report to King Rogan at once.

"He said not to make him come and get you." The boy finished. Gunter patted the boy on the head, sighed and rose to his feet. Then with a heavy heart, he looked down at the boy and said,

"Then I'd best not keep him waiting had I?" The young boy smiled and ran off to deliver Gunter's response, as he had been instructed to. Gunter adjusted his clothes and straightened his beard. Then with heavy steps, he headed towards the stables to prepare his horse for the journey.

"I'll probably pick the boy up on the way. Rogan's strong hold is two day's travel from here. It will probably take that boy three on foot." He told the smith who owned the stable. With a smile, he packed a few extra provisions just in case he was right, mounted his horse and rode North. Perhaps a day and a half into his journey, Gunter noticed the boy on the road ahead of him. He noted to himself what good time the lad had made. Spurring his mount on, Gunter caught up with the lad, and offered him a ride. Foot sore and tired, the boy eagerly accepted and Gunter leant down to lift the boy up behind him and placing him on the horse's rump, he warned him, "Hold on, don't fall or it will hurt." Gunter kicked his mount's flanks, coaxing it into a gallop. The boy threw his arms around Gunter's waist and hugged him tight. "First time on a horse boy?" Gunter called over his shoulder to the youth.

"Y.. yes." The boy struggled to reply as he bounced with the movements of the beast.

"Try to relax, move with the beast not against him or you will surely have a sore arse by the time we get there." Gunter called back, laughing as he did so. As Rogan's strong hold came into view, Gunter let his mount slow to a swaying walk. The boy sighed with relief and loosened his grip on Gunter's waist. "You hungry boy? Check that bag." Gunter pointed to a rough woollen bag hanging by the boy's left knee. The boy lifted and opened it, helping himself to some roast pork devouring it as though he hadn't eaten in days. Gunter laughed, but allowed the boy his fill as they continued their journey.

The lookout on the walls to King Rogan's strong hold called to the guards below that a rider approached. The guards took up their positions to challenge the rider once he was close enough as they always did, for the security of those within the strong hold. As Gunter and the boy approached, he was instantly recognised by the men and after a few brief greetings, he and the boy were allowed to enter. On reaching the stables, Gunter lowered the boy to the ground who immediately ran towards the Great Lodge to inform the King that Gunter was here. Gunter dismounted and handed his horse to the smith to take care of it. He was surprised to find that when he turned about, he was greeted by a welcoming committee of four of the King's guard. They escorted him directly to the King's council room, which was located to one side of the Great Lodge itself. Gunter fidgeted uneasily as he waited. It wasn't too long before the King entered the room.

"Gunter! It's good to see you. How have you been old friend?" He called in a warm greeting with outstretched arms. Gunter smiled and returned the gesture. They slapped each other's backs as they hugged momentarily.

"I'm good and you? You look well my Lord." Gunter said still smiling. Rogan stood tall again placing his hands on his hips. He was a big man, a little taller than Gunter and heavier too.

"Life has been good to me these last twenty years, mainly thanks to you and your son. I think things might well have been different without your support old friend." Gunter's expression altered at the mention of his son. Rogan noticed this so got straight to the matter at hand without any more niceties. "I sent for you, because I have received news of Lubeck." He said without any prior warning. Gunter gasped as his jaw dropped. Rogan continued. "He's not dead after all. Or at least he wasn't, about a week ago I think. Hard to tell with these birds." Gesturing round to a guard entering the room. On his arm stood a Hawk. Gunter frowned. "It was carrying this." Rogan continued holding up a rolled parchment. Fumbling at it to reveal the message written within. Handing it to Gunter, he suggested that he read it. "You can read it I take it? It's not quite our language, but it's not a bad attempt." Gunter took the parchment and began to read the message.

"By all the God's." He exclaimed. "Where did this come from?"

"An Island called Thanos by all accounts. Do you know of it?" King Rogan asked his old friend.

"No, no I don't, but by the look of this parchment, it's to the South somewhere."

"You may be right. You'll need a ship. I can supply you that at least for my old friend. I can let you take five in fact–"

"Five! This Ballan has at least four times that amount, can't you spare me more?" Gunter butted in.

Rogan frowned at Gunter deep in thought before replying.

"Your recent antics over the past few years have cost me dearly. The survivors of the settlements you destroyed in revenge for your son's death, have run to Akhola for protection pledging their allegiance to him. His armies are growing in number each week. This uneasy peace we enjoy is fragile. I believe that if Akhola sees my forces depleted any further than they already are, he will invade and attempt to overthrow me. I can't afford to send more with you. I need them here to defend our people and lands.

I'm sorry, five ships is all I can let go with you." Gunter went to protest, but then thought better of it. Instead he thanked his King and then asked,

"How do I find this Thanos?" Rogan turned to look at his former Chieftain and right hand.

"I don't know, but I will have my people questioned to see if any of them have ever been there. I'll let you know what turns up." With that Finn took to the air momentarily before landing on Gunter's shoulder. With a screech, he looked down at the parchment in Gunter's hand then lifted again only to land on a window ledge before turning to screech once more. The two men stared at the bird in silence and bewilderment. The bird took to the air, circled the Great Lodge and quickly re-entered the window to land on Gunter's shoulder again. A voice inside of Gunter's head urged him to follow the Hawk.

"I think the bird wants me to follow him." Gunter said hesitantly, not fully sure why he had suggested such a thing.

"Indeed, I have never seen a bird behave in such a manner before. Take it, after all it found its way here from whoever tied the message to its leg. I suppose it will be able to find its way home." Rogan replied, raising one eyebrow. Gunter nodded and waited impatiently. "Go!" Rogan continued, "Prepare yourself. Your ships will be ready at dawn." With that Gunter thanked Rogan and left to prepare to sail on the morning tide.

A long way to the South, on the Island of Thanos. The scars of battle were being healed as men filled in the deep pits they had dug in the sand. Bodies of the dead were lowered into the mass grave and Freyja spoke some appropriate words over them. The burned ships were being dismantled and cleared of anything useable. While the unscathed ships left behind from Ballan's defeated armada, were being taken care of and added to Lubeck's ever growing fleet. It had been a week now since the battle on the beach and between the men's hard work and the turning tides, most of the evidence of war had been swept away. The few charred hulls were already half buried by the shifting sand as the sea slowly piled sediment and sand against the wooden skeletons. Lubeck took a break from his labours and sat on the dunes in the midday sun. Malik joined him and the two men sighed as they enjoyed the welcome break. Agatha brought them some refreshment in the form of ale and salted pork. Malik chuckled to himself as he ate.

"Share the joke." Lubeck said swigging a mouth full of ale.

"I wonder what she is going to offer Tarique?" He said wiping his mouth with the back of his hand.

Lubeck frowned, not understanding for a moment then he too began to laugh.

"Perhaps she will offer him some ham?" He said, laughing louder at the thought.

"Actually, I have some roast chicken for him, if he wants it. We are not uneducated; I know he can't eat the salted Pork. Perhaps he would like some stuffed dates and mint tea?" Agatha retorted.

"Mint tea? By all the Gods, what does that taste like?" Lubeck asked.

"Here, try some, you might like it." Agatha said handing a small cup to Lubeck with a mischievous grin. Lubeck took the cup and sipped the warm liquid inside.

"Actually it's quite refreshing, but I think that I will stick to my ale, unless you have some mead in that basket?" Lubeck enquired with a chuckle. Agatha laughed as she shook her head.

"Mead, I will talk to Freyja and see what she can do about Mead." She replied as she continued to hand out refreshments to the rest of the men, as they took rest from their tasks.

"Sails! Sails! On the horizon to the North!" A man called down from the tower. Everyone jumped to their feet and rushed to the tower where their armour and weapons were stowed.

"Do you see their colours?" Lubeck enquired. The lookout replied that they were at the moment too far away to make out.

"By all the Gods, who comes at us now?" Thorsten spat wiping away the sweat from his brow and picking up his axe.

"Make ready, but stay out of sight." Lubeck instructed. The men did as ordered as Lubeck accompanied by Thorsten, Tarique and Malik climbed the stairs to the tower's highest point where the lookout was posted. They all squeezed onto the small balcony to try and spot the approaching ships for themselves. Squinting in the bright sunlight, it was Malik's sharp eyes that made out the vessel's colours first.

"It's Hagar! It's our ships returning from Altear. I can see the rams head on his blue sail." He exclaimed excitedly.

"If you can see that from here, then you must be part hawk. Perhaps we should have you up here all of the time?" Thorsten declared laughing. Lubeck laughed as Malik hit Thorsten on the arm with the piece of salted pork he was still trying to consume.

"Come lets go down and greet our friends as they land. But let's keep our numbers hidden, just in case Malik's eyes are not those of a hawk after all." Lubeck said moving towards the door. Tarique nodded and without further instruction, he descended the stairs and returned to the men hidden in the dunes informing them of Lubeck's intent.

On board the approaching ships, Hagar could now see the burnt remains of ships scattered along the shoreline. Unsure of what had unfolded there, he gave orders to his small fleet to make ready for battle. Within minutes all of the ships crews were armed and ready to defend themselves. Women and children hidden below decks. Archers and shields at the ready above. The ships glided to a halt just short of the shoreline. Hagar called out to anyone who may be there. Thorsten made himself visible and greeted his comrades inviting them ashore. At this, all of Lubeck's remaining men broke cover and came down to the beach to help with landing of the ships and their precious cargo. As Bjorn stepped onto the ships main deck, he paused looking at the giant standing on the beach welcoming everyone ashore. His heart leapt into his mouth, his eyes began to fill with tears of joy. It had been so long since he had seen his father with his own eyes, believing he had been killed many, many years ago. His breathing deepened and became erratic, and emotions swelled up inside of him to the point where he could no longer contain them. As he stood and stared, Bjorn could feel his body beginning to shake. A gentle hand took his and steadied it, followed by Morgana's soft voice telling him to go and greet his father. Bjorn steadied himself, smiled at Morgana thanking her for her caring and understanding during the journey. Then with a deep breath, he stepped to the edge and jumped down from the ship into thigh deep water and waded ashore. His tall figure caught Thorsten's eye as Bjorn strolled up the beach towards him. Recognition hit him like a hammer pounding on his chest. A little older and about two and a half feet taller, but yes, he could see his long lost son was in there walking towards him. A fine young man now, all grown like a young pine tree. Thorsten's heart fluttered with shock, excitement and relief all rolled into one. His body began to shake as his breathing quickened.

"Bjorn?" He questioned and then as certainty took hold, Thorsten dropped his axe and set off down the beach to meet the young man. Calling his son's name loud, not caring what others might think of him. "Bjorn! Bjorn!" He called as he ran, tears flowing down his cheeks. At seeing this, Bjorn too couldn't control his emotions any longer. He threw open his arms, tears flowing also and called out to the fast approaching giant.

"Father? Father! Is that really you?" The two men collided and threw their arms out hugging each other so tightly they thought they might crush each other's ribs. Lubeck watched from the tower window. A mix of joy and sadness flowed through him. Freyja touched him on the shoulder.

"He's not there?" She asked. Lubeck dropped his head shaking it solemnly.

"No." He said, his voice croaking and his heart breaking as he spoke. A single tear fell from his eyes landing on the window ledge with a tiny splash. At seeing this mightiest of warriors humanity breaking through his tough steely exterior, Freyja made a silent promise to herself to ensure Lubeck and Hafthor would one day be reunited. She would help in any way she could, but for now, all she could do was hold the formidable Viking in an attempt to ease his pain. Through watery eyes, Lubeck watched increasing numbers of his people greeting loved ones as they alighted from the ships. Freyja's grip around his huge shoulders tightened as she felt his massive frame shake with disappointment. She placed a gentle kiss on one cheek whispering to him that all would be okay one day.

"We will find him. He is alive. I feel it and we will not rest until we have him back with you here, safe and well. Now go down there and show yourself. We have many new mouths to feed." She assured Lubeck as she turned him to face her.

"No, give them this time to themselves. Let them enjoy the moment before I begin dishing out fresh orders and detailing working parties and stuff like that. Tomorrow is soon enough, let them enjoy tonight before reality has to return." He looked out of the Northern window towards the sea.

"There is still a man out there who wanted me in chains so that he could invade a peaceful land for his own gain. His ambitions have cost my family dearly. I have to find this man and right his wrong." Freyja nodded as she agreed with him, gently stroking back his hair and kissing him softly on the lips, she said,

"We will Lubeck, we will. Together we will find this man and he will answer for what he has done." Lubeck, taken aback, couldn't help but to react in kind, embracing her with his powerful arms and pulling their bodies together as they kissed again.

Families celebrated the return of their loved ones throughout the night and into the early hours of the next morning. Not all were quite so happy though. Not all of them had loved ones returned that day. Some, like Lubeck were still missing theirs. These men drank away their sorrows and did their best to rejoice with their colleagues for their good fortune. The celebrations continued all through the night.

Hagar awoke with a heavy head as the sun rose, as did a dozen or so more. Men, women and children had all slept where they had fallen or settled for the night on the beach amongst the dunes. Lubeck looked down upon them from the window of Freyja's chambers in the tower. A warm feeling filled his soul as he stared. He had achieved most of what he set out to. Most of his men were reunited with their families and loved ones. There were still a few, like himself that had not been so fortunate as yet. He knew that his path would lead him away from this place in search of his own son and his heart once again saddened. Lubeck liked it here. The time he had spent over the last two years building his fleet and army, had been good times in between the raids and fighting. He now commanded some of the finest warriors that he had ever seen. They were well trained and disciplined with superior armour and weaponry. No one could stand in their way, but now, as he watched them slowly awakening below, he knew that he couldn't ask any more of them. They had served him well without question and now they were reaping their rewards. A soft moan came from behind him. Lubeck looked over his shoulder to see Freyja's naked figure stirring in her bed. Guilt thumped his stomach and he dropped his head with shame. Thoughts of his wife raced through his head. What would she think? Would she ever forgive him? How can he face his son Hafthor after last night?

"And why should she not forgive you Lubeck?" Freyja's voice drifted over to him as he battled with his conflicting feelings. "You have not wronged her." Lubeck sighed and turned to face her. He leant back against the window ledge and shook his head.

"You're in here again aren't you?" He said tapping the side of his head with his finger.

"I couldn't really help it. Your guilt has raised your thoughts so high; I bet Agatha can hear them down there." Freyja replied nodding towards the window. "It troubles me to think that you regret last night." She continued.

"Regret? No, feeling as though I have betrayed my wife….." Lubeck paused and dropped his head once more. Freyja stepped from the bed and walked over to him.

"Your wife died Lubeck. I have seen that in your thoughts. I couldn't see it before because you were so focused on our quest, but last night, seeing everyone so happy, together once more. Your thoughts returned to her. They were loud and I couldn't help but hear them. You can't betray a memory." Lubeck frowned, wrestling with the feelings of guilt stirring inside of him once more. Freyja could see and feel his torment and reached out to him with her mind. She calmed his thoughts and lightened his mood just a little, so as not to alert him to what she was doing.

"I need to ready the Thunder Child for sea." Lubeck announced stepping away from the ledge he had been leaning against. "I have to sail in search of Hafthor and the others still out there somewhere." Freyja sighed as she dropped her head.

"Can it not wait a day or two? These people have just been reunited. Can you not give them some time together before you take their men away again?"

"I'm not taking anyone away. I will sail with just those who, like me, are still missing theirs." Lubeck declared moving over to the bed and beginning to get dressed.

"Then I will come with you." Freyja insisted. Lubeck stared at her before replying.

"What about the spell that holds you here? You can't." Freyja smiled replying.

"Agatha and Morgana are both here now, the spell can be lifted." Or at least that's what I believe.

"Then make it so, I want to sail in two days' time." Lubeck finished getting dressed and left the room descending the stairs to the beach and without a word to anyone, he headed along the coast to where the Thunder Child was berthed. Tarique watched as Lubeck strode away and discretely followed him remaining hidden as only the Saracen could. On approaching the ship, Lubeck saw Antonio rubbing down some slight damage to her hull.

"You not celebrating like the others?" Lubeck asked as he drew near. Antonio stopped what he was doing for a moment to reply.

"I did my share last night, but I wanted to get her repaired and ready to sail, for when you leave." Lubeck remained silent but looked surprised at Antonio's answer. Antonio began to elaborate.

"I figured that you would have need of her again and soon, since Hafthor wasn't among those who returned. She'll be ready in a few of days."

"I need her in two." Lubeck declared.

"Two it is, but I'll need some help." Antonio nodded. Lubeck removed his tunic preparing to help.

"What do you need me to do?" He asked. Antonio laughed as he pointed to a barrel of pitch.

"She needs that spreading over the repairs below decks. Once you have done that you can help me replace the main mast ropes. Some are slightly burned. I wouldn't want them to give when we need them." The two men set about their tasks as the morning sun started to warm the air. Tarique watched for a moment from his unseen vantage point before heading back towards the tower and the rest of the men on the beach.

Later that afternoon Freyja, Agatha and Morgana were all gathered in Freyja's chambers in the tower. They all knew this was the time to remove the spell that bound them all together. Agatha had imprisoned Freyja here for her own safety and Morgana had bound Agatha's powers while she remained here in order to protect Freyja. Jaffa had, unbeknown to the women, hidden himself in close proximity, to defend Freyja and Morgana if Agatha once unbound decided to wreak havoc. Thorsten also had a similar idea, having developed feelings for Morgana. He too had joined the women in the chamber with Malik there for moral support. Looking over Freyja's font and into the mist that formed within, Agatha spoke.

"Who goes first then?"

"I suppose that I'll have to in order to unbind your powers to let you remove the spell that holds Freyja." Morgana pointed out. Freyja agreed and so joining hands around the font, Morgana began to repeatedly recite a short verse. She paused for a moment then said uneasily.

"It's done, I think."

"Really? I don't feel any different. Shall I give it a try?" Agatha suggested. Thorsten tightened his grip on his axe. "Relax. You know, that after all of the help I've given you, you would all trust me by now." She continued. She lifted a single hand, made a small gesture in the air and waited for a moment. Thorsten's face filled with concern as he could feel the handle of his axe becoming hotter and hotter until it reached a point at which he could no longer hold onto it. He dropped it on the floor giving a small yell. Agatha laughed and clapped her hands. "It worked! It worked, wonderful." She exclaimed. Morgana reached out and grasped her arm.

"Now it's your turn." She said gesturing towards Freyja.

"Okay, Okay, no need to get all needy now is there?" Agatha closed her eyes and muttered inaudibly to herself. A moderate wind blew through the chambers momentarily and then all was still again. "There, it's done." She announced.

"How do we know?" Freyja asked.

"Well I guess you'll just have to trust me on that one won't you? Unless you want to take a ship and try to leave right now?" As they stood looking at each other, Finn landed on the window ledge with his usual screech. Freyja moved over to the window and peered out.

"Where did you come from? You are not supposed to be here, you were supposed to be with……" she trailed off not finishing what she had started to say.

"What is it?" Morgana asked.

"I sent him to find Gunter Jorgensen and deliver a message that I tied around his….." she stopped again, looking for the capsule she had tied to his leg. "It's gone. I guess he found him." She said in semi bewilderment. She looked out towards the sea, but saw nothing but sea and sunshine. The bird fidgeted a moment then took to the air again heading out to sea. Freyja returned to the font and peered into it closing her eyes. The others watched on with interest. After a moment, Freyja took a deep breath announcing. "He's here, he'll land tomorrow."

"Who? Who will land tomorrow?" Agatha asked.

"Gunter Jorgensen, with a small fleet of ships." Freyja replied. Thorsten growled and snatched up his axe, not caring about the heat in its handle. His hatred clouding his better judgment. He turned and stormed out of the tower.

"I don't understand. Who is Gunter Jorgensen?" Morgana enquired in bewilderment.

"Lubeck's father and Thorsten has sworn to kill him." Answered Agatha. With that Morgana fled from the room in pursuit of Thorsten. Agatha laughed a little as the absurdity of the situation dawned on her.

"Do you think that you had better tell Lubeck?" She asked, already knowing the answer. Freyja said nothing in reply, simply frowning at her sibling and exiting the tower in search of Lubeck. From a place of concealment, Jaffa moved silently out of the chamber and descended to the beach below, where he met with his fellow countrymen and informed them of what he had just overheard. Thorsten's initial anger had subsided by the time Morgana tracked him down. He sat by the dunes fidgeting with the sand in frustration as he thought about what he had just been told. Morgana sat on the sand beside him and tentatively began to talk.

"I know what you have sworn to do, but time has changed things don't you think? You and Lubeck have a great bond between you now. You are more than mere friends you are more like brothers now, brothers in arms if nothing else. You have suffered, fought and bled together as you have with Tarique and the others. Your son has been returned to you as Lubeck promised he would. Gunter did some bad things, in grief, but he is coming now to find his son. With him comes a small army. Do you want to die at his hands? Or maybe even Lubeck's? If you attempt to kill his father, Lubeck may well intervene and one of you will most probably die. Do you really want to destroy all that has been built and achieved here?" Thorsten grunted aggressively, but he knew that she spoke the truth, though this did nothing to ease his torment. His blood lust for revenge and his loyalty to his friends and colleagues were at loggerheads pulling him in all directions.

"What would you have me do?" He asked.

"Make peace with yourself; put your past where it belongs, in the past. Put it behind you and look to your future. You have just been reunited with Bjorn, think of him. If you follow this path, you may end up losing him again. He has just got his father back, surrounded by friends. A new life awaits. Put this oath behind you and look to a bright new future with Bjorn, and maybe a woman, perhaps…." She faded off. Thorsten stared at her, knowing that all she had said was true. Until a few moments ago he had been the happiest he had ever been. The joy he had felt being together with his son again, was something that he thought he would never again experience. But Lubeck had been good to his word and not just Bjorn, but many others had been recovered from these slavers and the slavers themselves all but wiped out. Such an Earl, he had never served before.

"The Gods mock me! Never have I been so blessed and cursed at the same time." He snarled.

"Then make peace Thorsten, make peace and enjoy what the Gods have bestowed upon you. Make a home here for you and Bjorn. Take a wife and sow the seeds of a future for you both." Morgana begged him.

"A home, a future, a wife?" Thorsten thought for a moment before a smile broke across his face. Morgana returned his smile, jumped to her feet, threw her arms around the big man and kissed him passionately before instructing him.

"Think hard Thorsten, choose well." With that she hurried away across the beach and returned to the tower. Thorsten sat stunned by her words and actions, but his smile broadened as he stood and walked off in search of his son Bjorn.

Freyja found Lubeck a little way along the coast, working on the Thunder Child with Antonio. The grave expression on her face told him that something was wrong. Antonio stopped work and made an excuse to leave them alone for a while.

"What troubles you?" Lubeck enquired putting down his tools and wiping his hands clean as Freyja approached.

"Your father is approaching with a small fleet of ships. He will be here by morning–" "How did he find us?" Lubeck interrupted. Freyja dropped her head still further.

"I sent Finn to inform him of your… our plight. I hoped he might help and it appears that he has answered."

"And this is why you look so worried?" Lubeck asked.

"No it's…" Freyja paused for a moment and Lubeck threw her a questioning look. Freyja fidgeted uncomfortably before continuing. "It's just that Thorsten has sworn to kill him for destroying his homestead, when Gunter sought revenge following your death."

"I can't let that happen. I will have to have words with the big ox before my father arrives." Lubeck sighed a long and heavy sigh.

"And if he won't listen? What then? Will you fight? Will you banish him? Will you…." Freyja stopped biting her lip with frustration.

"I will have words with him I said." Lubeck repeated with a new hardness in his voice. Freyja remained silent and Lubeck returned to his work without another word. Freyja turned to walk away, as she did, she paused, picked up an off cut piece of wood that lay on the ground nearby and hurled it at the warrior's back. It struck Lubeck across the back of his head causing him to drop the tools he had just picked up. "Ouch!" He yelled and turned to see Freyja already running away in the direction of the tower. He rubbed his head as he began to laugh.

"I think that one will need a slightly more delicate manner when discussing important issues." Antonio remarked as he returned to continue with the work at hand. Then with a broad smile and a quick look at the back of Lubeck's head, Antonio retrieved the tools Lubeck had dropped and the two men continued to repair the ship. Both laughing at the recent events.

The following morning brought a scene on the horizon that filled the men's hearts with both joy and dread. Five Viking long ships in full sail headed directly for the Island. Most of the men gathered on the shoreline to watch them as they approached. Horns sounded from the small fleet to announce their presence, indicating that their intentions were peaceful. Hagar raised a hand and a horn was sounded in reply. Lubeck leaned on the window ledge of Freyja's chambers and observed the fleet's progress. Feelings of joy began to swell inside and he couldn't help but smile. Thorsten sat on the dunes watching, tense with indecision. Malik, Tarique and the others all formed an informal welcoming committee on the beach to greet Gunter once he was ashore. The ships rolled in on the gentle breakers and their bows cleared the water as they bit into the sand. Sails came down and the first few crewmen dropped to the shoreline to secure the vessels. One by one, fierce looking Northmen dropped onto the beach all armed with swords, axes and spears. Each with a colourful shield strapped across his back. Their furs replaced, due to the increased heat, with chain mail over a light weight tunic. Their helmets covered most of their faces presenting an intimidating appearance of a faceless enemy. Hagar wondered down to the waters' edge to greet their leader as he too dropped from the bow of the largest ship. He was a big man, taller than Lubeck, but not as tall as Thorsten, no one was as tall as Thorsten. He, like Lubeck was heavily built with large well developed muscular arms and chest. He was an older man with greying hair and beard, but perhaps even more intimidating in appearance than his younger crewmen. Hagar bowed his head in respect and offered a hand in friendship. Gunter paused a moment surveying his surroundings before tentatively offering his in return.

"I am Hagar, Loyal servant and friend to Earl Lubeck who leads this settlement." Hagar announced. Gunter laughed as he replied.

"Earl Lubeck is it? My son has delusions of grandeur does he?" A murmur rolled around the beach as all within earshot were shocked to learn that this foreboding figure was Lubeck's father. A deep Booming voice bellowed from the dunes.

"Lubeck is far from delusional old man. He is our chosen Earl and we all follow him freely and would give our lives for him, as he would for any one of us!" Gunter peered through the crowd to see who would speak to him in such a way.

"Who dares speak to me in this manner?" He roared.

"I do!" Snarled Thorsten, standing to his full height and advancing at pace towards the arrogant elder on the beach, axe in hand and malicious intent carved into his face. Gunter slid a hand to the hilt of his sword in anticipation and a handful of men gathered around him to form a guard.

"Thorsten!" A woman called out with fear in her voice. The giant hesitated then began to move again. "Thorsten wait!" She called again. Again the giant paused. Again he resumed.

"Thorsten!" A deep roaring voice came from the tower. This time the giant stopped dead in his tracks. Everyone on the beach knew whose voice that was. All froze in anticipation of what might happen next. Morgana seized her chance and moved over to Thorsten's side reaching out to take hold of his arm begging him to rethink what he was about to do. An uneasy silence fell upon the scene; only the sound of the sea and the gulls could be heard. It was Malik, of course, who broke the silence and eased the mood.

"Earl Lubeck sounds in good voice this fine morning; shall we go and meet him? Or shall we just shout back to him?" Tarique kicked him on the rump and nodded towards the tower where Lubeck had just emerged onto the beach. The entire congregation bowed their heads in a grand show of respect women and children included. This was obviously done for Gunter's benefit. Something, that didn't go unnoticed by the aging warlord, who turned his gaze towards the advancing Earl. He squinted against the morning sun trying to make out the features of this mighty figure as he continued to walk methodically towards them.

"Can it truly be? By all the Gods, is it truly you Lubeck? My son, after all these years, can it truly be you? You are alive. The Gods be blessed, it is, it is you, Lubeck, it is you!" Gunter gasped. The old man's voice broke into a croaking quiver as the emotions rose to the surface. He let go of his sword hilt and raised his arms to greet his son as he took the final few steps. The two men embraced each other in a bear like hug, laughing with joy.

"It's been so long father. I thought you had forsaken me." Lubeck sighed.

"I thought you were truly dead and I still would be of that ilk if not for a strange hawk that brought news of your fate." Gunter replied looking around at the burned remains of Ballan's ships. "It appears that we are too late to assist in your struggles?"

"This one yes, but I have another that I would very much like your assistance with." Lubeck laughed.

"Just name it my son and I will be only too happy to help." Gunter bellowed for all to hear.

"I need to return to our homelands to rescue Hafthor who is being held by King Akhola." Lubeck announced.

"What? That son of a pig has my Grandson letting me believe all these years that the pair of you had perished? By all the Gods I'll gut him like a fish and bleed him like the pig he is when I get my hands on him, I'll......"

"No father. Akhola is mine when we get there. I will kill him, with my bare hands and watch his life diminish slowly and painfully for what he has done to us." Lubeck interrupted.

"Agreed! When do we sail?" Snapped Gunter.

"Once you are all rested and fed and once my ship is ready to sail. I have a few more repairs to complete before she is ready, a day or two perhaps." Lubeck smiled and headed to return to the tower passing Thorsten a stern look as he did.

Loyalty Can't Be Bought

Gunter's men came ashore and Lubeck's people welcomed them. All were fed and rested, had their fill of ale and overindulged in whatever they wanted for that night. Lubeck introduced Gunter to everyone, Freyja, Morgana, Malik the three Saracens and Thorsten.

"Thorsten has sworn to kill you father. You destroyed his settlement while you were rampaging a few years ago. Your armies killed his people and friends. While he was hunting you, his son was taken as slave and later he was too. I can't blame him for swearing to kill you." Lubeck informed the older man. Gunter gave Thorsten a stony stare momentarily before addressing the big man.

"I hope your oath can wait until I have helped retrieve my grandson and returned him to his father. Once this is done and I'm still living, I will meet you in combat so that you can attempt to kill me. If that is what you would desire?" He offered. Thorsten growled deeply in his chest and Gunter took this to be his answer. "Ok then. I'll do my best to stay alive long enough to let you attempt to kill me afterwards. Agreed?" Gunter spat into his palm and held it out to Thorsten. Thorsten curled his top lip in a snarl, and returned the gesture. The two men shook on it as Gunter announced. "Then it's agreed. I'll stay alive long enough to let you endeavour to kill me once my grandson is returned." Lubeck shook his head in frustration and thumped his fist weekly on Thorsten's chest. Then as the group sat down to eat, Gunter showed an interest in the three

Saracens. "Do you trust these men with their strange ways?" He asked Lubeck quietly. Lubeck laughed as he replied.

"I trust them with my life, as I do all of my followers. Thorsten there is my first mate aboard my ship. He is my second in command when we go into battle and he is more than just my friend, he is like a brother to me."

"It will be a shame for me to kill him then when the time comes." Gunter sighed as he passed a piece of chicken into his mouth hungrily.

"That's not going to happen, one way or another you two are going to sort this out before it comes to that. I don't want to lose either of you. So this has to be sorted before that point." Lubeck answered with a gruff and assertive tone.

"The man has sworn to kill me Lubeck, what can I do about that except defend myself and kill him when he tries?" Gunter replied in protest.

"What makes you think you can kill him? He's huge, strong and fast with it. You're getting old and you haven't been in battle for over a year now if I'm correct? When we go up against Akhola, you may not survive, I might not survive, none of us might survive." Lubeck's voice was becoming irritated. Gunter raised an eyebrow as he gestured towards Thorsten.

"Is he coming to help us when we sail?"

"No. I will only be accompanied by those who have not been reunited with their loved ones. Those that have been blessed enough to have theirs returned, I cannot ask them to risk all for my personal quest." Lubeck replied sorrowfully.

"Shame, if he's as good a warrior as you say he is, he will be missed when the fighting starts. What about them?" Gunter sighed, gesturing towards the three Saracens. Lubeck sighed heavily.

"Father, I don't lead by ordering men to fight for me like slaves. Any man who accompanies us on this quest will do so as a free man and of his own choice."

"Will you have enough to man a single ship then?" The older man laughed.

"I only need a single ship. The Thunder Child is enough to accomplish rescuing Hafthor." Lubeck replied settling back as he drank a little ale. Gunter on the other hand was not so comfortable with the thought of just his own five ships and one from his son. Akhola has a huge army; the odds did not look favourable at all. "Relax father. I know your concerns, but my ship is the finest you have ever seen. She is capable of destroying a stronghold without ever being in danger, sitting a half mile off shore. Trust me, my Saracens have passed some of their secrets of war and devices to me and the Thunder Child carries them. Plus I have a little witch at hand to help if needed." Gunter did not reply. He frowned at his son momentarily before raising a tankard of ale and taking a large gulp. Then he smiled, whatever tomorrow would bring, tonight he was going to enjoy his long lost son's company. He stretched out his arms and once again embraced his offspring with small tears filling his eyes. Nothing would spoil this moment for him. Tomorrow they would talk again about rescuing Hafthor, but tonight, tonight was a time to rejoice.

The morning found Gunter's men readying their ships. Supplies were loaded and minor maintenance carried out. Some town folk from the nearby village approached the tower and were met promptly by Malik and Tarique. A discussion ensued and grew louder as it appeared the villagers were disgruntled about something.

"I think I know what that is about. Those horses the Saracens rescued a while back I bet." Thorsten commented to Hagar.

"Shall we inform Earl Lubeck?" Hagar asked. Thorsten looked to the tower as he searched for Lubeck's whereabouts.

"No need, he already knows, see?" He pointed to the big door as it opened.

"I swear that man has eyes in the back of his head or he can see the future or something." Hagar responded.

"No, but the next best thing, Freyja sees everything doesn't she?" Thorsten said in reply, heading towards the quarrel as he spoke. The villagers stopped their objections, stunned into silence by the sight of the giant striding towards them. Malik sighed in anguish as Thorsten hoisted his axe onto his right shoulder in an intimidating manner. Lubeck touched him on the shoulder as he passed, assuring him that there was no need for violence. Thorsten had been right, the villagers were complaining about their horses being stolen and now they were unable to harvest their crops without them.

"This is not a problem. I will gladly pay you for them. What is their worth?" Lubeck asked in a light hearted manner. A young man with anger in his voice replied.

"Your gold can't harvest our crops. We need our horses back. If you don't return them, we will take them back by force." Thorsten stepped in front of the youth.

"Go ahead; you're welcome to them, just as soon as you get past me." He said in a very threatening tone.

"Thorsten, there's no need for bad feelings here." Lubeck countered as he turned to the older man in the group. "I take it you are the one with a brain? We borrowed your horses because we needed them more than you at that time. Things have changed since then. However, I would like to purchase said horses, for a fair price. I am also willing to let you borrow them, so as you can harvest your crops. As soon as this is done, I want them back."

"They're our horses, you have no right—" The young man was cut short by his elder.

"I'm not a warrior such as you clearly are. None of us in the village are. We know that to fight you over this would most likely result in many deaths, most probably ours and our village being put to the torch. But without our horses, we can't harvest our crops, which means we can't produce the food we all enjoy, you included. We need our horses all year round to plough, sow and harvest." The young man grew agitated as he watched Lubeck thinking deeply upon what he had just heard.

"Just give us our horses back!" He shouted, stepping forward in a menacing manner. A loud smack rang out and the young man fell backwards and landed on his backside on the floor. Lubeck shook his head as he raised his arm gesturing for everyone to calm down.

"Thorsten, help the young man to his feet will you? I apologise for my big friend, he gets a little over protective at times." Lubeck said in an attempt to suppress the rising tensions. The elder nodded in acceptance, turning to the young man and indicating for him to do the same. The young villager did as indicated to his disgruntlement. "I have a problem of my own to deal with." Lubeck began again. He then proceeded to explain what was about to unfold with regards to the forthcoming war across the sea. The elder listened intently and when Lubeck had finished, he replied.

"I understand your problem, but fail to see how this affects us in any way."

"Because if we fail, then Akhola will send a fleet of ships here to destroy what remains of our settlement. I dare say that he will not discriminate between us and you, do you understand now?" Lubeck replied watching the villagers. As the elder villager considered what he had just been told, Gunter joined the group. He made his way over to Lubeck and quietly whispered into his ear. Lubeck nodded in agreement then addressed the villagers once more. "We will pay you for the horses as I have already said and at a fair price. We will then let you borrow them for the time it takes to complete your harvest. We will then require most of them back to carry out our task. You can retain the rest to complete any other work on your farms. Once we return, the Gods willing, we will bring with us more horses for you to keep and work your lands."

"And if you don't return?" The elder asked,

"Then you have far more to be concerned about than a few horses." Lubeck replied in a sombre tone. The elder thought for a time about Lubeck's offer. Then nodding slowly he replied,

"It's not a perfect solution, but it is acceptable to me." Malik was dispatched to gather the horses for the villagers to return to their farms.

The two leaders shook hands and then Lubeck addressed the elder again.

"Before you go. Are there others like this one in your village?" He asked looking at the younger man who had shown such fire and readiness to fight.

"What do you mean? Young and healthy with no brain and a temper?" The village elder replied mockingly. Lubeck laughed in response but continued.

"Yes, but he has spirit. I could have use for such youths to join us on our task. In the long run, they would be helping your village if they joined our ranks and help boost our numbers."

"We have many such youths, but they are farmers not warriors. I fear they would be killed very quickly and not aid you much on the field of battle." The elder replied.

"The greater our numbers the better our chances of success." Gunter butted in.

"We will provide training and arms for them. As my father said, the greater our numbers the better our chances of success." Lubeck added.

"I will talk to the other elders and ask the young men in the village who, if any would be willing to join your cause. I will not order any of them to help, but I will not stand in their way should they wish to do so." With that, the villagers left, collecting the horses as they did.

"Let's hope they have enough men willing to help, the more we have the better, warriors or not." Gunter added before he addressed Lubeck directly. "Well, let's go and take a look at this ship of yours that you place so much faith in." Lubeck said nothing, but headed along the coast in the direction of the Thunder Child. Gunter followed as did Tarique. It was about noon the following day, as they reached the Thunder Child's berth. Gunter whistled his approval as his eyes fell upon the magnificent ship. Antonio was hard at work finishing off the last few jobs around the upper deck as the group approached.

"Ah Lubeck, good you're here at last. She's all but ready, just a few finishing touches required and she will be as good as new." His eyes looked upon the older figure following close behind. "Oh, who's this then?" He asked raising a smile and wiping his hands clean of the pitch he had been using.

"Antonio, this is my father Gunter Jorgensen, father, this is Antonio. He designed and built the Thunder Child." Lubeck announced introducing them.

"It's a fine ship." Gunter said in admiration of the vessel. Antonio was pleased to receive the praise and proceeded to show Gunter around. The men talked and laughed as the afternoon marched on. Tarique explained how the devices his compatriots had disclosed to Lubeck could hurl a rock, flaming with burning tar and oil across huge lengths, allowing the ship to strike at an enemy from some distance away. The old man was impressed and announced that he could hardly wait to see her in action. It was at this point that Tarique's sharp ears picked out the sound of horns being blown in the distance.

"Lubeck! Someone approaches, we must return to the tower at once." Without question, Lubeck grabbed his sword from where he had laid it earlier and slung it across his back as he ran. Gunter and Antonio followed close behind. As they ran along the cliff tops towards the tower, Tarique pointed to a mass of sails on the horizon. They all paused for breath and looked at the approaching fleet. "There must be more than fifty ships there." Tarique declared.

"And then some. But they look like Long ships, Northmen like us." Gunter added. Drawing on renewed energy, they all sped off again towards the tower and the alarms being sounded in the distance. They ran all night pausing for breath on occasion. By the time they arrived, it was a good way into the next morning and the beach was covered in men dressed for war. Thorsten had instinctively taken charge and his men were positioned strategically along the proposed landing site. Gunter's men had also taken up defensive positions alongside their hosts. Jaffa and Jamal had mounted the cliff tops with a group of archers and Gunter's ships were on their way along the coast with only a few crewmen on each in an attempt to protect them from being burned. By now the approaching ships were well within the bay. Their sails were gathered and their crews were crouched behind brightly coloured round shields lining the upper decks of each vessel. Large dragon and serpent heads adorned each and every bow as they glided majestically into the shallower waters near the shoreline.

"Hello ashore! Hello. We're coming ashore and would be very appreciative if we were not met with hostilities." A voice bellowed out from one of the ships. Hagar moved to reveal himself on the beach, then after a short pause he called back.

"Magnus, Magnus is that you? Is it truly you?" A roar of laughter bellowed out from the ship nearest the shoreline.

"By all the Gods, mother was right. My scrawny little brother IS still alive after all!" As he spoke, Magnus jumped down from his ship and landed in the waist deep water with a splash. Then dragging his feet against the water, he made his way up to the beach and stood hands on hips displaying no ill intent. Thorsten and a large group of men advanced down the beach towards Magnus and Hagar. Immediately, Two dozen armed Norsemen dropped from their ships and formed a guard around their leader, shields up and swords drawn. Archers took up positions at the bows of every ship within range of the beach and the remaining ships sat a little way out, moved closer to shoreline with the heaving of oars and splashing of water. All had happened without a single command and within seconds of Thorsten's advance. Magnus raised an arm to stand his men down, just as a horn sounded from the top of the cliffs. Everyone looked up to see

Lubeck, Gunter and Tarique making their way breathlessly down to the beach to join them. Antonio had remained with Jaffa and Jamal, who together with the rest of their archers, had at the first sign of aggression from their visitors, notched arrows and drawn them ready to let fly. Waving a hand as he caught his breath from the run along the cliff tops, Antonio indicated the archers to stand down for now, but just in case, Antonio too, picked up a bow and notched an arrow to make ready if needed. Magnus now pushed his way through his guards and stepped towards his younger brother with a broad grin on his face. Throwing out their arms, the brothers hugged slapping each other on the back. As Lubeck, Gunter and Tarique approached, Magnus ceased greeting his brother and dropped to one knee.

"Lord Jorgensen." He declared slamming his right fist against his chest in salute. "I did not know you were here my Lord." He continued. Gunter stopped alongside Hagar and indicated for Magnus to get to his feet. Magnus's men raised their heads from the bow of respect they had all adopted on seeing their Earl kneel in front of King Rogan's right hand.

"Earl Magnus, to what do we owe the pleasure of your company? And with such a large fleet?" Gunter enquired with joviality in his tone.

"I have come to the aid of my brother Hagar at our mother's request my Lord." Magnus replied.

"As I, to aid my son Lubeck here." Gunter responded gesturing towards Lubeck with one hand. "Lubeck is the appointed Earl here, and the Gods saw fit to reunite us after many years of me believing him dead." Magnus turned his eyes on Lubeck asking,

"Lubeck Jorgensen? The one they call the Valkyrie?" He bowed his head in respect and then asked, "Earl Lubeck, will you grant us leave to come ashore and discuss the matters at hand?" Lubeck nodded and Magnus gave the command. An audible sigh of relief swept across the beach as all stood down from their defensive position and assisted in the landing of Magus's men. Magnus joined Lubeck, Gunter and the others in Freyja's chambers. Lubeck introduced Magnus to her and her sister Agatha. Morgana entered the room followed by Thorsten moments later and moved to the far side of the room to sit with Malik and Antonio to listen to forthcoming discussion.

"It's a fine council we have here. Let's hope we can make decisions quickly and get on with the task at hand before we all grow too old and weary." Noted Gunter as proceedings began.

"Agreed" said Lubeck standing to deliver the tail of recent events and what is believed to have become of their remaining loved ones. When he reached the part about Akhola's ambitious plans, Magnus became agitated.

"Akhola's lands border mine and my lands are a long way from King Rogan's strong hold. Though he is the sovereign I serve. If we were to strike first, it would be an act of war. Does Rogan support such an action?" Magnus enquired.

"Rogan is unaware of Akhola's plans, something we need to remedy somehow. In the meantime, we need to strike first and stop or at least slow Akhola down before he marches on Rogan's kingdom." Gunter announced. Magnus sighed before answering.

"I have fifty five ships with me, another eighty at home. You I see, only have five ships with you and Lubeck has how many?"

"I have only one ship that will sail with us." Lubeck replied. Magnus snorted loudly in disgust.

"One ship? Just one ship? I would have expected a greater contribution than that from an Earl wanting to make war with such a powerful king as Akhola."

"The ship is magnificent and very large. Such a ship I have never seen the likes of before and it's a ship that is worth at least ten of yours." Gunter snapped raising his voice at Magnus. Magnus growled his disapproval then continued with his view on things.

"I have one hundred and thirty five ships in all, once we make landfall in my home lands. Gunter adds five more and Lubeck's ship, for all you're boasting, is still just one ship totalling one hundred and forty one ships in total. That gives us around three thousand, five hundred men. Akhola has more than ten thousand men at his disposal. I think it will be a very short fight if we meet him in open battle." On hearing this, Gunter stood to make his point.

"Once we get news of Akhola's intent to Rogan, I am sure he will support our cause and send men from the North to meet Akhola and drive him back to where he came from. Rogan commands some eight thousand men. With his support our forces would be equal, or perhaps even tilted in our favour."

"But how do we get word to Rogan? And how do we know that he will believe us and send aid?" Magnus countered.

"I can help there. I can send word to him as I did to Lord Gunter. Rogan will know of Akhola's intent before we even get close to landing in your homeland Earl Magnus." Freyja interjected.

"Yes, she's right! Her hawk can carry the warning to Rogan and he will join us when we land. I'm sure that he will." Gunter announced excitedly. The discussion continued into the evening, but finally it was decided that Freyja would send Finn as she had before to warn King Rogan of King Akhola's intentions. Gunter's ships and men would join Magnus's fleet along with the Thunder Child and sail for their homeland by the next new moon. If Rogan didn't receive the message or if he didn't come to their aid, by way of their forthcoming actions, war would be declared and Rogan would have no choice but to defend his lands and people from Akhola's invaders. Either way, they should get Rogan's support eventually. They simply hoped they would live long enough to see it.

Preparations began the following morning. Stores were loaded onto the ships, purchased from the nearby village. Swords and axes were sharpened and damaged armour repaired. The days passed and the preparations neared completion. It was decided that each chieftain would command his own men but all would work towards the common cause. As Magnus commanded the majority of the assaulting force, he would meet Akhola head on, blocking his path and slowing his advance towards Rogan's territories. Gunter and Lubeck would flank Akhola's forces and force him to defend on three fronts. Lubeck was well versed in engaging foes with much larger forces by now, so Gunter was more than willing to listen and take advice from his son on the best tactics in doing so. Strike from seclusion then disappear before a retaliatory counter could be mounted. Cut their numbers slowly but surely with strike after strike avoiding open combat.

"Hit and run? That doesn't sit well with me son." Gunter said with a sigh.

"I know, but it has been a successful tactic for us these last few years defeating foes much larger in numbers than ours. It is the only way, until King Rogan arrives. Then we can fight in open battle as you would prefer." Lubeck countered.

Later that day, preparations ceased as a herd of horses were guided down to the beach. Sixty young and middle aged villagers escorted them. Hagar met them and took charge of corralling the animals until they would be loaded prior to sailing. Thorsten discussed with the villagers their reason for being there. Then he informed Lubeck that they had come to join his ranks and bolster his forces. Lubeck accepted their offer and told Thorsten to begin training them immediately. There was no time to waste, they sail in two days. Training would continue during the voyage. This also meant that at least two more ships would be required to ferry them, Three would be better. The men that would have accompanied him on the Thunder Child would now have to be divided between the extra ships to ensure they all got there alive. Work began and extra ships prepared.

The day arrived. The Thunder Child glided into the bay like a leviathan, followed by three more smaller ships. All eyes turned to witness the splendour and magnificence of the huge ship. The bay now filled with sixty four ships, full and ready for war. Lubeck walked out onto the beach accompanied by Freyja and Agatha. Tarique as always, a few steps behind. A small fishing boat waited to ferry them across the bay to the Thunder Child as soon as they were ready. Most of the rescued families gathered to wave them off. Lubeck sighed with a heavy heart as he surveyed them.

None of his men were with them, none had turned out to see them on their way.

"Are you ready then?" Magnus asked, preparing to join his own ship. Lubeck nodded in silence and taking Freyja's hand headed towards the fishing boat. Gunter slapped him across the back and they all began to climb aboard. A horn sounded on the beach. They all turned to see what was happening. To Lubeck's delight and Freyja's relief Thorsten marched ahead of more than eighty men in full battle dress and armed with the enchanted weapons Freyja had supplied them some time ago.

"Gurlemek!" Tarique uncharacteristically called out. A roar emitted from them, as the Gurlemek soldiers advanced in unison. Their armour reflecting the bright sun as it clanked rhythmically with each step they took.

"And so the Thunder Comes." Freyja whispered with relief, gripping Lubeck's hand tightly.

"What's this?" Magnus enquired.

"I think our numbers and chances of success have just increased." Gunter suggested with a wry smile.

"Were you going to leave without us Earl Lubeck?" Thorsten called out in question, as he drew closer. Lubeck laughed and shook his head.

"I cannot ask this of you my friends. You all have your lives back, your families. I cannot ask that you risk all to follow me one more time into battle and a war we possibly won't return from." He replied.

"Without you, none of us would have anything. There's not a man here who wouldn't follow you now. So get your ships out of the way, so that ours can come in and pick us up." Thorsten yelled as he pointed to the open sea. Six more ships waited patiently for free water, to enter the bay and pick up their crews.

"They look the part, very professional. If they can fight as impressively as they look, we could really use them." Magnus commented surveying the soldiers on the beach. Lubeck roared the orders and the fleet began to move out as the fishing boat dropped each one to their respective ship. Thorsten turned to address his troops, dismissing them to board the ships once they came in. A tall young man stood close by, dressed in a similar manner to himself.

"You take care on this venture son. Stay close to me and do as I say. When war is unleashed, you stay close to me, do you hear me?" Thorsten instructed him. Bjorn nodded and smiled at the big man.

"I will father. I'll stay by your side at all times." The ships came in and the crews began to embark. Morgana kissed Thorsten and hugged Bjorn before returning to the rest of the women folk and children. Some older men also remained and just a few able bodied adolescent youths. Tears flowed as the women watched their men sail away beyond the horizon, all praying to their Gods for their safe return.

Outnumbered

For two days the fleet headed North with dual purpose. The main one being the safe return of family members. Lubeck and Gunter searching for Hafthor. Hagar and Magnus searching for Hagar's daughter Anna. Other crew men also searched for missing loved ones. Lubeck still insisted that if they lived, he would return them all. The other, to stop Akhola overthrowing Rogan. It was going to be a while before they would make landfall in Magnus's homelands. So training of the villagers had to continue, as well as practice for those who were already trained. Everyone had to be at their very best when they arrive. Lubeck took up his hooked weapon, twirled it around in his hands as one would a quarter staff or hand bow.

"You still carry that thing? I have never understood what it is about it that makes you think it is more effective than a good sword, which you also have." Malik enquired with curiosity. Lubeck placed an empty barrel on top of a full one in the middle of the main deck. The crew gathered to see what he was doing. Then, taking fifteen paces away from the newly placed target he addressed Malik directly instructing him to watch. Lubeck hoisted the weapon above his shoulder holding it like a javelin. He hurled it at the barrel. The spear like head sunk into the wooden target, knocking it from its base. Lubeck then walked over and placed a foot on the barrel while he retrieved the weapon, pulling it free. Then using the hooked appendage, he caught the edge of the barrel and tossed it into the air. The wooden target sailed upward some twenty feet before it began to descend.

Lubeck quickly twirled the weapon around and as the barrel reached head height; he swung the weapon round fast striking the target hard with the vicious mace at the opposite end, smashing the barrel and cascading shards of wood and buckled metal across the deck.

"It's very versatile is it not?" Lubeck asked as the crew applauded. "It's a spear, a hook, a mace and a staff all in one and I can quickly change between at will, depending on the situation in which I find myself. I can use it on foot as I just have or I can use it mounted from a horse. My sword is a good weapon when used correctly, but this, this is much more versatile and durable." Malik raised his eye brows and sighed in agreement.

"That's all very good, but we now have one less barrel to store fresh water in when we make a land the day after tomorrow." Antonio jovially reported. Lubeck dropped his head and laughed with the rest of the crew.

"I didn't think of that, do you think you can fix it?" He asked. Roars of laughter rolled around the deck as Antonio picked up the largest pieces of the shattered barrel, shrugged and tossed them overboard.

Gunter watched his son from his ship nearby. Many times they had rode into battle together in the name of King Rogan. Each time they had faced greater and greater challenges. This time however, was going to be extremely difficult. The odds were against them, they would be outnumbered and could easily be overwhelmed if they were not careful. Akhola was no push over. He was an accomplished warrior and his men were war hardened from years of fighting and raiding to the South. Gunter feared that this might be one battle too many and that having just found his son, he could easily lose him again within weeks. Jaffa touched him on the shoulder.

"There's no need to worry my Lord. Lubeck is a mighty warrior, like none I have ever seen before. Our weapons and armour are from the Gods themselves, gifted to us by Freyja. No blade or arrow can pierce this armour. Also, I and my fellow countrymen watch over him day and night." Gunter smiled and returned the pat on the shoulder.

"Let's pray to the Gods that you are right. I have seen my son in battle. He is fierce and skilful, but he is also reckless at times. I fear that this recklessness may cost him his life one day." Gunter replied with anxiety in his voice.

"He has many with him who would give their lives for his. He has Tarique to influence his thoughts and keep him from recklessness my Lord. Your thoughts should be on keeping your own skin safe." Jaffa reminded the aging General. Gunter smiled as he nodded in agreement.

"I'll do my best to do that." He chuckled.

King Rogan rested in his strong hold as his queen entered bringing him some refreshment. The aging King looked tired as he graciously accepted. He stretched his arms and clenched his fists, as he asked her,

"Am I getting so old my love?"

"So old, no, but you're not a young man any more. Even Gunter is getting old these days and he is younger than you dear. But to me, you will always be my heroic warrior that brought peace to these lands and gave us a secure home to grow old in." Rogan smiled at her as he replied.

"So I am old then, you just told me so.? This trouble stirred up by Gunter's rampage over the last few years. Do you think that our peaceful lives will come to an end because of it?" Queen Tanya smiled shaking her head.

"Not because of Gunter's actions, but maybe by another's." The foreboding in her voice gave rise for concern to Rogan.

"What do you mean by that?" He asked her. Tanya lowered her eyes and unrolled a scroll of parchment handing it to her husband. Rogan recognised the parchment; it was the same as the last piece he had seen some months earlier.

"I take it we have had a visit from that peculiar bird again?" He asked. Tanya nodded silently as Rogan took the parchment and began to read.

"Can it be true?" Tanya asked.

"It carries Gunter's seal at the base. I can only assume it is. If this bird took five days to get here, then Gunter and Earl Magnus should be landing within the week." Tanya looked mournful and worried. She moved close to her husband and clutched his arm.

"If Akhola is indeed planning to overthrow you my love, what are we going to do about it?" Rogan patted her hand reassuringly, smiled, sighed and then told her,

"Don't worry yourself my dear, Akhola may be many things, but to invade our lands and openly challenge my rule would be an act of stupidity, and one thing Akhola is not, is stupid. I will send out scouts to report back to me on his activities. If they find that my opinion of Akhola is incorrect and that he is in fact stupid enough to attempt to overthrow us, then I will gather all of my Earls and rally as many men as we can, to defend our homes. The royal guard has two hundred men and our regular army numbers over five thousand. If the worst happens, I can meet him head on at the Outland Pass between Magnus's lands and our own. I can hold him there until the other Earls can gather their men and join us. With their aid and numbers, our forces should amount to some eight to ten thousand. Akhola could theoretically muster about the same number I believe. I cannot march South without good reason, or that may bring open war upon us and I will not risk open war with Akhola without due course." The Queen gripped her husband's arm tighter and spoke with an uncharacteristic hardness to her voice.

"You dare not risk open war without due course? What of Akhola? I think my husband, that Akhola brings open war to you. Gunter would not lie about such things. I do not believe that he would send a warning like this without being sure. He knows the consequence of what such a message would bring. I for one believe your old friend and guardian. I believe that open war comes our way and if you do not act quickly, Akhola will be sitting in our Great Lodge with you dead and me chained like a slave destined to serve him for what remains of my life. You need to act, not ponder. Gunter and Magnus are attempting to intervene. They would not do so without being certain. Open your eyes my love, open war is upon us and you need to act." King Rogan sighed heavily and pondered a little more before he replied.

"I will send the scouts. If they confirm Gunter's warning, I will ride out to meet him at the Pass as I have already stated. While I am waiting for their reports however, I will send word to the other Earls to gather their men and make ready for war. If it comes to it, I will block Akhola's path at the Outland Pass with the five Thousand men from our regular army and hold him there until the other Earls arrive."

"And what if they don't?" Tanya spat back at him. Rogan raised his eyebrows and sighed.

"In that case my love. It will be a very short campaign, outnumbered at least two to one perhaps more. Gunter and Magnus sail here with seventy ships, which equates to almost two thousand men. Magnus will be able to gather another two thousand or so once he lands. They will try to stop Akhola before he crosses Magnus's lands." Tanya took a sharp breath.

"If they do that, they will surely be slain. Will you not ride out to join them? Will you let them face Akhola alone? Or will you one last time, don your armour and ride to the aid of your oldest friend and ally?" Rogan sighed, kissed her sweetly on the cheek and without further conversation, he left the room.

Three horsemen sat aloft a clifftop watching the impressive fleet of long ships entering the waters bordering King Akhola's Western most lands. This was exactly why their King had dispatched them. They dug in their heels to coax their mounts into a canter. Simultaneously, an arrow hit the first rider square in the chest knocking him from his horse. His two colleagues, alerted by this, kicked harder to speed away as fast as they could. A second arrow hit another in the thigh. The rider cried out in pain, but remained in his saddle and continued to ride with blood streaming from his wound. The riders weaved their way through the scrub and brush, ducking under low branches of the thin tree line. As they emerged, a Saracen leapt from a rocky outcrop as they passed. His two slender swords cutting deep into one riders flesh and knocking him to the ground as his horse continued to run. The third rider paused a moment to look back for his fallen comrade. At seeing him being cut down by the Saracen killing machine that had unseated him, the rider chose to hurry on. He turned his horse and kicked it hard. As the animal sprang into a full gallop, another arrow hit him between the shoulder blades felling him and allowing his horse to continue rider less. Now the Saracen moved from his first victim to the newly felled scout laying on the ground gasping for breath. He raised one of his slender swords and quickly brought it down, thrusting it deep into the wounded man's chest. With a sickening chocking sound, blood spouted from his mouth as the scout died. Tarique pulled his sword from the dead man and wiped the blade clean of blood as Malik emerged through the trees carrying a bow.

"Your aim needs to improve my friend. This one almost got away. If he had, our presence here would be known by now and we would have to face Akhola's forces on our own without the aid of the rest of Magnus's men." Tarique stated.

"I thought that I had done okay?" Malik slumped as he protested.

"Okay yes. Well, no. Okay is not good enough my friend. Well is the only standard we accept. You must improve." Tarique corrected him. With that he took hold of the body and dragged it into the scrub concealing it. Malik did likewise to another and then they both retrieved the third. Once the bodies were hidden, Malik asked Tarique.

"What about their horses? If they return to their settlement, won't that alert them to our presence?"

"Yes it would, but you don't know horses do you?" Tarique smiled at his comrade. Malik looked confused so Tarique continued to explain. "Horses won't run and run returning to where they are normally kept. They'll run for a mile or so, then slow and finally stop and begin to graze. We'll find them happily feeding a little way down there." Tarique pointed North as he began to move in the same direction.

On the deck of the Thunder Child, Lubeck looked to the clifftops as the fleet moved quietly on.

"I hope our friends are up there doing their job and keeping our presence concealed." He said with concern in his voice.

"I'm sure they are, all of them." Replied Freyja also looking to the clifftops. Lubeck had sent word to the other ships. The three Saracens, the two Mongols and the Oriental along with Malik and Mauro had all been dropped ashore to scout the land and ensure the fleet's approach remained unknown to Akhola. Lubeck knew that scouts would be wondering these lands mapping and reporting all movements back to Akhola as his army advanced towards the Outland Pass. This was where they had to stop him. Though it did not sit well with Magnus, he also had to agree that the pass was the best place to engage Akhola's forces and try to slow or perhaps even stop his advance. The fleet was going to continue North to the upper reaches of Magnus's lands and dock there. It would only be a few days march from there to the Outland Pass. The scouts were also to spread word amongst Magnus's people that he was calling together his forces to drive back an invasion and protect his people. To this end, Magnus had given each scouting party a scroll with orders and his seal to verify that the bearer's message was genuine. Two pairs of scouts had moved inland to spread the word; two pairs scoured the coastline ensuring that the fleet's existence remained unknown to Akhola. Magnus had shown the scouts the arm bands of allegiance his sworn followers would be wearing. This was common practice in the Norse culture, so they should be able to identify friend from foe. Akhola's men would also be wearing loyalty bands, but they would differ from Magnus's. The fleet moved quietly on and their guardians on the land worked hard to follow and remove any possible informants.

Tarique and Malik found the dead scout's horses just as Tarique had foreseen. They coaxed them in and removed their saddles and bridals. They set them loose and allowed them to roam wild. It would be some time before the scouts were missed, as scouts were often out in the field for weeks without returning with any news. If the horses were seen, they would simply be mistaken for wild and no one would be particularly alarmed by this. The saddles and tack were hidden. Then Malik and Tarique mounted their own horses and continued their mission along the coast.

Progress was good and the fleet landed unseen by Akhola as planned. The small bay where a port had been built struggled with such a large number of ships, but with some tight manoeuvring and well thought out planning, the task was finally achieved. Almost two thousand men disembarked from the vessels and made camp for the night. Lubeck, Gunter, Magnus and the others met in one large shelter to discuss the next step. Two hundred men would remain to protect the fleet and rescue whatever they could, should it come under attack. The rest would move out at first light marching at speed to reach the Outland Pass before Akhola. The port elder informed Magnus that he had received reports from further South that Akhola had indeed commenced marching North and had burned some of the Southern settlements as he moved. He had however, not met with much resistance, as most of Magnus's people had packed up and headed North following the call to arms, which Lubeck's scouts had delivered as they too moved North. Word had spread throughout Magnus's lands and the people were rallying to his call.

"Let's hope that enough of them turn up at the pass to give us a fighting chance." Gunter stated to the rest of the group.

"I know my people; they'll be there, but what of your friend, our King? Is there any word from Rogan? Will he join us at the pass? Or do we face Akhola alone?" Magnus grunted as if already knowing these answers and not liking them.

"Nothing has come from King Rogan as yet." Freyja replied, her eyes looking to Lubeck for support.

"I'm sure he will come." Lubeck stated with authority.

"Huh! Perhaps he waits to see if we cut Akhola's forces first, to allow him an easy victory and claim all of the glory for himself." Magnus grunted indignantly. Gunter slammed his fist onto the makeshift table they were seated around, raising his voice as he addressed Magnus.

"Rogan is no coward. He will come, of that I'm sure!" With that he turned and stormed out of the shelter and into the darkness. Lubeck raised one eyebrow as he stared at Magnus, which caused the chieftain to shuffle uncomfortably.

"What? What? I'm only saying what most of us are already thinking." He protested. Thorsten loomed over the disgruntled Earl menacingly as he spoke directly to him.

"Rogan is not my King. I only know of the man. But what I know of him is that he didn't become King by hiding away and letting others do his bidding. Lubeck trusts him and Gunter has served Rogan for many years. If they believe that he will come, that's good enough for me. I will fight with the faith that Rogan's army will flow through the Outland Pass like a mighty wave washing away everything that stands before it. If it takes longer than we hoped for him to arrive, then I will hold the pass until he does, or die trying. I thought as he is your King, that you might have a little more faith in him yourself." Lubeck patted the big man on the back. Thorsten stood tall again, nodded at Lubeck and then also left the shelter.

"He's right you know." Freyja snapped at Magnus as she too left the shelter. Lubeck sighed heavily, shook his head at Magnus then tapped the loyalty band around the disgruntled Earl's upper arm.

"Your men trust and follow you, that's why they swore their allegiance to you and wear your band. You also took an oath, to King Rogan, that's why you wear his band as did I and as does my father. The big ox is right. You should have more faith." Magnus exhaled frowning as Lubeck followed his friends and went in search of his father. Agatha, who had remained silent through all of this, now stepped forward and spoke.

"Rogan will come, this I know. So you should do as the others say and have a little more faith in your King. Lubeck needs you to lead your men. Neither he nor Gunter can do this without your support and I think you know deep down, that you have no choice other than to betray your King and side with Akhola. Your people will soon be safe, having traversed the Outland Pass. Your warriors need to wait there for us while your womenfolk and children move to the North and safety. We all have our own reasons for joining this campaign, but now that we are here together, we must stand as one."

"She speaks the truth brother. We may be outnumbered, at least until King Rogan arrives. But I have fought alongside these men, facing much greater odds than these and always we have emerged victorious. Lubeck has a mind for strategy like no other I have ever seen. He is also possibly the mightiest of warriors. You know him by another name my brother, Lubeck is the Valkyrie." Hagar informed his older sibling.

"The Valkyrie? By all the Gods that makes a difference." Magnus interjected beaming.

"Yes, the Valkyrie, and his warriors are known now as the Gurlemek. In Tarique's tongue this means Thunder." Hagar continued. Magnus looked up at his younger brother.

"I have heard this name mentioned across the seas. The Ports of Ibis and Altear were both sacked by these Gurlemek. I've heard said that they are demons that cannot be killed. Weapons glance off them, leaving them unharmed. I've heard that they are protected by a witch and they ride the seas on the back of a giant fire breathing dragon. Old wives tales, stories to frighten children nothing more." Magnus retorted with some distain. Agatha slammed her fist down on the table as she addressed Magnus.

"No. Think about it. Lubeck has lost but a handful of men in total throughout all of his raids, because of their blessed armour gifted them by the Gods. The fire breathing dragon, people speak of is the Thunder Child and the fire, is the burning tar covered rocks that are hurled from the Saracens devices mounted front and rear on her main deck. however the Gurlemek are not protected by a witch, Oh no, they got that bit wrong. The Gurlemek are protected by three witches." She objected and with that, she raised her hands and Magnus was thrown across the shelter like a leaf on the wind.

"Agatha! Cease at once!" Hagar commanded in a loud and clear voice. Agatha laughed, announcing,

"I'll go and find my little sister." She said heading for the door. Before she passed through it though, she turned to look at Magnus, "BOO!" She snapped. Magnus flinched and brought his arms up in way of defence.

Agatha laughed as she finally left the shelter. The two men inside could hear her laughter fading as she walked away into the darkness.

"What company you keep little brother." Magnus said climbing back to his feet. "If these friends of yours are indeed these fearsome Gurlemek of which I have heard, then this changes things quite considerably. We might be outnumbered almost three to one, but if these men are indeed the demons that nightmares are made of and Lubeck is in fact the Valkyrie….." he chuckled to himself, "And witches too, then we may just stand a chance, with or without Rogan's help."

The Morning sun made the disassembly of the crude shelters that little less tedious. Spirits seemed surprisingly good as everyone made light work of the necessary chores. Soon the amalgamated forces were ready to march and with the sounding of a single horn, they set off with rhythmic footsteps for the Outland Pass. Two days march lay ahead of them, leaving little time for preparations once there. Akhola would reach the Pass in five or maybe only four days if the information their scouts were reporting back was correct. They continued to march without incident, until they reached the Pass.

The Outland Pass was a former riverbed, now covered in lush grass and level footing. The river had been blocked a long time ago by earthquakes and volcanic activity, causing the ground to erupt forming a natural damn. To the North, was now a wide, flooded waterway connecting to fjords and eventually to the sea beyond. To the South, a lush green valley with just a shallow stream where once a wide river flowed. To the East and West rose high cliffs, steep and dangerous to climb. Only the winding gentle slopes of the Northern end of the Pass would bring a traveller up to the waterway beyond and then North to King Rogan's central lands where his strong hold stood, accessible by land or water. Before reaching Rogan's strong hold though, there were two subsidiaries feeding into the main waterway. Lubeck and Gunter both knew of these as did Magnus. They also knew that Akhola knew this too. He could utilise these subsidiaries for his ships, enabling him to transport men behind the Pass. Lubeck's council had agreed to send the Thunder Child accompanied by five other ships, to try and prevent this from happening. Under Hagar's command, they would defend the Northern waterways protecting the backs of the main forces in the Pass. But they would have to take the long way round which would take an extra days travel before the ships would be in place. If Akhola had sent ships to circumnavigate the Pass already, Lubeck's forces could be vulnerable during this time. Lubeck was regretting his decision to have Freyja remain at the port with the rest of the fleet. She had never experienced battle first hand before and he didn't want her to make mistakes under pressure and possibly even get killed. Instead, he had instructed Agatha, who had by way of her service to Ballan via Akhola in the past, a reasonable amount of experience in war. Freyja had the ability to, locally at least, control the weather. This he thought might have been useful to slow Akhola's ships and allow Hagar to arrive first. Akhola's forces were too large for him to transport entirely by ship. Therefore he would have to move the majority of them by land. By doing so, he had to come through the Outland Pass. Here his forces would be funnelled into the three hundred foot wide pass. Here his numbers would not be so effective. That is why they had to stop him here. Akhola would also know this and Lubeck was sure he would be taking steps to ensure he wasn't ambushed and his campaign halted. Lubeck needed information as to Akhola's movements. He needed his scouts to come in and enlighten him on this matter. But where were they?

Akhola was having similar thoughts to Lubeck. His scouts were long overdue for their reports. Suspicion ran through his head. He instinctively felt that something was wrong. Were his movements known to his enemies? His forces had met with little resistance as there were no people in the settlements he had come across. They had all fled. They were forewarned of his approach, which means that someone was out there spying on his movements. Now his scouts were late. Had they fallen prey to his enemy's spies? Whoever his opponent was, he was clever and shrewd, Akhola surmised. The timing of his unknown opponent's moves had left Akhola with little to no choice. His movements known or unknown, he had to press on as it was now too late to change course and try a different tactic. The Outland Pass it was and he would fight his way through if he must. He had almost ten thousand men at his back. The biggest army these lands had ever seen. Who could stand in his way? He would push on regardless. Once through the Pass, he would be well positioned to execute the rest of his plans and become the most powerful ruler in his country's history. Once Rogan was out of the way, no one could stand against his ambitions.

To the South West of the Outland Pass, crouching amongst the forest undergrowth. Jaffa and Mauro watched a group of Akhola's scouts from their secluded position. This was a larger group than they had come across before. Instead of the usual three, there were seven men in this group. The scouts were watching with great interest from their location at the edge of the tree line, where the forest gave way to a large open grassy plain. They studied the movements of the amalgamated forces fortifying positions around the approach to the mouth of the Pass. Jaffa knew that he could not allow these scouts to report back to Akhola as to what they had witnessed. He and Mauro would have to stop them. But there were so many. How could they be sure to take them all and not allow a single one to escape? Jaffa checked his quiver, only three arrows left, Mauro had only two. The last few days had been hard work removing scouting parties as efficiently as they had. Their supply of arrows being now depleted. Not enough remained to take them all from a distance. They would have to get close, close enough to ensure they didn't miss. They also needed to be able to kill the last two with swords or some other close quarter weapon. The pair moved closer trying to increase their options and improve their chances of success. When Jaffa thought they were in their optimum positions, he signalled to Mauro. They loosed their arrows simultaneously. Two scouts fell being hit squarely in their backs by the long slender shafts. The other five scouts scrambled to mount their horses. As they tried, two more arrows struck home killing their targets instantly. Mauro, now out of arrows broke cover and charged at the nearest scout, who was attempting to mount his frightened horse. The animal pranced, making it difficult for the rider to get cleanly into the saddle. Jaffa released his final arrow hurriedly. It flew wide of its intended target, striking the scout in the upper arm instead of his chest. The man cried out in agony as he fell from his saddle landing with a bone crunching thud on the forest floor.

Mauro now caught his intended victim. He grabbed him by the shoulders from behind and pulled him to the ground. Both men falling into a scrambling mass of arms and legs, kicking and punching in all directions. Jaffa advanced onto his stricken target. The man wailed in pain as he attempted to stand. Jaffa placed a foot against the wounded man's chest and pushed him to the ground once more. Now the sound of galloping hooves came thundering through the undergrowth. Jaffa turned to face the direction of the approaching horseman, only to see him strike Mauro across the back with his sword as he rode past at speed heading towards Jaffa. Mauro reeled in pain as he fell to the ground, blood spilling from the deep wound on his back. Jaffa drew a dagger from his belt and threw it at the advancing rider. The rider ducked to one side almost falling from his horse to do so, and the weapon sailed past harmlessly. As the rider regained his balance and drew back his sword in preparation to strike, Jaffa rolled forward and under the attempted blow. Drawing his sword as he did, he rolled and drove the blade deep into the scout that Mauro had been engaged with before he was injured. The man screamed throwing his arms into the air as the blade cut into him. Withdrawing his sword as quickly as he could, Jaffa spun around barely in time to deflect another attempt from the assaulting rider. The horseman thundered past fighting to regain control of his mount in the confines of the forest edge. The wounded scout with an arrow in his arm was now on his feet and running at the unbalanced Saracen. Jaffa made a snap decision, He hurled his sword at the rider catching him in the neck and almost removing his head with the long slender blade. The man fell lifelessly to the ground, his horse running on rider less. As quick as he was, Jaffa was unable to avoid the thrust of the remaining scout's sword. It cut deep into his side knocking him to the ground. Mauro seriously injured, struggled to his feet and lunged towards the scout. This attempt was deflected and the scout drove his sword through Mauro stopping him in his stride. Retrieving his sword from Mauro's lifeless body, the remaining scout turned readying to finish Jaffa. He swung his blade overhead bringing it down on his intended victim. Jaffa caught the blade with his left hand. The sharp steel cut sinew and bone as it progressed two thirds of the way through Jaffa's flesh. He screamed in pain, but managed to grip the arrow sticking out of his attacker's upper arm. He pulled hard and the head of the arrow ripped through flesh and muscle as it came away. The man screamed as pain shot through him. He reeled backwards pulling his sword free from Jaffa's hand. The two men lunged at each other simultaneously. The scout's sword plunged through Jaffa's abdomen and blood spilled from his mouth as he cried out in pain. At the same time, Jaffa drove the arrow he had retrieved, deep into his attacker's chest. With laboured breaths, the two men fell to their knees and limply rolled to one side as they fell into death's grim embrace.

Jamal and the Oriental scout emerged from the forest a little further East. They rode hard across the open plain towards the relative safety of the Pass. Noticing the fortifications being constructed by their allies, their hearts lifted with relief, their lonely mission now over. Jamal had news for Lubeck and was eager to deliver it.

"No sign of the others?" Thorsten asked him as Jamal dismounted.

"No, I haven't seen them in days." Jamal replied passing the reins of his horse's bridal to a nearby former farm hand and hurrying to find Lubeck, his Oriental companion close behind him. After finding Lubeck deep in discussions with Gunter and Magnus, Jamal disclosed everything he had noted about Akhola's movements. Akhola had dispatched ships just as Lubeck had foreseen. His main forces numbered almost ten thousand strong and were only a few days South of the Pass. He continued to inform them that they had encountered three scouting parties during their time out in the wilderness and noted that they would probably be missed by now.

"So he was expecting an attempt to slow or stop him at this Pass then? That's why he dispatched some ships to traverse around the mountains and approach from the rear, to clear the Pass for his main forces. Just as I thought he might." Lubeck hissed with venom in his tone.

"He knows that we're here waiting for him." Gunter added with deep foreboding in his voice.

"No. He knows that someone is here waiting for him, but not who. That is, unless other scouts made it back to Akhola to report our movements?" Magnus commented.

"None that we encountered." Boasted Tarique entering the shelter with a broad grin on his face and Malik hot on his heels. Lubeck greeted them both with relief and joy at seeing them safely returned. "What of Jaffa and the others?" Tarique continued. Everyone in the shelter shook their heads and shrugged.

"Your two groups are the first back, we haven't heard from any of you until just now. Do you have anything more to add to Jamal's report?" Gunter asked the Saracen.

"I would doubt it; we spent more time killing scouts than scouting ourselves." Malik answered before Tarique could draw breath. Tarique slapped him across the back of the head, "AAWWW!" Malik yelled rubbing his scalp with one hand and frowning at Tarique indignantly.

Lubeck couldn't help but chuckle at the pair's antics, but knew that Malik was probably right. Tarique was a very efficient assassin and enjoyed it, perhaps a little too much. However, it was a trait that reassured Lubeck when he knew that Tarique was close.

A disturbance near the mouth of the Pass caught everyone's attention. Men were shouting and arms were rattling as Thorsten's booming voice barked orders. The shelter emptied as its occupants ran to see what caused the alarm. A single rider galloping at speed was crossing the plain closely followed by three of Akhola's scouts. They were obviously unaware of the forces gathered at the Pass. This was a good sign Lubeck thought. If Akhola's scouts were unaware they were there, then Akhola himself was probably blissfully unaware too. As the single Mongol passed the rudimentary perimeter defences, a volley of arrows showered down onto his pursuers. The men fell as their horses stumbled, one crushing it's rider as it fell. The others were dead before they hit the ground, each pierced by as many as six arrows or more. Two of their horses continued to run into the Pass where they were caught and calmed by Magnus's men. The Mongol jumped from his horse and reported to Lubeck panting loudly after his dash for safety. The group returned to the large shelter to listen.

"And the other?" Lubeck asked. The Mongol scout dropped his head shaking it in silence. Lubeck sighed. He hated losing anyone. Now his attention turned to Jaffa and Mauro who were still unaccounted for.

"Don't fret lad. Jaffa is more than capable, I'm sure they'll be back before night fall." Gunter said placing his hand on Lubeck's shoulder.

"Eight scouts went out, only five have returned so far." Lubeck noted.

"So far yes, but by all accounts Akhola is missing many more scouts." Gunter replied.

"I will ride out to find them." Tarique announced

"As will I." Jamal added.

"No! We cannot risk losing you two at this point. Besides Jaffa and Mauro are probably on their way here as we speak." Magnus snapped.

"No. They are both gone. I can feel it. I wish my sister was here as she could tell you for sure. But I sense that their life force is gone. I can't reach them. I can't see them at all. I'm sorry, but they're gone." Agatha said quietly as she approached the group. The group lowered their heads with sadness and a tear fell from Jamal's eye as he fought back the urge to cry openly. Lubeck placed his hand on Agatha's shoulder, asking her,

"Are you sure? Could you be mistaken?" Agatha shook her head as she lowered her eyes.

"I sense that their life force is gone. I can't see or feel anything more. So no, I can't be certain, but I'm pretty sure. Freyja would have been able to tell you for sure with no mistake, but she's not here is she?" Gunter offered some words of solace before turning to Lubeck reminding him.

"These things happen in war son. You know that as well as I. Half of the people in this shelter might be lost come the end of tomorrow, maybe more, maybe all of us if it is the will of the Gods. Come, we need to finish planning, to try and prevent that from happening."

"Your father's right. We must finish the fortifications to improve our chances once Akhola comes knocking at our doors." Magnus advised. The council returned to their discussions, but the mood remained much darker. Preparations continued both to the South and now the North. Lubeck hoped that Hagar would arrive in time and undermine Akhola's plans to have them defend the Pass on two fronts. The few defences they could install quickly were not particularly effective, but they would have to do. At least they should slow down Akhola's men if they should come from the North.

The following day saw Gunter send lookouts to elevated positions at the entrance to the Pass. Early warning of Akhola's approach would be vital. Archers were placed at strategic points along the perimeter of the plain that lay before the mouth of the Pass. Akhola would have to cross this dangerous ground with little cover in order to enter the Pass. Gunter ordered rows of sharpened stakes to be placed in staggered positions across the plain to slow any mounted assault. Lubeck employed the methods that had worked for them against Ballan and Mormont before him, hoping they would serve him well again this time. Lubeck's council had mulled over many different scenarios and how best to defend against them. But when it comes right down to it, the only thing they could do now, was wait and see what actions Akhola would take once he arrived. Everything was set; all they could do now was wait.

Akhola's ships landed at the Southern end of the Northern waterway. Two miles North of the main Outland Passage. Ten ships in total, carrying around two hundred and fifty men. They disembarked and began to set up defences and an encampment. From here they would move South to engage their enemy from behind and force them to defend on two opposing fronts. They were unaware that Lubeck's forces were expecting them. Nor were they aware that Hagar was nearing the main fjord with the Thunder Child and his small fleet. Akhola had given his men orders to attack on a strict schedule. He wanted their offensives to be simultaneous to create as much chaos as possible. As his ships had made good time, they would need to wait until the following day before commencing their assault. Unbeknown to them, this would work in Lubeck's favour, allowing time for Hagar's arrival. Lookouts watching the Northern waterway sent word to Gunter, about the fleet's arrival and also informed him about the crew's movements.

"They're waiting for the main forces to arrive, catch us like rats in the middle leaving us no retreat." Magnus snarled on hearing the news.

"That's as maybe, but it also informs us of Akhola's intended assault time. When those ships crews head out South towards us, we know that Akhola will attack. He is unaware that we know of his plans. It might just give us a little advantage." Gunter grinned. Lubeck took a deep breath and sighed before answering.

"Magnus is right though. If Hagar doesn't arrive in time, our retreat if required is cut off and we are trapped like rats. We need Rogan to join us and soon."

In his strong hold, King Rogan had also received news of Akhola's ships landing. His Queen Tanya, rushed into his chambers agitated by the rumours she had heard. Rogan's aids, who were dressing their King in his armour stopped as she spoke with a concerned voice.

"Gunter and his allies are trapped in the Outland Pass. They are to make a stand there against Akhola's forces. Is this true my husband?"

"It is; my scouts have returned bearing this information." Rogan answered in an unconcerned manner.

"Yet you do nothing? Will you not ride to his aid? Will you sit in your chambers and let your oldest friend and his allies die in your stead?" Tanya questioned. Rogan coughed gently and indicated for his aids to continue. The men set about securing the leather straps to tighten his breast plate against his chest. Rogan tugged at it in discomfort.

"I don't remember it feeling quite so tight." He observed with an uneasy chuckle. Tanya stared at him open mouthed as she recognised what her husband was wearing. The noise outside of the Great Lodge caught her attention and she ran to the window to see what was happening. Shields, shields and more shields filed past the lodge and carrying them, men in full battle dress, swords slung across their backs, spears in hand with axes, daggers, bows and quivers filled with arrows. Horsemen also trotted past, with tails flicking, heads held high and a spring in their step. Thousands of men, an entire army had gathered over the last few moments.

"Where did all of these come from? How did I not notice them all before?" Tanya asked.

"I sent for them days ago my dear. You didn't notice them as I gave word for them to meet a couple of miles to the West. They have gathered there for the past few days at my command. Now time has run short and I must head South with those that are here. I have no more time to wait for the rest. Only six thousand have arrived so far. It will have to do. I hope that Gunter and his allies can hold Akhola for a couple of days to give us time to come to his aid." Rogan began to explain.

Tanya's eyes darted all over her husband. Her head in a spin. Rogan was riding to assist his friend, as she had begged him to. But now the day of his departure had arrived, she realised this could be the last time she sees him alive. Rogan tugged again, adjusting his armour. He walked to his wife, kissed her tenderly, then without further words he turned and made for his horse. Once mounted, he gave a nod to his master at arms, who raised a large curled horn to his lips and blew. At the sound of the horn, the entire body of men moved, heading South. The whole strong hold trembled as thousands of men marched, horses snorted and pounded their hooves and wagons creaked and groaned as they rolled, carrying their heavy loads of supplies and shelters. Shields and spears as far as the eye could see. Rogan's army was on the move.

Standing Fast

The sound of distant horns and the rhythmic beating of drums grew louder as Akhola's army advanced towards the Outland Pass. Earl Magnus stood at his vantage point in order to oversee and direct the battle that was about to unfold. Lubeck had joined Thorsten and the rest of the Gurlemek while Gunter was at the head of his own men. All were in their respective positions; all waited with baited breath and pensive apprehension for what was to come. All present were accustomed to being on the field of battle, but overwhelming odds and uncertainty of reinforcements made this occasion considerably more ominous. As they stood and listened to the beat of the drums and the sounding of horns growing ever closer. Each man quietly made his peace with his own Gods as they continued to watch for the smallest sign to indicate the battle would begin.

To the North, the crews of Akhola's ships formed up and prepared to move South. An early morning mist had developed across the water, but the sky showed signs of a bright clear day. One of the men towards the rear of the formation looked back over his shoulder as he joined the main group. His eyes befell a fearful sight. A huge dragon loomed out of the mist. Plumes of fire reached out before it crashing into one of their moored ships, setting it ablaze instantaneously. The man cried out in fear at seeing such a sight, which attracted the attention of his comrades. The formation scattered in confused panic and scrambled back to their ships as another burst of flames ignited a second. Now as they drew closer, Akhola's men could see this was no demonic beast come to devour them. It was a ship, a big ship granted, but a ship all the same. More ships began to emerge from the mist either side of the leviathan which bore down on them. More fire and another ship burst into flames, timbers smashed as its mast came crashing down like a tree falling in the forest. The smaller ships now moved ahead of their bigger companion. Moving swiftly to the shingle beach, the crews jumped ashore in a whirl of shields and weapons of all description. Now the mighty ship rammed into another victim, crushing it against the rocky shoreline. The bewildered men scrambling back down the low hillside launched themselves into an undisciplined attack on the disembarking crews.

Hagar roared at his men to form a shield wall, which they accomplished in seconds. Akhola's men hurled themselves at it suffering hideous injuries as a consequence. Their attack was uncoordinated and ineffective. Their captain screamed at them to fall back, in an attempt to regroup and try to restore order. Hagar was not about to let that happen. A wave of his arm brought another two flaming balls of fire sailing over the shield wall scattering the retreating enemy. The fire balls hit the rocky ground and exploded like volcanos sending flames in all directions. Men screamed and wailed as their clothes caught fire.

"Archers!" Hagar yelled. A volley of arrows clouded the sky, passing high over the shield wall and raining down onto their fleeing targets. Again men screamed, some holding their shields high in a vain attempt to protect themselves. Their captain desperately barked orders to try and reform his men. Again the fearsome fire balls crashed down on them, killing men by the score. Panic set in. Men ran in all directions trying to escape the onslaught. Chaos was ruling now. Taken completely by surprise, Akhola's plan to attack the amalgamated forces was beginning to fall apart. The rear figurehead of Freyja on board the Thunder Child tentatively opened its eyes and surveyed the scenes ashore. A few of Akhola's ships remained secured with their bows dug into the shingle that formed a narrow beach. The images were relayed back to Freyja as she watched, staring into a makeshift font, from the relative safety of the port. Everyone was preoccupied with the fighting. Hagar appeared to have everything under control and Akhola's men were scrambling around undisciplined and without direction. She closed her eyes and concentrated. Now the

Thunder Child's dragon creaked into life. It lifted a single mighty paw and brought it down onto the closest of the enemy's ships, smashing it like dried kindling. The ship broke in two, wood splintering and ropes snapping as it collapsed. The dragon lifted its huge head and emitted a thundering roar that shook the ground with its ferocity and volume. Too busy fighting, Hagar and his opponents paid little if any attention to the noise. Lives were being fought for and they would not be distracted from that goal. The immense roar did however carry to the nearby Outland Pass. Heads turned to look North and worried expressions covered men's faces at the horrifying sound. Thorsten glanced to Lubeck,

"The Thunder Child is here. Hagar must be engaging Akhola's ships." Lubeck assured him.

"Do we go to his aid?" Thorsten enquired. Lubeck looked through squinted eyes for any signs of Akhola's forces emerging from the tree line on the other side of the plain. He could see nothing yet. With a quick nod, Lubeck broke from his position followed without word by Thorsten and there after the rest of the Gurlemek soldiers heading North.

"Where are you going?" Demanded Gunter as the two hundred men filed past him at double pace.

"To protect our rear!" Thorsten called back over his shoulder.

"But….." Gunter didn't bother to argue. He knew his son and knew that he knew what he was doing. Barking orders and waving arms, Gunter moved his men to fill the spaces left by the Gurlemek. Magnus cursed and spat onto the ground at his feet, as he watched Lubeck's forces disappear through the Pass. Indicating to his lieutenants to backfill weak points in the defences left by the sudden loss of the Gurlemek. He ground his teeth and turned his attention back towards the open plains and the tree line beyond. Still no sign of any movement, just the relentless sounds of war drums beating menacingly from afar.

At the Northern waterway, the skirmish Hagar had so efficiently dominated was all but done by the time the Gurlemek soldiers arrived at the summit of the low hill supporting the narrow path to the Northern most end of the Outland Pass. Lubeck, Thorsten and the rest, stopped to survey the scenes before them. A handful of Akhola's men ran aimlessly in various directions attempting to avoid being killed by the far superior fighting men that alighted from the long ships earlier that day. Lubeck pointed towards them and a section of his men broke away to assist Hagar in resolving this small matter. Descending the hill in a guarded manner, the Gurlemek watched for would be assassins hiding amongst the rocks. By the time they had reached the shingle beach below, Hagar's men had finished off the remnants of Akhola's saboteurs.

"Has Akhola attempted to break through the Pass yet?" Hagar asked as the main body of Gurlemek assembled on the shingle.

"Not as we left." Thorsten replied looking over his shoulder and up the hill they had just descended.

"We should hurry then. Get back there before we miss all of the action." Hagar said with haste.

"No. We will return once we have rested a little. You and your crews will remain here to guard our rears, in case Akhola has foreseen this and has a second wave already heading our way to recover his original plans." Lubeck instructed. Hagar let his disgruntlement show, but accepted his instructions. He would take up a rear guard and defend it to the last if need be. Thorsten set about retrieving water from the ships secured by the beach and distributed it amongst the men. Hagar's crews were covered in dirty sweat and blood from their encounters, with some needing wounds tending. Lubeck looked North to see the mist over the waters lifting. All appeared calm now and the sun began to shine. As the mist cleared further, a long way off, on the Western shorelines, too far away to be certain, Lubeck thought that he could see signs of a dust cloud. He screwed up his eyes in an attempt to see further. The harder he tried, the more his eyes played tricks on him. "Malik!" he called. At hearing his name, Malik came quickly to Lubeck's side.

"Yes?" He enquired. Lubeck pointed as he addressed his young companion.

"Your eyes are the best in our numbers. Can you make out what that is?" Malik squinted against the bright sun light, shading his eyes with his hand.

"It is dust, lots of it. It's too low to be a storm, perhaps........" Malik trailed off, concern replaced his usual expression.

"What is it?" Lubeck asked.

"I can't be sure, but the only thing, apart from a titanic monster, that could disturb that much dust would be an army on the move."

"An army?" Lubeck frowned. His mind raced, Could it be that Akhola has somehow out flanked them? Is this why he hasn't attacked the Pass yet? His drums holding Gunter's and Magnus's attention while he took his main forces around the mountains to attack them from behind?

"No not a chance." Tarique's voice broke the train of thought flowing through Lubeck's mind.

"You are thinking that might be Akhola's army trying to flank us aren't you?" He asked. Lubeck slightly surprised, nodded silently.

"I told you in my report. Akhoa's main forces are South of here, moving North through the valley. Unless he has twice as many men than we know of, that, if it is an army cannot be his." Lubeck's eyes returned to the cloud in the distance and a wry smile crept onto Lubeck's lips.

"Rogan, I think our King may be coming to our aid. Tarique, take your scouts and confirm for me if that is indeed an army and if so, who's? If it is truly our King, then the news will lift the spirits of our men. They will fight so much harder knowing that help is on the way." Then turning his attention directly to Tarique Lubeck continued. "If it is Rogan, his banners will carry a golden spread eagle against a black background. Make yourself known to him and inform him of the situation. Rogan carries the reminder of a wound on his right hip. You won't be able to see it, but if you tell him of its existence and that he got it from a wild boar during a hunt twelve years ago. He will know that you are my men, as I was the only one with him when it happened. No one else knows of the incident. I tended his wounds for five days until we returned home. Bring him and his army to the fight. If it's not Rogan, get back here with haste, unseen and we will make the best plans we can to defend ourselves." Tarique jumped to it, gathering Jamal and the remaining Mongol and Oriental scouts to assist him. Travelling light, carrying only weapons and a little water, they jogged along the Western shoreline heading North. "You must take the ships onto the water, get them to a safe distance where land based forces cannot reach them. If it is not Rogan approaching, return to the port and get Freyja and the others to safety. Take them home, take them back to Thanos. We will do what we can and if the Gods are willing, meet you again, if not in this life, then in another my friend." Lubeck said addressing Hagar directly. Hagar bowed his head in acknowledgment, then began to assemble his crews to embark and follow Lubeck's instructions. Thorsten slapped Hagar on the back as a parting gesture then turned to Lubeck.

"We will have to make obstacles as we return to the battle at the mouth. Make it difficult for an enemy to move easily through the Pass. Set ambush points, whatever it takes."

"We will my friend, we will." Lubeck assured the giant as he prepared to return to his father and assist with the imminent battle ahead.

At the mouth of the Pass, Akhola's men were now visible, having set up a base just out of the tree line on the Southern edge of the open plain. Akhola stood and surveyed the fortifications mounted by Magnus and Gunter, with scorn. He had superior numbers, but he knew that the restrictions of the terrain ahead would reduce the impact his numbers would have against a fortified and well defended natural corral. He knew that to attack head on would result in heavy losses, but there was no way around that. To cross the plain slowly and cautiously, would invite archers to inflict devastating blows to his front lines. To rush the Pass defences at speed, could result in chaos and confusion. No, he needed a steady defensive approach. Advance a little, then set up protective shelters to allow his men to rest in relative safety. Advance a little more and repeat. This would take time, but hopefully result in fewer losses. He raised an arm, a horn sounded and Akhola's army began to advance. Three rows of men, their shields held in front of them forming a barrier, moved out onto the plain. Close behind them, more rows of men ready to fill any gaps left by fallen comrades. Behind them, row after row of archers then foot soldiers, carts with supplies and finally cavalry being held back until they were close enough to be effective. The Southern end of the plain filled completely with armed warriors moving slowly but surely towards the mouth of the Outland Pass.

"So it begins." Magnus uttered almost to himself, looking to Gunter for recognition of their opponent's manoeuvres. Gunter gestured that he was aware and both men readied their forces. Hearts pounded and pulses raced as the defenders watched Akhola's army slowly leave the cover of the tree line and advance onto the plain. The enormity of their task was now being realised, as they could see clearly what a ten thousand strong army looked like. Heavily outnumbered they were, but they had the advantage of being well protected by their fortified defences and the natural fortress of their environment. Gunter thought about his son's suggestions of guerrilla tactics and how they might have reduced Akhola's numbers. It was too late now. This path had not been followed and now they faced the full might of the Southern King's army. Now was not a time for fear. It was not a time for doubt or self-pity. It was a time for courage and fortitude, a time for belief that should death find you, you can only hope, it is such a glorious death that you take your place by your forefathers in Valhalla.

Akhola's men moved ever closer, crossing almost half the length of the plain before Gunter signalled to his archers. They raised their bows, aiming high into the air to gain as much distance as possible. Then at the drop of Gunter's arm, they loosed. The sky darkened accompanied by a faint whistling. The front rows of the advancing army raised their shields to protect themselves from the approaching projectiles. Five hundred arrows thumped into shields, earth and men alike. Screams of pain were heard all around the field as a large number of the forward ranks fell. Men from the rear ranks ran forward to fill the gaps left by their fallen comrades, as a second wave of hissing death poured down upon them. Now the rear ranks of Akhola's army hurried to form more cover, interlocking their shields to help protect them from above as well as in front. At Akhola's command, horns sounded and the first six ranks, some twelve hundred men surged forward at speed, charging head long towards the mouth of the pass.

Magnus pointed towards the middle of the plain and ordered his archers to fire. Horns sounded from the cliffs behind him and archers lit their arrows from braziers placed along their ranks. At the sounding of a second horn, they raised their bows lifting them high and loosed. This time the intended target was not the lines of quickly approaching shields, but the lines of pitch laid out as part of Gunter's defences. As in the battle on the beach at Thanos when Thorsten faced Ballan's men, the ground erupted into flame as soon as the arrows plunged to the earth. The flames licked across the plain like a fiery serpent more than ten feet wide and spread the entire width of the plain, effectively separating the twelve hundred off from the rest of Akhola's army. There was nothing Akhola could do but watch through the orange flames, helpless to assist as his men on the other side were reduced in number by wave after wave of arrows raining down on them from all directions. In desperation, the trapped men charged at the mouth of the Pass.

"Shield wall!" Gunter yelled as loud as he could. His men quickly formed the typical Viking shield wall, some distance inside the mouth of the Pass. Three shields high, all interlocking and totally traversing the Pass entrance. With rocky faces to each side and a well formed shield wall in front, Gunter's men were well protected as Akhola's descended upon them. The mouth of the pass was relatively narrow in comparison to the grassy plain. They had to close together, clustering and funnelling towards their waiting foe.

"Hold fast!" Gunter ordered as the charging enemy bore down upon them. Akhola's men crashed into the wall with ferocity. The sounds of battle filled the air, shield against shield, sword against sword. Men screamed as blades of all description bit into flesh and bone. Blood turned the ground red as it flowed like water. Bodies began to pile up in front of the shield wall, which held fast. Fallen warriors were speedily replaced as reinforcements moved forward to maintain the barrier. Again and again Akhola's depleting first wave crashed against the immoveable obstacle in front of them, losing their footing as they tripped and slipped on the bodies of their fallen comrades. At Gunter's command, the entire wall pushed back at their assailants forcing them to fall back and give ground.

"Push!" Each man in the wall shouted simultaneously. Another gain in ground was made and the wall moved closer to the mouth of the Pass pushing their enemy back towards the plain. Injured men lay on the ground as the wall passed over them. A dozen of Gunter's men followed close behind the advancing shield wall, killing injured enemy soldiers and rescuing their own as they moved. Unable to get around or through the shield wall and realising that their situation was hopeless, the attackers retreated back onto the plain in an attempt to flee the unexpected slaughter. But with a raging fire in front of them and Gunter's men closing from behind, it was a short lived attempt.

Akhola watched through the flames to witness the unbelievable events that unfolded in front of him. Helpless to aid, he turned and waved his forces to return to the relative safety of the forest. Twelve hundred men lost with no gain in ground. It appeared that he had underestimated his opponents on this occasion, a mistake he would not repeat.

Some hours later, the flames across the plain were burning low as the pitch that fed them became exhausted. Akhola had mustered his men ready to advance once again towards the Pass. As a steady controlled advance had failed before, he now threw caution to the wind and decided to try a full charge. Sheer numbers meant that most of his men would make it across the plain. Once across, in close quarters, weight of numbers would prevail. The order was given and horns sounded once more. This time his cavalry led the onslaught, racing far out in front and thundering towards the newly reformed shield wall positioned as it was earlier.

Arrows rained down at the advancing charge, but the speed of the horses made it difficult for the archers to find their marks, and only minor numbers were stopped this way. Some of the horsemen fell into pits which had been strategically dug hindering the cavalry's advance. Sharpened stakes lay at the bottom of these pits, which impaled the riders and horse alike. But through this, most of the horsemen made it to the mouth of the Pass. The shield wall this time could not hold the might of five hundred horsemen descending upon them. Horses ploughed through, battering holes in the defences and trampling men underfoot. The cavalry turned about and began to engage the remnants of the wall from behind. Horses snorted and stamped. Men cried out in fear and pain as they were cut down by the mounted foe.

Fortunes were now turned in favour of Akhola. The rest of his army were running across the flat to join the fight on seeing the defences breached. Magnus searched for a solution. His archers were running very low on arrows, some had abandoned their positions, opting to try and help their comrades with sword in hand. Gunter's forces were being overwhelmed by the mounted assault that had destroyed his shield wall giving refuelled hope to the Akhola's advancing forces. It was then, that Agatha climbed to a ledge and chanted an ancient verse. She raised her arms to the sky, then as her incantation reached its climax, she brought her arms down thrusting her outstretched hands towards the advancing army. The ground began to shake and rumble. Her eyes turned deep red as she stared towards the plain. Freyja's voice echoed in her head as the two worked together to raise an unearthly storm. The sky darkened and thunder rumbled overhead. Rain began to fall in torrents and chasms opened as the ground split causing hundreds of Akhola's men to fall to their deaths. Akhola stopped to stare at the witch standing on the ledge.

"You!" He snarled as another clap of thunder crashed overhead. Lightning bolts hit the floor close to him and he dived for cover. At the site of the devastated shield wall, fierce fighting continued. Gunter's men fought against the overpowering force of the swift mounted warriors. As the inevitable outcome was becoming clear, Gunter called for his men to fall back. As they retreated further into the Pass, a volley of arrows flew over their heads and thumped into riders unseating them and causing their horses to bolt. One Horseman threw a lance at Gunter barely missing him. The rider continued his assault with a sword. Gunter found himself backed against the rock face on one side of the Pass. He fought hard, but there was no way to escape his opponent's relentless attack, he was trapped. Blow after blow rained down onto the aging warlord but he managed to deflect them with his shield. Gunter used his sword, but found no avenue for attack. The rider dug his heels into the animal's flanks and the horse reared up onto its hind legs. With four legs flailing, the horse kicked Gunter knocking him back hard against the rock face and causing him to drop his sword. The rider now slammed his sword down onto Gunter's shield, as he held it high in an attempt to protect himself. The shield broke and split into two halves. Now his attacker moved his mount to give him a better angle to strike at his quarry, he raised his sword high, then, reeled in his saddle, arching his back and dropping his sword. Blood spilled from his mouth as the stricken horseman fell to the ground. There embedded deep in the middle of his back was a huge double headed axe. The horse bolted as Thorsten's immense figure towered over its stricken rider. He reached out to Gunter, offering a helping hand which was accepted with gratitude. Then retrieving his axe Thorsten turned to join the fight.

"The Gurlemek are coming! The Gurlemek are coming!" One of Akhola's men screamed as he turned to run. With the rain cascading down, thunder roaring overhead and lightning flashing all around, it did indeed appear as if some unworldly demons were taking to the battle field. Lubeck charged towards the mounted men who had broken their defences. He moved with such speed and ferocity that they could not defend against him. Killing more than six horsemen before they realised they had a new foe to face.

Disengaging from their fight with the remnants of Gunter's shield wall, Akhola's cavalry turned to face Lubeck and his men, as they advanced. But these were not just tribesmen bundled together as a rudimentary fighting force. These were Gurlemek soldiers. Two hundred well trained and well armed men working together with a common goal. As the cavalry reformed to charge, the Gurlemek formed a shield wall of their own. These shields though, were not made of wood. They were shields made from a strange metal gifted to them by the Gods. Their weapons too, were no ordinary weapons. These also, were from the same gifted armoury Freyja had disclosed. As the lightning reflected off the shiny metal wall, the horsemen charged. The Gurlemek braced, angling their bodies for the best resistance against the inevitable impact. This wall held an extra unexpected surprise for the charging cavalry. As they drew close, in response to a sharp order from Lubeck, spears were passed through small gaps between the interlocking shields. Now the horsemen were not charging towards a dull wall of man and shield. They were hurtling towards more than a hundred sharp, menacing, metal teeth now standing proud of the wall by three feet or more. This transformation happened just as the cavalry drew to close proximity leaving them no time to withdraw.

Man and horse alike found themselves impaled as they crashed into the unmoving metal obstacle. Lubeck's voice rang out loud and the spears were withdrawn then just as quickly redeployed. Horses collided into each other throwing their riders onto the waiting spears as the remaining horsemen tried to halt their attack. Those that were not unseated tried to retreat, only to find their way blocked by the remnants of Gunter's shield wall, now reinforced by three hundred of Magnus's men. Caught between the two barriers, with no room to manoeuvre their beasts, the cavalry fought to the last against an impenetrable enemy. The two shield walls moved methodically towards each other, cutting down anything in their paths. Frightened horses reared and bucked, riders fell to the ground and were trampled by the very animals they had been riding. Others were slaughtered where they lay as Gurlemek forces stepped over them during their advance. The screams and wailing finally silenced as the last cavalryman was executed. His body lay in a river of blood that was forming along the entrance to the Pass. Man and beast alike, their bodies cut and bleeding, some with limbs missing and others with multiple fatal wounds. All now motionless and sinking into the muddy mixture of rain and blood. Lubeck and his men did not take time for breath. They quickly deployed themselves to the mouth of the Pass, ready to engage Akhola's main forces once they had crossed the plain.

Out on the plain, the fortified entrapments positioned by Magnus and Gunter combined with the fierce storm the mystic sisters had conjured, were hindering Akhola's advance considerably. But finally his forces were within striking distance of the Outland Pass. His archers returned fire from protected positions, quickly erected by his forward ranks using the panels and wooden frames they had carried with them. Just three hundred feet to go and Magnus's archers would not be able to shoot clearly for danger of hitting their own. Akhola peered over one of the wooden panels. He could see more clearly now, the massacre of his cavalry at the hands of the combined enemy forces. He could also see now, the shining shield wall being erected across the mouth of the Pass.

"Lubeck. I thought you surely dead by now. Still time to remedy that." He hissed, indicating to his men, to advance still further. The panels were lifted and carried out front blocking wave after wave of arrows which thumped into the long wooden barriers harmlessly. Dead and wounded warriors from both sides littered the ground in front of them, as Akhola's forces surged ever closer to their goal. Now only a hundred feet away from the Gurlemek shield wall, Akhola resisted the urge to charge at it. Instead he waited for his main forces to gather around, forming a long barrier of wooden panels. Sitting behind these with their shields raised over head, Akhola and his men were well protected from the probing arrows that still occasionally thudded into their protection. Grasping the opportunity to peer through small gaps at his enemy, Akhola could see that the amalgamated forces had suffered heavy losses also. One last push might just achieve his goal and break through into the Pass. But this storm was making it increasingly difficult to move. Lightning continued to strike, smashing holes in his wooden panelled barrier. The ground continued to shake and caverns opened to swallow men by the dozen. Akhola scanned the rocky cliff faces looking for Agatha.

"There you are!" He snarled as his eyes focused upon the dangerous beauty, stood overlooking the plain and destroying his army, almost single handed. "Kill her! Kill the witch!" He shouted to a pair of archers nearby. They moved their aim and let fly. The arrows hissed through the darkened sky until they reached their mark. Agatha was stunned as the first of the two arrows glanced off the rocks close by her, but the second caught her mid chest. She gasped as the breath was knocked out of her by the force of the impact. Staggering backwards, her eyes looked down to see the slender wooden shaft embedded in her ribs, blood oozing from the wound. Pain seared through her body as her fingers closed around the projectile. She coughed as she sat against a rock, leant back and closed her eyes.

In the safety of the port, Freyja took a sharp breath and gasped also. Pain shot through her like a hot knife. The telepathic contact she and her sister shared was broken. Tears filled her eyes until they over flowed down her cheeks as she wailed her sister's name loudly. She stepped back from the font, sat on a chair and began to weep uncontrollably.

With Agatha mortally injured and Freyja no longer assisting, the storm over the Outland Pass broke. Akhola rejoiced and ordered his men to charge the Gurlemek shield wall. Sensing victory was nearing, Akhola and his army raced towards the Gurlemek with renewed vigour. Running short of arrows, Magnus's archers released their remaining few, striking down a handful of enemies. They descended the rocky faces of the Pass entrance to assist in the defence behind the shield wall. The Gurlemek braised and the tremendous impact hit. Shields and swords clashed as ferocious fighting ensued before the metal barricade. Blood flowed in torrents; limbs fell to the ground as they were severed from their hosts. Men emitted blood curdling screams of agony as the relentless onslaught pressed against Lubeck's tiring troops. Gunter and what was left of his men came to their aid and filled gaps which were starting to appear, as even the mighty Gurlemek began to fall under such weight of numbers. Magnus's men also joined the fight at the mouth of the Pass. Bodies piled high in front of the wall, which started to become problematic for Akhola's men. Footing became precarious as they tripped and slipped on the blood soaked corpses.

"Hold! Hold!" Thorsten yelled putting all of his might into bracing part of the upper most rows of shields. Magnus too, joined the support, picking up a dropped spear and thrusting it through a small gap purposely left between a pair of shields. The deadly weapon found its mark and another of Akhola's men fell. The pressure of the attacking forces began to tell and the Gurlemek shield wall began to weaken. Magnus could feel this as well as any man behind the shields. In a desperate attempt to relieve the strain, he led a score of men up one side of the rocky faces that formed the mouth of the Pass. From this elevated position he could see the barrier beginning to buckle. Magnus and his men began to hurl rocks down upon their enemies below. The tactic worked at first, as the forward line of attackers cowered from the rocks raining down at them. Distracted as they were, they became easy targets for the spears thrusting back and forth from the barrier of shields. Akhola directed his archers to kill Magnus and his men. Arrows flew and the men on the rock face crouched behind their shields for cover. Some cried out as projectiles bit into unprotected body parts. Again Magnus's handful of men launched rocks at the men below. Again archers caused them to crouch behind their shields. This distraction gave Lubeck and the others enough time to reform a strong blockade. This time though, the wall opened just wide enough to allow Lubeck and a group of Gurlemek soldiers to file through and counter attack their assailants. Thorsten, along with Malik and twenty others spilled through the opening which closed quickly behind them. As they moved, men fell before them and Akhola's attack began to falter. At seeing the Gurlemek's daring move, Magnus descended from the rock face with his men to assist. As the pressure against the wall began to ease, Gunter ordered them to push. The Men forming the shield wall pushed in unison emitting a loud roar as they did. Slowly but surely, push after push, the wall moved forward forcing Akhola and his attacking forces to give ground.

Freyja, still sobbing pulled herself together and peered back into her font. With a wave of her hand and peeping through tear filled eyes, she could see the reckless action Lubeck had taken. Fearing for his and the others safety, she hastily chanted in an old and almost forgotten tongue. As she concentrated, she felt a presence on the astral plains in which she worked. The presence was faint, but definitely there. Her spirits lifted and heart raced.

"Agatha! Help me!" She called. At hearing her sister's voice deep within her mind, Agatha's eyes flickered open. Grimacing against the pain, she struggled to her knees and leant her hands against the rocks in front of her. Being careful not to press against the shaft of the arrow protruding from her ribs, she surveyed the scene below. The Gurlemek were standing fast at the mouth of the cavern. Lubeck and his most trusted companions were fighting fiercely slaying everyone within an arms length of them. Thorsten's huge axe swung from one side then the other, clearing space around himself and his friends with powerful blows which cut clean through his enemies decapitating or bisecting them as the immense blade barely hesitated. Akhola was now losing ground and being forced back, away from the mouth of the Pass. Answering her sister's call, Agatha unsteadily raised her hands and recited the verse, her chanting synchronised with Freyja's. The sky began to grow darker once again. The winds picked up and distant thunder rumbled once more as the rain resumed. Akhola looked to the sky and cursed.

"Damn the Gods this day! Where are you my pretty witch? I'll kill you myself this time!" He snarled as his eyes scanned the rocky ledges frantically trying to locate Agatha. She was much harder to find this time, as she knelt behind the rocks. "There you are." Reaching out and retrieving a spear from a nearby body, Akhola moved a little closer to his intended target. Magnus noticed Akhola's predatory movements and followed his gaze. Agatha was deep in concentration and was not taking steps to avoid being spotted. Striking down one more opponent, Magnus surged forward to intercept Akhola's advance. Leaping over another stricken adversary and sailing through air towards the invading King, sword thrusting as he came. Akhola turned instinctively and diverted the spear into his flying attacker. The weight of Magnus's considerable frame carried them both to the ground, the spear passing straight through and protruding more than a foot from Magnus's back as they fell. He cried out in pain and anguish as he realised that his attempt to end this battle had failed. Coughing and choking as blood spilled from his mouth, Magnus rolled to the side as Akhola struggled to free himself from under the heavy Northern Earl.

Fingers of steel, with a vice like grip, caught Akhola by the throat and dragged him from under the fallen chieftain. Akhola clawed at the powerful hand that gripped him so tightly, gasping for air. He looked up at his assailant, straight into two burning sapphires beneath a crown of golden hair. Lubeck dragged Akhola by the throat clearing him of Magnus's limp body with such fury and hatred, that Akhola became dizzy with the lack of oxygen. The power of the grip was crushing his throat. Holding his victim firm against the muddy ground, Lubeck raised his sword with his left hand, only to be struck from behind by an attempt to kill him. The blow glanced against the armoured vestment he wore, knocking him to his knees and forcing him to relinquish his grip on the gasping King. Lubeck's attacker raised his sword for a second attempt, but froze in horror and shock as Malik drove his sword though the man's back driving it completely through, causing his blade to protrude from his victim's chest.

Akhola coughed and spluttered as he rolled in the mud gasping for breath and attempting to get to his feet. Lubeck too, slowly and tentatively rose to his feet. Lightning flashed as Akhola rested his eyes on Lubeck's imposing figure, now streaked in other men's blood from head to toe. Rain drenched mud splattered across his armour and a look of contemptuous hatred filling his eyes. With his gaze firmly fixed on Akhola, Lubeck reached to the ground to recover his sword, but instead, his hand found the smooth shaft of the hooked weapon he had dropped in order to grasp Akhola by the throat. His fingers closed around the weapon raising it menacingly. Akhola looked about him for a weapon to defend himself. The battle continued to rage all around them as two more attackers attempted to strike Lubeck down. Lubeck slammed the mace pommel of his weapon into the skull of the first. His victims head caved from the impact of the blow and the man fell to the mud lifeless. The second brought his sword round in a downward arc aimed at Lubeck's head. Lubeck parried the attempt with the shaft of his own weapon and quickly rotated it to drive the spear like head deep into his attacker's chest. This distraction allowed Akhola time to recover both sword and shield from a fallen countryman. He leapt towards Lubeck trying to catch him off guard. Lubeck though, was far too quick to be caught. He rotated around and out of the path of the approaching sword blade causing it to thump harmlessly into the mud. Then, spinning the hooked weapon around, Lubeck smashed it into Akhola's shield, splintering it and rendering it useless as Akhola reeled from the impact causing him to reach out and take hold of one of the sharpened defensive stakes to regain his balance. Lubeck, fuelled by hatred, slammed the pommel of his weapon into Akhola's abdomen. The force of the blow knocked the wind from his lungs and caused Akhola to drop to his knees, struggling to breath.

Now the storm began to break, but rumblings like thunder could be heard over the battle's noise. The ground began to shake and the fighting at the Gurmelek shield wall faltered. The rumblings grew louder and the ground shook like an earth quake. Akhola's men broke off their attack at the mouth of the pass and began to retreat back towards the plain. The men defending the Pass took a tentative look over their shoulders. Their eyes were met by the most welcome of sights. Thousands of mounted warriors filled the Outland Pass as far as the eye could see, all following the banner of King Rogan. The exhausted Gurlemek broke formation and cleared the way for the horsemen to pass unhindered onto the battlefield. Akhola's men fled, but were easily caught by the much faster horsemen, who cut them down as they rode.

Akhola, seeing victory becoming defeat, launched himself once more at Lubeck, his sword cutting dangerously close to Lubeck's head. Lubeck in counter, once again skilfully rotated around and out of harm's way striking a blow of his own which found it's mark between Akhola's shoulder blades. Akhola fell forward and struggled to maintain his footing. He span round quickly swinging his sword once more towards Lubeck. Lubeck lunged forward catching Akhola by the arm, then, throwing him over his shoulder, he slammed Akhola into the mud with immeasurable ferocity. Dazed, frustrated and angry beyond comprehension, Akhola scrambled to his feet and hurtled towards his tormentor screaming as he came. Lubeck slammed the pommel of his weapon into Akhola's stomach stopping him in his tracks. Lubeck then spun the weapon around and brought it home against the side of Akhola's head. The blow stunned Akhola causing him to freeze. Lubeck proceeded to slam his head into his enemy's face, breaking Akhola's nose in a fountain of blood and cartilage. Then dropping his weapon and grasping his opponent with both hands, Lubeck hoisted Akhola high overhead. Akhola cried out in horror and agony as Lubeck dropped him onto one of the broken defence's sharpened stakes that cluttered the battlefield. Akhola choked as blood spouted from his mouth. The blood soaked point of the stake pierced through Akhola's battered and broken body as his weight slowly dragged him further and further down the wooden shaft. Lubeck took hold of Akhola by the jaw and turned his tortured face, to face his own.

"Tell me where my son is and I'll ease your passing." Lubeck offered to the agonized Southern King. Akhola's contempt knew no bounds as he spat blood and cursed at Lubeck. "Then die slowly and without honour, and may you never stand by your forefathers in Valhalla." Lubeck spat in reply as he turned his back.

The battle was short lived now, with the arrival of King Rogan and his army. His horsemen ran down all those who would not throw down their arms and yield. Lubeck surveyed the scenes in front of him. His huge chest heaving as he panted for breath following the exertions of battle. Akhola screamed in agony behind him and in an act of malice, hatred and rage, Lubeck turned and slammed his fist into Akhola's face once more, breaking his jaw to add to the immense pain the invader was already suffering. The force of the blow rendered Akhola unconscious and pushed his body a further few inches down the wooden shaft of the stake on which he was impaled. Lubeck roared with rage as he delivered the blow and roared some more as he believed that the location of his son Hafthor would now never be known. Malik tired and bleeding from his encounters now stepped forward and took hold of Lubeck's wrist. He pulled it towards Akhola's battered head and placed Lubeck's hand on it.

"Think Lubeck, think of Hafthor, quickly before this scum dies. Think of your son and your prayers will be answered I'm sure." Lubeck frowned at his friend in puzzlement, but did as he was urged to. Freyja, who was sobbing loudly over her stricken sister, suddenly caught a vision. A young man, big in stature, with golden hair and burning blue eyes wearing torn clothing and feeding pigs from a wooden bucket drifted into her mind. Her sobbing stopped as realisation hit her.

"Found you. Found you at last." She whispered. The words echoed inside Lubeck's head and he removed his hand from the blood soaked scalp of the suffering Akhola. The sounds of battle began to fade as Horses hooves approached. Lubeck raised his head to look upon the approaching horsemen. King Rogan himself brought his mount to a halt just feet away from the mighty warriors now beginning to gather around Lubeck. Thorsten lifted his axe in a threatening manner before Lubeck placed his hand on his friend's shoulder and reassured him that they were no longer in any danger. Rogan sighed as he surveyed the devastating scenes and the thousands of dead. He sheathed his sword and wiped away the blood that covered his face.

"The crows will feed well this day, Lubeck. I owe you and your men a great debt. Had you not delayed Akhola here, he would surely have brought great sorrow and destruction to my lands before I could have intervened."

"Your words are received most gratefully my Lord." Lubeck replied lowering his head in a respectful bow.

"This will take some time to clear. My men will recover your dead so that you may send them to the afterlife as you see fit. Akhola and his men can be food for crows and wolves, unless you would prefer otherwise?"

King Rogan announced. Lubeck shook his head without a word, but turned slightly in the direction of the impaled Akhola. Rogan lifted his gaze just enough to follow Lubeck's. "Is he dead?" Rogan asked.

"Not yet my Lord." Lubeck replied.

"Then we shall remedy that this instant." Rogan countered as he dismounted. He walked over to his defeated and dying foe and gripped the blood soaked mass of matted hair, lifting his head back to gaze upon his enemies face. "Your work?" He asked as Lubeck approached. Lubeck nodded without further words. Rogan sighed as he released the head allowing it to drop unceremoniously. "Tell me you discovered the location of your son before you did this?" Rogan asked. Lubeck took a deep breath.

"I know where he is my Lord." He replied.

"Good. Then as soon as you are able, you must go and retrieve him, but for now, you rest and get that seen to." Lubeck looked to where Rogan was pointing. Blood poured from a wound on his upper right thigh. The presence of which he had been totally unaware. The adrenalin and ferocity of battle had numbed his body to pain, but now as his mind and body began to relax, he felt it searing through him from several injuries. Rogan drew a dagger and drove it into Akhola's neck. Blood gushed out of the severed artery. Rogan wiped his blade on part of Akhola's tunic, then turned and indicated for Lubeck to walk with him. As they began to move away from the now dead Akhola, Lubeck instructed Thorsten to find Agatha. The big man nodded and took Tarique, who along with the rest of his scouts, had led Rogan's army to the battle.

Gunter stood over the body of Magnus, the spear still protruding from his chest. Gunter knelt beside his fallen countryman and removed the offending weapon. He struggled to lift the large chieftain, but managed it to spite being injured himself. Carrying him to a more acceptable location, Gunter lowered Magnus to lie on an abandoned cart and placed a sword into his dead hands.

"Your forefathers await you to take your place by their sides. May you have safe and free passage to Valhalla. We will meet again. When my time comes." He said. Moments later, Thorsten and Tarique arrived. The giant carried the lifeless body of Agatha, the arrow still embedded in her chest. Gunter looked to Thorsten with hope, but Thorsten shook his head gravely.

"Remove that thing, so that we may return her to her sister for a proper burial." Gunter commanded referring to the arrow that had taken Agatha's life. Thorsten grunted as he turned to place her on the ground. Then gripping the arrow tightly, he pulled firmly. The head of the arrow was not barbed and came relatively easily for the big man. He tossed it to the floor with disgust, then resumed carrying her towards the Northern end of the Pass.

"Do you intend to carry her all of the way to the Thunder Child?" Malik enquired as he raced to Thorsten's side.

"If need be." The giant answered abruptly.

"No my friend, there is a cart over there, place her in it alongside Magnus. We will hitch up some horses to pull it to the ship." Malik countered, pointing towards one of the carts used by the invading forces. Thorsten paused, then moved slowly towards the cart and placed Agatha carefully down beside the body of the fallen chieftain.

"Hagar will be saddened, to see his brother so." Thorsten stated. Malik sighed as he responded.

"We know, but the news of Magnus's death is already on its way to him. Jamal has gone ahead to deliver the message and to tell Hagar to ready the ships for our return." Four of Rogan's men brought two stray horses and hitched them up to the cart. Then in sombre silence, they led them away towards the Northern end of the Pass.

Out on the plain, vast numbers of King Rogan's men were already retrieving their fallen allies from the apocalyptic aftermath of that morning's battle. Crows cawed and buzzards had already begun to circle overhead as the afternoon grew older. Rogan ordered an encampment be erected and the wounded to be tended to. Exhausted, battle weary troops filed into the quickly erected shelters where they received the medical attention they needed, Lubeck included. As Lubeck's thigh was being stitched, Rogan sat with him and talked. Gunter and the others were not far away as always.

"I would like you to come back home and take up your place in my court again at your father's side." Rogan began. Gunter stood and smiled.

"You want me to return to your court and take charge of your guard again my Lord?" He enquired.

"Yes, I would like everything to be just as it was, all those years ago. My two most trusted servants and friends at my sides and overseeing the safety of my family and subjects alike." Rogan replied. Lubeck sighed and shook his head slowly.

"As tempting as your generous offer is my Lord, I have to respectfully decline. I have to find my son and I have a new home I want to return to. I have a new life waiting for me in Thanos. If it pleases my Lord, I'm sure that with my father by your side, your house and followers will all be in safe hands. If he can't take care of things, just send for me. I will return to your aid if needed."

"No! I don't want you to leave again. I want you to stay here where you belong." Gunter objected to his son's reply.

"I must say that I agree with your father." Rogan added. Lubeck looked around the shelter at the many faces staring expectantly at him. His father, sorrow slowly etching its way across his troubled brow. Rogan with hope slowly fading into reluctant acceptance and his trusted and loyal friends, each waiting with anticipation and hope for Lubeck to give the reply they all longed for. Lubeck sighed heavily and dropped his head. Then slowly looking up to his saddened father he said,

"I'm sorry father, but I have many responsibilities now. These men and their families have placed their faith and trust in me as their Earl. I cannot turn my back on them now, even if I wanted to, which I don't. I now have a settlement in Thanos, with over five hundred subjects to protect and govern. I also have a chance of a family again. Hafthor is out there somewhere and I will find him. There is a woman that I wish to be with. It has been some time now since Ilka died. She left a hole in our lives, Hafthor and me. But now there is a real possibility to have something special again."

"But you could have all of that here, with us." Gunter protested. King Rogan raised a hand in gesture for Gunter to be quiet as he commented.

"You must respect your son's decision. I too will regret not having him back by my side, however an Earl must fulfil his duties as must the captain of my personal guard." Then turning to address Lubeck directly, Rogan continued. "I do not fully agree with your decision. However I respect it and accept it. When do you intend to return to Thanos?" Lubeck glanced at his friends across the shelter, before responding.

"As soon as we are able to my Lord." Rogan and Gunter sighed simultaneously. Then Rogan patted Lubeck on the shoulder announcing.

"Then I shall personally escort you to the coast accompanied by a thousand men, to provide you safe passage. Akhola may be dead, but some of his followers are still out there and may well desire revenge. Have this magnificent ship of yours that I've heard so much about, brought to Keterik. I believe that's where you landed yes?"

"I believe that's what Magnus called the port." Lubeck nodded. Rogan stood and placed his hand on Gunter's shoulder.

"Make your peace with your son old friend. You must respect his decision and accept that life does not always play out the way one would desire. Take up your reappointed position and make ready to move. We ride at….." Rogan paused as he turned back to Lubeck before querying "Dawn?"

"Yes my Lord, dawn would suit very well." Lubeck responded in a whisper. Gunter slammed his fist against his chest in salute to his King as Rogan left the shelter and accompanied by four of his guard, moved away towards his own shelter. Lubeck hesitantly tested his leg and stood to see how it would bare weight. He winced as the stiches pulled tight and pain shot through his thigh, but regained his composure quickly before addressing his father.

"Don't be saddened father. It is a time to rejoice. You are going to take up your rightful position by Rogan's side and I will begin to build a new settlement far to the South. I am an Earl now with people to lead and protect. I have plans for Thanos, and if Freyja is agreeable, her tower will be central to the new settlement, where I intend to develop an exciting new centre for trade. Rogan's ships will always have safe haven there and they will always be welcome."

"As yours will here, my son. But it does sadden me. I have just found you, only to lose you again so soon." Gunter objected. Lubeck stopped his father from continuing, by embracing him in a loving hug. Gunter's eyes filled with tears which he struggled to hold back as he sighed in reluctant acceptance.

"I will send word when I have recovered Hafthor. Then you must sail to Thanos to see him." Lubeck assured his father.

"Odin himself would not stop me. We have a few days until we reach Keterik. Let's make the most of the time we have and enjoy the journey then." The old warrior replied. With that, Gunter patted his son on the back and turned to leave the shelter, stopping as his eyes fell upon Thorsten.

"I want to thank you for what you did out there today, I know how you feel about me. It was fortunate for me, that you had a change of mind I think." Thorsten grunted almost inaudibly as he nodded in response. Gunter smiled and left the shelter walking quietly into the advancing twilight of the approaching evening. Lubeck moved to stand by the big man and patted him gently on the arm.

"I too, thank you for your interventions my friend. My family owes you a great debt."

"Your family owes me nothing Lubeck. If not for you, we all would still be imprisoned aboard that Galley in chains and my son Bjorn would still be a slave in Altear. I owe you a lifetime debt." The giant replied.

"The debt you think you owe me is repaid my friend, you owe me nothing anymore." Lubeck said again patting his big friend on the arm and turning to the rest of the group he announced. "None of you owe me anything. Fighting alongside me as you all have over these few years, I feel it is I who owes you." Malik drew attention to himself, as he spoke.

"As Thorsten said. We all owe you our freedom, but that is not the reason we follow you. We are friends are we not? We fight alongside you because you are our friend, not because we think we owe you a debt." Lubeck smiled as he looked around the small shelter at each of the friends staring back at him. Then with a lighter tone to his voice, Lubeck announced.

"Then let's go and eat, drink and rejoice at surviving to fight another day. Also to salute our fallen comrades and wish them safe voyage on their journeys to their chosen afterlives." The shelter erupted with calls of agreement as each of them followed Lubeck through the low, draped door and out into the evening air.

HOME

The following morning saw the encampment being disassembled and packed onto carts. Men worked with frivolity and good humour, as spirits began to rise with the knowledge that they were to return home. The fighting was done. Akhola's scheming treachery was thwarted and the men from all tribes were looking forward to being with their families once more. Large funeral pyres were lit and their dead were honoured in the traditions of their forefathers. Just a few selected fallen were placed onto carts to be transported to their loved ones for burial at a later time. Magnus and Agatha were among them. Each body cleaned and wrapped, was then placed carefully with the others for transport home. By midmorning all were ready to move. King Rogan dispatched the bulk of his army to return North and on to their respective homes. One thousand of his own stronghold guard were to escort him as he would travel to Keterik with Lubeck and the Gurlemek, before watching them sail on their return journey to Thanos. The two groups set off in their separate directions. Crossing the open plain to head South was not a pleasant path. The sound of buzzing flies filled ears with a low droning hum and crows picked at bodies littering the field. Lubeck surveyed the scene as he rode slowly past. Akhola's body still hung limply on the stake on which he had been impaled. Buzzards had also begun to feed on the carrion that such a battle had left in its wake. At the tree line ahead, Lubeck noticed the movements of wolves, still wary of the large number of humans at the scene. They waited patiently for the men to clear the field, before making their move to feed on the veritable banquet of meat the bodies of the dead provided.

Idle chatter slowly built as the men moved South. Lubeck told King Rogan of his plans to create a centre of trade at the tower by the beach in Thanos. Rogan was impressed by Lubeck's ambitions and promised to send ships on regular visits to help establish this goal. Gunter's heart began to warm as he listened to his son's plans and he was encouraged by Rogan's response. But always there was the uncertainty over Hafthor. Lubeck seemed inexplicably sure that he would find and recover his son. Something that Gunter found hard to understand. But, if Lubeck was so sure that this would happen, who was he to disagree? Thorsten laughed with Malik and Tarique as they shared some private joke and all seemed well in the world as they travelled uneventfully to Keterik.

As they approached the port, Rogan commented on the magnitude and magnificence of the Thunder Child as she sat, dominating the middle of the bay with smaller ships all around. A horn was sounded to announce their approach and people left their daily duties to welcome the King to their humble port.

Freyja stepped out to try and glimpse a view of the returning warriors. One in particular she wanted to see more than any. There he was, riding beside the King, surrounded as always by his trusty companions. Her heart pounded with excitement and tears of joy escaped from her eyes as she ran to the square to greet them. Hagar too, waited with mixed emotions. The loss of his brother overshadowing the joy of seeing his friends returned safely. But on seeing Tarique slapping Malik across the back of his head, yet again in response to some stupid comment, lifted his spirits enough to allow him to chuckle to himself. Bjorn had now come ashore from the Thunder Child. Thorsten had insisted that the young man, inexperienced in war, should stay with the ship under Hagar's watchful eye. He was no longer inexperienced at war. The brief skirmish with Akhola's men in the Northern end of the Outland Pass had been a fitting baptism. Now all he wanted was to see his father's safe return.

On entering the main square, Rogan's men dismounted and immediately began to unload carts and erect the temporary shelters around the outskirts of the town. Lubeck dropped from his saddle onto his good leg and was no sooner on the ground, when he was almost bowled over by Freyja greeting him with a tight hug. Returning the embrace, Lubeck kissed her tenderly before turning to the King to introduce her. Rogan acknowledged her as she uncharacteristically bowed her head in respect.

Thorsten grinned with delight as he gripped Bjorn in a tight hug looking over the new minor wounds that now decorated his young face and body.

"You saw some action boy? Ha! You're not a boy anymore then." Thorsten asked mockingly. Antonio eagerly volunteered to escort the King, to show him around the Thunder Child. Then accompanied by Gunter and a couple of guards, they were ferried out to where she was moored. Hagar approached Lubeck and the others with a sombre demeanour. Thorsten offered to take him to his brother as Lubeck did the same for Freyja. Agatha's and Magnus's bodies had already been placed in a small room in a nearby cabin, along with others from the little port. The group entered with bowed heads. The families of the dead were sobbing and holding each other as the group entered. Thorsten braced himself expecting a verbal onslaught from the widows and children, however this didn't occur. Lubeck informed them, that their sacrifices were not in vain and that families who had lost their men, would be taken care of by the rest of the port and provided for, if necessary, by the King himself. They had King Rogan's word on that, Lubeck assured them.

Freyja sobbed quietly as she touched her sister's arm and Hagar's eyes filled with tears as they looked upon his slain sibling. Thorsten informed them both that their bodies would be taken back to Thanos where they would have proper funerals with whatever beliefs they held. The news was received gratefully and Freyja insisted on reciting a verse. She informed them it would preserve their bodies during the long voyage back. Hagar insisted that Magnus should be returned to their mother, so that she could arrange the funeral she would desire for her oldest son. Hagar continued to inform them that he would not be taking his brother's place as Earl in these parts, but would leave that to his cousin Horik. Instead Hagar would be returning to Thanos with them. Anna had not been found yet and until she had, he would continue to serve with the Gurlemek by Lubeck's side. Only then might he think about taking his brother's place. All this he would explain to his mother once Magnus was returned to her. No objections were voiced, so plans were made.

On returning from his tour of the Thunder Child, King Rogan enquired as to when Lubeck intended to return to his new home.

"I think it will be on the morning tide, the day after tomorrow, if that fits with Antonio?" Lubeck informed him. Antonio thought momentarily before nodding as he raised an eyebrow replying.

"The day after tomorrow should be fine. The morning tide will be early though, but still, an early start never hurt anyone." The rest of the day passed with festive celebration. The villagers of Keterik enjoyed the unexpected honour of their King visiting their humble homes personally. A feast was quickly arranged in his honour and festivities continued late into the night.

As morning came, many were feeling a little worse for wear after too much ale, but began the arduous tasks of preparing to sail once again. Stores were loaded onto the ships that were going to make the journey back to Thanos. Everyone worked in good spirit, in spite of the pounding heads. It is said that 'Many hands make light work' this was proven to be true as hundreds of helping hands from King Rogan's men made short work of the toil.

"All's ready Lubeck. All of our ships are loaded and ready to sail, just as soon as you give the order." Antonio reported.

"Very good Antonio. Let us pray for fine weather and a fair wind tomorrow. A safe and uneventful voyage home would be pleasing." Lubeck replied. Antonio laughed as he returned to the harbour side calling back over his shoulder.

"Uneventful, HA! The Gods have too much fun with you Lubeck. You entertain them far too much for our voyage to be uneventful." Lubeck snorted at the comment knowing it to be true. But, after all they had endured; he hoped the Gods would indeed grant them safe passage home. His thoughts were interrupted by the approach of Gunter and King Rogan. Once again Rogan invited Lubeck and his people to stay, but once more Lubeck politely refused the offer. His plans for a trade centre and a new life on Thanos were all he wanted now, once Hafthor had been returned to him. Lubeck looked at his father's disappointed face and tried again to reassure him this was not goodbye, merely farewell and that they would meet again soon.

"I will return to my stronghold once you and your people have sailed." Rogan commented to Lubeck.

"As you wish my lord. Your continued presence here is both an honour and a pleasure." Lubeck replied. Gunter escorted the King wherever he ventured as he took the time to view how his subjects were living in this little port. He could see that life has it's hardships in these remote places and he instructed Gunter to make a mental note, so that the matter could be investigated further and hopefully resolved upon their return to the grand lodge. Gunter nodded obediently assuring Rogan that he would do so.

"I have seen the way your son's people admire, no, love and respect him so. He treats them all as equals and this has earned their love." Rogan remarked. Gunter shifted a little uneasily as he replied.

"He is loved by those who have chosen to follow him my lord, but perhaps it is that he was elected to be their leader by the people themselves? Lubeck has demonstrated fortitude and valour alongside compassion and humanity for all. But most of all, my lord, I think it is because he keeps his word. When Lubeck makes a promise, then the vow is fulfilled. He never forgets and always puts the needs of others before his own." King Rogan paused as he mulled over Gunter's words. Then stroking his chin in thought he answered.

"Your son is very special and does not RULE his people but leads them. I believe that I too would want my people to follow me as Lubeck's do him. I want my people's love as his love him and you my dear old friend, will help me achieve this. So where do I begin to change the way things have been? How do I get things to be the way I would like them?" Gunter coughed as he cleared his throat nervously before answering, choosing his word carefully.

"To begin with my Lord, you are a popular King. Your people do not hate or feel bitter towards you, but to reach the kind of following that my son has achieved, you must keep your word to these people. You must not forget their struggles and hardships and you must find a way to keep your word to ease their hardships. That would be a very good place to start I think. Then you will begin to feel your subjects love."

"Wise words my friend, wise words indeed." Rogan responded as he watched Lubeck walking with Freyja. They stopped to help a fisherman stretch out his nets ready for repair, before continuing their stroll in the afternoon sun. King Rogan watched enviously as Lubeck walked without guard or fear, among the people of Keterik with Freyja by his side. Unconcerned about the possibility of an assassin and not afraid to get his hands dirty helping those around him. He joked and played with children as he passed and was not above playing practical jokes of his own. Demonstrated by pushing Thorsten off the jetty and into the water just to make the others laugh. He was also not above permitting himself to be launched into the cold waters of the bay, as Freyja, assisted by Malik and Tarique, bundled him off the jetty to join his spluttering friend. The children looking on cheered and laughed at the spectacle, as they watched the two warriors playfully ducking each other below the water's surface, as they tried to swim ashore.

"This is what I would have for myself." Rogan began gesturing towards the frivolous scenes and beckoning Gunter to look. "I want that freedom to move as he does, without caution and without fear. Everywhere I go, I am accompanied by guards, even within my own home in case of attempts on my life. Your son has no such fear, no such doubts. He is truly free and truly loved. I must have this." Rogan's eyes returned to his old friend as he spoke. Gunter sighed as he hesitantly offered,

"Lubeck is free my lord yes, but to become so, he first suffered as a slave. In order for him to be truly free though, he needs to find his son, my Grandson and return with him to make a new life together. He will not be truly free until he has accomplished this."

"Then he will have any assistance he requires to make it so." Rogan replied as he moved his gaze back to the dripping figures lifting themselves from the cold waters of the bay. "Your son and I must maintain a solid friendship and alliance. You my old friend will ensure this can be done. Establish a trade route to Thanos and support Lubeck's plans to build a trading centre there. Links between us must remain strong, for the mutual benefits of both our Kingdoms." Gunter slapped his fist against his chest and bowed his head in salute, acknowledging his Kings instruction. With a glance over his shoulder towards his frolicking son and friends, Gunter smiled as he followed his old friend and King.

The rest of the day passed uneventfully. The port busied itself with the usual chores of day to day life and the Gurlemek crews rested before their forthcoming voyage home. All was peaceful and unhurried. There was no indication of the brutal battles that took place just a little over a week ago. The men's bodies were healing and expended energies returning. An air of excitement and expectation built as the time to sail drew closer. Every Gurlemek crewman was longing to be reunited with their waiting families back on Thanos. Even those who had no family were eager to sail for home. Some of the men were becoming a little irritable with the waiting and questioned why they could not sail immediately. Lubeck tried to assure them that waiting for a favourable tide and wind would be a better tactic than simply plunging headlong into the oceans and wrestling against unfavourable tides with no assistance from the wind. This would make for a very arduous voyage, tiring and slow. The following morning would bring more favourable conditions, this Freyja had foreseen and so they wait.

Soon enough, the day arrived. The early morning was shrouded in a thin mist as the sun began to climb. A steady breeze swirled gently around the port and rocked the ships as a mother would an infant in a crib. Hagar stepped onto the dock and raised his face to the sky taking a deep breath and exhaling loudly.

"It's a fine morning for a voyage." He declared as Thorsten accompanied by his son Bjorn stepped onto the dock beside him. "There is no scent of rain in the air and the wind is building nicely. The tide is turning and shall be ebbing within the hour I'd say. It appears that Freyja was right and Lubeck was right to listen to her, yet again." The older man chuckled to himself as he spoke.

"We have a long voyage ahead. Let's hope the Gods see fit to let us return to Thanos without incident, just for once." Thorsten commented before kneeling to reach into the water and cover his face with a handful of cold bracing brine.

Dogs barked in the distance as the little port began to wake. The dull murmur of indistinct chatter carried on the breeze and grew as more people began to prepare themselves for the day ahead. Some men began to board a solitary fishing boat, which then headed out towards some of the ships moored in the bay. One by one they were distributed amongst the fleet, each man with tasks to perform. Ropes were passed from ship to ship and when all were ready a signal was given and all anchors were raised.

Heaving on the recently passed ropes, the ships slowly moved towards each other. One by one they bumped gently against the docks and each other alike, until finally they were tethered together, to form a pontoon. Now a man or even a child could step from ship to ship with ease. All but the Thunder Child, who's size made it unsafe to include her in these manoeuvres. So, she sat alone in the bay awaiting her crew to be ferried out to her by fishing boat. The smaller ships were ready within hours and the earlier gentle chatter had now grown into a continuous hum of conversation. All sounds lowered and finally stopped, as the King stepped onto the docks. Gunter, as was expected from his post, was by his Kings side. Malik rushed to get Lubeck, who was overseeing the ferrying of the Thunder Child's crew. Lubeck followed Malik to the dock where the King and his entourage waited.

"Apologies my Lord, I was engaged with the day's tasks and did not know that you would be here so early." Lubeck commented as he approached Rogan with his head respectfully lowered.

"No apologies necessary. I simply wanted to wish you and your men a pleasant and safe journey. May you reach your homelands with speed." Rogan smiled reaching out a hand in friendship. Lubeck returned the gesture. Gunter hugged his son slapping his back as he did. Freyja appeared and joined the farewells. Thorsten and the others hit their fists against their chests and bowed their heads in salute to the King, then turned to man their posts aboard the ships to which they had been assigned. Lubeck returned to where the little fishing boat was secured and dropped into it. Freyja, assisted by King Rogan lowered herself to join Lubeck and once everyone was aboard, the little boat moved away from the shore and headed towards the huge ship in the middle of the bay. Once there, they climbed aboard and as Lubeck ordered the oars to be deployed, a horn sounded to inform the rest of the fleet to do likewise. More horns sounded in response and soon the whole fleet was headed for the open sea. Cheers from the crews roared rhythmically and singing broke out as the fleet moved swiftly away. King Rogan turned to his trusted friend and right hand stating,

"I think that perhaps we should do likewise and return home ourselves?"

"As you wish my Lord." Gunter replied bowing shallowly and moving away to arrange for their departure. One last look out across the bay at the receding fleet caused a sigh with a heavy heart. Then without further delay he barked orders readying the men to leave.

The early morning mist had cleared by the time the fleet reached the open water. The sun was beginning to shine and the breeze had swollen into a bracing wind. The oars were stowed and sails unfurled. They bellowed as the air caught them and the ships lurched into life, majestically skimming over the waters at great speed. Hagar grinned with delight as he manned the tiller of the great ship.

"We will be home in no time at all if this keeps up!" He called to Lubeck standing a few feet away.

Lubeck returned the smile and then looked out towards the South.

"The Gods willing." He said, almost to himself.

"I'm sure they are." Freyja interrupted him "They must see you and all that you have accomplished. They surely can't expect more of you so soon?"

"We shall see." Lubeck muttered under his breath. "But you my little witch, need to take me to my son. You told me as I placed my hands on Akhola's head before he died, that you had found him. Do you know where he is?" Lubeck stared at her with anticipation. Freyja smiled and nodded her head vigorously,

"I have. He is safe enough and in no danger, but he is a slave and we must go and retrieve him. Just as soon as we have returned our people to their homes." Lubeck sighed heavily. He wanted to go and retrieve Hafthor now, as they were returning home. He wanted to turn the fleet around and head for wherever Hafthor was being held. But, he had learned that Freyja was usually right about such things. So, if she urges him to wait a little, then wait he will, for now. Though his disappointment showed on his face.

They sailed without incident for the following weeks and made good time with perfect weather, until the tower by the beach on Thanos finally came into view. The crews could hear the sound of horns coming from the shoreline as the fleet approached. Sails were lowered and horns sounded in response as the ships slowed and glided gently towards the beach. Crowds began to gather and shouts of excitement and expectation erupted as the ships grew closer. Loved ones called out as they recognised their husbands, fathers or sons. The smaller ships beached their bows in quick succession and families rushed to greet their men as they jumped ashore. The Thunder Child loomed over them and anchored a little way out. Some of her crew jumped overboard and swam to the shallower waters, too eager to wait for smaller vessels to ferry them ashore. As they waited patiently, Lubeck and Freyja watched the giant figure of Thorsten wade through water and onto the beach where he was greeted by a very relieved Morgana. She threw her arms around his neck and kissed him passionately; stopping only to hug Bjorn as he also waded onto the beach following his father. Malik, Tarique and Jamal, all of which had no families here to greet them, simply dropped to the sand and lay on their backs laughing with relief that their adventures were over—

"Over?" Interrupted a youth as he sat listening to the old man's tale. "How can their adventures be over? The tales I have heard of these Gurlemek go far beyond this."

"Me too." Agreed another, shuffling dissatisfied as he tried to move closer to the fire. "How did Lubeck become a mighty Chieftain? How did he command such a vast army and rise to lead so many people?" Murmurs of discontent rippled around the fire. The old man's eyes darted from face to face with concern for his traveling companion's change of mood.

"You asked me about the warrior Lubeck." The old man started in response. "I have told you of him. Why are you so displeased?" The men in the group around the fire grunted before one spoke up again.

"We listened to your tale old man. The younger ones among us fixed on your every word, but now we feel cheated–"

"Cheated?" The old man interrupted. "Why do you say you feel cheated?" He asked. The man looked at him again, before responding.

"Cheated because you promised to tell us of Lubeck's rise from slave to chieftain and more, but now you end your tale before it has fully begun. You tell us nothing of his rise at all and you haven't even told us how or if he ever found his son Hafthor." The old man laughed and clapped his hands.

"You want to know all about the mighty Lubeck?" He questioned, laughing as he waited for a response.

"Yes, yes we do. Did he find his son? Did he rescue him?" A young man asked eagerly. The old man watched the group's expectant faces. He stretched his legs, shifted his seat and addressed his audience.

"All of this and more I can tell you if you refill this." He said holding up his empty tankard. One of the group took the tankard and filled it, then handing it back he asked.

"Will you continue then?" The old man laughed again, took a gulp from the tankard and replied,

"Does Lubeck find Hafthor? How does Lubeck become a powerful chieftain and lead so many people? All shall be answered. Now settle back, get comfortable and let me tell you a tale……."